THE
TRACKS
BOOK THREE

SHADOW
TRAIN

THE
TRACKS
BOOK THREE

SHADOW TRAIN

J. GABRIEL GATES
AND CHARLENE KEEL

HCI
TEENS™

Health Communications, Inc.
Deerfield Beach, Florida

www.hcibooks.com

**Library of Congress Cataloging-in-Publication Data
is available through the Library of Congress**

ISBN-13:978-0-7573-1739-2 (paperback)
ISBN-10:0-7573-1739-1 (paperback)
ISBN-13:978-0-7573-1740-8 (ePub)
ISBN-10:0-7573-1740-5 (ePub)

©2013 J. Gabriel Gates and Charlene Keel

Publisher: Health Communications, Inc.
    3201 S.W. 15th Street
    Deerfield Beach, FL 33442–8190

Cover design by Dane Wesolko
Interior design Lawna Patterson Oldfield
Formatting by Dawn Von Strolley Grove

CHAPTER 1

VALENTINE'S DAY.

Ignacio stood quietly, staring at the array of demolition vehicles lined up across the street: two bulldozers and a big backhoe. His Flatliner brothers sat on the curb next to him in various postures of defeat. They always walked home from school along this route, and today the sight of big machines revving up for action had made them stop to watch. Beet was slouching and staring down at the pavement beneath his feet. Josh had his head in his hands. Benji kept fidgeting, nervously zipping and unzipping his jacket. But Emory sat perfectly still, staring intensely at the three-story apartment house that stood before him. He and his family had lived in that building since he was a baby. Now, it was about to be destroyed before his eyes.

Ignacio couldn't imagine how bad that must feel—on top of the fact that Emory and his mom, dad, and little sister were still living like refugees in Beet's dad's garage.

"Don't worry, man," Josh said, putting a hand on Emory's back. "We'll find you a new place—eventually."

Emory didn't respond.

"Maybe somebody'll stop it at the last minute, like in the movies," Benji said hopefully, with a glance at Ignacio. "Right, Nass? Maybe city hall will accept your petition after all."

"Nah." Ignacio shook his head. "They rejected it on a technicality. They said the margin on the edge of the page was too big. Jerks. I watched them throw it in the trash. Nobody's going to stop it," he finished, dejected.

They all stared in silence at the vacant building. The sound of an engine, then another, drifted toward them from across the street as the workmen turned the bulldozers on.

"Gentlemen, start your engines," Benji said. Nobody laughed.

"If Raph were here, he'd know what to do," Beet said glumly, and they all breathed a collective sigh.

For the last two and a half months, they'd searched every day for their friend and leader. They felt like they'd turned over every log in the forest and peered behind every tree trunk. They'd gotten flashlights and explored Middleburg's infamous, creepy railroad tunnels, and then traversed the slopes of the mountain through which the tunnels ran. They had hiked around Macomb Lake and ridden their bikes down country roads calling his name. They had even organized Flats residents to do a block-by-block search of the town, including Hilltop Haven. Still, Raphael Kain was nowhere to be found.

The only traces of him that remained were the shards of the treasure he'd held just before that phantom train struck him. With superstitious reverence, each of the Flatliners—and most of the Toppers—had picked shards of the broken crystal ring from the spot where the explosion happened. Even though the ring's magical glow disappeared once it broke and the shards became nothing more than translucent glass, they had all wanted a piece of it. Nass knew without asking that his fellow Flatliners each carried a small fragment of that mystical ring with them everywhere they went, just as he did. As he thought of it, his hand slipped into his pocket, his fingers tracing along the jagged edge of the broken bit of crystal.

Maybe the Shen magic contained in the crystal was responsible for Raphael's disappearance, Nass thought with a stirring of hope that felt like a ray of sunlight trying to pierce the cloudbank of his depression. Maybe it had transported Raph to another time or place, and he'd find his way home. Maybe he would come walking back into Middleburg any day now. But the prospect seemed too much to hope for. Raphael was gone. And for all they knew, he wasn't coming back.

For all they knew, he was dead.

Across the street, a huge backhoe inched across the apartment building's overgrown lawn, raising its big yellow bucket across the cloud-paled, late winter sun.

"I took my first steps in that apartment," Emory said quietly, speaking for the first time all afternoon. "It's where my sister said her first word. Don't get me wrong, it sucked—but it was the only home I've ever had."

Nass looked over at his friend, half expecting to see tears in his eyes, but there were none. Emory's face held no expression, which was worse. He just stared across the street as the backhoe reached slowly toward the roof of the building, as if the sight made him feel nothing at all, as if he were completely numb. Nass guessed that all the Flatliners probably felt that way. He felt numb, too, ever since Raphael disappeared. Numb and empty, except for a subtle, nagging pressure in the pit of his stomach that never seemed to go away.

"I wish I had a trumpet," Benji lamented. "I'd play taps." He started humming it, doing an impression of a bugle that would have been funny—if the occasion wasn't so depressing.

"Well, if it's any consolation, Emory, I'm sure they'll knock down the rest of the Flats soon," Josh said. "Nass's eviction is scheduled for next week, and my family has to be gone in a month."

"Thanks," Emory said sarcastically. "I feel much better now."

Just as the backhoe was about to crunch into the roof of the building, there came a roar of engines and a squeal of tires, and Nass looked over to see a shiny, black SUV whip around the corner, followed by an identical vehicle.

Reflexively, all the Flatliners scrambled to their feet, and Nass backed up from the curb onto the sidewalk. In Middleburg, only rich Topper brats had shiny, new SUVs—and with Raphael gone, tension with the Flatliners' rivals was higher than ever.

But when the doors to the vehicles opened, it wasn't the Toppers who emerged. It was a bunch of muscular guys in black suits, all of them with military-style haircuts. The man who got out on the passenger side of the first vehicle took the lead, pulling some kind of official-looking badge out of his jacket pocket as he hurried up the lawn toward the apartment building.

"Stop," he barked, and instantly the heads of all the Shao Construction workers snapped toward him. The backhoe that was about to tear into the roof of the building froze.

"Yeah! City hall! The petition worked!" Benji shouted, and he plunged excitedly across the street, toward the building.

But Nass wasn't so sure that it was city hall they were dealing with. Jack Banfield had local government sewn up pretty tight, so when he wanted something done it usually got done. If he stood to make money by having the Flats torn down, Nass doubted city hall would stand in his way. Besides, the six guys in suits who were swarming toward the building didn't seem like city bureaucrats to him—they looked more like the secret service agents who guarded the president of the United States. But the other Flatliners were already hurrying across the lawn, so Nass followed.

As soon as they were within earshot, he heard the leader of the suits talking to the Shao Construction foreman. "This property is hereby seized by the federal government. We are placing an injunction on any redevelopment within the city of Middleburg until our investigation here is concluded."

"Investigation into what?" the foreman asked. He didn't seem upset by this new turn of events, only confused.

"That's classified," the man said indifferently. "You can direct your questions to your local law-enforcement agency. But I want nothing touched, you understand? No renovation, no demolition until we've gone through every inch of this place."

The foreman shrugged and glanced at his crew members. "All right, no problem. But, uh, my boss ain't gonna be too pleased. He's going to ask for your name and badge number and stuff."

"The name is Hackett," the man said.

Nass noticed that Hackett's fellow black-suits had already pried the front door of the building open and were swarming through it into the vacant apartment house.

"And what agency are you with exactly? My boss'll want to know," the foreman asked, and Nass could see that he was appropriately intimidated.

"Local law enforcement," Agent Hackett reminded him. "Direct your questions to them."

The foreman nodded to his crew members, who shrugged and began retreating toward their trucks. As they went, he pulled out his cell phone. *Calling Jack Banfield or Cheung Shao, no doubt,* Nass thought. Man, he would love to see the look on their faces when they heard that the feds had come in and squashed their little real-estate deal.

"Dude, that was kick *ass*! High-five!" Benji said, and held his hand up for the agent to slap him one.

The man, Agent Hackett, turned toward him slowly, with an air of threatening calm. He was tall, with a salt-and-pepper crew cut and a pair of aviator sunglasses so dark it was impossible to see his eyes. He chewed a piece of gum slowly, as if, Nass thought, he enjoyed the feeling of smashing things between his teeth. He did not move to give Benji five.

"We're the ones who did the petition," Benji blurted, obviously thinking that an explanation was in order. The man merely stared at him. "I'm so glad you guys showed up, man. This neighborhood isn't much, but it's all we got, you know?"

"Benji . . . let's go," Nass said. The *knowing* was kicking in, and over the past few months, he'd learned to trust his psychic instincts when that peculiar little feeling came over him. Right now, his instincts were telling him to get out of there. But Benji was still talking.

"It was so cool, man—you guys riding in to the rescue at the last possible minute—just like in the movies!"

Agent Hackett reached up and slowly removed his sunglasses, revealing narrow brown eyes, the folds around them tightly creased like those of a cowboy who spent his days squinting into harsh sunlight and blowing dust. He stared at Benji.

"You're one of Raphael Kain's friends," he stated. "A Flatliner. Your name is Benjamin Case, isn't it?"

Benji finally got the message that something was off, and he started slowly backing away. "Um, yeah. Yes, sir. Anyway, thanks. I should be heading home . . ." His voice faded into silence.

"I don't think so," Hackett said tonelessly. "I'm going to need you to answer a few questions about Raphael Kain."

When Benji tried to take another step back, Hackett reached out to grab his arm. Instinctively, Nass stepped between them, pushing Hackett's hand away.

"I can speak for all of us," he blurted. "You should talk to me."

Before he knew what had happened, Nass found himself lying in the grass face-first, his arm twisted painfully behind him. From his awkward vantage, he looked up to see several agents step up next to Agent Hackett.

"Don't ever touch me, boy. Understand?" Hackett said evenly, leaning close to Nass's ear.

"Go! Now!" Nass shouted, and the other Flatliners obediently took off across the street, running as fast as they could.

"You want us to grab them?" one of the other agents asked, but Hackett shook his head.

"No, let them go," he said quietly, and glanced down at Nass, giving his wrist a final, painful twist. "We can pick them up later if we need to. But I have a feeling this one is going to tell us everything we need to know."

Rick Banfield sat in front of his father's broad mahogany desk, tapping his foot impatiently. His dad, who occupied a large leather office chair behind the desk, scowled as he held the phone receiver to his ear. Jack Banfield's lavish office was on the top floor of the tallest building in downtown Middleburg, and its sixth-floor windows provided the best view in town. There was Main Street, with its historic brick buildings, then the blocks of old, well-cared-for houses that surrounded downtown. Beyond it, to the east, Rick could see the rise that led to Hilltop Haven, the beautiful gated community where he and his fellow Toppers lived. Further south there was a second hill—a small mountain, really—through which Middleburg's railroad tunnels ran. Further to his right, he could see the ragged rooftops of tenement houses in the distance. That was where the trouble was happening, Rick surmised; he'd overheard his father say something about a redevelopment deal getting screwed up, and that's where the work was taking place. Besides, Rick thought, every bad thing that ever happened in Middleburg came from those filthy, lazy slobs who lived south of the tracks. Rick's patience for his Flatliner rivals had long ago disappeared, and he yearned more and more for the day when he could make Middleburg a better place by exterminating them all, like the rats they were.

"You've got to be kidding me," his dad growled into the phone. "On whose authority? Well, where did it come from? There has to be some . . . uh-huh. Right. Listen, I'll make a couple calls to my friends at city hall and see if I can get to the bottom of this, all right? I'll call you as soon as I know something."

Jack slammed the phone down and glared at his son. "Yes?" he prompted impatiently. "As you can see, I've got a pretty full plate today. What's on your mind? Spit it out."

"You were going to leave me some cash this morning," Rick said. "For Valentine's Day?"

"Right." Jack sighed and dug his wallet out of the pocket of his sport coat. "You taking Maggie to Spinnacle?"

"Something like that," Rick said quietly. He didn't want to tell his dad what he was really doing for Valentine's Day. It was kind of embarrassing—but that was part of the thrill. The fact that his date had to be secret made it even more illicit. *Dirty.* Something he could relish. Besides, it wasn't exactly a lie—he would do something for Maggie, send her flowers or something. He had to keep her on the hook in case he needed her for something later. But tonight, he had more interesting plans.

"What was the phone call about?" Rick asked, trying to be casual. "Is something going on in the Flats?"

Jack, who was sifting through the contents of his wallet, shook his head. "They were supposed to start bulldozing the first apartment building down there today, but some bozo who claimed to be from the federal government showed up and ordered them to cease and desist."

Immediately, the wheels in Rick's head started turning. "The feds? Why would they give a crap what we do in the Flats?" he asked. "You think it's because of the petition the Flatliners started?"

Jack shrugged, clearly irritated, as he pulled a few bills out of his wallet. "Who knows? We'll take care of it. Everybody has a price. Two hundred okay?"

He tossed the bills onto his desk and Rick scooped them up. "How about three hundred—and I'll see what I can find out about what's going down in the Flats?"

Jack laughed. He took a hundred-dollar bill out of his wallet. "You're learning, kid. You'll make a businessman, yet. Just remember, when I pay somebody for something, I expect results. Next time the bulldozer starts rolling, there better not be any sad teenage faces watching, you got me? We don't need any pictures like that in the paper. *No bad press.*"

"Deal," Rick said eagerly. "Don't worry. When I'm done with them, they won't be making trouble for you anymore." And he snatched the bill from his father's outstretched hand.

As the door shut behind his son, the smile disappeared from Jack's face. It was always something, he thought, shaking his head. And why did this snafu have to come up today, of all days? He reached out and pressed the button on his phone's intercom, buzzing his secretary.

"Yes, Mr. Banfield?"

"Everything ready for tonight?" he asked.

"Yes—it's all taken care of," she said. "I'm sure Ms. Kain will love it."

"Thanks, Patrice. That's all," he said, and he heard the intercom click off.

So, everything was ready for the surprise he'd prepared for Savana. It had been a long wait, but it would all be worth it, he thought with a rare sense of satisfaction.

Jack gazed out at the picturesque view of his downtown. That's how he'd always thought of Middleburg, as *his* town. It was a beautiful place. And when he was done with it, it would be perfect.

Tonight would be perfect, too. This would be a Valentine's Day no one in Middleburg would ever forget.

Ջ

"Hey."

The voice that called to Rick as he stepped out the back door and into the alleyway behind his father's office was sultry, dark—and familiar. Clarisse emerged from the recessed doorway where she'd been waiting and eyed Rick seductively. She wore tight jeans and a low-cut sweater that revealed just enough. Her dark brown hair was pulled back in a tight ponytail, and her blood-red lips curved in a little pouting smile that started a fever of desire burning in Rick.

The night Raphael Kain disappeared, after the big fight, Rick had found Clarisse and taken her out to Macomb Lake. He'd been robbed of the revenge that she had promised him, and he was fully prepared to take his frustration out on her. He had all sorts of wicked plans—to drive her out into the middle of nowhere, rough her up a little and leave her there, to take her money, to smash her cell phone—and even darker things, too. Dangerous, exotic things. He'd been in a foul mood when he'd picked her up that night after the fight, but something surprising had happened: the meaner he got, the more she seemed to like it.

She'd been a little nervous at first—a little shaken—maybe it was seeing her Flats rats buddies getting their butts kicked or seeing that train smash into Raphael. But whatever it was, she seemed to be kind of turned on by the way Rick manhandled her—forceful and demanding, not caring if he hurt her. It was like she took some kind of weird comfort in it. He knew some girls liked it rough—and he liked that she liked it. She'd been following him around ever since, popping up in unexpected places like some kind of stalker. The word filled him with a disdain that bordered on revulsion, but it turned him on, too. The little Flats tramp was stalking him . . .

Be careful what you wish for, little girl, he thought. *Because it just might sneak up on you and grab you by the throat.* Visions of what he could do to her flashed through his mind. He was strong enough now. He was strong enough to do whatever he wanted.

He shook his head, clearing it of the visions. He was having more of them lately—flashes of violence that shot through his brain at unexpected moments—but they no longer bothered him. Now, he almost welcomed them.

When Clarisse had shown up at Spinnacle after a Topper meeting a few nights after their first encounter, he had been disturbed to find that he was actually happy to see her.

"I thought you might turn up soon," he had said, trying to repress the smile that was tempting his lips.

"I saw your car," she'd said, gesturing to the silver Audi SUV that was parked in the lot.

"I told you, I don't date Flats girls."

"I told you, I don't want to be dated," she'd replied.

"Why are you here? Spying for the Flats rats again?"

She shook her head. "I'm done with them," she'd whispered. "I'm here to see you."

"What do you want?"

She hadn't said anything else. She'd only smiled and pulled him into the backseat of his Audi, where they had spent half an hour making out. When his friends started calling his cell phone, looking for him, he'd made her leave. He hadn't even offered to drive her home. Not even that discouraged her.

Then, about a week ago, she'd knocked on the door of his house in Hilltop Haven, brazenly unapologetic. She didn't say a word, not even about how she'd gotten past all the security. She'd just grabbed him and slammed her lips against his.

And now here she was, waiting outside his dad's office. The clever little stalker must've seen his car in the lot.

Rick knew that they were both aware of exactly where this was heading. But being mean to her was part of the fun. It was way more of a turn-on than the handholding, slow-dancing crap that Maggie Anderson insisted on. An idea suddenly came to him.

"My dad just bought the Starlite Theater two doors down from here," he told her. "The upstairs is vacant—and I snagged the key. You don't leave me alone, I'm going to drag you over there and teach you a lesson," he said.

Her deep brown eyes narrowed with wicked excitement. "So drag me," she said. "Or is that just an empty promise?"

Finally, Rick allowed the grin he'd been holding back to spread across his face.

☙

Nass found himself unceremoniously shoved into the Middleburg police station's interrogation room.

"You going to read me my rights?" he asked the secret service–looking dude who was doing the shoving. "Or just—" but the big man was already out the door. It clapped shut behind him.

"Alrighty, then. Guess I'll make myself at home," Nass grumbled. Looking around the room, he realized that wasn't going to be so easy. It was just four white walls, one of them covered with a mirror—one of those two-way interrogation mirrors, he guessed. There was a tile floor, a single light fixture on the ceiling, and that was it. Not even a table and chairs. Nass sighed and looked down at his watch. It was five minutes after four, an hour and a half before he was supposed to pick Dalton up at Lily Rose's for their Valentine's date—and he still had to go home and get ready first.

With the loss of Raphael, his family's impending eviction, and all the normal drama and stress of high school, the pure bliss of being with Dalton was the only thing that had gotten him through the last couple of months. If these jack-holes in the suits made him late for his date, he'd really give them a reason to read him his rights, he thought.

A few uneventful minutes passed, and just as he was about to lie down in a corner and catch a nap, the door swung open. The ugly face it revealed didn't give him any reassurance, though. The guy looked like a human version of an English bulldog, and his expansive body was covered by a Hawaiian shirt that Benji and Emory could both have worn at once. It was Detective Zalewski.

Detective Z had never been a friend to the kids from the Flats, but he had been even more of a pain since Raphael went missing. For some reason, Z seemed to take the mystery of Raphael's unsolved disappearance as a personal affront. He became especially furious whenever any of them tried to tell him about the magical ring or the train or the crazy explosion of Shen power that had happened at the moment Raphael had vanished. It seemed to Nass like he thought the Flats kids were all playing a big practical joke on him and laughing behind his back, and he was determined to get his revenge. It didn't help that the Flatliners were getting increasingly angry with the police for their failure to make any headway in Raphael's case. The result was a nasty rivalry between the police and the Flatliners that made living in the Flats harder than it had ever been. The cops had already dragged Nass down to the station twice now for questioning, and the second time he was pretty sure the only reason they let him go was because his mom showed up with Lily Rose, who talked them into releasing him.

Now, Z glowered at Nass as he unfolded a metal chair he'd brought into the room with him.

"Aloha," Nass said, unable to bite back his sarcasm. "What am I in for now, Z? Existing?"

Zalewski's jowls quivered into a grin as he settled into the chair. "How about assaulting a federal agent?"

"Assaulting?" Nass's voice rose on the word. "I barely touched him! I have witnesses, too. All I did was step in between him and my friend."

"Relax," Z said. He seemed to be enjoying himself. "Nobody's sending you to the electric chair, all right?"

"Then what am I here for?" Nass asked.

"We're going to revisit what you've told me about your friend Raphael Kain," Z said, and he flipped open a file he'd brought in with him. "In amongst all the other BS you tried to feed me, you told me that on the night he disappeared you saw two Asian men in derby hats. Is that right?"

"Yeah. I told you about them. They were Obies. From the Order of the Black Snake."

"You want to describe them again for me?"

Nass shrugged. "They were Chinese. One was a little shorter than average, the other one was a little taller. They had on black suits and derby hats."

"Right," Z said, rolling his eyes. "These were the guys who had the half-invisible giant cobra with them, right? And they were fighting Oberon Morrow's son, Orias, who was battling them with some kind of magical ring . . . I remember the story." He reached into the folder, took out two photos and handed them to Nass. "These the guys?"

"Sure. I mean, I didn't get a real good look, but that looks like them. And those are definitely the hats they wear."

Z took the pictures back and stuck them in the folder, then gave a pointed glance at the mirror that was built into the wall. Without another word, he left the room. A few minutes passed and then the door swung open again. This time, Agent Hackett entered and took the chair Z had just vacated.

"Order of the Black Snake. What do you know about them?" Hackett asked, his tone calm and matter-of-fact.

"Not much. They're this mystical Chinese gang or something. Dangerous guys. My friend Raphael told me about them," Nass said.

Hackett flipped open a file and glanced down at a sheet of paper. "Raphael Kain, sixteen years old, disappeared two and a half months ago. What really happened to him?"

For probably the fiftieth time in the last two months, Nass recited the story of what happened the night Raphael disappeared. He told the truth, going through every detail just as it had really happened.

With every word, the events of that night played through his mind again. The night had been cold, shrouded in a swirling blizzard. The Flatliners and Toppers were locked in another of their duels down by the tracks when the Obies had shown up with the giant cobra that was their god. They had tried to take the crystal ring of power from Orias. Instead, Aimee Banfield had ended up with it, but when Raphael stepped in to protect her from the giant snake god, he took the ring. Then, a mysterious black locomotive had thundered out of the tunnel and struck him, and there was an explosion powerful enough to knock down dozens of trees in the surrounding forest. It knocked the Toppers and Flatliners down, too, and when they got up and looked around, there was no sign of the train, or of Raphael. They were simply gone.

He had only gotten a few sentences out when Hackett stopped him. "Listen, Ignacio. From what I hear your life is tough enough already, so I don't want to make it any tougher, all right? But if you're not straight with me, I will. And believe me when I say I can make it much, much tougher."

"I'm telling the truth," Nass said. "I want to get my friend back and I didn't do anything wrong, so why would I lie? Besides—" What he was about to say next made him think of Raphael, and the sudden swell of emotion cut the words off in his throat.

"Besides?" Hackett prompted.

"Besides, kids from my neighborhood are called Flatliners—"

"Yes, your little gang," Hackett interrupted with a derisive chuckle. "Way out here in the boonies . . ."

Nass ignored the insult. "We have a law we live by," he went on. "The Wu-De. We're not supposed to lie."

Hackett eyed him shrewdly. "Okay—that makes my job a lot easier," he said. "Tell me about your interaction with the guys you call the Obies."

"They were looking for something. A treasure that was hidden in Middleburg. It was this big crystal ring about the size of a dinner plate. But it got destroyed—it exploded—when Raphael disappeared. I mean, at the *exact moment* he disappeared."

"And have you seen the two Chinese men since that night?"

Nass shook his head. Hackett reached into a manila folder, pulled out another photo, and held it out to him.

"You recognize this man?"

Nass stared at the picture. It was a Chinese man, about sixty years old. His neck looked thick, muscular. He had short, slicked-back hair, a pencil-thin moustache, a small goatee that had been slicked into a knife-like point, and pale eyes that Nass could only describe as scary. Even in a photo, the man's piercing gaze was enough to make him shiver.

"No, I never saw him before," Nass said. "Who is he?"

Hackett sniffed and snatched the photograph from Nass's hand.

"I'll ask the questions," he said brusquely. He stuck the picture back in his folder, stood, and headed for the door.

"You're letting me go now, right?" Nass said hopefully.

Hackett turned back to him with a slow, smug smile.

"I think we'll let you hang out in here for a while and think about whether or not you have anything else to tell me that might be helpful. I'm sure your girlfriend won't mind. What's her name again?" He glanced in his folder. "Oh yes, Dalton." As he closed the folder, the picture of the sinister looking Asian man slipped out and fluttered to the floor, face down, at Nass's feet. As he stooped to pick it up, Nass saw that there was writing on the back:

Name: Feng Xu, Deputy Director of China's Ministry of State
Security Leader, Order of the Black Snake
Last Suspected Location: Middleburg, Kansas

Nass picked up the photo and as Hackett approached he quickly offered it to him. Wordlessly, Hackett took the photo and headed back to the door. As he left, he shut off the lights, leaving Nass locked away in complete darkness.

໑

At seven that evening, a stretch limousine pulled up in front of the Kain's apartment building and the driver honked its horn twice. Savana Kain, still putting one earring on, hurried from the bathroom vanity to look out the window. Despite the misery that weighed her down ever since her son, Raphael, had disappeared, the sight of the limo made her smile.

"Oh, Jack," she said. Then, grabbing her coat off the back of her couch, she hurried out the door. He had called to let her know he was sending a car, but she hadn't expected anything so lavish.

Instead of taking her to Spinnacle, the nicest restaurant in town, or to Jack Banfield's house, the limo driver surprised Savana by stopping downtown, just outside the front entrance of Jack's office building. Even though the driver opened her door for her and helped her out of the car, her distended belly almost caused her to lose her balance. She was still a couple of months from her due date, but the pregnancy seemed to be wearing on forever, and she felt as big as the Goodyear Blimp and twice as unstable. The baby was kicking and moving often now; he was so active she often thought of him as her little Olympic gymnast.

The joke just made her sad, though, because the person who would have laughed the most, the person she normally shared her jokes with, was gone. Every time she thought of Raphael, her firstborn, she felt like someone had twisted a length of barbed wire around her heart and was squeezing it tighter and tighter. Raph had been doing so well, too. He had lots of friends, and a girlfriend. He was even starting to accept the idea of Jack and the baby. Well, at least the baby. It didn't make sense that he had just up and run away—and the explanations his friends offered made even less sense.

No, she thought as she pushed through the glass doors and into the opulent lobby of Jack's building. She was not going to allow herself to get all morose again and ruin the night. She had to be strong. The police were doing everything they could to find her son, and she had to believe that they would and that Raph would be okay. She knew he wasn't dead. She was as sure of that as she was sure of the strong, new life she was carrying. She had to stay positive. Jack reminded her of that every day, and he'd even talked about hiring a private detective if the police didn't turn up something soon.

She took the elevator up to the top floor, and when it opened she found a trail of red rose petals on the carpet, leading to a stairwell on the far side of the office. She waddled up it as best she could, feeling the growing weight of her baby even more, and pushed her way out the exit door she found there. It opened onto the rooftop. Violin music greeted her instantly, and she found Jack sitting at a small, candlelit table, wearing a charming grin and one of his customary charcoal-gray suits. There was a string quartet set up behind him, playing a soft, romantic melody. The night was unseasonably mild, but Jack even had a portable heater set up near the table, just in case.

She cupped her hands over her mouth, amazed. "Jack! Oh my God!" she exclaimed, as a server in a white tuxedo approached and escorted her to the table. Jack rose, kissed her, and held her chair for her as she sat.

"This is too much, really. You didn't have to do all this," she chided.

"Oh, I've done way more than this, sweetheart. I told you I'd move heaven and earth for you, didn't I?" He reached under the table, brought out a black lacquered box and placed it on the table. On top of it, he set another box, a smaller one. A ring box.

Savana felt her eyes filling with tears.

"Pedro, pop the champagne," Jack commanded the waiter, then turned his attention back to Savana. "Don't worry; it's just sparkling grape juice," he said with a wink.

She laughed. In all the time she'd known him, she'd never seen him so happy and playful. He gestured down to the gifts on the table. "Go ahead, baby. Open it."

With trembling hands, she picked up the smaller box. Inside, she found exactly what she'd been hoping for—and dreading. The ring was stunning, perfect. She was no diamond expert, but she was pretty sure a rock like this could buy a whole block of the Flats. When she looked up from the sparkling stone, she found Jack on his knees before her, a tender smile gracing his handsome features.

"Marry me," he said. Without waiting for an answer, he took the ring out of its box and took Savana's left hand in his. Just as he slipped the ring onto her finger, she pulled away.

"What about Emily?" she asked.

Jack's smile faded a little, but not much. He nodded at the box still on the table.

"Open the other one," he said.

Slowly and carefully, she opened the black lacquered box. Inside, she found a single folded piece of paper. She unfolded it and read only the first few words before it slipped out of her hands.

Smith County, Kansas
Death Certificate
Emily Banfield

Suddenly, Savana's heart felt like it was galloping in her chest. Jack's wife had been gone for months now, but somehow Savana had never imagined that she was dead.

"What? They . . . they found her body?" she asked, holding her breath as she waited for his answer.

Jack shook his head. "Oh, no. Nothing like that. But she's been gone for so long and no one's heard a word from her. So, I filed some papers and took care of it."

Horrified, Savana asked, "But—doesn't it take seven years or something like that?"

He nodded. "Three years if there's some kind of disaster, like a tornado. But I pulled a few strings at the state Office of Vital Statistics." He chuckled and squeezed her hand comfortingly. "Don't worry, if she turns up—which she's not likely to do—we'll get it straightened out with a quick divorce. I love you, Savana, and I need to move on. I want you to move on with me. So what do you say? Don't you love me?"

"Jack—you know how I feel about you, but it's not that simple—"

"Sure it is," he interrupted. "You know, I bought that condo on Black Lake just for you and me, for weekend getaways. I know how much you like it. I can give you all the things you like, my darling. Everything you need. Everything you want."

She fought back her tears, but she had to say it. "Can you give me back my son, Jack?"

Jack's smile wavered for an instant and then returned. "I promise you—just like I promised after he went missing. We're going to keep looking for Raphael. We'll find him and bring him home. You have my word on that. In the meantime, let me take care of you. Let me give you the kind of life you deserve."

She was staring down at the paper that had slipped from her fingers, back into the box. All she could see now were the words: *Death Certificate*. And she dreaded to see Raph's name on such a document.

Jack kissed the finger with his ring on it. Then he held her hand up and pointed to the ring. "Look at it," he said. "It's just a symbol of the wonderful life I'm going to give you." But she could hardly see it through her tears.

Suddenly, a cascade of beautiful fireworks lit up the Middleburg sky.

CHAPTER 2

AIMEE BANFIELD SAT IN THE FLICKERING CANDLELIGHT that threw weird shadows against the wall of Orias Morrow's dining room, gazing down at her plate. Orias had prepared the meal himself, and as usual it was exquisite: a delectable piece of bloody-rare filet mignon, garlic mashed potatoes, sweet-potato medallions, and lemon-sautéed green beans. But as usual, Aimee wasn't hungry. She took a sip of Orias's delicious tea, the one he made from tea leaves that grew on his family's plantation in India.

"You told me once that there is a secret ingredient in your tea," she said.

He nodded, his eyes glinting with uncharacteristic emotion. "Yes," he said softly.

"What is it again?"

"A drop of water from the River Lethe," he replied.

"Oh yeah," Aimee said. "It's really good. Comforting." She took another sip. "Where is it? The river?"

Orias smiled, and she loved how the candlelight made him even more handsome. "South. Way South."

"We should go there sometime. Slip there, I mean." By slip, of course, she meant teleport. Using Aimee's newfound ability, they'd slipped all over the world the last few months, going everywhere from Bangladesh to Antarctica. By now, Aimee's powers of teleportation had grown so strong that it was as easy for her to slip to Paris as it was to hop on one foot.

But they hadn't been traveling much lately. On all their journeys,

Aimee had an unsettling feeling that she was supposed to be looking for something she'd lost, and it haunted her. It wasn't her mom—she remembered that she still had to look for her, as soon as her powers were strong enough. It was something else. She had a feeling it was incredibly important, but no matter how hard she tried, she couldn't remember what it was, and wherever she looked, she couldn't find it. It was so frustrating that after a while she'd gotten sick of traveling. These days, she preferred to stay in Orias's beautiful, old-fashioned, luxurious home with the shades drawn.

Her father and her brother seemed to have less time than ever for her now, and she was less and less able to tolerate their company. Anyway, Jack Banfield seemed delighted that she was spending so much time with Orias. Orias had even allowed Jack to partner with him in the renovation and reopening of Hot House Strip Club as Elixir, a tea and coffee shop that featured all kinds of natural herbal beverages, and Jack credited Aimee with helping him close the deal. She'd finally been able to do something that pleased her dad. Since then, she'd had a blank check to hang out with Orias as much as she wanted—which was basically all the time.

Tonight, Orias had styled her hair (at his urging, she had dyed it from the rebellious shade of raven black back to its original blond). She loved having him fuss over her and was fascinated by his stories about how his ancestors—his Nephilim brothers—had been the first to teach human women to adorn their faces with powders and rouge and their hair with flowers and jewels. He had also gotten her a lovely dress for Valentine's Day—a crimson ball gown that looked like something a princess would wear. It was stunning, and once she'd put it on and Orias had helped her with her makeup, she had to admit that she looked as amazing as he told her she did.

But it didn't change her mood. She felt restless and apathetic. Lately, Orias even had to insist that she go to school. To her, it seemed much nicer to sit in his parlor in front of the fire, dozing, making out with him, and occasionally sipping his specially brewed tea.

"I have something for you," he said, and from somewhere beneath the table he produced a long jewelry box. He popped it open to reveal a gorgeous necklace of white gold and diamonds set around a ruby the size of a baby's fist.

"Wow. Thanks," she said. "It's really pretty."

It was probably the most beautiful piece of jewelry she'd ever seen, and a year ago if someone had given her a gift like that she would probably have freaked out with sheer joy. Now, she accepted it as easily as she would a Target gift card. Looking at the dazzling jewels, she knew she should be thrilled, but she couldn't get past the feeling that something was missing—something important—and she wouldn't be able to get excited about anything until she figured out what it was.

"Here, let me put it on you," Orias said eagerly, getting out of his chair to stand behind her and drape the gold and diamond band across her chest. His fingers tickled the back of her neck as he did the clasp, and it instilled in her the sweet, familiar longing she felt whenever he touched her. "Happy Valentine's Day, my love," he whispered in her ear.

But her thoughts had already drifted away, like a slip of teleportation.

"I had the dream again," she said.

"What dream?"

"About the man. The blind man in the tower. He's been locked in a room up there, and he wants me to let him out. But he's furious, you know? He's so angry that I'm afraid of him. But in my dream I let him out anyway . . ." Her voice trailed off briefly, as she remembered the feeling of terror the dream always gave her. "What do you think it means?"

Orias didn't answer. Instead, he took her hand, helped her to her feet, and led her to a big gilded mirror that hung on one wall near the window. He stopped her in front of it.

"Don't you look stunning?" he asked as they both gazed at her reflection.

She stared at herself in the mirror, looking like the princess her little-girl self had always imagined she would grow up to be. And Orias, standing behind her, was every inch the prince, with his perfectly sculpted face, his long dark hair, and those startling blue eyes. She should be the happiest girl in the world.

A flash caught her eye, and she went to the window.

"Oh, look! Fireworks. Aren't they beautiful?" She tried to sound enthusiastic, but the words came out tonelessly. She watched as the sky lit up with spirals, stars, pinwheels, and spinners that fizzled, then crackled and sparked to life again and again above the treetops of Middleburg.

"Yes, it's beautiful," Orias said, gazing first at the fireworks and then at her.

"Where did you say it comes from?" she asked vaguely. "The water for the tea?"

"The River Lethe," Orias said, and he levitated her gently off the floor and floated her toward him. She laughed softly, and when she was close enough he reached out and pulled her into his arms.

"I've never heard of it. Where is it?" Aimee asked.

"In my father's homeland. The Dark Territory," Orias answered. "Perhaps we'll go there one day."

"Oh," Aimee said. Then another gorgeous multicolored pinwheel went crackling and reeling across the sky, like a scattering of diamonds. As its sparks faded, her uneasiness disappeared, too.

"Lovely," Orias said, his lips brushing her ear as he spoke.

She nodded in agreement and took comfort in having his arms around her, the missing element that troubled her slipping away from her mind.

⁂

As Zhai Shao approached Lily Rose's door, he adjusted his tie. He was dressed in the new clothes he'd asked Lotus to pick up for him on her last shopping trip to New York, and in his hand he held a special bouquet of exotic flowers from his stepmother's florist. Before the door opened, he went through a quick mental checklist to make sure that all his preparations for the evening had been completed, and by the time Lily Rose was greeting him, he was feeling a little more relaxed. Besides, the old lady's eyes were utterly unique: one was a rich hazel color that bordered on amber, the other a clear pristine blue, and when she looked at him with them, it was impossible to stress out.

"Well, hello, Zhai. Don't you look nice?" Lily Rose said warmly, the dark skin around her mouth crinkling into a smile. "Come in, come in. Go on back—they're almost ready."

He followed the sound of laughter to Dalton's bedroom door, which was ajar.

"Knock, knock," he said, slipping inside.

He found Dalton and another Flats girl, Myka, standing in front of a broad mirror. Next to them was Kate—and she looked spectacular. She was wearing a beautiful green velvet dress that Zhai guessed Lily Rose had made for her and her fiery red hair, which Dalton had probably styled, looked fantastic. She'd lost a little weight while recovering from the wound she'd suffered during the battle at the tracks, but the color had returned to her cheeks. Lily Rose, Master Chin, and the local doctor all agreed that she had healed wonderfully. Miraculously, in fact.

"Zhai!" she said when she saw him, and hurried over.

"You look gorgeous," he told her. He summoned up the courage to take her hand and give her a kiss on the cheek as he handed her the bouquet.

"You can't steal her away yet, Romeo," Myka teased, her trademark edge of sarcasm in her voice. "I still have some finishing touches to put on her makeup."

"Yes, ma'am," Zhai joked as he sat down on the bed. "I'll wait quietly. Don't mind me."

Myka, as usual, was dressed as Goth as possible. She wore a torn black T-shirt with a faded red image of an anatomically correct heart on it, paired with a puffy black skirt, high black leather boots, and livid-red lipstick. Her nails were painted black and her hair was streaked with red; her nose and one eyebrow were pierced. Before he got to know her Zhai thought she was a little scary, but his attitude toward a lot of the Flats kids had changed since Raphael's disappearance.

Zhai had spent a lot of time with all of them as they combed the woods around Middleburg looking for his former best friend. Sometimes at the end of a long afternoon of searching he'd spring for pizza, since he knew money was tight for the Flats kids. He also spent a lot of blissful time at Lily Rose's, hanging out with Kate while she recovered from the injury those monstrous Black Snakes had inflicted on her. In the process, he'd ended up spending a lot of time with the Flatliners, too. And gradually, a strange thing happened: they all started becoming friends.

"Where are Emory and Nass?" Zhai asked, breaking his promise to sit quietly.

"Nass was supposed to be here an hour ago. The boy is late as usual," Dalton said with a sad shake of her head that Zhai knew was meant as a joke. She would definitely give Nass a hard time about it when he showed up, but that was just the way they were—always teasing each other. Their comic banter cracked Zhai up, and it gave him hope that one day he'd be comfortable enough with Kate to joke with her that way.

"Emory should be here any minute," Myka said, as she carefully applied Kate's eyeliner.

"What about Aimee? Has she hung out with you guys lately?" Zhai asked. He'd always been closer to Rick than to Rick's little sister, but like the Flatliners, he was worried about her new choice of companionship.

"Nope. I've barely seen her since the gym got demolished at homecoming," Dalton said. "We don't have as many classes together since we started the new schedule. Besides, she doesn't come to school much these days—and she hardly talks to me at all when she does. It's like she's a totally different person."

"Still spending all her time with Orias?" Zhai asked.

"I guess," Dalton replied with a frustrated shrug.

"I don't know how," Myka said as she brusquely applied blush to Kate's cheeks. "I work for him, you know, and he freaks me out. Always running around all perfect and gorgeous and always saying the right stuff. I watch him in meetings all day—he's cold, like a snake charmer. I'm telling you, Aimee is in way over her head."

Dalton nodded and sat down heavily in an old Papasan chair in the corner, as if the whole conversation depressed her.

Just then, the doorbell rang. "That's probably Emory," Myka said.

They could hear Lily Rose's muted greeting to the new guest, and a second later Emory poked his head into the room. He was wearing a black stocking cap, a pair of black pinstriped dress pants, and a black leather motorcycle jacket. He and Myka were the perfect couple, Zhai thought—they were the two most emo-looking kids at Middleburg High.

"I'm sorry," Emory whispered as soon as he was in the door.

"What?" Myka asked. His sudden, unexplained apology seemed to worry her.

"She begged me to let her come," Emory whispered. "And I can't say no to her. Ever since she almost got killed—" He shut his mouth the moment he realized Zhai was in the room. After an awkward pause, he looked back at Myka. "I just couldn't leave her at home," he finished.

"You have fun with the big kids!" they heard Lily Rose say from down the hall, and then a drumroll of quick, excited footsteps thumped toward them and a young girl appeared in the doorway. From the resemblance, Zhai knew she had to be Emory's little sister, and he guessed she had to be about ten. He didn't remember seeing her before, but for some reason she seemed slightly familiar.

"Hi, Myka!" the girl said, and she ran over and fiercely embraced her brother's girlfriend.

"Hey there, shrimp!" Myka returned cheerfully. "God, Haylee—you're strong! What are you, part gorilla?"

"I'm going out to dinner with you and my brother! You don't mind?"

"'Course not!" Myka said, giving a warm, reassuring smile to Emory, who smiled back at her apologetically.

"Emory said you might do some makeup for me!" Haylee said eagerly.

"Sure. Sit down in the chair here. Kate's all finished, right Kate?"

"Indeed I am," Kate replied in her pert Irish accent. "And my everlastin' thanks to you, Myka." She turned to Emory's sister and said, "She'll do you up right, lass! Myka's a regular Leonardo da Vinci of makeup!"

"You look beautiful, Kate," Zhai agreed, and as he spoke, the little girl's gaze fell upon him. Instantly, she went pale and began to back away. She turned and tried to run out the door, but her brother caught her.

"It's him!" she shouted, burying her face in Emory's jacket.

"It's okay," Emory said, stroking her hair. "He won't try to hurt you again, Haylee. Zhai wasn't himself that night, but he's okay now. Alright?"

Zhai finally understood. This was the little girl he'd tried to kill when he was under the control of the Order of the Black Snake. He felt suddenly sick with shame and remorse.

No wonder Emory, out of all the Flatliners, was the one who still looked at him with distrust. When Zhai had first shown up to help search for Raphael, he'd felt like Emory wanted to kill him. The anger in his eyes had lessened somewhat as the weeks passed and he saw that Zhai truly wanted the best for Raphael and the Flatliners—but it hadn't disappeared completely. Emory looked at Zhai again now, and the coldness in his eyes faded.

"It's okay, Haylee. Zhai is . . . a friend," he said at last.

Zhai came forward. "I'm sorry. I never meant to hurt you. And your brother is right—I'll never do it again. That's a promise," he said, and he extended his hand. Haylee moved tentatively out of her brother's embrace and took Zhai's hand for a moment. Everyone in the room smiled.

"Well, I guess we'll call and change our reservation to three," Emory said.

"Definitely," Myka agreed brightly, as she led Haylee over to the makeup chair.

"Oh, Dalton," Emory said. "Nass ran into a little trouble earlier, but I'm sure he'll be here soon. We were watching the apartment demolition and—"

Dalton raised a hand, waving away his explanation. "Don't tell me," she said. "I like to hear my excuses direct from the source, thank you very much."

Everyone laughed, imagining the trouble Nass was going to get into when he showed up late.

"Well, try to take it easy on him," Emory said.

"Shall we?" Zhai asked Kate. The unspoken truce that he and Emory had forged felt good, but he still didn't want to make Haylee uncomfortable.

"Bye," everyone called as Zhai and Kate headed out of the room, hand in hand.

Zhai was eager to get going—his driver was waiting outside to take them back to Kate's train car home, where Zhai had lots of exciting surprises in store.

∞

It was night by the time Rick stood at the second-floor window of the Starlite Cinema, his dad's newest downtown acquisition, watching Clarisse make her way across the parking lot. *That's my kind of girl,* he thought.

Up until this point in his life, the only place he'd really been able to be himself was on the football field. The rest of the world was riddled with all kinds of etiquette, rules he didn't like and didn't care to understand. He was supposed to watch out for people's feelings, help the less fortunate, be polite, and tolerate those who were weaker than him. To him, it was all a bunch of nonsense. The code of selflessness was like Chinese to him—some complex language he could never hope to understand.

But with Clarisse, everything was simple. Sometimes they desired each other. Sometimes they hated each other. But they were always eager to use each other, and to Rick, that made sense.

As perverse as it would seem to other people, Rick felt like Clarisse, even though she was a dumb Flats rat, was the only person in town who got him. With her, he could be his truest, purest, most animalistic self. She seemed to love it—and he almost loved her for it.

Once she'd disappeared from sight—heading, he guessed, back to the Flats—he took out his phone and made three calls. The first was to the florist, to send some lame bouquet to Maggie. Even though he had little interest in her these days, she was still head cheerleader and homecoming queen, and he still wanted her on his arm for social functions, so he knew he had to appease her with some sort of pathetic gesture. The second call was to order two large loaded pizzas. He was famished. The third call was to his best friend, Bran Goheen.

"What's up, slick Rick?" Bran answered.

"I'm downtown. Remember, I told you my dad bought the Starlite? Well, I snagged a key. The whole second floor is vacant."

Rick looked around. The room he was in was a wide-open loft space with ancient wood floors, high ceilings, and exposed brick walls. On the other side of the room, four high windows looked down on Middleburg's main street.

"This place is pretty cool. We should have a party or something. Come down—bring the guys. I already ordered pizza."

Bran hesitated. "I don't know, man. It's Valentine's Day. I'll come down, but I think most of the guys have dates."

Rick shook his head, feeling his ever-present anger rising again. What a world! All anyone seemed to care about was hugging and kissing and being fake with one another. He couldn't even understand his own friends sometimes. "Buncha wusses," he grumbled. "You're coming down though, right?"

"Sure, bro. I was in the car anyway. I'm like a block away. Be right there."

As Rick stared out the window at the parking lot, he caught sight of something that stirred his feelings even more than Clarisse had.

"All right, see you then. I gotta run," he said and ended the call.

In the parking lot below, one of the Flatliners, Emory, was getting out of the car with a couple of girls—probably heading for the back door of Rosa's Italian restaurant. And, Rick knew, Emory was the one whose apartment building was supposed to have been torn down today. He was the perfect Flatliner to make an example of, Rick thought, and he laughed out loud, hardly able to believe his good luck.

A few months ago, he would have held back, afraid of what Zhai might say if he started trouble, but these days the so-called Topper leader spent half his time hanging out with those Flatliner losers and looking for Raphael Kain. As far as Rick and the other Toppers were concerned, Zhai was a traitor—and most of the guys were now taking orders from Rick. That meant there was nothing to prevent him from going down there and unleashing every delicious drop of his hatred on that little Flats punk Emory. And, Rick thought gleefully, that was exactly what he was going to do.

"Time to earn that extra hundred bucks," he muttered to himself, and hurried toward the stairs.

∾

Myka had made an ironic mix of the fifteen cheesiest love songs of all time in honor of Valentine's Day. As Emory pulled his dad's beat-up Subaru station wagon into the parking lot behind Rosa's Trattoria, Myka and Haylee were singing along at the top of their lungs to Celine Dion's "My Heart Will Go On."

"All right, divas. We're here," he said as they pulled into the parking space, and he killed the stereo.

They all got out of the car and walked together across the dimly lit alleyway that ran behind Middleburg's main street. As they went, Myka took Emory's hand. Haylee sidled up to him on the other side and gave him a big bear hug around the waist, and they kept on moving. Ever since that traumatic night when Zhai, under the Obies' mind control, had almost killed her, Haylee was like a different person. Her former snotty attitude was gone. She obeyed her parents, and she clung to Emory as she hadn't done since she was a toddler.

"Thanks for being my Valentine, guys," she said, and Emory and Myka exchanged a smile.

"No problem, kiddo," Emory said. "You can hang with us any time."

Just then, a rocket sizzled across the sky and exploded in a brilliant fireworks display of spinners, snakes, and spirals. Haylee stopped and pointed up. "Oh—wow!" was all she said as the dazzling display was reflected in her eyes.

Emory looked up, too, at the scattering of fire sizzling across the heavens, just as a bright green explosion burst above them. It seemed so close that it might shower them in magical emerald embers.

Haylee squealed with delight and giggled.

At that moment, Emory caught movement in his peripheral vision. He glanced to his right to see a nondescript metal door on a building a few doors down drifting shut. Then, he saw a shadowed figure moving toward him. There were no lights in the parking lot, but in the glow cast by the next fireworks explosion he recognized the intruder: it was Rick Banfield.

"Guys, why don't you go inside and get us a table?" he said quickly, trying his best to sound casual. He had no idea why Rick was lurking in an alley after dark, but whatever was going on, Emory had to make sure his sister and Myka didn't get mixed up in it.

"No—I want to watch the fireworks!" Haylee protested.

Rick was coming closer now, and Myka followed Emory's sight line.

A look of fear crossed her face as she saw what Emory saw.

"Come on, Haylee. We have to go in," she said quickly, grabbing Haylee's arm and leading her toward the back door of Rosa's.

"But . . . but . . ." Haylee objected, but Myka was stronger than she looked. She dragged Haylee all the way to the door and shoved her gently but firmly into the dimly lit hallway.

As Rosa's door opened, Emory saw the burgundy carpeting inside, and smelled the comforting aromas of garlic and tomatoes and melted cheese. He heard the clink of dinnerware, the bustle of the kitchen, the soft, lilting melody of a strain of classical music. He saw Myka, silhouetted in the doorway, her slender figure framed in illumination. The features of her pale, beautiful face were rendered invisible by the backlight, but he knew exactly the look of love and concern she'd be wearing as she turned back to look at him.

They had grown close since his family got evicted. At first he imagined that she would dump him, that she'd want no part of dating some loser who was basically homeless—especially when she had a decent job working after school at Morningstar, Inc., and all he had was a paper route. But she'd stood by him. And at this moment, for the first time ever, he admitted to himself that he was in love with her. What he wanted now, more than anything in the world, was to be walking into that restaurant with her, holding her hand and listening to Haylee's stupid knock-knock jokes over a plate of steaming lasagna.

But before he could take a step toward the door, Rick emerged from the shadows, only a few feet away from him now.

"What's up, Flatliner? I hear you've been signing petitions," Rick said darkly. He cracked his knuckles. Suddenly, Emory was overcome with a feeling of blinding, electrifying rage. It was because of Rick and people like him—Toppers—that Emory's family had to live in a garage. It was because of them that they'd had to huddle together in the cold all winter while his sister cried herself to sleep at night. It was because of them that

Emory had lost the only home he'd ever known. Everything bad in his life was because of them. And here Rick was, king of the Toppers, ready to make fun of him for it.

"It's time for you to learn that little rats like you shouldn't be sticking their noses in places where they don't belong, *Emory.*"

Emory and Rick were eye to eye now, although Emory had to stand on his tiptoes to do it. He wanted to say something back, something clever, but the rage and adrenaline coursing through his body were too strong to allow him to speak. His hands were trembling, his whole body shivering. He didn't trust his voice not to quaver if he tried to talk.

"Emory, come on," Myka called from the doorway. Emory glanced over at her. Thank God, at least Haylee was hidden behind the big, solid wood door, unable to see the confrontation.

"Yeah, Emory," Rick whispered. "Go on inside with your skinny-ass Flats bitch and your little brat sister. Just don't forget that the next time you meddle in my dad's affairs, I'm going to take both of them and—"

"Go inside," Emory shouted to Myka, and then his eyes flicked back to Rick's.

"Emory, no! Come on," Myka said, her voice rising.

"GO INSIDE!" Emory yelled. "Take Haylee and shut the door!"

This time, he was so commanding that Myka obeyed immediately. The door clapped shut, and the light and the sounds of the restaurant disappeared, leaving Emory alone in the darkness with Rick. Another rocket burst overhead, painting the shadows with an eerie red light.

"Well, well," Rick said. "You're a man after all. All that eyeliner and those black-painted nails of yours, I thought you were girl for sure." He shook his head in disgust. "You people are always making things harder for my family, you know that? I can't even stand the sight of you."

Once again, Emory wanted to speak—a dozen retorts came to his mind—but he couldn't. His body convulsed once more with adrenaline, and without another word he snarled and threw the first punch. It caught

Rick in the eye and made him stumble back a few steps, but an instant later the Topper regrouped and was on the attack.

Emory managed to get his hands up in front of his face to block the first few blows, using the kung fu techniques that Raph had taught him. He even clipped Rick's cheek with another punch and caught him with a good kick to the thigh. But Rick's fists were as huge and heavy as sledge hammers, and with the next blow Emory tried to block, he felt a terrible pain in his forearm and knew instantly that it was broken. Before he could back up, Rick's other fist blasted him directly in the face. He was aware of being in mid-air, then landing hard on the ground, the back of his head cracking against blacktop. He must have blacked out for a second, because the next thing he knew he was on his back on the grimy pavement of the alley, moving all his limbs in a desperate but futile attempt to scramble away, like he was doing a backstroke on the pavement.

An elbow fell heavily on his stomach and vomit gushed into his mouth. Choking on it, he rolled onto his side to spit, then Rick's fist blasted into his temple, sending his head clacking off the pavement. His tongue slipped across his teeth, finding their edges no longer smooth and uniform, but broken and jagged. Two more blows hit him in the ribs, sending starbursts of pain through his chest and abdomen. Every shallow breath he took sent a sizzling lance of pain through his chest.

The world was spinning violently, and he couldn't see anything—but whether it was because there was blood in his eyes or because he'd somehow gone blind, he didn't know. His hands groped above his head, and he felt what had to be the edge of a Dumpster. He pushed with his legs, trying to clamber behind it, but the blows kept coming with mechanical precision, one after another after another. Someone was shouting. Someone was cursing. He was wet—with blood? Maybe urine? He didn't know. There was no order to the spin of his mind. He thought once more of Myka, standing in the doorway of the restaurant. His last thought was of the Valentine's Day card he was going to give her. It was in his jacket pocket, and he hoped it wasn't crumpled.

Another firework shimmered above, like an explosion of stardust. As it faded, Emory's mind surrendered to darkness.

CHAPTER 3

WHEN BRAN PULLED INTO THE PARKING LOT behind Rosa's Trattoria, he didn't see Rick at first. He got out of his car and walked across the parking lot and the darkened alley at his normal ambling pace, occasionally glancing up at the fireworks. July Fourth had always been his favorite holiday as a kid, and even though he would never admit it to Rick or any of his other macho friends, he loved watching the beautiful colors tracing across the sky.

He was almost to the back door of the Starlite when he heard the sound: a rhythmic thumping, like someone dribbling a basketball, with a few grunts and curses mixed in. His heart rate quickened, and he jogged toward the sound. There was movement in the shadow of a big green Dumpster and he hurried toward it, but the sight he witnessed there made him freeze.

It was Rick, and he was kneeling over someone. There was so much blood the guy's face was unrecognizable, but whoever it was made no effort to defend himself. He just lay there, completely limp, no more animate than a pile of dirty laundry.

For a second Bran felt like his brain had come untethered from his body and he watched, frozen with a bizarre sense of horrified detachment, as Rick cocked his fist back and brought it down once more on the distorted, unrecognizable face beneath him.

Then Bran was moving, grabbing Rick from behind, yanking him hard enough to haul his much bigger frame halfway across the alley in one mighty heave. He was talking, too, though he didn't remember when he'd started to speak: "Rick! What the hell are you doing? Stop! Stop! What did you do?"

Rick thrashed, but Bran was so juiced with adrenaline that it took Rick a moment to shake free of his grasp.

"Get off me!" Rick shouted. "That little Flats bitch had it coming, all right, for screwing around in my father's business."

Bran stared down at the figure on the ground. That was one of the Flatliners? The face was so bloody and broken he couldn't tell which one it was.

His body shivered violently, and for a second he thought he was going to throw up. Fumbling in his pocket, he pulled out his cell phone.

"What the hell are you doing?" Rick demanded.

"Calling an ambulance—what do you think?" Bran shouted.

Rick grabbed him and started dragging him away.

"Let go of me, Rick!"

By now, Rick had hauled Bran into the dimly lit parking lot between his SUV and a big delivery van. Sheltered from prying eyes, he grabbed the front of Bran's shirt and jerked him like a rag doll, so hard that his cell phone fell out of his hand.

"You listen to me, Bran. Listen carefully. You are part of this. Do you understand me?"

"We have to call, man. We don't, and he's going to die!"

"And what does that make you, tough guy? An accessory. Think about it. We have to get out of here."

Bran was shaking his head.

"Yes," Rick snarled. "We're getting out of here."

"No—Rick! We can't leave him like this! What's wrong with you?"

Rick jerked Bran again, so hard his teeth clacked together.

"You want to sell me out, Bran? You sure about that? You want your dad to lose his job? You want your parents to get tossed out of their house like a lousy Flats rat? And they'll lose their son, too, because I'll make damn sure everyone knows you helped me do it. Who do you think the police will believe? Jack Banfield's son—or you?"

Bran felt a tide of remorse and desperation like he'd never felt in his life. He suddenly realized that he hated Rick, that he'd always hated him. Why had he ever been friends with this guy in the first place? Just because he could throw a football? Because he hung out with all the hot cheerleaders? At that moment, Bran would have given anything in the world for a button he could press to rewind his life, so he could do it all again and never talk to Rick Banfield. What would it matter if he never played football, or if he wasn't popular? But there was no magical rewind button; it was too late.

And Rick was right. What good would it do anyone for Bran to end up in jail? For his father to lose his life's work? The kid was already hurt—nothing was going to change that.

"Listen. Spike Ferrington is having a training intensive in Topeka this weekend," Rick said. "We're going down there until Monday when all this has blown over. Now, we're going to stop by your house and drop your car off. I'll follow you, then you get in with me and we roll to Topeka. Got it?"

Spike was Rick's mixed martial arts instructor, Bran knew. He was one of the best in the state.

"Sure," Bran said, so quietly he could barely hear himself. "But what about school tomorrow?"

"Don't worry—my dad will work it out. Now go!"

As he pulled out of the parking lot, Bran looked back and saw the restaurant door opening, casting a puddle of warm yellow light across the concrete. Even from inside the car, he could hear the scream of whoever it was that discovered the kid Rick had brutalized. And he felt a measure of relief. It would be okay. Whoever it was would call an ambulance.

After they left his car in his driveway, parked next to his mom's little Smart Car, Bran jogged over to Rick's SUV and climbed into the passenger seat.

Rick, behind the wheel, was looking down at himself. "Dammit—would you look at this? I got blood on my brand-new shirt. Typical . . ." he grumbled.

"Who was it?" Bran asked.

"Who was what?" Rick seemed perfectly calm now—relaxed, even.

"The kid in the alley."

"Oh—it was that fairy Emory. Look, man—it had to be done. He was messing up my dad's business in the Flats. Somebody had to teach him a lesson."

Bran stared at the dashboard. In the sky above them, one final firework ignited, its fast-fading glow drizzling across the windshield before disappearing again into darkness.

The worst part, Bran thought, was that he didn't even know which Flatliner was Emory. As much as he'd hated the rival gang members and wanted to hurt them and blamed them for his and his friends' problems, the sad fact was that he didn't know them at all.

✧

Clarisse hurried up the alley as fast as she could without breaking into a run.

After leaving Rick, she had doubled back to sit on the curb outside the parking lot, out of the reach of streetlights, and watch the door to Rick's little upstairs lair. She knew they weren't exclusive but somehow knowing it made her feel even more possessive, and she'd decided to spy on him to see if that conceited cheerleader Maggie was going to show up. The thought of catching Rick in a lie gave her a painful satisfaction, she thought, like when you wiggle a loose tooth with your tongue: even though it hurts and you can taste your own blood, somehow it's impossible to stop.

When she had first started following Rick, if someone had asked her what the attraction was, she wouldn't have been able to tell them. Sure, she'd always had a thing for bad boys—her fling with that drug dealer back home after Nass had moved to Middleburg proved that. Her relationship with Oscar Salazar had been sick—so sick that she'd scammed him out of a ton of money and had to flee Los Angeles in fear for her life. But never, even during her thing with Oscar, had she obsessed over a guy like she was doing with Rick.

It wasn't just because he was hot or rich or because he was a football star. She liked those things, but they didn't fascinate her. Rick had a certain indefinable primitive power about him, like some kind of exotic jungle beast. She liked the way he just grabbed her when he was in the mood to make out, without bothering to see if she was up for it. That, she just thought of as taking charge (which she really liked in a guy), but there was something more, something deeper in him that she was trying to discover. It was like . . . a kind of dark, uncontrollable energy bordering on violence that was always on the edge of erupting. And if she could discover what drove Rick, what gave him the brute strength that was somehow connected to the darkness, she might be able to control him.

She had been sitting there on the curb, in the shadows, thinking about all this when Emory, Myka, and Haylee had emerged from the car. She'd seen Rick come out of the doorway. She'd inched silently forward behind a row of hedges that formed one border of the parking lot, and from the hidden shelter of their boughs she'd watched what Rick had done to Emory. In the fleeting glare of the fireworks, she'd even caught a glimpse of the same thing she'd seen the night of the big fight on the tracks when she thought she'd lost her mind. The thing she watched for every time they made out, and both hoped and dreaded to see: *Rick's face transformed into that of a snarling demon.*

That night, the sight had filled her with fascination that had quickly turned into lust, even though she had been sure she had imagined it. But tonight, she knew it was real. Maybe she should have felt revulsion after witnessing the beating he gave Emory, but her fascination with and desire for Rick hadn't diminished at all. The truth was, it had increased tenfold.

After Rick and Bran took off, she lingered long enough to see Myka emerge from the back door of the restaurant. She heard Myka's scream, and she saw her push Emory's little sister back inside. She'd heard Myka's words coming out in sobs as she called the ambulance. Then, as stealthily as possible, Clarisse split. If growing up streetwise in one of the worst neighborhoods in L.A. had taught her anything, it was the skill of selective amnesia. It was not a good thing to be the only witness to a crime, especially when the perpetrator was rich and well connected. *No,* she told herself, *she hadn't seen anything. If the cops ever found out she'd been with Rick that night, she'd make sure they knew she'd left Rick and headed straight home, and that she was blocks away when the fight had happened.*

It wouldn't be as easy to manage Rick as it was to manipulate Nass, she thought as she cut up the next side street toward the brightness and relative bustle of Middleburg's main thoroughfare. She'd fallen for Rick because she thought he was dangerous. She was a little afraid of him, and the fear was delicious—and there could be a great advantage to having a demon for a boyfriend. If her plan worked out, all her problems with Oscar and his drug-dealing crew back in South Central would be solved—permanently.

♥

The sound of the scream jerked Maggie out of her meditation and caused her eyes to snap open.

Just a few months ago, the idea that she would be happy sitting at home alone and meditating on Valentine's Day night would have been completely inconceivable. But tonight, that's just what she'd done. She had taken a bath, caught up on her homework, read a book for a while, watched some stupid videos online, texted back and forth to some of her friends to check up on their night, and then settled in for her daily meditation, just as Lily Rose and *The Good Book* had instructed her to do. The book the old woman had given Maggie not long after homecoming, when she'd felt so lost and confused, did give her comfort and guidance even though she didn't quite understand how it worked. At first, she'd thought it was a Bible, but when she'd opened it she'd seen that it was something very different. Its blank pages were luminous, like clouds at night with the moon shining through them. And just when you needed an answer most, words would appear on those pages. But they hadn't yet told her what to do about Rick.

A flower-delivery guy came by earlier with his pathetic bouquet, his attempt at maintaining the charade of their relationship. Even that hadn't dampened Maggie's mood. She had no idea what had made him relax his controlling attitude toward her over the last couple of months, but whatever it was, she was grateful. He still went through the motions. Sometimes he'd force a kiss from her in the lunchroom, where she wouldn't be able to pull away without causing a scene. Sometimes he'd coerce her, with veiled threats about her mother's health, into going with him to one of his Topper dinners at Spinnacle. But more and more he left her alone, and that was fine with her.

The only boy she really wanted to spend Valentine's Day with had been vaporized on the old railroad tracks by a spectral locomotive. The memory sent a blinding howl of agony through her soul.

She didn't know where Raphael was or what had happened to him, but for some reason she held out hope that somewhere, somehow, he was still alive. She'd seen enough magic in this weird old dump of a small town that nothing would surprise her. Sometimes when she meditated she could almost feel Raphael's presence; it felt like if she just concentrated hard enough, she would be able to reach out her hand and find him there. She was having that extraordinary, heavenly feeling on Valentine's Day night when her mother's scream cut her meditation short.

Maggie galloped down the stairs and into her mother's breakfast-room-turned-art-studio in seconds.

"What, Mom? What happened?" she asked, but as soon as the words were out of her mouth, she saw the answer.

The tapestry her mother worked obsessively on day and night was suspended in front of her, the fabric held taut by a huge wooden frame. And the part of the picture her mother had been embroidering was now covered in blood.

Violet sat in a chair in front of the tapestry, gripping her wrist.

"I—I didn't do it!" she stammered as Maggie hurried over to assess the situation.

Her mother's half-eaten New York strip steak sat on a plate nearby. The steak knife lay discarded on the floor near her feet. Even without picking it up, Maggie could see blood on its edge.

"Let me see," Maggie commanded, gently taking Violet's injured arm and pulling her fingers away from it. A thin stream of blood drizzled from the wound, and Maggie felt her stomach turn.

"Oh, Mom!" she shouted, and she grabbed the linen napkin off the table and hurried to bind up the cut.

"I wasn't trying to hurt myself, Maggie. I swear! I fell asleep—I—and when I woke up, I was bleeding."

"Mom . . ." Maggie began, but she didn't know what to say. She wanted to chastise her mother. In the long progression of Violet's mental illness, this was a new low. But what was the point in yelling at her? Violet had never understood or cared how her erratic actions affected Maggie, and anyway, the priority now was to get her medical attention.

"We have to get you to the clinic in Benton," Maggie sighed. "I'll get my purse."

"No! Just call Master Chin."

Maggie rolled her eyes. "He's an old kung fu teacher, Mom. Not a doctor."

"He's a healer, and he's better than anybody over in Benton," Violet said defiantly. "And anyway, I'm not leaving. I have too much work to do."

Maggie couldn't keep the disdain out of her voice. "Work? On what, the tapestry? In case you didn't notice, Mom, it's ruined. Just like my night." She tried to swallow the bitter thought: *Just like all my nights, trying to take care of you.*

At the mention of the tapestry, they both glanced at it. This design was huge. It was by far the largest tapestry her mother had ever undertaken, and she had been working on a small section in one corner when the "accident" had happened. As Maggie stared at the bloodstained cloth, a bizarre realization struck her. The scene her mother had been working on was of a young man lying prostrate in an alleyway. Violet's blood had stained the canvas in such a way that it looked like the blood was seeping from the body, onto the ground beneath it. The design wasn't ruined, Maggie realized with morbid fascination. Quite the opposite—the blood had completed it.

She knew from overhearing conversations between her mother and Master Chin that the scenes depicted in the tapestries sometimes seemed to reflect things that were really happening in Middleburg or things that were going to happen. And she didn't care to imagine what ramifications this image might hold.

Maggie studied the creepy scene for a moment longer and then blinked and shook her head, as if trying to dislodge the image from her mind. "I'll call Master Chin," she said.

∽

Zhai sat in the flickering candlelight in Kate's train car. They'd finished the dinner she'd prepared on her new electric stove, talked for a while, and then Zhai had shown her how to load the dishes into the dishwasher he'd had installed as a surprise while she was staying at Lily Rose's. He'd had the whole place decked out while she was away.

When he'd flipped a switch and the lights had come on (thanks to the gas-powered generator) her sudden, awed intake of breath was captivating. She squealed with delight when he turned on the faucet of the new sink and water flowed through it from a well he'd had drilled. She was thrilled with the stove and the small refrigerator, too. In her little living room section, he'd placed a Bose iPod SoundDock that played romantic music throughout their meal. He'd had a bathroom installed, complete with a shower, and there was even a 3-D HDTV mounted to the back wall of the car connected to a satellite dish affixed to the roof.

She'd been especially delighted with the television set, but they hadn't turned it on yet tonight. Oddly enough, the only thing that fascinated Kate more than the TV was the dishwasher. As it churned away quietly in the kitchenette section of the train car, she kept glancing over at it with a look of wide-eyed, childlike amazement on her face. She hadn't really believed him when he'd told her it was a machine just for washing dishes.

"To think!" she said. "'Tis a wonder, truly!"

Kate's reactions to modern conveniences were not lost on Zhai. She also had a strange, old-world way of talking that was just as charming as her accent, and he had several theories about where she might have come from in Ireland. He knew from the Internet that there were Amish communities in Ireland, and there were convents; it was entirely possible that Kate had grown up in one of them.

So far, she had volunteered little information about how she'd come to America or what her life was like before she arrived, and Zhai respected their unspoken agreement by not asking too many questions. Still, he found her sense of wonder at the simplest things fascinating, and infectious.

"Really, Zhai, you shouldn't have done so much for me. You've turned my little home into the eighth wonder of the world!" she exclaimed, and reaching across the table, she took his hand.

He felt his heart rate increase, and he took a deep breath, trying to steady himself. "It was nothing," he said. "I still wish you'd think about staying with my family. The guesthouse is hardly ever used—" But Kate was already shaking her head.

"Thank you. You're so sweet to me, but I've never been one to accept charity. And I don't expect I'll be stayin' in Middleburg much longer. . . ."

Zhai looked into her eyes, and this time, for once, he didn't let himself look away.

"Kate, I know we don't talk about that much—why you came, when you're going back—but if you're having trouble getting home, if you need a plane ticket, I'd be happy to get one for you—round-trip, so you could come back whenever you like. Or I could loan you the money."

Kate's smile was sad and joyous at once. "Fly on one of those big silver monsters?" she exclaimed with a laugh. "Actually, I would love it, but I'm afraid it isn't as simple as all that . . . I wouldn't leave Middleburg at all if it weren't for my family."

Zhai nodded. "I just want to help you however I can. And when the time comes, I want you to do what you need to do to be happy. Even if that means going away from me for a while."

Kate smiled; she looked radiant, and as always, it made him want to kiss her and never stop kissing her. He forced himself to continue.

"But in the meantime," he said, his heart now beating out of control and beads of sweat slipping down his forehead and his sides beneath his shirt. "In the meantime," he repeated, fighting to keep his voice steady, "I was hoping that maybe you might want to . . . to be my girlfriend."

"I've been wondering when you'd get up the gumption to ask," she said sweetly. "Certainly! Of course I will!"

Zhai was so delighted he laughed out loud, and Kate joined in. Her laugh seemed like music to him, and it was the most carefree sound in the world. It made him laugh even louder.

"Well, I expect you should kiss me now, don't you?" she asked.

Suddenly serious, Zhai's gaze softened and he leaned across the table. "Yes," he whispered and his voice was steady and sure. "I believe I should." Just as their lips were about to meet, something buzzed loudly in his jacket pocket.

"Just, um . . . just a second . . ."

He dug into his pocket for a moment before finally pulling out his cell phone. He was about to shut it off when he looked at the screen and saw that it was Master Chin. Phone calls from Zhai's kung fu instructor where rare. If Chin called, it was usually for something really important.

"I should take it," he said apologetically, and he answered the call.

The conversation was brief. Chin was at Maggie Anderson's house, and he needed Zhai to come there right away; it was urgent.

"I'll be there soon," Zhai promised and ended the call. "Sorry," he said as he turned back to Kate, who was eyeing the phone in his hand. They'd had a few conversations about how cell phones worked, but Kate was still almost overcome with wonder every time Zhai made or got a call. That would have to be his next gift to her, he vowed to himself: a cell phone.

"I really have to go," he told her. "Master Chin is waiting for me in Hilltop Haven. I guess it's something important. You can come, if you want," he added hopefully.

"Oh, I'd love to, my dear—but if it's all the same, I'd like to stay here. I can't wait to see the dishes when they come out of the washer machine!"

Zhai laughed. "Okay," he said. "You remember how to open it?"

She nodded.

"Thanks for being my valentine, okay?"

Kate beamed at him. "Always," she said.

∾

It was getting pretty late by the time Zhai got to the palatial Anderson house. He was surprised when Maggie answered his knock.

"Hey, Maggie," he said. "I figured you'd be out with Rick."

She gave him a mysterious smile. "Nope. He let me off the hook tonight. Come on in. Master Chin and my mom are in the sewing room."

Zhai followed Maggie into the room and found Master Chin sitting with Mrs. Anderson, taping a fresh bandage on her arm.

"Zhai, I'm glad you came," Master Chin said as Zhai entered the room. He finished securing the bandage and then stood and went to Zhai, speaking quickly. Whatever was going on, Zhai knew, it had to be urgent.

"Look at the tapestry with me," Chin said, steering him toward the large expanse of fabric suspended within a wooden frame. It was a large swatch of heavy, off-white cloth, and about half of it had a scene embroidered onto it; the rest was blank. Chin pointed to the bottom right-hand corner of the tapestry, which had been completed, and Zhai's gaze followed his gesture. The scene depicted a person lying face down in a pool of what looked to Zhai like real blood that had soaked into the canvas.

"This scene in particular," Chin said. "I think it might have recently taken place—or it's about to. Have you seen anything like this? Or heard about anyone injured recently?"

"No," Zhai said, studying the picture. Staring at the image seemed to evoke a swirling of Shen energy, like a cold ball deep within his chest cavity. It wasn't the normally warm, life-affirming Shen he was used to experiencing. This feeling, he was sure, was a warning—or a premonition.

"What about the rest? What does it bring to mind?"

Zhai squinted at the part of the tapestry just above the fallen person. It appeared to depict a different scene, this one of a darkened space with a bright, arched doorway leading out of it. In the center of the dark space there was a ring-shaped object—it looked solid at first, but upon closer inspection, it appeared as if it was broken and had been pieced back together.

As Zhai stared at it, the dark room on the tapestry suddenly seemed to shift, and his eyes picked out a pattern of threads that were a slightly lighter shade of black than the others. He was able to make out the outline of a person who floated, ghost-like, above the ring. The figure was featureless, but Zhai could see that it had broad, masculine shoulders and long hair. *Raphael,* he thought instantly. As his eyes traced downward, he noticed something else that hadn't jumped out at first glance: a subtle pattern at the bottom of the embroidered room that looked like crossed railroad tracks.

"It's Raphael," Zhai said quietly. "Or his ghost. And it looks like he's in the old rail tunnels, at the Wheel of Illusion. The ring is there too, and it's been put back together. It's like . . . like it's making him materialize."

Master Chin nodded eagerly. "I thought so too," the sifu agreed. "Do you still have your shard of the ring?"

"Yes," Zhai said.

"Meet me outside the east tunnel at noon tomorrow, and bring it with you. If you can get any other shards, bring those too—and I'll bring mine as well. Perhaps there is still enough Shen in them to spark the Wheel back to life."

"You think that's what this means? That if we get the shards back together we'll be able to bring Raph back from wherever he is?"

"I don't know," Master Chin said darkly. "But I think it's important that we try."

"Okay. Noon," Zhai agreed.

"I'm coming too," Maggie said quickly, and the guys both turned around and looked at her.

Zhai glanced at his sifu, expecting him to contradict her, but instead he said, "Good. Zhai will pick you up."

It seemed like a surprising turn of events, until Zhai remembered the blast of Shen that Maggie had unleashed during the last battle at the tracks—the one that had sent the Obies' Black Snake God flying. She had been wearing her homecoming queen crown, and some kind of energy had seemed to flow from it, and through Maggie, with incredible force. With power like that, no wonder Master Chin wasn't too worried about her safety. Besides, Maggie had taken part in all the searches for Raphael so far. Zhai didn't know why, but she seemed just as eager to find him as any of the Flats kids were. If she wanted to come along, Zhai would be glad to have her.

He glanced at his watch. "I'd better go," he said. "I'm ten minutes past curfew. After Li's illness and then my disappearing with those Black Snake guys, my parents get pretty jumpy when we're late these days."

"Zhai—one more thing," Master Chin said as he gazed at the blood-stained cloth. "Keep your eyes open for this injured person, whoever he is. If there's any way you can, try to prevent it from happening. I fear that once this event takes place, there will be no stopping what will follow."

"And what's that?" Maggie asked.

"Middleburg's darkest destiny," Chin replied.

෨

Nass had been lying on the floor of the windowless interrogation room for hours, drifting in and out of sleep. This time when he woke up, however, something was different. There was warm air blowing on his face, and he could hear voices. They sounded like they were echoing to him from far away, but he could hear them clearly. It only took him a moment to determine that the two voices belonged to Agent Hackett and Detective Zalewski.

"Listen," Z was saying. "These kids are full of crap. You saw their statements. They read like the freakin' *Lord of the Rings*."

"Thank you, detective, but I'll decide that for myself," Hackett replied, his voice icy calm.

"These kids are scum, agent. The dregs of Middleburg. We're talking broken homes, alcoholic parents, flunkin' out of school, getting into fights. They'd say Martians landed in Hilltop Haven if they thought it would get them off the hook for something. Their stories are nonsense."

"Are they? What if I were to tell you that the National Ocean and Atmospheric Administration satellites registered a massive energy disturbance in this region at the exact time these kids are claiming their friend disappeared in an explosion? Would you still say they are all liars, detective?"

"Well, okay, sure," Z stammered. "We noted some trees had been knocked down in the area. You'll see that in the reports. Probably some stupid teenager's cherry bomb or something. What does this have to do with your case, anyway? I thought you said this was a manhunt."

Hackett's voice lowered in volume, so that Nass had to inch toward the source of the sound in order to hear him.

"Detective, I'm sure you've heard in the movies where a spy says, 'I could tell you, but then I'd have to kill you'? Well, I'll tell you this, but it's absolutely classified. So if you repeat it to anyone . . ."

"Understood," Z interrupted gruffly. "I just want to be in the loop so I can cooperate with you, Agent Hackett, that's all."

There was a pause and then Hackett continued. "The guy we're looking for is a Chinese secret agent, specializing in advanced energy generation and weapons system technology. He works completely off the grid, and his men are insanely loyal. According to our reports, they operate almost like a cult. Now as lovely as Middleburg is, I don't think Feng Xu and his agents are here looking to take a five-star Kansas vacation."

"So what are they after?" Z asked. "It's not like we have any advanced energy generation equipment or weapons systems in Middleburg—do we?"

"That's what I intend to find out, detective. One thing all these kids' stories have in common is some treasure—a ring—that exploded, releasing so much energy that it was detected from space. Whatever it was, it sounds like it vaporized this Raphael Kain kid. And before this ring surfaced, Chinese agents were combing the town looking for it. I think you can connect the dots."

"So . . . what? You stopped the demolition in the Flats because you think the ring is still hidden there someplace?"

"My mission isn't to find the ring," Hackett said. "The witnesses all say it was destroyed in the blast, anyway. All I care about is capturing Feng Xu. He's clearly here because he's after something. Maybe it's some technology associated with the ring, maybe something else. Whatever it is, I won't allow one scrap of evidence to be destroyed until I've got him. That means nothing gets bulldozed, nothing gets renovated, and no one leaves town. I've already got more men en route, and we're setting up checkpoints on all roads in and out of Middleburg."

"What about the Flats kid?" Z asked.

"I'll worry about him. Your job is now PR. As the investigation unfolds, residents are going to call with questions. Your job is to BS them until they stop asking. Got it?"

"Whatever you say, Wade. I'm a team player."

Nass heard a groan of chairs scraping across the floor, as if both men had stood up from a table. A second later, he heard the door open, and Agent Hackett entered and flipped on the lights.

Nass looked over and saw where the voices had been coming from: there was a hot-air vent in the floor right next to the spot where he'd passed out. The voices must have traveled to him through the heating duct. He was glad he'd heard the conversation, but he still wasn't sure what to make of it—or what it would mean for him now.

Hackett sat down in the room's only chair once again and calmly flipped through a file as Nass sat up and squinted at him, his vision adjusting to the sudden glare.

"What time is it?" he asked.

Hackett ignored the question. "The statements of several witnesses mention a glowing ring of some kind that was seen on the night that Raphael Kain disappeared."

"Yeah, there was a ring," Nass confirmed.

"And where is it now?"

"It disappeared. In the explosion."

"Where there any remains? Any pieces of it left lying around?"

The knowing flared once again, an overwhelming feeling that urged Nass to keep silent. He could tell the truth about everything else, but something told him that telling this guy about the ring shards would be a bad idea.

He shrugged. "My friends and I walked all over those tracks while we were looking for Raphael. Maybe it vaporized."

"Or maybe those Obies picked up whatever was left of it?"

"Maybe," Nass said. "After the explosion I never saw the Obies again."

Hackett's shrewd gaze lingered on Nass for a long moment before he spoke again. "You remember that picture I showed you?" he said finally. "I expect you to let me know if you see that man or any of his minions again. I know you and your pals are out running the streets all the time. Keep me posted, all right?"

He handed Nass a plain white business card. It had his name printed on it, *Agent Wade Hackett,* and a phone number—nothing else.

"You help me out, I can be your best friend. If not, not. You feel me, Ignacio? Do we understand each other?"

"Yep. Got it," Nass said, unable to restrain his irritation any longer. "Can I go now, please? I have a date. It is Valentine's Day, you know."

Hackett chuckled, glancing at his watch. "Not anymore, it isn't," he said.

≈

Dalton sat on the edge of her bed, staring at a picture of herself and Nass from the Middleburg High School annual play. It was slightly warped from the spots where her tears had hit it, but it was dry now. She had finished crying a long time ago.

She heard her grandmother's gentle knock at the door and looked up.

"Just wanted to say goodnight, sweetie," Lily Rose said, peering around the edge of the doorframe. She moved to walk away, and then paused. "Don't you worry, sugar. Nass is a good boy. If he stood you up, I expect he had a good reason."

Dalton forced a sad smile. "He always does," she said.

She knew exactly what her grandmother was saying: be kind, be patient, forgive and forget. But those were just words. Actions were what mattered. Nass had blown her off for Clarisse at the homecoming dance, and now he'd stood her up on Valentine's Day. Of course she wanted to be forgiving, as her grandma always urged her to be. But she also knew that she deserved a guy she didn't have to forgive all the time. And she was afraid she'd have to accept the heartbreaking fact that Nass wasn't that guy.

Her grandmother's sigh seemed to contain enough sympathy to match the pathos Dalton was feeling—and then some.

"Goodnight, little girl of mine. See you in the morning shine," she said.

"'Night, Grandma," Dalton said. And with a heavy heart, she reached over and turned out the light.

CHAPTER 4

BY THE TIME NASS REACHED THE DOOR of his family's apartment building early Friday morning, the faint, pale glow of dawn was illuminating the eastern horizon.

Great, he thought. His mother was an early riser, and their apartment was tiny. There was no way he could sneak in unnoticed. And missing curfew on Valentine's Day (especially since it was a week night) would probably give him an even steeper penalty than usual—maybe even a speech about responsibility, unplanned pregnancy, and traditional Catholic values. Explaining that he'd spent the night at the police station would result in another round of lectures. And that was nothing compared to the punishment he would receive soon, when he got to Middleburg High and got hold of Dalton. Nass braced for the onslaught to come as he stepped through the door and found his mother seated at the kitchen table, head bowed, and gazing pensively down into her coffee cup. Softly, he closed the door behind him and she looked up, her eyes wild with worry and red, as if she'd been crying.

He sighed. This wasn't going to easy; he might as well just be direct. "Don't get mad," he began. "I can explain where I was . . ."

But she stood and rushed eagerly to him. "Oh, 'Nacio! I heard, honey. How is he?" She seemed gravely concerned.

Nass was confused. "How is who?"

"'Nacio, this is no time for jokes. Myka's mother said he's in critical condition!"

Instantly, Nass's mind leaped to Raphael. Had they found him while

Nass was at the police station? Was he hurt? Sick? Two feelings struck him at the same time—excitement that his friend and leader might be back and dread at what his mother had said: *he's in critical condition.*

She was still talking. "Is it true? She said they added a critical-care unit to the little hospital at Benton and they're going to keep him there until he stabilizes. You're such a good friend for spending the whole night with him. Was everyone else there, too?"

Nass felt numb. His mind wheeled wildly as he tried to process what had happened. "I need the car. I need to go there," he said.

"You want to go back to the hospital?" she said. "Oh, dear God—it must be really bad! Of course—go, *mijo.* Go!"

Nass grabbed the keys off the hook by the door.

"Tell his family we're praying for them. And drive carefully!" But Nass barely heard her words as he raced out the door and down the steps.

ॐ

Friday morning, Aimee gazed out the car window at the gray wintery streets of downtown Middleburg as Orias went through his almost daily ritual of convincing her that she had to go back to school.

"Your father wants you there at least four days a week *from now on,*" he scolded her sweetly as they drove along Main Street toward Middleburg High.

She turned and made a little face at him. "Why?" she asked. "I can't learn anything there that you can't teach me. Anyway, I'm keeping up—turning everything in on time."

"He has laid down the law, it seems," Orias told her. "I think he's concerned about your reputation."

"If he only knew. I'm safer with you than in a convent."

"He does know. He's worried about what other people think. And he wants you to spend some time at home this weekend."

"Again—why?" she asked.

"He said he has something important to talk to you about—and

Monday, he's having a big dinner party that we're both invited to. He said he's going to make some kind of big announcement."

Aimee groaned. "I can hardly wait," she said, her tone touched with sarcasm.

Orias pulled his Maserati into the student lot and put it in park. "You should probably get a ride with Rick after school and check in at home," he said.

"No, pick me up, please. Don't leave me with my brother—he's getting creepier by the minute," she said. "Or I can just slip."

"We've talked about that, Aimee" he reminded her. "Someone could see you. I'll pick you up."

"Won't you be busy with the contractors over at Elixir?"

"Never too busy for you." He leaned over and gave her a quick kiss. "See you later then. But give your dad a call and let him know, okay? You'll have to see him sometime."

Aimee took a deep breath, as if preparing herself to face an enemy, and got out of the car. Watching her head for the auditorium's side entrance, Orias hoped she would look back—but he knew she wouldn't. He wondered if she forgot him as soon as he was out of sight.

That didn't matter, as long as she forgot Raphael Kain.

He didn't know how much longer he could dose her with the tea. Oberon, his father, had told him once that drinking too much of it over an extended period of time could drive a human insane.

Orias uttered a low curse, annoyed. He should have let her go by now—sent her back to her father or gotten rid of her in some other way. Once the crystal ring exploded and lost its glorious power, she was of no more use to him.

But, he had told himself, since she had been the one destined to retrieve the ring, perhaps she could help in his bid to permanently take over his father's holdings and assume control of the Dark Territory. Aimee Banfield was part of it—part of the whole tapestry. The Big Picture. She still had an important part to play in it all—and once he figured out what it was he would be able to make a new plan to take his father's holdings, and his power, for good and forever.

Anyway, he would have found it almost impossible to get through the aftermath of the explosion without her. He had been so enraged and so devastated at losing the ring that he'd wanted to destroy Middleburg and everything else in his path. If the explosion hadn't drained his strength, he would have gone on a monstrous rampage. But Aimee had been amazing—unaffected by the blast and so solicitous, so genuinely concerned about him. She had gone home with him, put him to bed, and cared for him for three days and nights, until he started coming around.

That's when she'd started staying with him, insisting that he needed her, but even when he got better, she avoided going back to the Banfield house. That should have bothered Orias. If it were anyone else, their constant presence would have felt like an awful invasion of privacy, but with Aimee it was different. Everything was different.

The truth was that even once he got over the effects of the blast and was able to think more clearly, he still liked having her in his life. He wanted her for as long as he could have her.

And Orias Morrow was accustomed to getting everything he wanted.

❧

In her continuing efforts to avoid Rick, Maggie had arrived at school as the first bell rang, just in time to make it to first-period study hall, which was held in the auditorium. Dalton, who sat next to her, already had her history book open.

Some things had changed—besides class schedules—since Maggie had raised her voice at the homecoming dance and destroyed the gymnasium. She and Dalton now had a few classes together and the icy situation between them had thawed considerably since Maggie had insisted on helping the Flatliners search for Raphael. The thing they had most in common, and probably what they liked best about each other, was that neither of them hesitated for one second to say what she thought.

Maggie hardly ever saw her old friends anymore, including the other cheerleaders, Lisa Marie and Bobbi Jean, and it wasn't only that she no longer had that much in common with them. Spending time with them would have meant hanging out with the jocks—and that would have meant seeing Rick. She was about to ask Dalton about one of their homework assignments when she saw Aimee coming in. She nodded in Aimee's direction.

"He dropped her off again this morning," she said when Dalton looked up and followed her gaze.

"Orias?" Dalton asked.

Maggie nodded. "I saw them as I came in. Kissing." After a moment she added, "Does she ever mention Raphael?" She almost dreaded to hear the answer.

"No." Dalton shook her head. "And if I mention him, she acts like she doesn't know who I'm talking about—most of the time."

"Really?" In spite of trying not to allow it, Maggie's hopes rose just a little. It wasn't clear to Maggie exactly what Orias was doing in Middleburg, but she was pretty sure it wasn't a good idea for Aimee to be practically living with him. She still felt guilty that she hadn't tried to help Aimee that day in the auditorium, when Orias had taken Aimee's hand and filled her aura with his strange energy—but she couldn't help being glad that Aimee showed every sign of having gotten over Raphael.

"You really like him, don't you?" asked Dalton. For the first time, Maggie heard real sympathy in her voice.

Maggie gave a little shrug. "Everybody likes Raphael," she replied.

Dalton reacted to Maggie's noncommittal response with one of her trademark "yeah right" looks. That was another reason their friendship had blossomed over the last few months: nothing got past Dalton.

But now, Maggie fell silent as Aimee took the seat next to her.

"What about you, Aimee?" Dalton said. "You *used* to like him, right?"

The second bell saved Aimee from answering right away. "Who?" she asked when the clanging stopped. She took off her coat, threw it over the back of the chair in front of her, and balanced her notebook and purse on her lap. She had neither books nor backpack.

"Raphael," Dalton said, and when Aimee just looked blank and remained silent, she added, "Raphael Kain, Flatliner bad boy that you hung out with all during the play?"

"Oh—him," Aimee said. "He's okay, I guess."

Mr. Brighton, their study hall teacher as well as their drama instructor, didn't verbally call the roll; he sent an attendance roster around for everyone to sign. And he wasn't strict about the no-talking rule, as long as it related to homework and didn't get too rowdy. The three girls signed the attendance sheet and passed it on. Maggie turned her history book to the same page Dalton had open.

"Aimee . . . what's wrong with you?" Dalton whispered. "You know you and Raphael had a major thing. During the play you guys were—"

Aimee interrupted again, as if she didn't want to be reminded. "Right—the play," she said. "Yeah, I guess. But then the play was over and whatever I thought I felt for—for that boy—that was over too."

Dalton frowned and Maggie could tell she wasn't buying it. "But you went to the homecoming dance with him," Dalton argued.

Aimee's brow furrowed slightly as if she was trying to remember. "I guess . . . I did," she said vaguely. "I don't know why. My dad says I was just going through my rebellious stage. Anyway, then I met Orias," she finished, as if that explained everything.

None of them noticed Mr. Brighton approaching. "Okay, girls," he said softly, glancing down at the open books. "Are we talking American history, or the history of who likes who at Middleburg High? Aimee, do you need to borrow a book from someone?"

She looked at him, her expression dreamy. "Yes, thanks," she said pleasantly. "I must have forgotten mine."

It was time for Friday morning classes to start, but Nass wasn't at school; he was driving, on his way to Benton. As he drove, he looked at his cell phone for perhaps the fifth time, and then reminded himself that it was dead. Agent Hackett had taken it from him when he locked him in the police station, and when he got it back, the battery was spent. He wished desperately that it was working so he could call and check in with Beet, the only other Flatliner with a cell phone, but he didn't have a car charger. He'd just have to wait until he got to Benton to find out what was going on.

When he finally arrived the sun was up. Its bright, clear golden rays soared through the trees, streaking across a pale blue sky. It looked to Nass like the banner proclaiming the arrival of an early spring, but the beauty around him made the sickening worry and exhaustion he felt even worse.

When Nass had first moved to Middleburg, Benton had been the location of the nearest walk-in clinic and a pretty lame one at that. With the recent opening of the Benton Regional Medical Center, however, the town now boasted a full-fledged hospital, complete with an ER, an intensive-care unit, and an outpatient surgery wing—at least according to the sign. The place even smelled new, Nass noticed as the automatic doors slid open, ushering him inside. But he didn't take more than a second to look at the décor of the place. He was already hurrying up to an information desk when he caught sight of Beet pacing in a pastel-colored waiting area with furniture covered in a thick, plastic floral motif. He glanced around and saw that the rest of the Flatliners were there, too, all of them sitting silently together with downcast eyes.

And then he saw Emory's family sitting in the corner. His sister, Haylee, was wearing a fancy dress and crying quietly while her mother cradled her in her arms. His father just stared at the far wall, looking completely rigid and empty, like a wooden carving of himself instead of a real person.

Myka sat a little ways away from everyone else with her arms crossed over her chest and her eyes closed.

Benji was the first to notice Nass, and he nudged Josh with his elbow, causing him to look up. When Josh saw Nass, he stood and hurried over to him.

"What's going on?" Nass asked, and he followed as Josh led him across the lobby, away from everyone else.

"It's Emory," Josh explained. "He got jumped."

"Is it bad? I mean, it must be bad or he wouldn't be here, but—he's going to be okay, right?"

Josh raised his gaze to meet Nass's. There weren't tears in his eyes; instead they were filled with a cold, hard pain.

"They don't know," Josh said quietly. "I guess he has brain swelling from the beating. They did some kind of surgery to relieve the pressure, but they're not sure . . ."

In the silence that followed those words, Nass's gaze slipped down to the brand-new polished floor at his feet. He wished his body could slump down there, too. He suddenly felt a crippling exhaustion, as if every over-taxed cell of his body would give way, his bones would crumble, his muscles would melt, his brain would seize up, and he would fall down and sleep for a thousand years. His wasn't an exhaustion of the body. It was exhaustion of the soul.

But as much as he wanted to, he couldn't collapse now. He had to stay strong for the rest of the Flatliners, for Emory and his family. He forced himself to speak again. "What happened?"

Josh repeated what Myka had told the Flatliners and the police.

"So it was Rick?"

"Myka didn't actually see the fight, but it had to be him, obviously," Josh said. "The cops supposedly went to talk to him. They told Emory's dad he was out of town."

"When are they going to know about Emory?"

"I guess he's in no condition to be moved, so they're bringing in some neurosurgeon from Topeka to perform another emergency surgery. He hasn't been conscious since it happened."

Nass only shook his head. There was nothing he could say.

"Myka was with him while they were waiting for the ambulance, and I asked her how bad it looked." Josh's lip quivered for a moment, and he paused and regained his composure. "It's bad."

Nass looked over at his friends, all of them sitting in chairs in the waiting area, their faces wracked with misery. He thought of Emory, lying in the hospital room, fighting for his life. He thought of Rick Banfield, wherever he was, probably plotting another horrific attack. And soon, Agent Hackett would leave and the Topper companies would start bull-dozing the Flats, leaving the Flatliners and their families on the streets. All these thoughts hit him once, like the scattershot from a shotgun, and as the sting of their impressions receded only one thought remained: *Where is Raphael Kain?*

CHAPTER 5

FENG XU WAS NOT IN A PLEASANT MOOD. The journey from the Zhanjiang naval base in southern China to Cuba had been miserable. Although the People's Liberation Army submarine he'd ridden on had been the flagship of the fleet (and vaguely and pleasurably snake-like in shape), his quarters had been cramped and dank, and the trip had dragged on far too long for his liking. The journey from Havana to Cape Coral, Florida, on the cigarette boat had been pleasant enough, though. Feng Xu had enjoyed skimming across all that clear, azure water and breathing the rich, primordial-smelling, brine-filled air. But the rest of the trip, from Cape Coral to Middleburg, Kansas, in the back of a black Lincoln Town Car, had been as dull as it was tiring, a blur of gray skies, drizzling rain, and dismal small towns punctuated only by a seemingly endless series of brightly lit signs for American fast-food restaurants and gas stations. If this was all his enemies had to offer—greasy beef sandwiches, French fries, and petrol—Feng Xu had thought, then retrieving the treasure he had sought for so long would be easier than he'd imagined.

Now, at last, the illustrious leader of the Order of the Black Snake had reached his destination—the Order's makeshift base, set within a drafty, abandoned brick factory building. Before him stood the two most senior, most trusted, and most powerful members of his brotherhood—and yet both had failed miserably. They held their derbies in their hands and stared subserviently down at the cracked concrete floor, literally trembling before him.

"I remember when I found the two of you," Feng Xu said slowly, practicing his English. "Two brothers—one twelve, one fourteen. So smart, so eager, so full of promise . . ." he shook his head sadly. "If I had known then how you would fail me, I would have fed you to the Snake God before the whole assembly."

The taller one, the eldest, winced at his words as if at a blow, but Feng Xu continued: "But no. You would not have been worthy food for our lord," he said softly. "Likely you would have given our master indigestion."

The four men who stood behind Feng Xu laughed. They were dressed identically to the two brothers he had sent ahead to Middleburg—in the same suits and the same derby hats.

Feng Xu allowed himself a smile. He stood tall, with his arms at his sides, as if he were standing at attention, but he was completely relaxed. In fact, it was only in moments like this that he felt truly at ease. He was enjoying himself.

"In honor of the potential that those two bright-eyed young pupils displayed so many years ago, I will allow you the honor of deciding which of you will pay for your incompetence and which will live. So tell me: who will sacrifice himself to our lord, the Black Snake?"

The taller brother stepped forward first; the shorter one, who had a fresh scar on one cheek, hesitated for a second, and then he stepped forward, too.

Feng Xu smiled again and stepped up to the shorter brother who, if Xu remembered correctly, was the younger one. "Ah, you let your brother step forward first. Good for you. There is some selfishness left in you after all. The selfish man is predictable, reliable. I can work with a selfish man. As long as you hold his fate in your hands, he remains utterly true. But a man who cleaves to so-called loftier ideals . . ." Feng Xu clucked his tongue at the taller brother. "Such a man is as unreliable as a drunken rat. And as such, he is good for only one thing—snake food."

Feng Xu laughed, and his men laughed as well, in the very same manner. All the while, Xu watched the taller brother, watched his face grow pale, his brow beading with sweat, his teeth beginning to clench. Xu waited patiently for him to lash out, eager for the fun, and when it happened, he was ready.

The condemned man dropped his hat and whipped out his double daggers, stabbing them both at Feng Xu's eyes. It was a particularly bad move. Since the blades were close together, Xu was able to parry them both with a single *Tan Sau*, then gather up both the man's arms with a *Huen Sau*, and snap both his elbows with a quick but ferocious armbreak. It was as simple as trapping the arms then striking the elbow with his forearm, with a sharp shift of the hips. The brother screamed in agony, and both knives fell from his hands. Before they had hit the ground, Feng Xu had snapped his opponent's left knee with a stomp kick and blinded him with the Bite of the Snake—a single finger strike to both eyes.

The result was devastating, Feng Xu thought with businesslike satisfaction: only a single second had elapsed from the moment the man pulled his knives until he was reduced to a crumpled, trembling mass of broken limbs and bloody tears.

Feng Xu gazed down at him for a long moment, as he gently wiped the blood from his right hand with a black silk handkerchief he'd pulled from his suit pocket. When one became a master of the Venom of the Fang fighting style, the reward was not a sash or a belt or a silly American-style trophy—it was a set of steel fingernails, implanted on the middle two fingers of each hand. It was these nails, the Fangs of the Snake, that Feng Xu had used to blind his opponent.

Now came the fun part. The shadows of the rusted machinery, broken-down conveyor belts, old smelting ovens, and rotten crates began to coalesce, then to slither, moving slowly but inexorably toward the blind and squealing sacrifice Feng Xu had prepared. By the time the form reached him, it was visible for what it was: a great black cobra.

All the men of the Order watched in rapt silence as the blind man on the ground shrieked, begged, and cried, as first one leg, then the other, then his entire lower half, then his whole torso, was swallowed up by the giant, shadow-black serpent. Finally, only one hand was left visible, its fingers wriggling strangely in the same gesture as a child would use to wave goodbye. Then in one more chomp, the hand was gone too. The Snake God rose up then, over their heads, coiling itself and flaring out its hood as if poised to strike its next victim, and everyone—including Feng Xu—bowed subserviently.

Out of the corner of his eye, Feng Xu watched the surviving brother to see if any rebellious thoughts might be coursing through his mind. Fighting off his shock, the man hesitated only for a second before he too bowed before the Black Snake God.

The snake hissed once, a sharp sound that seemed to cut to the bone, and then in one swift blink it was gone, disappearing as if it had never been there at all.

Feng Xu rose and smoothed out his shirt, making sure that there was no blood staining it from his short-lived fight, and then he looked around, gauging the morale and the loyalty of his remaining men. They were all looking at him as he expected they would be, with the perfect mixture of awe, fear, hatred, and admiration—even the scar-faced brother.

"Very well, gentlemen," Feng Xu said in his usual businesslike fashion. "I believe we have a treasure to find."

He knew from his latest briefing that the ring had been shattered and the shards scattered throughout Middleburg, but that prospect didn't concern him at all. It was simply a matter of gathering them together again. And he had a feeling he knew exactly where to begin.

❧

Friday after school, Zhai, Maggie, and Master Chin marched together through the Middleburg tunnels, toward the mystical railroad round-house they called the Wheel of Illusion. In his pocket, Zhai's fingers closed on the three pieces of the shattered crystal ring that he'd managed to round up. One was his, and the others belonged to Dax Avery and

Michael Ponder, two of the Toppers. Zhai had tried to reach Rick, Bran, and the Cunningham brothers last night after he'd seen Violet Anderson's tapestry, but Rick and Bran hadn't answered their phones, and D'von Cunningham had told Zhai that they weren't following his orders anymore; they reported to Rick now.

"Rick says you've been helping the enemy search for Raphael Kain," D'von had said coldly. "That's treason, man."

"If I help find Raphael, maybe the Flatliners won't be our enemies anymore, D'von," Zhai had patiently replied. "Did you and Rick think of that?"

There was a pause on the other end of the phone line.

"Look, I gotta go. Rick told me not to talk to you," D'von had said and ended the call.

Dax and Michael had acted a little weird, too. Standing on his front porch, Dax had glanced around furtively before turning his shard over to Zhai, as if he expected Rick to be hiding in the bushes watching them. Once he'd handed it over he quickly said goodbye and slipped back inside. Michael wouldn't even see Zhai; he simply left the shard in an envelope and put the envelope in his mailbox for Zhai to pick up.

Zhai worried about the fact that his control on the Toppers had slipped. For years now, he'd been the voice of reason and the advocate of calm and peace within the group. Without him, there was no way of telling what the Toppers would become. But as dangerous as it was to cede his position as leader of the gang, finding Raphael was more important, and he wasn't going to let anyone's opinion stand in his way.

So, Zhai had three shards of the magical crystal ring in his pocket, Maggie Anderson had one, and Master Chin had one—that made five. It only accounted for about a third of the ring, but they would have to hope it was enough.

"We're getting close," Chin said, and Zhai immediately abandoned his extraneous thoughts and focused on the task at hand. The tunnels were dangerous—it was important that he remained mindful and present.

"I've never been in here before. Are we going to the X?" Maggie asked quietly. "It's kind of creepy." But she seemed more fascinated than scared.

Zhai knew what she was talking about. There had always been legends circulating in the school about a spot deep inside the tunnels where the railroad tracks crossed. According to the stories, no one saw the X and lived to tell about it—because the Middleburg monster would eat them alive. Zhai, however, had seen the X and survived. He also knew that the stories were true, and he hoped that when the ring shattered, the giant shadow monsters that guarded it had also disappeared.

"Yes—the X is just up ahead," Chin whispered, and as he did they passed from the stone tunnel into an open space so massive and vacuous that their flashlight beams were unable to penetrate the blackness surrounding them. The Wheel was housed in a vast stone dome, Zhai knew—a space so huge that it had to take up half of the mountain.

"Be on your guard, my friends," Chin whispered. "We are not alone."

Moments later, the companions reached the fabled X where the tracks crossed. Zhai and Maggie each handed their ring shards to Chin, who held the five pieces in his hands and closed his eyes in reverent meditation. For an instant, Zhai thought he saw a glimmer of light through Chin's fingers. Maggie gasped, too, but in the next second, the spark faded, and the shards were dead again, like ordinary pieces of broken glass.

Chin opened his eyes and shook his head. "There is still some power in them," he said, "but not enough."

It was at that moment that Zhai saw a movement just out of range of his flashlight beam. The figure materialized so suddenly that Zhai's breath caught in his throat. When the man stepped into the light and Zhai recognized his face, his unease only grew.

He was Asian, with long dark hair, a thin beard, and penetrating, dark brown eyes. He was tall and imposing, with limbs that seemed to Zhai as long and strong as the branches of an ancient oak. But perhaps it was his garb that made Zhai think of a tree. Instead of the robes he'd worn before—the one of bloody, autumn red or the austere, icy bluish-white garment—this time, the Magician's habit was the tender green color of the first newly born buds of spring.

"Greetings, Man of Four, our Dark Teacher," Chin said and bowed.

Silently, the Magician returned the bow.

"You know the one whom we seek," Chin said. "Will you help us find him?"

The Magician stared at Chin without moving, without breathing, as still as a corpse. In their previous encounters, Zhai had found the Magician's maniacal laughter and endless questions disturbing and frightening—but neither was half as terrible as his current stillness.

As Zhai's desperation rose, he could no longer contain it or remain silent. He moved closer to Chin and spoke to the Man of Four: "Please, how can we get Raphael back?" he asked. "Tell us what to do and we'll do it."

Slowly, the Magician's gaze shifted to Zhai.

"Have you the treasure?" the Magician asked.

Zhai had expected to feel relieved when the Magician finally broke the horrible silence, but his voice was terrifying, too. It was somehow deep enough that Zhai could feel its rumble but also shrill enough that he wanted to cover his ears.

"Yes," Zhai answered quickly, and Chin held out the five ring shards.

The magician's terrible, dark eyes scanned Master Chin's outstretched hands.

"A broken wheel cannot turn," he said, and Zhai felt his hope crumbling to despair. Then, he had a realization.

"Wait—so you mean if we get all the shards and put them back together, then the Wheel *will* turn, and we can get Raphael back?"

It would be hard to get the shards back from all the Toppers and the

Flatliners—but if there was a possibility it would work, they had to try. Zhai wouldn't rest until they'd exhausted every effort to get Raph back.

A slow smile curled across the Magician's face.

"That's it!" Zhai said triumphantly. "We have to reunite all the shards!"

He looked to the Magician for further confirmation, but the man's smile had disappeared. He sniffed the air, frowning.

"What is it?" Chin asked, his brow furrowed with concern.

The Magician looked at him, a hint of his smile returning. "I smell snake," he said, and he receded quickly into the darkness, disappearing even as he went.

At the same instant, Zhai heard the sound of a footstep on the railroad ties behind them and whipped around, his flashlight slashing through the darkness. The man who stepped out of the shadows was handsome and muscular, with a thin moustache and pale-gray eyes. He wore a black silk shirt, and he was Chinese.

"Greetings, Chin," he said. But his inflection was harsh and the words seemed more like a command than a greeting. Zhai's mind spun as he tried to figure out who this stranger might be, and he widened his stance, preparing for a potential attack. A moment later, his worries were confirmed: five men wearing derby hats stepped out of the darkness and took their positions behind the stranger.

Master Chin, as usual, remained perfectly calm. "Hello, Feng Xu," he said.

Zhai noticed a stirring in the shadows behind their adversaries, and for just an instant he was able to see the outline of the God of the Black Snakes—a massive, half-invisible cobra, rising behind them.

A pang of crippling fear hit Zhai in the gut. So it would be just him, Chin, and Maggie fighting against Feng Xu, five Obies, and an ancient Snake God? It didn't look good. What they desperately needed was backup.

Please, All! Please, Shen! Zhai entreated silently, fighting back the desperation that was trying to surface. *Where is Raphael?*

CHAPTER 6

RAPHAEL KAIN AWOKE FROM A LONG AND DREAMLESS SLEEP.

Before he even opened his eyes, he was aware of a sound, a single deep, sonorous note that seemed to him like the mingled howl of a mighty wind and the low hum of a huge, powerful motor, combined into the single, soul-thrumming chord of a Gregorian chant.

Ooooooooooooooooooo . . .

He sat up and looked around. He was on the floor of a small room, perhaps 10-feet-by-10-feet wide. Windows ran along three sides, but they were too high up for Raphael to see what was outside them. In the front of the room, strangely enough, was the control panel from the Wheel of Illusion—or a panel that was almost identical to it, with the same polished-wood body and old-fashioned gauges. There was a single high leather seat in front of the control panel, as if one were meant to sit there to operate it. Slowly, Raphael rose to his feet.

Standing, the sound he heard rushing and moaning all around him seemed to condense into a vibration that ran from the soles of his feet up through his shinbones and all the way into his chest and his head, where he felt as if it was jiggling his heart and his brain at once. It was a weird feeling, but not entirely unpleasant. Now that he was upright, he was able to look out the windows. Outside, a thick gray fog was racing past. It seemed to be blowing toward him from the direction that the chair and the control panel faced, and Raphael suddenly understood. It wasn't the fog outside that was moving—it was him. And he had to be moving at an incredible speed.

Only then did he remember what had happened on the train tracks back in Middleburg.

In his mind, he retraced the events for himself, trying to make sense of it all. There had been a battle raging between the Flatliners and the Toppers, then between the Obies and Orias. Raphael remembered saving Aimee from the giant cobra, then Maggie saving him from the slithering, raging beast. Then, he had picked up the treasure that everyone—the Order of the Black Snake, Orias, the Flatliners, and the Toppers—had been searching for. The glowing crystal ring. He had grabbed it, and when he looked up, he had seen the train coming—a massive, ancient-looking steam-powered locomotive thundering toward him. But instead of being scared, he had felt mysteriously grateful. And he'd stood his ground without moving, without flinching, without fear, until the engine hit him.

The next thing he remembered was waking up in this room—and of course it was not a room. It was the cab of the train that had struck him. Somehow, he was inside it now. He stepped up to the front of the car, placed one steadying hand on the back of the big leather engineer's chair and gazed out the windshield, hoping to get some idea of where he was.

The fog he was passing through was the densest Raphael had ever seen. He stared into it for perhaps ten minutes as it flowed past, but it was as thick and heavy as cotton candy, and it obscured every feature of the land that might lay behind it; he couldn't catch a glimpse of a single tree, or a house—nothing. Raphael had never been on an airplane, but he imagined this must be what it would look like to be jetting through a massive cloudbank.

For a moment, it occurred to him that he might be dead. Maybe this was what people saw when they passed away, he reasoned. The famous tunnel leading to the white light. But when he went to the side window and looked down, he found that he was not racing through the heavens. There was land below him, featureless brown earth that shot by so fast it was a total blur. He stared down at it for a moment, then looked out the front window again, trying to estimate how fast he might be going. But, he decided, it was impossible. Without any landmarks to watch, there was no way to judge. All he knew was that he was moving fast.

"Very fast," he said aloud. "But where am I going?"

Of course, there was no one to answer him. He was alone in the cab of the train, and judging from the terrain around him, he might be alone in some strange world or dimension that he'd somehow been blasted into when the train hit him.

He left the window, went back to the control panel, and looked down at it. There were six gauges, each one with a dial and a red needle. But the markings on the gauges were not numbers or letters—to Raphael, they looked like the nonsense squiggles a child would make up before they learned how to write for real.

"Oh, great," he said to himself, "we're going squiggly-mark, lopsided-circle, leaning-triangle miles per hour."

A brass lever extended from the side of the panel, similar to the slot machine–type lever that operated the Wheel of Illusion. Raphael considered pulling on it to see what would happen, then thought better of it. For all he knew it would make the train blast off into space. No, he decided, the train had started moving by itself. It would stop by itself. But he was worried. Where would he be when it stopped? Where was it taking him?

If the Wheel that was meant to turn the trains in different directions could take its operator to different times, what could the trains themselves do? Wherever he was going, was it a round-trip or a one-way ticket? How long had he been gone? He had this weird feeling that he'd been sleeping for a week. What was happening back in Middleburg? Was his mom worried about him? How would she survive if he never came back? She could barely take care of herself, much less a new baby. And what about Aimee? He had to get back to Aimee and find a way to get her away from Orias.

He reached into his pocket and took out his cell phone, but when he looked down at the screen, he wasn't surprised to find that it was dead. He held down the power button and waited for the screen to light up. Nothing.

When he put the phone back into his pocket, he felt something else there and took it out. There, in the palm of his hand, was a jagged shard of crystal about three inches long. It was flat and rounded. It took him a long moment before he realized what it was: a piece of the crystal ring, the treasure he and his friends had searched so hard for. It must've broken when the train hit him. The light that had once shone through it had disappeared now, and it looked dead in his hands, like nothing but a piece of broken glass.

Just as this thought crossed his mind, however, a blink of greenish white light winked through the shard, as if reassuring him: *oh, no, my friend. I am alive.*

But whether it was alive or not, Raphael doubted it would do any good. He stuck it back in his pocket.

Questions swarmed through his mind, thick and fast, but he realized quickly that none of them had answers. Whatever was happening in Middleburg, he couldn't do anything about it. As for where he was going, the track had already been laid. He had no choice but to follow it.

With a sigh of surrender, Raphael settled into the surprisingly comfortable, old-fashioned leather armchair and gazed out the windshield. Soon, his thoughts were as featureless and serene as the fog that roiled past.

☙

"There is no need for anyone to get hurt, Chin. All I require are the pieces of the ring."

Feng Xu's words gave Zhai a moment of hope. If the Obies were after the shards, then maybe there really was some Shen magic left in them, and maybe they could use them to get Raphael back—but they'd have to get out of here alive first.

Master Chin's eyes traced the forms of Feng Xu, the five Obies, and the indistinct, looming shape of the Black Snake God, and Zhai knew from his years of training that his sifu's brain was racing like a Pentagon computer, calculating whether or not this was a battle they could win—and if so, how.

After a moment, Chin replied, "Certainly. I will be glad to give them to you, *sihing*. I'll give them to you freely. All you have to do is beat me in a fair fight."

Feng Xu barked out a laugh, but his narrow eyes remained mirthless. "And to think your father called me the tricky one. Of course you would prefer a duel. You know that in an all-out battle, your dear student Zhai and his pretty little friend would perish along with you—and I would take the shards anyway."

Chin nodded, never taking his eyes from Feng Xu's. "You could try to take the shards," he agreed. "And you might succeed. Certainly, you are a man who values winning his objective at any cost. But think of your pride. We both know you will never find another opponent so worthy of your consideration. If you don't fight me now, you will spend every day for the rest of your life wondering who would have won—me or you."

Chin handed the shards to Zhai and took a small step forward. When he did, there was a collective metallic *click* as all the Obies whipped out their weapons—twelve-inch-long switchblade daggers. But Feng Xu stayed them with a gesture.

Chin placed the fist of one hand against the palm of the other in front of his heart and bowed to Feng Xu. The Black Snake master hesitated only for a moment before he stepped forward.

"Very well, then. To the death," he said, and returned the bow.

As one, the Obies put away their knives and settled into a semi-circle to watch the duel unfold. The massive, half-visible cobra that loomed behind them seemed to fade out of existence as the two masters each assumed their fight-ready positions. As they did, Zhai noticed something strange about Feng Xu. He had long nails on the middle two fingers of each hand, like two deadly steel fangs.

It was all happening so fast, Zhai could barely process it. As he looked upon Chin's opponent, he felt a rising panic. Feng Xu looked bigger and stronger than master Chin, and although Zhai had great faith in his master's tremendous martial arts ability, Zhai knew firsthand how incredibly potent the snakes' Venom of the Fang martial arts style could be. Neither he nor Raphael had been able to win against it, and Feng Xu was the grand master of the style.

What if Chin loses? Zhai wondered, suddenly alarmed. *What if he dies?*

Maggie Anderson nudged him with her elbow. "What's happening?" she asked. "Should we do something?" He had almost forgotten she was there.

"No," he said quickly, even though he wished with all his heart that there was something he could do. "For a student to interfere with his master's duel would be a major violation of the Wu-de," he told her. "That's the code he taught us—Raphael and me."

"So we're just supposed to stand back and hope for the best?" she demanded.

"We have no choice," he said.

Chin and Xu were circling around the center of the crossed railroad tracks. Feng Xu's arms undulated hypnotically in front of him, and his feet barely seemed to move as he circled, as if he were slithering rather than stepping. Chin, on the other hand, looked just as he did in his *kwoon* during Zhai's weekly lessons. He seemed as relaxed as ever, but there was a look of sublime focus on his face that was as intense as it was placid.

Feng Xu tried several feigns, designed to distract Chin and get him off balance, but the master didn't flinch. After almost a full minute of circling, Xu made his move, attacking Chin with both hands at the same moment, as if his arms were a pair of striking vipers. Chin parried both blows and countered with a *Po Pai,* shoving Xu with both hands so hard that he stumbled backward and fell into a sitting position on the burnished brass surface of the Wheel of Illusion.

A look of rage crossed Feng Xu's features, but he quickly suppressed it, replacing it with a smile. "Well, Chin," he taunted. "It seems you have not lost your touch. I'm glad. That will make this more fun."

Xu windmilled his legs, using the momentum to spring to his feet, and shot toward Master Chin. The barrage he unleashed then was fearsome; it was like he had six arms and all of them were striking, blocking, shoving, and trapping at once. Zhai stood there in awe, watching his master fend off the incredible assault.

Finally, a blow got through Chin's defenses, leaving two gaping slashes across his face, instantly drawing blood. Zhai's tension mounted with his concern and he wanted to cry out, but his sifu remained as poised as ever.

"Come now, Chin," Feng Xu chided, circling again. "Why do you cling to that outdated style of yours? Just because your grandfather taught it to you? You know the Venom of the Fang is superior."

"The last time I used it, I took a man's eye," Chin said. "I swore I would never use it again."

Xu smirked. "A noble fool, just like the rest of your family—all of them dead now," he said, and attacked again.

There was a blurred flurry of strikes, and the exchange was so fast that even Zhai's trained eye couldn't follow the movements. After a moment, both men stepped away bloodied and started circling again.

Zhai was ready for more taunts from the Snake master, but instead of speaking, he struck again, lashing out with a whip-fast kick that caught Chin off guard and sent him sprawling. Chin tried to get to his feet, but before he could rise Xu caught him with another kick to the gut, then one to the face, keeping him down. Zhai's heart was pounding. He had to do something. If things kept going on like this, Master Chin would end up dead. He couldn't stand by and watch it happen, but he couldn't stop it, either—not without violating the Wu-de. And he knew that Chin would rather die than see Zhai violate the law of their art.

Chin was on his knees now, reeling, and Feng Xu grabbed him by the hair and looked into his eyes, one fanged hand poised to strike.

"Do you feel it, Chin? The Venom of the Snake is coursing through your veins already. Feel its poison, choking your heart, wrapping its coils around your brain? It is a slow, miserable death. Shall I put you out of your misery? I could impale you through both eyes now and snuff out your brain—it would be almost painless. What do you say, *sidai*? Will you beg me for mercy?"

Chin's brown eyes shone up from a face covered in his own blood. "My grandfather tried to show you a path of light, but you preferred the darkness. Let's see how you fight in it," he said.

Chin clapped his hands together, and there was a crackle of lightning. Zhai felt a shockwave of Shen energy blast into him. It blew the flashlight out of his hand, and he heard it land somewhere behind him. As it hit the tracks, the light bulb in it shattered—and the same thing happened to the lights the Obies had, too. Now, they were all in total darkness.

From the spot where Master Chin and Feng Xu were standing, Zhai heard the sounds of grunts and the thuds of violent blows, but he had no way of knowing who was winning. He felt a hand on his arm and started.

"It's me," Maggie whispered into his ear. "Give me the shards and I'll sneak out."

"How?" Zhai asked. He could see nothing in the pitch black around him.

"I can see, okay? Just give them to me."

Zhai hesitated for only a second before realizing that she was right. The Obies had no honor. Win or lose, when the duel was over they would be trying to take the shards anyway; it was better to get rid of them now and keep them safe. He dug them out of his pocket and pressed them into Maggie's hand. Immediately, he heard her footsteps receding as she jogged away down the tracks.

Meanwhile, the unseen battle was raging on, marked only by the sounds of a thousand rapid blows. After a moment, two small sparks of illumination appeared, and Zhai saw that two of the Obies had found lighters. By the light of the quivering twin flames, Zhai could see that Chin had forced a bloodied Feng Xu to his knees, with his fist cocked back, ready to strike. Zhai knew that a blow like the one Master Chin had prepared for his enemy could be deadly.

"Go ahead, Chin," Feng Xu said, a drizzle of blood coming from his mouth as he spoke. "Kill me, if you dare. But know that your beloved student dies with me."

As he spoke, his eyes flicked over to where Zhai was standing. Chin's glance followed, and at that moment Zhai sensed a malevolent presence behind him, hovering over him. Slowly, he turned his head to look. It was the Black Snake God, poised to strike him from behind.

In that moment of distraction, Feng Xu lashed out, his fang-like nails stabbing into the side of Master Chin's neck. Chin fell to his knees, choking violently. At almost the same instant, Zhai heard the faint whistle as the snake's jaws sped toward the back of his head, and as fast as a gunshot he whipped around and blocked the deadly fangs with a double *Biu Sau,* then struck the Snake God's nose with one elbow as hard as he could. There was a crackle of lightning-like Shen energy, and the beast's head snapped back. The whole creature flickered twice, like a movie going out of focus, and then disappeared completely. Zhai turned back toward the others to find Chin lying on the ground with Feng Xu standing over him. The Black Snake master glared at Zhai, and then seemed to taste the air with all his senses.

"The shards are gone. The girl must have them—find her!" he shouted, and his men sprang into motion. One of the Obies moved toward Zhai, but Feng Xu admonished him. "Forget those fools! The old man is dead anyway. All that matters now is the ring."

And the Obies and Feng Xu all ran off soundlessly down the tunnel, their lights receding. In total darkness, Zhai felt his way down the track, toward his sifu.

"Master Chin?"

"I'm here." Chin's voice was a mere whisper, but Zhai followed it to its source and gripped his teacher's hand.

"You all right?" he asked.

"Venom . . . of the Fang," Chin muttered. "Deadly. From his nails . . . struck me in the neck."

Already, he was barely able to speak. His words came out slow and heavy.

"Don't worry, Sifu. I'll save you. We'll get you help," Zhai said, although he had no idea how. Without a flashlight, it would be impossible to get out of the tunnels.

"Lily Rose," Chin croaked.

"I'll carry you there if I have to," Zhai said. "But how do we get out? I can't see."

"Follow the tracks. Close eyes. Use . . . Shen."

Zhai was about to protest—he'd used Shen for healing and for fighting, but to close his eyes when he was already in total darkness and use the energy of the All to see?—it seemed impossible.

"Trust it," Chin said, as if Zhai had spoken aloud.

Zhai nodded. He would trust it, because if he didn't, then the most important person in his life was going to die right here in these tunnels.

Carefully, Zhai scooped his sifu up in his arms and began walking down the train track.

At first he stumbled, but after a few moments he began to see the tracks in the darkness on the backs of his eyelids, traced out in faint streams of light, like a sketch made from the streaks of fast-moving fireflies.

"It's working," Zhai said, and for a moment the giddy feeling of Shen flowing through him eclipsed the urgency and terror of the situation.

"Hurry," was Master Chin's only response.

☙

Maggie raced down the blackened tunnels, listening with dread for the sound of pursuing footsteps behind her. After a few minutes, she heard them—the relentless thud of booted feet—gaining on her.

It was a passage from Lily Rose's magical *Good Book* that had given her the power to flee her attackers in the complete darkness:

> *Vision not of light*
> *Eyes not required for sight*
> *Close them, and see right*

Maggie had learned the passage by heart. It had taken several weeks of experimentation for her to realize that the axiom applied not only to her using meditation to discern the truth about the people around her; it also meant that she could close her eyes and sense the world around her even in complete darkness. She'd had fun walking around her house in the wee hours of the morning with her eyes closed and all the lights off. She had even been able to fix herself snacks in the pitch darkness, using the vision that the invisible homecoming crown projected inside her mind.

She hadn't seen any practical use for the power when she first discovered it, but she was certainly putting it to good use now. As she fled, she wracked her brain to come up with another *Good Book* passage that might be helpful in escaping her pursuers, but nothing occurred to her. By the time she burst into the moonlight of the crisp, late-winter night, the Obies' footsteps seemed to be echoing all around her, although when she looked back, she couldn't see them—not yet, anyway.

Her mind whirled and her eyes scanned the terrain around her. She could try to hide in the woods, she thought, but the trees were bare. The Obies would spot her for sure. She could try to outrun them, but that seemed impossible, since they were already catching up to her. Her final option was that she could turn and fight. The last time she had fought the Snake God, her otherworldly blast of energy had sent it flying—but it had taken a lot out of her. She was doubtful she could demolish the demon and his minions all in one shot.

The steps were coming closer. Maggie looked up at the series of boulders that stood at the top of the tunnel mouth. If only she could fly, she could hide up there. Unfortunately, flight was one ability that the crown hadn't given her and The Good Book hadn't taught her yet. It was weird—she could move objects, but she couldn't make herself move through the air, which somehow didn't quite seem fair.

Her heart was racing. The footsteps were almost on top of her now. She heard the Obies shouting in Chinese and their voices sounded terrifyingly close. She was about to run again, to take off into the woods, when she spotted a large section of a rotting fallen tree trunk lying a few yards off next to the tracks, and she ran to it. If she could levitate it—and she was on top of it—that would be almost as good as flying. She hoped it would work because there was no time for anything else.

She hopped onto a portion of the tree trunk and, standing on it, she focused her energy and willed it to rise. As it lifted from the ground, it bobbed slightly, almost causing her to slip off. She fell to her knees and then sat down and straddled it, as if it was a horse and she was riding bareback.

Up, she commanded silently, imagining the energy in her mind was a laser beam she was directing at the trunk, and she felt it move again. Clinging to it tightly, she rode it to the top of the tunnel mound. Willing it to settle quietly into the soft earth there, she disembarked and crouched behind it, peering cautiously around one end.

Moments later, the Obies burst from the tunnel's entrance. They scattered instantly, two of them rushing into the woods to the right of the tracks and two looking to the left of it, with one charging ahead between the rails. A few seconds later, the leader came out. He barked a few words in Chinese and his men responded. The man shook his head angrily and shouted again, and they all moved together down the tracks.

When they had disappeared from sight, Maggie rose from her hiding place and rested one sneakered foot on top of the tree trunk.

"Well, it's no broomstick, but it worked," she muttered to herself. She slipped one hand into her pocket to make sure the shards were still there, and then she headed off through the woods, away from the tunnel mouth. She considered heading back into the tunnel to check on Zhai and Master Chin, then thought better of it. If the Obies doubled back they might catch her, and she couldn't risk losing the shards they had, especially since it was now clear that they were still important.

The best plan was to head back to Hilltop Haven on foot, she decided, and she set off, proud of outwitting the Obies, escaping from them, and discovering a new ability, all in one night.

CHAPTER 7

FRIDAY AFTERNOON.

Bran Goheen's body ached all over, and his hand trembled as he brought the Styrofoam cup to his lips. It was the end of a brutal day of mixed martial arts training, filled with running, jumping rope, bag work, ground work, and sparring. He'd spent hours pounding a heavy tractor tire with a sledgehammer, then flipping the tire end-over-end down the length of Spike's Gym and back. He'd taken a heavy rope in each hand and jerked it up and down, making it undulate in waves until his arms burned so much he felt sure his muscles would ignite. Halfway through the day he threw up, but five minutes later he was back in the cage, working on his Brazilian jujitsu takedowns. He'd worked harder than he had ever worked in his life, but he still had a hard time keeping up with Rick. And despite all the distractions, he couldn't forget what had happened back in that alley in Middleburg—not even for a second.

"So what do you think of Spike's weekend intensive so far?" Rick asked. They were sitting at a smoothie place just up the block from Spike's Gym in downtown Topeka, gulping down a couple of protein shakes.

Bran laughed weakly. "You were right, man. It's pretty hardcore."

"I told you, Spike doesn't play," Rick said, and he went back to downing his smoothie. Just then, his cell phone rang and he answered it. "Hey, Dad. We're about to head back to the gym. . . . What?" He paused and a slight furrow creased his brow for a moment.

"Why would they want to talk to me about it?" Another pause and Rick looked at Bran, grinned and winked. "Sure, I know him from school, but—" He frowned, annoyed, and then went on. "Yeah, I saw him that night. I had a few words with him in the parking lot, but I didn't put him in the hospital."

Bran's heart was pounding faster than it had during the hardest part of the day's workout. Before he died, his granddad had always told him never to lie, that everything secret would come into the light sooner or later. That's what he dreaded: the moment when someone would connect him and Rick with what happened back in Middleburg.

"Uh-huh . . . good," Rick was saying. "Don't worry, I won't. No one saw anything. His girlfriend and sister went inside before we even started talking." Rick paused again, to listen. "Okay. See you then." He ended the call and looked at Bran, his eyes filled with equal parts amusement and annoyance.

"The cops had the nerve to call my dad and ask where I was on Valentine's night. You believe that?" he said with contempt.

"What did he say?" Bran asked, the words coming out a whisper.

Rick shrugged casually. "He told them to go to hell and gave them our lawyer's phone number. It doesn't matter; they can't do anything. Those stupid Flats girls admitted to the cops that they didn't see anything except me walking up to Emory and talking to him. The lawyer says they can't do anything unless someone saw us actually fighting. And no one saw that," Rick said pointedly.

No one except me, Bran thought.

"As long as neither of us talks to the cops or the newspaper, it'll all blow over in a week or two," Rick said.

Bran felt sick. "You think it'll be in the newspaper?"

"Nah—probably not. He's just a punk Flatliner. But if we have to give a statement to anybody, we'll do it through Dad's lawyer. They can't touch us."

Bran said nothing; he had no idea where to begin.

Rick stretched his long arms out then tilted his head, first to one side and then the other, cracking his neck. "Crap, I'm starving. Let's pick up some fried chicken on the way back to the hotel. It's gonna be a long weekend, man. We need our protein."

"What about Emory?" Bran asked quietly.

Rick was looking down at his cell phone. "Who?" he asked.

"Emory," Bran said a little more forcefully, but when Rick looked up at him he was quick to make his voice even. "Just wondering if he's okay."

"Oh, he's in the hospital," Rick said proudly. "Relax—he'll be fine. But he's not getting out any time soon. Did you see that elbow I laid on him during the ground-and-pound? It was wicked, man. I wish somebody got it on video. Bam!" Rick mimed the move that had knocked Emory unconscious and then went back to messing with his phone.

Bran sat perfectly still, watching Rick. The Banfield heir sat slumped in the chair, his long, muscled legs carelessly sprawled, his chin raised in an attitude of arrogant defiance as he tapped out a text message. And Bran suddenly realized that Rick truly, genuinely didn't care what happened to Emory.

"What's wrong with you?" Bran asked. He hadn't meant to say it aloud; it just came out.

Rick's eyes flicked from the screen of his phone up to meet Bran's and they were empty, with a complacent kind of coldness in them, and no emotion at all. "I just told you," he said. "I'm hungry."

࿇

Zhai paced outside the closed door of Lily Rose's tiny guest bedroom.

Around forty-five minutes had passed since he arrived at her door with Master Chin in his arms. He had been exhausted and out of breath from running all the way from the tunnel to the Flats, carrying Chin, but they were close enough to the old woman's house that it made more sense for him to go on foot than to wait for an ambulance or for his family's driver. Besides, the paramedics would have insisted on taking Chin to the medical center in Benton. They never would have agreed to take him to

Lily Rose's. But when the door opened and Lily Rose saw Master Chin, Zhai began to doubt the wisdom of that choice. All the years Zhai had known her, he'd never seen so much as a glimmer of concern cross her face, but when she saw his sifu's ashen skin and his shallow breathing, then examined the two livid, swollen puncture wounds on his neck, she'd looked like she might actually faint.

"The venom," she'd whispered. "Oh, Lord help us. Come on, get him inside. Put him in the guest room and meet me out in the garden."

Zhai couldn't imagine why Lily Rose would want to go for a stroll in her garden at a time like this, but he had followed her orders. He gently placed Chin on a neatly made antique twin bed, and then hurried down the hall, through the back door, and out into the yard. There he'd found Lily Rose already hard at work, her age-gnarled hands moving quickly and deftly, snapping off sprigs of herbs and flowers and placing them into a basket. She pointed to another basket and another set of clippers sitting on the stoop, then to a low green vine spilling from a ceramic pot.

"Get me twenty-five leaves from that plant," she ordered, and Zhai had gotten to work. There was a moment when he wondered how Lily Rose could have so many flourishing plants in her garden only a few days after the last freeze of a harsh winter had subsided—but he didn't bother to ask her. Such things didn't matter now, with Master Chin's life in danger. Besides, over the last few months, Zhai had come to accept the seemingly impossible with the calm acceptance of a battle-hardened veteran facing enemy fire.

Once Lily Rose was content with the array of herbs, flowers, and roots they'd collected, she led him inside to the kitchen. There she got a small cast-iron pot, filled it with water, and set it on the stove to boil. She took out a mortar and pestle made of what looked like white marble, placed all the plant parts inside the bowl, and ground them down until they were as fine as flour. Then she dumped them into the pot and allowed the mixture to simmer for a few moments before she poured it into a shallow bowl.

"Fetch me a piece of burlap from that drawer," she commanded, pointing to the tallboy in the corner. "It's the brown, coarse cloth."

Zhai obeyed, and Lily Rose folded up the fabric and submerged it in the bowl, letting it soak. She placed the bowl onto a tray, along with a clean white dishtowel.

While she was working, Zhai's phone beeped. It was a text message from Maggie, saying that she'd made it to Hilltop Haven safely. He breathed a mighty sigh of relief. More and more he was impressed by Maggie. He wondered how she could possibly have escaped the Obies. He would ask her next time they were together, but for now it was enough to know that she was okay and that she still had the shards.

Now finished in the kitchen, Lily Rose walked wordlessly down the hall and into the bedroom, and Zhai followed her as closely and silently as a shadow.

As the old woman placed the tray on the bedside table, Zhai looked at his teacher laid out on the bed and felt suddenly ill with fear. Master Chin already looked half dead. His skin had turned a frightening shade of pale, grayish blue, and his chest moved erratically in a series of shallow, staccato breaths.

With businesslike efficiency, Lily Rose took the burlap from the bowl, squeezed the excess liquid out of it, then wrapped it in the dishtowel, and placed the whole thing over the wounds on Master Chin's neck. Instantly, a jet of steam rose from it, as if it had been placed on scorching metal. Chin bucked and a tortured groan escaped his lips, but his eyes did not open.

"It's hurting him!" Zhai said, and he reached to take the towel from his sifu's neck, but Lily Rose placed a hand on his shoulder, stopping him.

"Yes, it hurts," she said. "But it's also the only chance we have of saving his life. If we're lucky, that poultice will pull the venom out."

"And if we're not lucky?" Zhai asked. He had seen Lily Rose's miraculous healing powers at work when she'd helped Kate recover from her recent dagger wound, but even at her worst, Kate had never looked as bad as Chin did now.

"If we're not lucky, it won't work," Lily Rose said. She sounded weary, Zhai thought. It was the first time he'd seen her be anything but cheerful, and that, too, filled him with fear.

"What else can we do?" he asked.

"Remember when you healed your sister?" Lily Rose asked, and Zhai remembered the extraordinary light of Shen that had filled him and helped him to rouse Li from her coma. "It will take much more faith than that to heal the wound your teacher has suffered."

"But he can still live, right?" Zhai asked hopefully.

Lily Rose gazed down at Chin. "Within the All, everything is possible," she said and left the room.

Immediately, Zhai stepped near his teacher's bedside and took his hand. Master Chin's callused palm felt like it was made of granite; his powerful fingers, as if they were carved of wood. Zhai had seen these hands punch through boards and blocks of solid concrete. It seemed impossible that the life could ever disappear from them—but if Lily Rose's poultice didn't succeed, that was exactly what would happen. Without wasting another moment, he closed his eyes and let the healing light of Shen fill him.

ॐ

"I didn't say I was mad at you—I said I was disappointed!" Dalton tossed over her shoulder as she stepped onto the front porch of her grandmother's house.

"That's what people say when they're mad," Nass replied, following her. "And I don't think it's fair. What did I do wrong? I got arrested for no reason. And my phone died, because I was texting *you* all day, so I couldn't call. And I didn't make it to school because I was at the hospital with Emory."

"I know," Dalton replied, relenting a little at the mention of Emory.

"I'm not saying you did anything wrong—specifically. I'm just saying, you seem to have this uncanny knack of building up my expectations—and then somehow I end up feeling like crap."

"It wasn't my fault!" Nass insisted. He was trying to stay calm, but the idea of Dalton being mad at him was excruciating, especially when so many other things were going wrong, too. She was the last person in the world he wanted to disappoint, but she was right. Somehow it kept happening—and it was so frustrating, it made him want to scream.

"Nass, I know. I'm not saying it's your fault," Dalton returned. "All I'm saying is that it keeps happening, and it's not making me happy."

Sitting down heavily on the porch swing Nass rolled his eyes. "Okay, so now I don't make you happy?" he said. "I mean, our friend is lying in the hospital in a coma, my family is about to be evicted, *I* get detained by the police because *they* can't figure out what happened to Raph and that stupid crystal ring—and *I'm not making you happy?* I don't know what I'm supposed to do about that."

Just then, the door swung open, and Nass instantly felt bad for fighting on Lily Rose's porch. But it wasn't Dalton's grandma who emerged from the doorway; it was Zhai Shao. For a moment, the surprise left both him and Dalton speechless.

"Oh—hey, Zhai," Dalton said. "You get Kate settled? Did she forget something?"

Zhai shook his head. "No, I'm—it's Master Chin. He's hurt." And then he told them what had happened when the Obies attacked. Nass rose from the porch swing.

"So you still have the shards?" he asked.

"Yes. Maggie took them," Zhai answered. "They're safe."

Nass paused for a second, trying to decide if he should trust Zhai with the information he'd picked up at the police station or not. Finally, he decided he had no choice. Besides, even though Raphael had a problem with Zhai, he definitely would have put their differences aside with their sifu's life on the line.

"I was hauled down to the police station for questioning yesterday," Nass said. "There's this government agent in town named Hackett. He's looking for that guy you were talking about—the leader of the Obies, Feng Xu. I guess they must have known that he came into the country somehow and tracked him here."

Zhai seemed to consider this. "It makes sense," he said.

"If Feng Xu came to town after the ring was destroyed, that must mean he thinks it still has some power," Nass continued. "Maybe he's right. Maybe it does."

Zhai nodded eagerly. "Master Chin thought so, too. That's why we were in the tunnels—we were using the broken pieces to try to activate the Wheel and get Raphael back. It sparked a little, but not enough."

"So . . . we have to get all the shards," Dalton guessed. "We have to put the ring back together for it to work."

Nass and Zhai both nodded.

"It won't be easy," Zhai said. "Not with the Obies looking for it. And if these government guys are trying to track Feng Xu, that probably means they're looking for it, too."

"Well," Nass said. "We know all the people who picked up the pieces. All we have to do is get everyone to give them back to us, so we can put the ring back together. How hard can that be?"

But the minute the words left his mouth, Nass knew it wouldn't be so easy. He didn't think Zhai could get the Toppers to cooperate—he wasn't hanging with them much anymore. And after what had happened to Emory, getting the Flatliners to cooperate with Zhai might not be so easy, either.

"I'll talk to the Toppers," Zhai promised.

"I'll call a meeting of the Flatliners, too, and fill them in on the plan."

Somehow, Nass felt that if they could just get Raphael back to Middleburg, everything would be okay. But the more he thought about getting the two gangs to cooperate, the more worried he got.

On Saturday afternoon, Li Shao sat at the kitchen table at her friend Weston Darling's house, her math homework laid out in front of her, along with a glass of untouched milk and a plate of uneaten cookies. It was impossible for Li to understand why his mom insisted on serving them such unhealthy snacks day after day, seemingly oblivious to the fact that Li never so much as nibbled on them. She only ate food that her mother's kitchen staff prepared for her—fare that was perfectly nutritionally balanced. But whenever Mrs. Darling appeared with that big Stepford-Wife smile and asked, "How about a little study snack, you two?" Li always smiled back and said, "Sure, that would be great."

The studying was also a charade. Neither Li nor Weston needed any help on their homework—not in any subject. In fact, Li was certain they were probably the two smartest kids in the school. Li knew Weston believed that she came over on the pretext of doing homework together because she had a romantic interest in him. In fact, the idea almost made her laugh. Although not entirely without charm, Weston was a skinny, ineffectual pretty boy with shiny, blond hair and glasses that seemed to swallow up his face, and he dressed like a sixty-year-old college professor. If Li could have chosen, she would have much preferred spending her evenings with someone hot—like Raphael Kain. Too bad he'd up and disappeared like that. Bran Goheen didn't come up quite as far as Raph on the heat scale, but he was a pretty close second. But Li was not at liberty to choose who she spent her time with; she was here for a purpose. And today, it looked like that purpose might soon be fulfilled.

"That guy my dad's talking to," Weston mused, causing Li to glance up from her schoolbook. "I wonder who he is."

"Why?"

"Dad used to have to meet all the time with guys who looked like that, when we were living back in D.C. He called them spooks—they were government agents. I wonder if that guy is a spook."

Li had caught a glimpse of the mysterious visitor when he'd arrived earlier, and she thought Weston was dead on—the cheap black suit, the crew cut, the humorless face—all of it screamed clandestine operations. But instead of agreeing, she said, "What would a government agent be doing in Middleburg?" Her tone was musical, innocent—and perfectly controlled.

"I don't know," Weston confessed, lowering his voice. "But I always wondered why we moved *here* of all places when my dad's job at the White House was over. I always thought there had to be a reason."

"Huh," Li said and shrugged, feigning a lack of interest. This was a game she enjoyed very much. Her brother Zhai played the violin, but Li's instrument was people—and she played them like a virtuoso. After all, she'd learned from the best. She had learned from her mother.

Footsteps sounded, coming down the hallway, and Weston's father appeared in the kitchen. He was a heavyset man with thinning gray hair and thick glasses, and like Weston, he was wearing a sweater vest. Despite his stout physique, his deportment was that of a military man; he stood straight, with his shoulders back.

"Weston, can I have a word with you, please?" he said calmly, and then turned to Li. "Would you excuse him for a moment, Li? Our guest is an old friend of mine and I'd like him to meet Wes."

Li smiled. "No problem, Mr. Darling."

Weston gave Li an apologetic shrug and went with his father down the hall.

Li waited for a count of three before she followed. A cat could not have moved as silently as she did. It took her only a few moments to track the sounds of muffled voices to the room Weston and his father had entered. Silently, she pressed her ear to the door.

"Wade, this is my son Weston." She recognized Weston's father's voice. "Wes, this is Agent Hackett."

"Weston, good to meet you," the voice that belonged to Agent Hackett said. "Listen, son, your father and I go way back—to the first Gulf war, isn't that right, Charlie?"

"Right," Mr. Darling agreed. "Back to the good old days of George Bush Senior!"

"We're all friends here, Weston, so I'm going to be blunt with you," Hackett said. "But everything I'm telling you is confidential. I need your help, but you can't repeat what I'm about to tell you, understand? You can't tell anyone."

"Yes, sir," Weston said quietly.

Li pressed her ear more tightly to the door. If she missed even a word of this exchange, her mother would be very displeased.

"My men and I have come to town looking for a man by the name of Feng Xu. He's an agent of the Chinese government and a very dangerous person. We believe he's come to town searching for some kind of treasure, an energy-generating ring. Have you heard anything about an item like that?"

"Yes, sir," Weston replied, and he related the story, which everyone in school had heard by now, of Raphael Kain's disappearance.

"Here's the thing," Hackett's voice replied. "From what I've heard so far, the ring was destroyed in the explosion. But the man I'm after wouldn't have come here all the way from China unless he thought there was still something important he could get his hands on—you follow me, Weston? What I'm trying to figure out is if there might be a part of the ring—or some of its technology—still floating around Middleburg somewhere. If we could locate it, we could use it as bait. Do you have any idea where it is—or who's got the pieces?"

"No," Weston said. "I mean—not really."

There was a pause, then Li heard Hackett say, "What do you mean?"

"Well, I saw some of the pieces—a while back. Some of the Topper kids were showing them around in the lunchroom one day. There were probably a dozen of them, at least. But no one's mentioned them lately."

"And the names?" Hackett pressed.

"What?" Weston asked, and Li had to stifle a giggle. He sounded so nervous, like he was a fugitive being questioned by the FBI.

"The kids who had the pieces—what are their names?"

Weston proceeded to rattle off the names of all the Toppers and the Flatliners, and Li could hear the faint scratching of a pen as the man—Agent Hackett—wrote them down.

"Listen to me very closely, Weston," Agent Hackett said. "We have to get all the pieces of the ring—but we have to be subtle about it, you understand? You willing to work with me here?"

"Yes, sir. I guess so."

"Okay—here's what I need you to do. I'm going to give you my card. If any pieces of that ring turn up—if any of the kids mention that they still have them—I want you to call me. If you can manage to get your hands on any of them and bring them to me, that's even better. Can you do that, Weston? If you could, your country will be grateful—and I'm sure your father will be very proud."

"Absolutely," Weston's dad agreed.

"I'll do my best, sir," Weston said. His voice was naturally quiet and timid-sounding, but there was an unusual hint of determination in it that Li found admirable.

"You'll have to be careful, Weston. Feng Xu and his men are extremely dangerous."

As Agent Hackett launched into his warning, Li slipped back down the hallway. She'd heard enough.

A few minutes later, the agent departed. She only saw him for a moment, as he peeked into the kitchen to wave goodbye to Mrs. Darling, but Li made a mental note of his every feature.

When their schoolwork was done, Weston invited Li to go up to his room to play video games. Li knew that was just an excuse—he spent these video-game sessions trying to work up the nerve to kiss her, and she found it quite amusing to watch him squirm. This time, however, he didn't even bother to turn on his Xbox. Instead, he immediately confided everything that Agent Hackett had just told him, putting special emphasis on how important and dangerous the mission was. As usual, he was trying desperately to impress her.

"So I'm basically a government spy now," he summarized, blinking wildly behind the fishbowl-like lenses of his glasses.

"Wow!" Li said, and she gave her trademark little giggle—the one her mother had taught her to use whenever she needed to convince someone that she was nothing but a pretty, inconsequential little creature, as delicate and placid as a flower—and not even half as threatening.

"So what do you think?" Weston said, breathless with excitement. "Will you help me? Will you help me track down the pieces of the ring?"

Li smiled sweetly. "Of course, Wes. You know I'd do anything to help you," she said.

Inwardly, she was laughing. *Mother will be very pleased,* she thought. And she stood and gave Weston a big, lingering hug, just to spin her web a little tighter.

℘

On Sunday evening, Bran and Rick rolled back into Middleburg. Bran was pretty much wiped out from three days of intense training and was looking forward to gorging on a meal of his mom's special spaghetti and flopping into his bed. But when he checked his voice mail, he found a disturbing message from his dad. The police had come by twice asking to talk to him. Rick checked his messages and found one from his father, too.

Two hours later, Bran sat in the waiting area of Jack Banfield's office. He had showered, and he was now wearing a dress shirt and a tie that felt like it was choking him to death. Mr. Banfield, irritated that the local authorities dared to insinuate that his son might have done something wrong, had made his lawyer drive in from Topeka so the boys could make a statement. Rick was recording his now.

Bran looked down at his hands folded in his lap, and his grandfather's admonition played through his mind once more: the truth always comes to light sooner or later. His grandpa had been a Korean War veteran and a staunch church-goer. He had taught Bran how to shoot a basketball, catch a football, and throw a punch. Before he'd passed away two years ago, he'd been Bran's favorite person in the world, even though he'd lived back in Alabama and Bran didn't see him much during his last few years. Still, he knew the old man would want him to tell the truth now—and that knowledge was eating him up. Because he also knew that his social life, his dad's job, and maybe even his survival required him to lie. The conflict seemed to be tearing a hole in the pit of his stomach.

He heard the door open, and Banfield's lawyer, a fat man with a catfish moustache and a gold pinky ring, invited him into the conference room. Bran took his seat and cleared his throat. Rick's dad, seated on the other side of the table, gave him an encouraging nod. Rick was leaning back in the leather office chair with his big feet kicked up onto the table, checking basketball scores on his cell phone. The lawyer—Bran thought his name was Mr. Davis—coughed and then activated a small digital recorder sitting in the middle of the table. He rattled off the date and time, stated his name, and then asked Bran to state his name.

"All right, Bran. We're going to get right down to business," the lawyer rumbled. "On the night in question, did you see Rick Banfield harm Emory Van Buren in any way?"

A second passed, then two seconds. Bran could feel the sweat forming on his forehead, dripping down his temple, soaking through his shirt at the armpits. The lawyer leaned forward in his chair. Mr. Banfield's eyes narrowed. Rick looked up from his phone.

For a moment, Bran was frozen. Finally, with a mighty effort, he cleared his throat. "No," he said. "I didn't see anything."

CHAPTER 8

AT NOON ON MONDAY, MAGGIE SAT at her old table in the lunchroom, but she felt like she was in another world. Dalton had gone to Miss Pembrook's room for a meeting of one of the numerous clubs she was in, and when Maggie had entered the cafeteria alone, Lisa Marie snagged her and led her over to her old place at the table where the cheerleaders and jocks always sat.

"We miss our Magsie!" she'd said sweetly, and Maggie knew resistance would be futile. It would invite more questions than she was willing to answer.

She looked around for Rick and found him at the far end of the table with his Topper crew. Lisa Marie, Bobbi Jean, and the other girls Maggie usually hung out with took up a big space in the middle, and Maggie was at the other end—as far from Rick as she could get. She hoped he wouldn't notice her.

By now, Maggie had grown accustomed to the special gift of insight that had suddenly, instantly, filled her at the homecoming dance, when the queen's crown was placed on her head. But it was more than insight. It was a special way of seeing what people were under the surface—what they were in their hearts, in the core of them. It was like she could see into their souls.

Lily Rose, Dalton's grandmother, who had given her *The Good Book* to help her try to understand it, said that it was a good thing. Maggie wasn't always so sure of that. She was getting used to it, but that didn't necessarily make it easier, especially when she looked at her so-called boyfriend. That was when it was strongest—when she looked at Rick. More and more often he appeared to her as a hideous, malformed demon, but this morning had been the worst.

When Maggie saw him standing at his locker before homeroom, she'd almost run the other way. His hands were big and grotesque, his face was hard and crusty like a moss-covered tree trunk, and his teeth were jagged, shark-like, and dripping with blood, as if he'd disemboweled someone on his way to school. Maggie had heard the rumors that were spreading quickly around the school as everyone speculated about what had happened to that poor Flatliner, Emory Van Buren, who now lay in a coma in the hospital, but Maggie *knew* Rick was responsible.

Some students had set up a shrine in the hallway of the school in the spot they called Four Corners. At its center was a large picture of Emory, surrounded by candles, photos, cards, stuffed animals, and other mementoes. Principal Innis had ordered all the candles extinguished—it was a fire hazard or something—but from where she was sitting, Maggie could still see, through the plate-glass windows of the lunchroom, the glow that surrounded the memorial. Its energy, bright with the prayers and good wishes of so many kids and teachers, outshone even the brightest auras of any she'd seen that day.

All, that is, except the aura of Aimee Banfield, who was just entering the cafeteria. Aimee drifted between the crowded tables as if in a dream, oblivious to everyone around her. She took a seat at an empty table across the room. As she moved among them, the white, star-like radiance of her aura still shone brightly, as it had the first time Maggie had seen it; only now fluttering fissures of blackness—the spoils of Orias Morrow's influence—shot through it like small flashes of morbid lightning, as if a storm were moving through her soul.

Rick's little sister had undergone a total change since returning to Middleburg High the previous autumn. Her short, black-dyed hair was blond again and was growing out at a rate that made Maggie wonder if she'd gotten hair extensions. Her nails, which she used to nervously bite down to nothing, were now long and she had a perfect French manicure. She had replaced her jeans and T-shirts with dresses that had long, flowing skirts and delicate floral patterns, and every day a new diamond, sapphire, ruby, or emerald sparkled from her wrist, her finger, or her earlobes.

In some ways, Aimee seemed to have reverted to the girl she had been before the traumatic death of her old boyfriend Tyler and the subsequent breakdown that had prompted her father to send her away to a boarding school in Montana. In other ways, she seemed like a different person altogether.

Before all that—before Tyler had died, or had been murdered—Aimee had been part of Maggie's crew and she and Maggie had been best friends. But when she came back to town, Aimee had forged a close friendship with Dalton—not that Maggie could blame her. She hadn't been so nice to Aimee back then—and she really didn't know why. Maybe she had been afraid of Aimee, afraid that the stories were true, and that Aimee had taken Tyler's life, like everyone said.

Since Maggie had come into her new power, her special way of seeing people, she was no longer afraid—and she no longer believed that Aimee had killed Tyler. But Maggie's gift, her new sense of strength, was no match for Orias, and Aimee had changed even more drastically since she'd started dating him. Now she was aloof and distant with everyone, even Dalton, and as unbelievable as it seemed, Aimee had even dumped Raphael Kain for Orias. Maggie couldn't help being glad about that—she still couldn't get that one kiss she had shared with Raphael out of her mind—but she didn't feel good about seeing Aimee with that slick manipulator, Orias.

She wished now that she had interceded the day she saw Orias take Aimee's hand, when he'd first infested her aura with the darkness of his incredibly magnetic energy. But now, it seemed, it was too late.

Maggie was lost in these thoughts (and half listening to Casey Swaddock ranting about her favorite reality show) when Zhai Shao came and took the seat across from her.

"Hey," he said. "You got them?"

"Yeah. I've got them."

Zhai glanced at the Topper girls sitting next to Maggie, as if afraid that they might overhear his conversation, but they were now engaged in a heated discussion about makeup. He relaxed as Maggie took a manila envelope from her purse and pushed it across the table to him. Inside were the shards of the ring she'd rescued from the tunnels, just before the Obies attacked.

"You still haven't told me how you got away from them," Zhai said as he folded the envelope carefully and put it in the inside breast pocket of his blazer.

"A girl has to keep her secrets, right?" she tried to joke but somehow it fell flat. Often now she felt that in Middleburg, the time for joking was over.

Zhai smiled and shook his head. "Wow, Maggie. You're seriously the last person I would ever expect to be my ally in all this—but the way you've helped out, looking for Raphael, going with Master Chin and me to the Wheel, hiding the shards . . . thank you."

"No problem," Maggie said. "How is he? Master Chin?"

Zhai's smile disappeared. "Lily Rose is working on him. I stayed there all night, using my energy—" Zhai seemed to catch himself. "You know, my prayers and good wishes—to help him. But I'm worried. I'm going there again after school, if you'd like to come by."

Maggie nodded. "I'll have to check with my mom first to make sure she doesn't need anything, but yeah. Anything to help." She picked at a piece of her turkey wrap and nibbled on it.

"I talked to Nass yesterday," he continued. "We both think it's really important to put all the pieces of the ring back together. It could help us get Raphael back."

She gestured to Zhai's coat, where the shards were safely tucked away in his breast pocket. "Mine is in there too," she said. "If I can get my hands on any others, I'll give them to you."

Zhai nodded. "Thanks. I'm going to talk to Rick right now and call a Toppers meeting tonight, to get their shards back. Nass is going to call a meeting of the Flatliners, too."

"Sounds good," Maggie said.

"Just be careful, okay? As long as those Obies are out there, none of us is safe." Zhai stood. "One of these days you're going to tell me how you got away from those guys."

"Never," Maggie said with a smile. "I'll take it to my grave."

Zhai smiled. "Thanks again," he said and headed over to Rick.

Good luck reasoning with—whatever he is now, Maggie thought with a shudder.

"Just who the hell does she think she is?" Bobbi Jean was saying resentfully, and Maggie followed her gaze to where Aimee was sitting alone.

"Look at me with my fake blond hair, I'm so cool I don't even need friends," Casey mocked, and Bobbi Jean and Lisa Marie laughed.

"Why don't you guys shut up?" Maggie said sharply, and all three of them turned toward her, their eyes wide.

"What's wrong with you?" Bobbie Jean asked.

"What's wrong is that I'm sick of hearing you guys making fun of people," Maggie snapped. "You want to judge somebody, judge yourselves." She shouldered her purse, picked up her lunch tray, and walked away. Their stunned silence trailed behind her as she crossed the room and sat down across from Aimee Banfield.

∽

It was three-thirty, and as the Flatliners invaded their usual booth in the back of Rack 'Em Billiards Hall, they had the place pretty much to themselves. Raphael had worked there before he disappeared, and it gave Nass an ache of sadness to see its familiar worn booths, the flashing pinball machine and the dark, polished wood of the bar, and know that his friend wasn't there. Every time he turned around, he half expected Raph to burst through the big swinging door that led to the kitchen with a bus tub in his hand and a look of hardworking determination on his face. Every time he didn't, Nass's disappointment stung anew. As painful as it was, the Flatliners came to Rack 'Em even more often now than they had when Raphael was with them. Nass knew it made all of them feel closer to him to be there, in the place he'd loved so much.

Nass wished desperately that he was here now. The meeting hadn't even begun, and already it wasn't going well.

"I just want to sit on the outside, okay?" Benji carped at Josh.

"Quit being a baby. Move over and let me in," Josh snapped.

"Just for that I'm not moving at all. You can drag a chair over," Benji said, crossing his arms over his chest.

"Don't be a jackass. Just scoot," Josh said, pushing Benji. Benji pushed him back.

"Guys!" Nass said, unable to take it anymore. "Come on. We got important things to talk about. Benji, let Josh in. Josh, let Benji sit on the outside. He was there first. What's the big deal?"

There was a general grumbling as everyone settled down.

Nass reminded himself to cut his friends some slack. They were all stressed out about everything that had happened: Raphael was gone, Emory was in a coma, and it seemed like every family in the Flats was getting evicted. He was stressed out too, Nass thought as he glanced at his phone. Today was the deadline for the eviction notice his family had received. His dad had gone down to the rental office one more time to try to fight it, but so far Nass hadn't heard any news. When they were tossed out on the street, Emory's family had been forced to watch a crew of Jack Banfield's men throw all their stuff out into the front yard. The thought of going home and finding his mom, his dad, and Clarisse waiting on the lawn made him angry and afraid—but not knowing what was going on was even worse.

He exhaled sharply, trying to release all the pent-up frustration he was feeling, and plunged his cell phone back into his pocket.

"All right, let's get this meeting started," he said. It didn't feel like much of a meeting. With Raph and Benji gone, it was just Nass, Beet, and across from them Josh and Emory. Four of them against the world.

"Okay, what's the big news?" Josh asked irritably. He'd been closer to Emory than anyone, Nass knew, and he was taking the attack on their friend even harder than the rest of them. He was snapping at everyone, and Nass was finding his attitude increasingly hard to take. But he forced himself to be patient and began.

"I talked with Zhai yesterday," Nass told them. He says those kung fu guys in the crazy hats—the Obies—they're still around, and their leader is here now. He's this bad dude named Feng Xu. They attacked Master Chin yesterday. He's at Lily Rose's house, and from what Zhai said, he's barely alive."

The guys reacted to this news with a mixture of shock, rage, and despair. Nass understood what they must be feeling. If Chin couldn't defend himself against the Obies, the Flatliners wouldn't stand a chance.

"What are you saying?" Josh asked. "You think it was the Obies that attacked Emory?"

Nass shook his head. "I don't think so. The knowing tells me it wasn't them . . . anyway, there's more. Remember those government guys who stopped Emory's building from being torn down? They're here looking for Feng Xu. And Feng Xu—he's looking for the shards of the ring."

Beet frowned. "But—it's broken. Why would they want it?"

"Chin and Zhai think that it still has some powers," Nass said quietly. "They think that if we put all the pieces together we'll be able to bring Raph back."

Beet's and Benji's faces lit up, but Josh didn't look impressed.

"Look, Nass. I've been biting my tongue for a long time with this magic crap, but don't you think enough is enough? I mean, we've got real problems to deal with. Somebody almost killed our friend. Emory is in Benton right now barely hanging on to his life, Raph is gone, Chin is almost dead, and we're sitting here scheming about how to gather up the pieces of a magic crystal? Come on, it's ridiculous."

"I know it sounds nuts, but think about the way Raphael disappeared," Nass said. "Think about that crazy, ghostly train, man. Whether we want to accept it or not—whether we even believe it—there's supernatural stuff going on here. Now, we need to get Raphael back, and we think we can do it. All you guys have to do is give me your pieces of the ring. Zhai is gathering up the pieces the Toppers have, then we're going to put them together and—"

"Stop right there!" Josh interrupted, outraged. "You're just going to hand our pieces of the ring over to Zhai?"

"No—I'm not *giving* them to him," Nass said. "I'm going to hold on to ours, he's going to have the ones from the Toppers, and then we're going to put them together."

"I see," Josh said. "And has it ever occurred to you that it might be kind of a stupid idea to trust the leader of our enemies, when he and his friends just beat Emory into a coma?"

Nass closed his eyes for a second, focusing his energy on staying calm. "Josh, I think if Raph were here—"

"Well, I got news for you, Nass," Josh cut him off again, his voice rising. "Raph's *not* here. And who are you to tell us what he would want, anyway? You've been a Flatliner—what? A few months? Who died and made you the boss?"

"I'm not trying to be the boss," Nass said mildly. "I'm just trying to—"

"To get all the pieces of the ring for yourself?" Josh broke in again. "I can see that." Now he was shouting. "I'll tell you what. You're not getting mine, and you can't tell us what to do!"

"Well, what do you suggest?" Nass countered. "You got a better idea?"

"*I suggest,*" Josh said firmly, "that we get some new leadership. I propose that we vote on it right now." He glanced around the table at his friends. "You vote for me and the first thing I'll do is find Rick Banfield, challenge him to a fight, and put him in a hospital bed right next to Emory. That should be our priority—honor. Survival. Revenge. Not messing around with some stupid pieces of broken glass."

As Nass looked at Josh, the knowing kicked in, and he was able to see beyond his friend's paler-than-usual skin and the dark circles under his eyes. He saw the sleepless nights, the tears, the guilt he'd felt that he'd been out with his girlfriend, Beth, on Valentine's night instead of at his best friend's side. All this came to Nass in a flash of realization, and instantly diffused the ticking bomb of irritation that was about to explode within him. But understanding Josh's point of view didn't change the situation. Josh was about to take control of the Flatliners and lead them down a very dangerous path, and Nass couldn't let that happen.

"I'm nominating myself for leader of the Flatliners," Josh continued. "Anyone want to run against me?" He looked at Beet.

"Not me," Beet said quickly. "I don't want to be the leader."

Benji just shook his head and gnawed nervously on the straw from his Coke.

Josh looked at Nass next, and Nass sighed heavily.

"I think we should all just work together until we get Raph back," he said. "But if you insist on being the leader and dragging us into a war, then all right, Josh. I'll run against you."

"See, that's how I can tell you're not really a Flatliner, Nass," Josh said coldly. "If you were, you'd realize we're already at war."

Josh's eyes were locked onto Nass's, and Nass wouldn't let himself look away.

"Okay," Nass said. "Let's vote."

"All in favor of me?" Josh said.

Beet raised his hand. "Sorry, Nass, but Josh is right," he said. "We gotta get revenge—for Emory."

Josh's hand was already up. All eyes drifted to Benji.

"Benji, think of Emory," Josh said.

"Think of Raphael," Nass countered. "If we don't work together to get Zhai's shards, we'll never get him back."

"We don't know that," Josh said.

Benji drummed his fingers on the table. "Well . . . I think we should try to work with Zhai to get Raph back," he said slowly, and then gave Nass an apologetic glance. "But Josh has been a Flatliner longer than you. He has seniority. Plus, we gotta stand up to Rick. Sorry, Nass." And Benji raised his hand.

"Three to one," Josh said. "I win."

Nass stood up from the table, his shoulders slumped, too frustrated to sit anymore. It was like everything was unraveling around him. He knew going into the meeting that tempers were flaring and it might be tough to keep the peace, but he never thought it would turn out like this.

With Nass on his feet, the rest of the guys rose, too, sensing that the meeting was over. They stood next to the table in a loose circle.

"Congrats, man," Nass said. "I hope you'll be the wise leader these guys deserve, and I'll follow you, too. To the death, just like the Wu-de says. But I'm telling you, a war with the Toppers right now won't help Emory recover, and it won't help get Raphael back, either."

"No. It'll get us back our honor and our pride," Josh said. "It'll allow us to walk around town without having to look over our shoulders and without having to worry about our brothers and our sisters and our friends. Maybe if you had to worry about your family's safety you'd get it. Except, oh yeah—Clarisse is hooking up with Rick, isn't she? She's safe."

At this revelation, Nass looked stunned. "What are you talking about?" he demanded.

"Yeah, that's right," Josh said. "Beet and Benji saw them parked down by Make-Out Lake—as if you didn't know."

"I didn't," said Nass.

"Anyway," Josh went on, "you're best buddies with Zhai now. You're practically half Topper yourself."

Finally, Nass couldn't take it anymore. He shoved Josh. Josh shoved him back, causing him to stumble backward and knock over a chair. Nass was just getting ready to lay into him again when he heard a shout from behind the bar.

"Hey!" It was Rudy, the owner of Rack 'Em—and he looked pissed off. "I ask one thing of you guys: no trouble in my place, then I come out and find you all acting like a bunch of animals? Get out."

There was a heavy silence, and then the guys started trudging toward the door—Benji first, then Beet, then Josh. Nass was the last to go.

"Hey, look, we're really sorry," he said.

"Come back next week—if you can act like human beings," Rudy snapped. "Out."

Outside, a fitful breeze met the Flatliners. The sky was full of wispy gray clouds that seemed on the verge of breaking up to a blue sky—but didn't. The Flatliners lingered on the wide front stoop of the bar for a moment, unsure of what to do. Josh was the first to depart, striking off across the parking lot alone.

Benji and Beet exchanged a couple of low words, and then Benji approached Nass. "You were right in there," he said. "Raph would want us to work this out." He dug into the pocket of his jeans, pulled out his ring shard, and handed it to Nass.

"I'll get you mine, too," Beet promised. "Just don't tell Josh, all right? He's taking this whole Emory thing pretty hard."

Nass gazed down at the shard in his hand, looking desperately for a spark or a glimmer—any hint that there was still some magic left in it—but there was nothing. It remained dead and gray.

"Later, Nass," Beet said over his shoulder as he and Benji departed.

Nass stood alone for a long moment, gazing across the empty parking lot at the bare, brown skeletons of trees that bordered the abandoned railroad tracks, at the implacable emptiness of the sky, and then he too started walking. He passed an old Pepsi can and booted it as hard as he could, watching it clatter lamely across the blacktop—but it didn't make him feel any better. He walked all the way home as fast as he could, trying to use the motion and the exertion to burn off the anger and frustration he was feeling, all the while examining his problems in his mind, turning them over, twisting them around, groping for solutions that simply weren't there.

By time he was home, his foul mood was finally beginning to subside—until he reached the walkway leading up to his building and looked up. The first thing he saw was his chest of drawers sitting under a big, leafless maple tree. All the rest of his family's furniture was there too. His mother was pacing back and forth and shouting at his father in Spanish. His dad stood with one hand against the tree's trunk, leaning on it as if it were the only thing in the world that was keeping him from falling to the earth and never rising again. Clarisse was carrying a cardboard box from the porch of the building and putting it with a stack of other boxes, near the rest of the family's possessions.

Nass stared at the scene in utter disgust and disbelief. It seemed impossible that it could be real. All this time he'd never thought it would happen; he'd been certain something would save them. But now, his nightmare had come true. On top of everything else that had happened, his family was being evicted.

CHAPTER 9

STANDING IN THE CENTER OF THE TILED FLOOR in the largest of the three upstairs bathrooms in Orias Morrow's house, Aimee gazed into the full-length mirror. She wore only her bra and panties, and her hair was tied back from her face with a silk scarf. Her skin was smooth and radiant and, now that her hair was back to its natural blond, it was the perfect color for her deep blue eyes. The delicacies Orias constantly shipped in from all over the world—foie gras, white truffles, Alaskan king crab, Japanese Kobe beef, succulent blue lobster—had helped Aimee to regain the weight she'd lost while at boarding school, and her body was firm and beautifully toned. But she wasn't really looking at her appearance. She was looking at her technique.

Knees bent, hips tilted forward, arms relaxed yet firm, body erect, she went through the movements of the form, then began practicing her strikes over and over, counting silently with each one: *yut, yee, sarm, say, ng, look, chut, bart, gau, sap,* then again on the left side. *Yut, yee, sarm. . .* It didn't seem strange to her that she was counting in Chinese, nor did it trouble her that she couldn't remember who had first taught her the moves she was practicing. All she knew was that if she wanted to find her mother and bring her home, it was important to train each and every day.

Aside from this, she kept no other secrets from Orias. She had surrendered her will to him completely, the way a baby helplessly abandons himself to the protection of his mother's arms—except for this. Except for the one hour a day that she went into the bathroom, locked the door, and practiced her kung fu.

The strangest part was that when she was there practicing, locked in the bathroom alone, she sometimes felt a presence there with her, guiding her, correcting her, silently whispering encouragement, somewhere in the recesses of her mind. Today, the feeling was stronger than ever.

Keep your elbows in. Good. Feet parallel. Watch your centerline . . . very nice.

She didn't think much about who or what this presence might be. The truth was, she didn't think very hard about anything these days. She just drifted, slipping from moment to moment with the same effortless abandon with which she was now able to slip through space.

Actually, this thoughtless existence was an incredible relief. Sometimes, when Aimee remembered the person she'd been before Orias came into her life, she found that girl to be completely baffling. All the angst, the rebellion, the aching need for freedom, the thirst for truth—all those things seemed like such a waste of energy to her now. She had Orias, and he was wonderful. Her father and brother finally approved of her and maybe even loved her. She enjoyed her classes when Orias insisted that she go to school. And she looked forward to a day when she and Orias could be together completely, as husband and wife—as they had been the first time she'd teleported and had seen her future, ending up in that red tent, alone with him, on the top of the temple.

Just as she had surrendered her will to him, she would have been happy to surrender her body as well. When he kissed her and stroked her hair, when he looked into her eyes and held her close, she wanted him more than she had ever wanted anything else in her life. But Orias was careful. He let it go only so far and no further. She had his love and his respect, he told her, and he protected her as if she were made of spun glass, insisting that they wait until their wedding day. Even though she desired him, that was also a relief. And now there seemed to be nothing to be upset about, nothing to fear, nothing to hide.

Of course, she still needed to find her mother, but the urgency of the quest had dimmed. She knew where her mother was—in Middle-burg, sometime in the 1800—as unbelievable as it seemed. Judging from the picture Aimee had found while helping Miss Pembrook, her history teacher, with some research, Emily Banfield was perfectly happy living back in the olden days, as if she belonged there. But Aimee missed her terribly and would go there and retrieve her just as soon as her teleporta-tion skills had developed enough.

The only thing that troubled Aimee these days was her recurring nightmare about the angry man locked up in the tower that stood imposingly at the rear of Orias's house. In her dreams, the man was pounding on the door demanding to be released, and with each dream he got more frantic, more insistent, and more enraged—but she always woke up before she could see his face. When she told Orias, he assured her that it was nothing, just a bad dream and, comforted, she would fall asleep again in his arms. The nightmare was coming less frequently now, and so was that vague, unsettling feeling that haunted her almost constantly—the feeling that she'd lost someone very precious to her, someone besides her mother, someone she needed desperately, someone who had once meant the world to her—except that she couldn't quite remember who it was.

One by one, those troubles had also dissipated, until finally only this one quirk remained. Aimee loved the times that she spent locked in the bathroom, training with the invisible teacher who seemed to speak inside her mind . . .

Again. Yut, yee, sarm . . .

Suddenly, a pounding on the door jolted her from the focus her train-ing required.

"Aimee, what's taking so long?" Orias demanded, clearly trying to contain his irritation.

"Be out in a minute," she answered sweetly.

"We're going to be late, you know," he said. "We're supposed to be at your house for dinner in fifteen minutes. Your father made it clear that it's very important."

"Yeah, okay. I'm about to hop in the shower," Aimee said.

For a moment he was silent and then, barely covering his exasperation, he said, "Fine. But please hurry. I'm not in the mood for a lecture from Jack." Then, after a moment, she heard his footsteps retreating down the hall.

Aimee made eye contact with herself in the mirror and then performed one last ferocious kick. Her foot made a whistling sound as it shot through the air, and she froze there, balanced on one leg, her body stretched out parallel to the floor, her foot hovering inches away from the spot on the mirror where her face had been just seconds before. If her reflection had been an opponent, she could have smashed it, she thought with satisfaction.

Yes, came the voice of her unknown teacher. *When the time comes, you will be ready.*

She retracted her kick, stood up straight, and, placing the fist of one hand in the palm of the other, she bowed to her reflection.

"Doh je," she said quietly. She knew that was Cantonese for "thank you," although she didn't know how she knew.

Orias was knocking on the door again. She was surprised. She hadn't heard his footsteps returning. "Aimee," he said, his irritation growing.

"I'm hurrying," she said pleasantly. She wiped the sweat from her brow with a washcloth and turned on the shower.

ॐ

Dalton, her grandmother, and Zhai Shao were at Master Chin's bedside. Dalton didn't know Chin very well, but she knew that her friend Raphael had loved him dearly, and her grandmother had known him and thought highly of him for years. It broke her heart to see the old man suffering so much.

She and Zhai exchanged a glance as Lily Rose took the fresh poultice she and Dalton had prepared and moved to the head of the bed. The second she pulled the old poultice away, the fetid odor of disease filled the room, and Dalton was disturbed to see that the skin around the two puncture wounds in Master Chin's neck was gray and marbled with the dark, branching red lines of infected veins.

Zhai's eyes widened, too, when he saw the wound.

"Is he . . . ?" Zhai began, but he was interrupted by a loud moan that escaped his teacher's lips as he thrashed beneath the covers.

"He'll be all right," Lily Rose said sternly. "If he stops doing harm to himself. He needs to lie still, but the pain from the venom is too much. Dalton, go around the other side of the bed and swab his brow with a cool, wet cloth."

Dalton did as she was told, gently wiping the sweat from Chin's forehead. She could feel the heat of the fever beneath the cloth, and she could see his eyes snapping back and forth beneath their lids. As his body twitched, he spoke, his speech guttural and mumbled: *"Yut . . . yee . . . sarm . . . say . . . ng . . ."*

"I think he's trying to tell us something," Dalton said.

Zhai shook his head and squinted down at his teacher, perplexed. "It's Cantonese Chinese. He's . . . counting," he said.

"Either way, what he needs is to rest," Lily Rose said. "Go on home now, Zhai, and thanks for your help. Close the door behind you."

Zhai started to leave, then hesitated in the doorway. "That Flatliner, Emory," he said. "Do you think with your healing ability, maybe you could . . . ?"

Lily Rose shook her head sadly. "I already went to see that boy in the hospital," she said, her voice a low, somber drawl. "There are some things I can fix, and some I can't."

Zhai seemed to deflate a bit at this news, but he managed a smile and a little wave before exiting.

As soon as he was gone, Dalton felt her grandmother's unusual eyes settling on her. Those insistent, probing eyes were two different colors—one amber and one blue—and there was no mistaking their power and no arguing with their wisdom.

"What?" Dalton asked, a little defensively.

"You know what I'm going to say. Chin needs rest, Dalton," Lily Rose said gently. "We've tried herbs. We've tried prayer. I can't make him get the rest he needs. Only you can do that. I need you to do it now."

Dalton sighed heavily and sat down in the antique chair near the foot of the bed. She'd known this day was coming, ever since that first time, so many years ago, when she'd first opened up the copy of *The Good Book* her grandma had given her. She'd expected a little poem, a piece of folksy wisdom, or one of the mysterious axioms that her grandmother was always imparting to her. Instead, she had found a song.

It wasn't in the form of regular musical notation (even at the age of seven, she'd already been in the church choir for two years and had learned to read music). The page she was looking at was blank. She was stunned and delighted, however, when the book actually sang to her. She remembered looking for the switch that would turn it off and on, as if it were a toy, but there was none. It was just a book—but she heard the melody loud and clear. It was a simple melody, and as she hummed along with it, she thought it was perhaps the most beautiful music she'd ever heard. She hummed it again and then she had started to sing, making up words as she went. She was amazed that so simple and so exquisite a melody hadn't been discovered by a hundred songwriters over the years. It seemed to her like the perfect tune every composer throughout time had tried but failed to capture.

The next day when she'd gone to school, she'd heard the melody everywhere, and lyrics came easily to her mind to fit whatever the circumstances were. It wasn't just that the music was stuck in her head for days (although it certainly was). It was repeated everywhere—in the twitter of the birds, in the laughter of the other children as they played, in the wind and the rain and the leaves that skipped down the street in front of her grandmother's comfortable old house. Variations and harmonies of it came from the engine of the plane flying high above, from the insects that chirped and buzzed in the deep grasses outside of the playground, from the bass notes of a lawnmower grumbling in the distance. The footsteps of her scampering playmates formed the percussion and the gentle whisper of the wind through the trees played the strings.

That Sunday in church Dalton was to sing a solo, a gospel version of "How Great Thou Art." But in the instant of anticipation before she began, when all those devout eyes were trained upon her, when the pianist's fingers hung suspended above the keys waiting for her to begin and the only sounds were the occasional cough and shuffle of the faithful, something within Dalton said, *Sing the other song.* And she had.

The result wasn't at all what she expected—although in truth, she hadn't known what to expect. During the first half of the thirty-second song, a radiant smile budded on each parishioner's face. By the time it was finished, their eyes had drifted closed, their necks had gone limp. When the last note faded from her throat, no one clapped or shouted amen. In fact, there was no movement, no reaction from the congregation at all. The only sound was a faint snore coming from a heavyset man named Mr. Barnes who sat in the back row of pews. Everyone, every last person in the church, had fallen asleep, except for herself and her grandma.

Little Dalton had stood there stunned, looking around with a rising sense of confusion, when one by one, the congregants began to wake up. Each of them was smiling, grinning broadly, as if they were bubbling over with so much joy that their mouths were simply powerless to contain it. They started clapping and one by one they got to their feet to give Dalton a standing ovation.

She'd asked her grandmother about it when they got home that evening.

"That's the Song of Peace," Lily Rose told her. "What a mighty fine song it is! And you sing it better than anyone, sugar plum." That was all the old woman had ever said on the subject.

Dalton had consulted *The Good Book* a few times in the ensuing years, looking for answers to all kinds of questions, but it never showed her anything else. Her grandmother was always asking her to sing the song for people—for the geezers at Middleburg Retirement Park, for the kids at the nursery school, and of course for the church—anywhere people might be in need of a little solace and rest. She tried to arrange a tour, so that Dalton could perform at all the churches in the area, and she was always urging Dalton to practice her singing. Dalton knew her grandmother's dream for her was to be a famous recording artist, sharing her talent and that special, mysterious song with the world, but Dalton had always resisted. For a while she wanted to be a lawyer, then a dental hygienist. Lately, she'd been thinking of going into architecture. She was open to doing just about anything, except being a singer.

It wasn't that her first performance of the song had freaked her out or anything like that. It was simply that no other songs she sang could compare to the one she'd learned from *The Good Book*. Singing them was like eating dry rice cakes when you knew you could be feasting on a por-terhouse steak. She was always hesitant to sing the Song of Peace, and only did it when she couldn't talk her grandma out of it. She never told anyone why, or even admitted it to herself, but the truth was, deep down in her soul she wasn't sure she was worthy to perform that glorious, tran-scendent song.

"I don't know if I can do it, Grandma. I haven't sung it in so long," she protested now.

Lily Rose came over and put a comforting hand on her shoulder. "I know you're scared, honey bun," she said. "But that venom old Master Chin got a dose of is powerful stuff, and even in someone as strong as he is, it moves fast. Faster than all the herbs and poultices and magic and prayers we have. The only chance he has is to go into a deep, deep sleep—

so deep that his heart almost stops beating. Then the venom will stop spreading, and we might be able to save him. But if you don't sing for him, Dalton, he is going to die."

Lily Rose's age-worn face was as kind as ever, but there was such gravity in her extraordinary eyes that it filled Dalton with alarm.

Dalton looked from her grandmother to Master Chin, who was still twitching, sweating, and muttering in his sleep, and she sighed. She hardly ever cried, but she felt like she might now.

"I know, darlin'," her grandmother soothed. "There's nothing in the world scarier than your own power. But I'll tell you a little secret: the only thing scarier than using it is not using it."

Dalton felt her grandmother take her hand and squeeze. She felt the old woman's thin, loose skin; her swollen, knobby knuckles; and most of all the strength and vitality that Lily Rose still had, despite her age.

And, Dalton suddenly realized, the greatest fear she had wasn't of her own power or her singing or how it might affect people. Most of all, she feared letting her grandmother down and not living up to the beautiful, saintly, unattainable example she'd always set.

"You're good enough, Dalton. Always have been, always will be," Lily Rose said simply, as if she could read her mind. "You can do it—and you must."

She squeezed Dalton's hand once more, then turned and left the room, shutting the door behind her.

As soon as she was gone Dalton moved closer to Master Chin's bedside and gazed down at him as he tossed fitfully, his brow furrowed and sweaty. Taking a deep, slow breath and closing her eyes, Dalton began the song.

Outside, the birds went silent as if they didn't want to miss even one exquisite note. The melody washed over Dalton, lifting her up with each soaring phrase. Lyrics came to her in a language she didn't understand, and yet they soothed her as they seemed now to soothe Master Chin. The sound of her own voice gave her goose bumps.

And when she looked down, Master Chin had settled into deep and peaceful sleep, with a placid smile on his face.

の

The Toppers sat around a large round table in Spinnacle's VIP area in chairs made of sleek, burnished steel with black leather cushions. The floors were of polished hardwood. Expensive abstract paintings graced the walls and fine silk curtains framed a huge picture window that looked out across the barren winter fields north of town. A deepening twilight seemed to descend upon them through the skylights above, its luminous purple fading fast to the desolate blackness of night.

Once, this place and all its sophistication and luxury had been a symbolic refuge for the Toppers—the one place in town where their Flatliner enemies could never follow them simply because they couldn't afford it. That had never bothered Zhai before. Now he felt like he was in enemy territory.

Normally, the guys would have been laughing and joking around, but now they all waited, staring at each other in stony silence.

Zhai glanced at his watch. Seven-ten, and still Rick hadn't shown up. The way things looked, none of the other guys would say a word until he did.

Just as that thought crossed Zhai's mind, he heard the sound of heavy footsteps pounding up the steps to the second floor, and a moment later Rick entered the room with Bran a few feet behind him. Zhai noticed something different about their demeanors at once. Rick's usual arrogant grin was even more brazen and cockier than he'd ever seen it. Bran, on the other hand, looked exhausted and nervous. If Zhai had believed in vampires, he might have thought that Rick was growing more powerful by sucking away the lifeblood of his best friend.

"Hey," all the guys said to Rick and Bran, almost in unison. Bran returned the greetings, but Rick remained silent as he took his usual place in the corner, slumped into his chair and put his size-thirteen feet up on the table.

Zhai cleared his throat. "Okay, thanks for coming, guys. It's been a while since we all hung out like this, huh?"

His icebreaker was met with an awkward silence, so he continued. "Look, I know some of you are pissed that I've been helping the Flatliners look for Raphael Kain, and I get that. I really do. But what you all need to understand is that whatever problems we've had, Raphael and I are bound by the Wu-de. That means we're brothers, training under Master Chin, no matter what our differences are. So even though he's sworn himself to be my enemy, I'm obligated to look for him. Besides, think about it: if I help bring him back, that's also the best way to end our feud with the Flatliners. Raphael can't keep hating us if we save his life, right?"

Michael Ponder was the first to speak up. "Even if we agree," he said, "how do you expect to save his life or find him or whatever? He got hit by a train in case you forgot. And he got vaporized. We all saw it. He's gone, Zhai. And good riddance."

Some of the other guys nodded.

Zhai tried a new tack. "All right, look—I'm not asking you to agree with me or even understand where I'm coming from. All I'm asking is that you let me borrow the little pieces of broken crystal you picked up from the tracks after Raphael got hit. I'll even buy them from you, if you want."

"Why?" Cle'von Cunningham asked. "What are you doing with them?" He didn't seem angry or concerned, just mildly curious.

"Well . . . okay, this may sound strange," Zhai said. "But . . . the thing is, those guys are looking for them—the guys in the Derby hats we saw that night, with the snake. If they get hold of them, something bad is going to happen. They already attacked us—Master Chin and me. And Chin got hurt—badly."

"So we won't give the pieces to those guys," D'von said. "But that doesn't mean we should give them to you. Unless you need them for something."

"Yeah," Cle'von agreed. "Why exactly do you need them?" Everyone looked at Zhai.

A waitress came in with a pitcher of water and put it on the table. Sensing the tension in the room, she turned quickly and walked out.

Rick took his feet off the table and leaned forward in his seat. It was the first time he'd moved during the conversation. "He wants to use them to find Raphael Kain," Rick said, his eyes burning into Zhai's. Zhai noticed a greater intensity about him than usual, and it was unnerving. It was all Zhai could do to keep from looking away.

"Is that right?" Michael Ponder asked, his tone verging on outrage. "Is that why you want them?"

Zhai looked around the table at his friends. He felt them all slipping away from him, like a tide receding from a deserted beach, leaving him stranded, alone.

"Yes," he said simply. "We all saw what happened during the blizzard. There are things going on in Middleburg. Crazy things. Supernatural things. Those guys in the hats belong to a cult called the Order of the Black Snake—Obies for short. And Master Chin said that if we don't bring Raphael back and keep the crystal shards away from them, we're all going to be in very serious trouble."

"And he knows this how?" Rick asked smugly.

Zhai hesitated. "There are these tapestries," he explained. "Maggie's mom does them—"

D'von blurted out a big, deep laugh, cutting Zhai off. "That crazy old broad who leaves her house about once every three years?" Cle'von laughed too and all the other guys joined in, except Bran. He sat there the whole time, perfectly still, taking everything in, as if his slightest movement would cause the whole world to shatter.

"No," Zhai argued. "You need to listen. She's not crazy. She works on the tapestries all the time—that's why she never goes anywhere. They're important—they have some kind of strange power. Maggie's mom draws all the designs and then embroiders them—and they show the history of Middleburg. And its future."

"Zhai, come on!" Dax Avery scoffed. "You sound as crazy as old lady Anderson. This is ridiculous."

"Is it?" Zhai asked. "You all saw what happened that night. The giant snake, the Obies, Orias, Aimee, the train—and what about that thing Maggie did? All that power that came out of her when she put the homecoming crown on her head and went after the cobra? You guys can't deny that you saw it." Zhai's voice rose with desperation on each word.

"Sorry, man," D'von said, and Zhai couldn't believe how much in denial they were. "Those Flatliners are blabbing all over school about how they're going to kick our asses for beating up their friend. And we're supposed to help them? Gimme a break! It's not happening."

All the Toppers looked at Rick to make sure he was in agreement, and then they nodded, too.

Coming into this meeting, Zhai believed that the friendship and respect he shared with the Toppers would be enough to convince them give him the shards. Now, he saw that the regard they'd once had for him was nothing compared to their hatred for the Flatliners—and their fear of Rick.

"I'm still your leader," Zhai said sternly. He stood and looked around at each of them, one by one. "And I'm ordering each of you to bring me your piece of the ring—by nine tonight."

Something in his tone—true authority, he thought, perhaps a gift of Shen—was making them take him seriously. They all looked like little kids who'd just been yelled at by their parents—except Rick, who was chuckling.

"Something funny, Rick?" Zhai asked.

"Yeah," Rick said, slowly coming to his feet. "It's funny that you still think you're the leader here."

The energy in the room changed as the group, frozen in silence, waited to see how Zhai would respond to Rick's challenge.

"I seem to remember that the last time we talked about leadership, I beat you down in your backyard. So, yes, I am the leader," Zhai said, fighting to stay calm.

"You betrayed every one of us the minute you started looking for Kain," Rick snapped. "You're a traitor, Zhai. I'm the leader now."

Zhai glanced around the table, gauging the reactions of the other Toppers. They were all staring down at the table cloth, avoiding eye contact with him. The only one who looked back at him was Bran, but he still had that wild, vacant expression in his eyes.

"The law of the Toppers says you can only become the new leader by beating the current leader in a fight," Zhai said.

"Let's do it," Rick said, already rolling up his sleeves. "And we can make it even more interesting."

"How?" Zhai asked.

"You win," Rick said. "And the guys will all give you their pieces of that useless broken glass." He looked at the others for confirmation. "Isn't that right?"

They all nodded but kept silent. Rick smiled lazily, enjoying himself. "If I win, I get control of the Toppers and all the pieces of that stupid ring—which I will then grind into dust. So if it's true—if that is the way to find Raphael—we'll never have to look at his miserable face again." He chuckled again, and it sounded guttural, almost unnatural. "Deal?"

Zhai stared at Rick. There was something different about him, but Zhai couldn't figure out what it was. Was he bigger somehow? Maybe. Cockier? Definitely. Whatever it was, it gave Zhai an uncharacteristic feeling of dread. Still, this might be his only chance to gather up the shards of the ring and, by extension, his only chance to save Middleburg from the Obies.

"Deal," Zhai said.

CHAPTER 10

FINALLY, RAPHAEL COULDN'T TAKE IT ANY LONGER. He'd napped in the big leather command chair for hours, gone through his kung fu form no less than ten times, and done pushups on the cab's ancient-looking floorboards until his muscles trembled. He'd even tried to decipher the strange markings on the train's gauges. When every other option was exhausted, he'd stared out at the billows of fog whooshing past the windshield until he felt like he was being hypnotized.

But still, the train continued its inexorable and meteoric forward motion. It didn't slow or speed up or turn. And the fog didn't abate or change, not even for an instant. Though he was rocketing toward some unknown destination, Raphael felt like he was in an eerie state of suspension.

He had no clue how much time had passed—minutes, hours, or *days*. He was leaning toward days, although strangely enough, he was neither hungry nor thirsty. For hours, he'd obsessed over what might be going on in Middleburg and how he might get back there, but after a while he'd simply decided it was out of his control and pushed it out of his mind. He was terribly bored for a long time, but eventually that receded, too, leaving him pleasantly vacant, neither happy nor sad, neither relaxed nor anxious, utterly devoid of expectation.

He'd also given up trying to guess where the train might end up. For all he knew, it would go on like this forever. The thought terrified him at first, but now he was strangely okay with it.

This feeling of complete surrender reminded him of his Master Chin's *qigong* training, and he immediately settled down in the leather armchair and began to meditate.

More time passed—again, he had no idea how much—but sometime during his meditation, the thought came to him: *Pull the lever. Stop the train.* Abruptly, he opened his eyes, stood up from the chair, and approached the train's control console. Before, he had been afraid to touch the brass lever that he guessed was the throttle. Now, he grasped it confidently with both hands and in a slow, smooth motion he pulled it backward, toward himself. The all-consuming hum of the engine lowered in pitch with each inch the lever moved, and Raph kept pulling until the brass shaft was perfectly vertical. It clicked into place, and the massive locomotive gave one final lurch and stopped.

The sound of the train's engine had disappeared, leaving in its wake a silence that was even more eerie than the drone of the engine had been. As he stared out the window, he thought for one disorienting moment that he was still moving—the fog remained outside, just as it had been since he'd first awakened on the train. But a second later, he realized that the billows and wisps were no longer moving. They stood in heavy, static sheets, like an infinite series of gray curtains that slowly drifted closed or opened, revealing more gray curtains behind them.

Despite his desolate surroundings, he felt a shock of excitement at the prospect of getting off the train and exploring, and he hurried to the door of the cab and opened it. Clambering down a metal ladder, he sighed in relief as his sneakers hit the hard-packed earth.

He looked around. A warm breeze hummed softly around him, stirring the fog, but that was the only sound or movement he could detect. Off to his right, he could see railroad tracks stretching away until the haze and mist swallowed them up.

The train looked just as he remembered it from the glimpse he'd gotten back in Middleburg. The engine was huge, probably over thirty feet tall and a hundred feet long—and black, as if the whole thing was made of cast iron. Here and there, the black was accented with another metal he couldn't identify. This strange, greenish alloy formed the stairs, the seams around the engine's massive, barrel-like boiler, and the menacing triangle of the cowcatcher. The engine's single headlight, too, gave off a strange, vaguely greenish glow.

Attached to the engine was a series of boxcars, as huge and black as the engine. They were all identical, just big, black rectangles, and Raphael counted nine of them before their lineup disappeared into the fog.

I wonder what's inside them, he thought. What kind of cargo would a supernatural train speeding into oblivion carry?

He hesitated for a second and then decided to find out. In a few strides, he made his way to the nearest boxcar. There were a few steps of greenish metal leading up to a massive, square doorway, and when he mounted them and grabbed the door handle, he got a closer look at the material the car was made of. Leaning closer, he ran a hand over it. Sure enough—it wasn't made of metal at all. It had been carved of some black, granite-like stone. It reminded Raphael of a slab that would cover a grave, and he quickly pulled his hand away.

That's when he heard a sound from inside the car.

Footsteps.

"Hello?" he said, leaning closer to the door, but the only answer was the wind, whispering across the flat, empty land.

Taking a slow, steadying breath, he reached up and gripped the greenish metal handle. He expected that the huge, stone door would be too heavy for him to pull aside, but it seemed to be perfectly weighted, and as he pulled the handle, the latch released, and the big granite slab slid to his right.

The sun or moon—or whatever indistinct light source it was that illuminated this world—shone into the black interior of the train car as Raphael peered inside.

At first, he could see nothing but formless shadows, then came the sound of quick footsteps approaching. It was a man with a heavy paunch at his beltline, a balding head, and dim, squinty eyes. Raphael thought for a second that he recognized him, but before he could figure out how he knew him, the guy charged at him.

"Close the door!" the man said. The desperation in his voice was frightening, and he had a wild look in his eyes. Something about him—the urgency of his tone, the glazed intensity of his expression, or maybe the way he appeared from the recesses of the shadows so suddenly made Raphael think of an insane ghost.

"Close it! Close it! Close it!" the man said, charging Raphael with rising fury.

Raph heaved on the heavy door with all his might, and the last thing he saw before it slammed shut was the man's eyes staring at him, electrified with madness, and his grease-stained hands, groping toward Raphael through the fast-closing gap of the door. When it shut with a bang, Raphael jumped down from the ladder and the sudden overwhelming fear he felt sent him running away from the train.

Wisps of fog clung to him like spiderwebs, slipping around him as he ran and his heart beat fast, pounding in his chest. After a moment, the fear of getting lost overcame the fear of the man in the boxcar and he slowed to a jog, and then to a walk. When he turned around he could no longer see the train.

This can't be good, he thought, and ran back in the direction he'd come. He ran toward the train for as long as he had run away from it, then twice as long, but it was gone. There was no sign of train or tracks. There was nothing but the fog, endless and listless, enshrouding him.

"Hello?" Raphael yelled, his fear coalescing into a wave of frustration. "Hello!" he shouted with all his might, but no one answered his call. There wasn't even an echo.

With a groan, he fell to his knees and buried his face in his hands. He'd been lost before, when he was a kid exploring the woods around

Middleburg with Zhai. That was scary, but it was nothing compared to this. This time, he hadn't just lost his way, he had lost his world. And this time, there was no friend to keep him company.

"Hello."

The voice seemed to come out of the mist, and as it swirled away, Raphael saw a familiar figure standing before him: black fingernails, long black hair, dark eyes. Only his outfit was different. Now, he wore a robe the color of fresh, spring green.

"Magician," Raphael said. "Why am I not surprised?"

The Magician's cunning eyes narrowed as he laughed. "Ah, asking me questions now, are you?" he said.

"Just tell me where I am and how I get back to Middleburg," Raphael said. Then, on second thought, he added, "Please."

"Very well," the Dark Teacher said. "You are in the borderland of the Dark Territory."

"Dark Territory . . ." Raphael said. "I thought that was just a railroad term."

"It is," the Magician said. "The Dark Territory is the destination of the train you have been riding. Middleburg is its second-to-last stop."

Raphael thought of the man in the boxcar. Suddenly, he remembered where he'd seen him before: he was a gas-station attendant from Middleburg. He remembered the guy's name, too. It was stitched on the front of the uniform he always wore: *Don*. But the last time he'd seen him wasn't behind the counter of the gas station; it was in Middleburg's newspaper. There had been a photo of him next to an article. Raphael remembered the headline, too: *LOCAL MAN HIT BY TRUCK AND KILLED*.

Raphael balled his trembling hands into fists and addressed the Magician again. "There was a man on the train, in one of the boxcars. I know him."

The Magician nodded.

"Where is the train taking him?"

The Magician scowled. "I will not repeat myself," he said and turned to disappear back into the fog.

"Wait!" Raphael called after him, his mind racing. "Why is the train taking Don to the Dark Territory?" he asked again, desperate to know.

When the Magician turned back to Raphael this time, he was smiling. "You know why."

The breeze that had been warm and calming a moment before seemed, to Raphael, to drop a few degrees. He shivered.

"Because . . . he's dead," Raphael said. The Magician didn't respond. He didn't have to. Raphael already knew it was true.

If what the Magician was saying was right, Raphael had just been on a train full of ghosts, speeding toward . . . what?

"What will happen to him in the Dark Territory?" Raphael asked warily.

The Magician gazed at Raphael. "That information is usually withheld from the living," he replied sternly.

His answer made Raphael feel a little better: it meant he was still alive. For a second, he had been afraid he was a ghost, just like Don. But another thought followed closely behind the first: if the Dark Territory was where people went when they died, maybe his father was there, too. And maybe that meant Raphael could see him again. The idea filled him with a dizzying feeling that was half elation and half terror.

"If I get back on the train and go there—to look for my dad—will I be able to get out again?"

The Magician's grin faded. "You can get back on the train, but know this: those who enter the Dark Territory are rarely the same when they come out."

Raphael frowned. "What does that mean?"

"They are re-formed," the Magician said.

Raphael wasn't sure if he meant *reformed* or *re-formed*, but either way it sounded a bit ominous. Getting back on the train also sounded like a bad idea—besides, he didn't even know where it was anymore.

"Okay, so if I don't want to get back on the train, where should I go?" Raphael asked.

The Magician pointed to his right. "This direction is time." He pointed the opposite way. "This direction is space."

Raphael looked in both directions through the featureless haze.

"And which way to Middleburg?" he asked.

The Magician pointed in a third direction, which was also obscured by fog.

"That is the way. But beware, Raphael Kain. Those who inhabit the borderland are restless souls, rebels who have rejected their re-formation. If you attempt to cross the wasteland, you will have to fight them every step of the way."

Raphael nodded. Phantom trains, parallel worlds, and creepy magicians all frightened and mystified him—but fighting was one thing he understood.

"Thanks," he said to the Magician. He started off in the direction the Dark Teacher had indicated, then paused and turned back.

"You said something about time," Raphael said. "Does that mean if I go in that direction, I can get to anywhere in time from the borderlands?"

"Of course," the Magician said.

Considering the Magician's words, Raphael stared off into the distance, in the direction the Magician had identified as time. He had so many regrets; he had inflicted so many wounds in the past, and those he loved had suffered so much. If only he could go back and change things. He could make it so that Aimee never met Orias, Emory and his family never got evicted, or his mom never started dating that bastard Jack Banfield.

But there was one thing, more than anything else in the world, that he wanted to go back and change. The first time he'd heard of the Wheel he'd secretly thought of it, and with every mention of time travel since then, it had lingered in his mind, a dark and forbidden hope that he longed for with every thread of his being. . . .

He wanted to ask another question, but when he turned back to look for him, the Magician was gone.

"Disappeared again. Typical," Raphael muttered.

No, he decided firmly. It was too risky to go charging through time or to try to take the phantom train to visit his father in the Dark Territory. The safest bet was to go back to Middleburg now and make sure his mom and Aimee and the Flatliners were all okay. Once he did that, maybe he could find his way back and explore the borderlands.

"Middleburg, here I come," he said. He was about to start walking when he remembered the Magician's warning. Enemies would confront him at every step, he'd said. *Well,* Raphael thought, *bring 'em on.*

He started walking and before long a figure appeared in the fog. The man was short, probably only four feet tall. He was naked and looked like he was more monkey than man, with his long face and hairy, apelike limbs. He shouted a shrill, inhuman battle cry at Raphael, and with both arms flailing, he attacked. Raphael managed to block his fists and sweep his front leg, causing his opponent to do the splits. As the monkeyman fought to keep his balance, Raphael caught him in the face with an elbow and he tumbled backward and disappeared into the mist.

Raphael started moving forward again, but he'd gone no more than two paces when a stone-tipped spear appeared through the fog and jabbed at his face. It almost stabbed him in the left eye before he managed to block it with a *Pak Sau.* The man wielding the weapon looked something like a Neanderthal, just as the first one had, only he was a bit taller and wore a furry loincloth. Raphael grabbed the shaft of the spear he was holding and used an arm-break technique to snap it. In a flurry of swift motion, he spun close to his opponent and impaled him with his own broken-off spearhead, and then he charged onward.

When he looked up, he saw more figures coming toward him out of the fog, and he felt his optimism flagging. The Magician was right. If this was the path back to Middleburg, he would literally be fighting every step of the way.

ℴℴ

Aimee watched as her father stood at the end of their beautifully decorated dining room table. He gave Savana Kain a flash of his charming smile, then raised his crystal champagne flute and saluted her. Aimee was there with Orias, Cheung and Lotus Shao sat at the far end of the table, and Maggie was sitting next to Rick. Aimee wondered what Maggie looked so anxious about.

Aimee already had an idea what was coming; her father had hinted at it before their guests arrived, probably to make sure that she didn't get upset by the news and ruin his little announcement. She wasn't sure if Rick knew or not. Certainly, he was too oblivious to notice the huge diamond that sparkled on the ring finger of Savana's left hand. Aimee watched her brother now, wondering how he would react to what their father was about to say.

"First, I want to thank you all for being here," Jack continued. "Some of you are family. Some of you are almost as close as family, and all of you hold a special place in my heart. That's why it's such a pleasure for me to share this great news with all of you. As I'm sure many of you know, Savana and I have been seeing each other for quite a while now, and as you can see, we're about to welcome a new little life into the world. So, we're getting married," he finished. "On Saturday, at city hall. And you're all invited."

There was a pause before Lotus and Cheung broke the silence with their applause.

"Congratulations," Orias said smoothly, smiling, and Aimee thought he was sincere. Rick scowled, pushed his chair back from the table, and stalked out of the room.

Aimee sat perfectly still for a moment, unsure of her feelings. It was like that moment of uncertainty where she knew she felt queasy, but didn't know if she was going to throw up or not. She couldn't tell if she was happy or devastated, furious or apathetic, and she wondered how her father could replace her mother so soon, so casually. Finally, with everyone looking at her, she reacted, and it was so spontaneous she couldn't stop herself. She laughed, then she laughed again, and after a moment she was laughing so hard that tears of helpless mirth were rolling down her face. It wasn't until Orias squeezed her hand under the table that her laughter finally subsided.

"Sorry, I thought of something funny," she said. She had thought of what her mother would say when she returned and discovered what had happened while she was gone. The chaos Aimee imagined taking place on that day in the future was as hysterical as it was heartbreaking.

She was sure that her outburst would make her dad angry, but he was distracted. Savana was leaning close to him.

"Wait, Jack," Savana protested. "Saturday? That's too soon. We need time to plan. I need a dress. We have things . . . things to discuss."

Jack brushed a stray hair from her face and soothed her with a whisper: "Plenty of time for discussion later. We're getting married before the baby is born. You know how I feel about that."

"But city hall? I told you I wanted it at Middleburg United."

"The church is booked this weekend, and my buddy in the mayor's office got us in downtown—opening city hall as a favor to me, even though it's Saturday. Don't worry. It will be fantastic. I got you set up at Lotus's flower shop—get anything you want. I don't care about the cost. The lady at Middleburg Couture will make your dress—you have a fitting tomorrow. It will all work out. The main thing is that we're together, like we talked about—right, baby? Right?"

Jack spoke gently, but the customary firmness never left his voice. It was as if he were negotiating with a child, Aimee thought—he spoke quietly, humoring Savana a bit, but there was no question that he was going to get his way. He finished his little speech by smiling at Orias and Cheung, like a stage actor pausing in his scene to ham it up for the crowd.

Savana started to protest again, then seemed to remember that everybody was looking at her. She added her smile to Jack's. "Of course," she agreed.

"I'm sure it will be a beautiful wedding," Lotus said. "Let me know if you'd like any help with planning—especially with the flowers."

"Nine A.M. at city hall," Jack said. "I hope to see you all there."

A loud crash reverberated from the other room. Probably Rick breaking something, Aimee thought. Across the table, she saw Maggie go pale, but her father went on as if nothing had happened.

"Well, let's have some dessert and celebrate, shall we?" he said and called toward the kitchen. "Lily Rose, would you bring in the cake, please?"

∽

After Orias, Maggie, and the Shaos departed, Jack directed Aimee to sit on the couch in the living room with Rick.

Aimee could hear the familiar and comforting sounds of clacking plates and rushing water from the kitchen, as Lily Rose cleaned up the celebratory feast. She seemed always to be around during the scariest, most volatile moments at the Banfield household. Aimee found her presence infinitely comforting, and this was a moment, she thought, when everyone in the house needed some comfort.

Her father and Savana Kain stood in front of Rick and Aimee as a pair of burly movers passed through the hallway and up the stairs, hauling a load of suitcases and boxes. At least Jack had waited until their guests had left to tell them that Savana was moving in.

Rick was still steaming.

"Listen, Rick, I understand that you're upset," Savana was saying. "But I promise, I'm not trying to replace your mom."

"Yeah—like that could happen," Rick said sullenly but clamped his mouth shut at a look from his father.

"And this baby isn't going to replace you or your sister, either," Savana went on. "Your dad has made it very clear that you kids are his number-one priority—"

"I don't care about you or your stupid baby," Rick broke in.

"Exactly what is your problem?" Jack asked flatly. Aimee knew what it meant when he talked like that; his patience with Rick was gone.

"I can't believe you're marrying the mother of a Flats rat!" Rick exploded.

"I don't recall asking for your opinion, and I don't need your permission," Jack returned sharply, but Savana put a hand on his arm, stopping him.

"Okay," she said to Rick. "I get it. I know that you and Raphael had some problems, but when we find Raph and you get to know him, I'm sure you'll be able to work it out. He's really a good person—and I'm sure he'll see that you are, too."

"I know him as well as I want to," Rick sneered. "Did you know he called my dad a murderer? He stood right there in our foyer and threatened him—threatened our whole family. He vandalized our property. He broke my friend Cle'von's arm. Knocked Bran Goheen out. Now you expect me to act like we're brothers?"

"Rick," Jack warned.

"If he tries to move into this house, I'll kill him!" Rick shouted. "How's that for brothers?"

"That's it. To your room, *now*," Jack said.

Rick's eyes ignited with fury and his fists clenched. For a second, Aimee thought he might actually attack their dad. Then he simply stood and walked out of the room. They all winced at the sound of his feet pounding up the stairs.

Savana looked at Aimee. "What about you, Aimee?" she asked gently. "You've been so quiet tonight. Are you okay with all this?"

Aimee shrugged. "Sure," she said. "I guess so."

"I know you and Raphael were close for a while," Savana pressed on. "Will it bother you if he comes to live here when he gets back?"

Aimee was looking at her fingernails. The tip of one of them was broken. "What?" she asked distractedly.

"Raphael. I know the two of you dated. How do you feel about him now? About him living here?" Savana asked.

"How do I feel?" Aimee asked. It was strange, she knew what Savana wanted to know, but she was finding the conversation difficult to follow. It was like trying to talk to someone on a bad cell phone connection, where she could hear only about half of their words. It was frustrating.

"Yes," Savana replied, her voice kind and concerned. "It's not like I'm asking for your blessing, you know—about me marrying your dad. I know that will take time. I just want to know that there wouldn't be any bad feelings between you and Raphael if—*when*—he comes home."

"Oh," Aimee said vaguely.

"So stop stalling," Jack said impatiently. "And tell us how you feel about him."

"I don't know," Aimee answered. "I guess . . . I don't feel anything."

"So if he comes back, it won't bother you to have him here?" Jack asked. "And I won't have to worry that you're going to start something up with him again?"

"Oh—no, of course not," Aimee thought it was a ridiculous question. She had Orias now. She wondered why her father thought she would be interested in anyone else. She had gone to some dance with Raphael— at least that's what Dalton had told her—but she couldn't even remember what he looked like. Right now she was wondering if she would be allowed to go back to Orias's tonight or if her dad would insist that she stay home. The idea of sipping Orias's delicious tea in front of the fire with his powerful arms wrapped around her made this and everything else in life seem like a meaningless waste of time.

"Well, I'm glad to hear that," Savana said with wary optimism. "I was a little worried. I just want you to know what I said to Rick is the truth. I'd like to be your friend, but I don't want to replace your mom. I know how hard all this must be for you. And I want you to know that when you're ready, I'm here for you."

Aimee smiled. "Thanks, but there's just one thing—no offense, Mrs. Kain," she said and turned to her dad. "What about Mom? Aren't you even going to look for her? She could be out there somewhere, hurt or something."

"That's enough, Aimee," Jack told her harshly. "Of course I looked for her. But we have to accept it. She's gone and there's no trace of her anywhere. She's been declared legally—"

"Jack, wait," Savana interrupted him. "This is not the time."

"Yes it is," Jack insisted, his frustration clear. "Aimee, your mother has been declared legally . . . deceased. You're just going to have to accept it. No matter how much we miss your mom, she isn't coming back. She's gone and you'll never see her again. But my life—our lives—must go on. Okay?"

"Okay," Aimee said, but silently, to herself, she added, *Oh, I'll see her again. As soon my teleportation skills are up to it, Orias will help me find her. And, boy, is she going to be mad when she gets back.*

෨

Savana sat wearily at the table in the Banfield's kitchen as Lily Rose set a steaming cup of herbal tea in front of her.

"Got anything stronger?" she asked. Lily Rose gave her a reproving look.

"Kidding! I'm kidding," Savana said. She stared into the teacup for a moment, absently swishing the bag around in the hot water. "Those kids hate me, you know."

"Well, they've been going through a lot. We all have lately, haven't we?" Lily Rose replied complacently as she loaded the dishwasher.

"You can say that again," Savana agreed.

"You just keep yourself calm and cool and have faith that everything will be all right," Lily Rose advised. "What you don't want to do is worry that baby. Stress is just as bad for those unborn little ones as it is for you and me."

"I know, and there's something I need to ask you. I know you gave up your midwife practice a while back—"

"I know what you're going to ask," Lily Rose interrupted. She put down the serving platter she was rinsing and joined Savana at the table. "Have you asked Jack about it? You know he always wants the best—and to him that's a big shiny hospital and a high-priced doctor. Not some tired old woman who cleans his toilets."

"But you *are* the best," Savana said earnestly. "Everyone in town says so. They say you can perform miracles. And I need your help. Because there's something . . . this baby, Lily Rose. Something is . . . different."

She was about to say more when she looked up and saw Jack standing in the doorway.

"What?" he asked. "What about our baby is different?"

Savana hesitated for a second. "It . . . oh, it's nothing," she said finally. "It just kicks more than usual. Here—feel."

Jack came over and put his hand on her stomach.

"I don't feel anything," he said. She could tell he was in a bad mood again. It was hard to keep up with Jack. One minute he'd be so sweet and kind and charming, then something would go wrong and he would turn cold and distant, as if his relationship with her was just another frustrating business transaction he had to endure.

"Jack, did you know Lily Rose is a licensed midwife?" She turned to the old black woman. "How many babies did you say you've delivered, Lily Rose?"

"Two hundred and five," Lily Rose said proudly and went to the dishwasher again.

"That's nice," Jack said, taking a bottle of Scotch from the cabinet and pouring himself a glass.

"I was thinking of asking Lily Rose to deliver the baby," Savana said.

"Well, stop thinking about it," Jack replied and then took a sip of his drink. "No offense, Lily Rose, but Dr. Rosenberg at Stormont-Vail in Topeka is a friend. We'll go there."

"But what if the baby comes early, Jack? We can't drive all the way to Topeka—"

"I've rented a condo in the city for you to move into a couple of weeks before the due date. I'll be there every weekend, and I'll have a driver on call in case you go into labor when I'm not there." He smiled at Savana. "You see, my darling—I think of everything."

"That's great, Jack, and I appreciate it, but—"

"It's nonnegotiable," he said harshly and then added gently, "my love." He downed the last of his drink and walked out of the kitchen.

Lily Rose turned on the dishwasher and wiped her hands on her apron. "Well, I guess I'm just about done here," she said, giving Savana a sympathetic smile. "But if you need me, you know right where to find me, don't you?"

∞

Aimee sat on her bed and looked around her room. It had been so long since she'd spent time here that everything seemed unfamiliar. But even stranger than her surroundings was a sudden recollection of the girl she had been before she met Orias. If she was still that girl, she would have freaked out tonight, when her father had grabbed her arm after Savana went into the kitchen with Lily Rose, marched her up the stairs, and thrust her into her bedroom. She would have been wracked with misery at the threat he had snarled at her, that she would be sorry if she tried to see Orias again until after he and Savana were married. If she acted up again, he had promised, he would send her back to boarding school immediately.

"You think just because I'm going into business with Orias that you can do whatever you want," he'd said. "But you're going to do what I want for a change—and that is to keep your butt at home and make Savana feel welcome and help her get ready for the wedding. Got it?"

Without waiting for her to answer, he'd slammed the door and locked it. The sound of the lock clicking into place would have sent the old Aimee into a downward spiral of hurt and anxiety. That familiar crippling, gnawing fear that came from feeling trapped and powerless would have crept up her spine until it paralyzed her. But now, as she dangled her feet off the bed, she was only amused.

Serene, she rose from the bed, smoothed her skirt with her hands, and looked at her closed door. "Bye, Daddy," she said and teleported out of her room.

It took less than a second. It felt something like a shiver, and Aimee was so good at it from all her practice with Orias that it took no more effort than a sneeze. When she opened her eyes, she was standing in the middle of Orias's parlor in front of a crackling fire. He sat in his usual spot on the couch, gazing into the trembling flames, and sipping from his chalice. As Aimee appeared, however, he started, almost spilling his drink.

"You've got to stop sneaking up on me like that!" he exclaimed. He put down the drink and pulled her into his arms. "You'll give me a heart attack."

Aimee laughed. "Oh, I didn't know that Nephilim have hearts," she teased.

"I don't," Orias said tenderly. "Not anymore. I gave mine to you."

Aimee smiled and pressed her head against his broad, powerful chest, inhaling the strange incense and musk scent that marked his divine presence.

"I thought your father wanted you to sleep at home," Orias observed.

"He did," Aimee said, nuzzling her face into his shirt. "But I didn't want to. And thanks to everything you taught me, no one can control me anymore."

She lifted her head and looked at him. He seemed strangely disturbed for a moment, but the expression disappeared quickly, replaced by his usual charming smile.

"Anyway, I can slip back into my room before school tomorrow, right?" she said.

"Of course, my love. Now . . . how about a nice cup of tea?"

Zhai stood for a long time in the shadowed hallway, staring at the swirling patterns of the wood grain in his father's study door. For the last few months, curiosity and resentment had risen within him like a cresting flood, but as many times as he'd approached this door, something had always made him shy away from confronting his father about his association with the Order of the Black Snake. For a long time, he'd thought it was respect, but lately he'd begun to think it might be fear—fear of what his father might tell him.

Either way, there was no more time for hesitation. Master Chin was barely hanging on to life. The Toppers were falling apart. And if Zhai lost his duel with Rick on Saturday, the shards the other Toppers possessed might be lost, too—at least until the Obies tracked them down. And once they presented the reassembled ring to their serpent god, who knew what would happen?

Ironically enough, it wasn't any of these potential calamities that had finally driven Zhai to his father's study. It was the phone call from Nass. His family had been evicted from their home by a company Zhai's father and Jack Banfield owned.

Before the search for Raphael started, Zhai had been certain that he wouldn't like Nass. He remembered watching the Flatliner's break-dancing routine during his first week of school and thinking that he was just a loudmouthed showoff, a ham who cared about nothing but stirring up trouble and being the center of attention. But when the two had joined forces in the search for Raphael, Zhai had been amazed. When other Flatliners began giving Zhai attitude, it was always Nass who reminded them that they were all working together to find their friend. Nass was truly hilarious, but his jokes were good-natured and inclusive, not the boastful, crass humor Zhai had expected. And often at the end of a long day of searching, Zhai, Maggie, and Nass had been the last three still out looking for Raphael. The more he observed Nass's work ethic, his leadership, and his generosity, the more he admired him. At times, it felt like they were a two-man gang of their own—the only two people in town fighting for peace, when everyone else was clamoring for a fight.

So when Zhai had learned that Nass's family had been thrown out of their home, he had decided he could no longer stand by while whatever his father was doing went forward.

Nass said that the Flatliners were sure that the evictions in the Flats had been part of the Obies' search for the ring. That search was over, yet the evictions continued. Zhai intended to find out why. He also had a few other questions he wanted his father to answer.

Before he could lose his nerve, he reached out and knocked on the door.

"Come in," his father's voice sounded from within.

As usual, the moment Cheung had returned home from the Banfields' party he'd barricaded himself in his study. Zhai entered it now and found his father sitting at his desk, looking at two computer monitors set up side by side. He gazed at them for a moment longer before pulling his eyes away.

"Hello, Zhai," he said. "What can I do for you this evening?"

The last phrase was one Cheung Shao had picked up many years ago in an English for Business course, and he was particularly fond of it. Zhai would have preferred a less impersonal greeting, but he was in no mood to correct his father—not tonight.

He placed both hands on the desk, palms down. Four puffy, crimson lines on the back of each of his hands showed clearly in the lamplight. If anyone looked closely, they would be able to see the remnants of the defaced markings beneath the scars—black tattoos that had been the Chinese symbols for the word *slave*. So far, Zhai had kept the scars and the marks beneath them hidden from Cheung Shao. Now he made sure he saw them.

His father stared down at his hands and then cleared his throat. His face was so rigid with tension that his lips barely moved as he asked, "What happened?"

"The Order of the Black Snake," Zhai said. "They marked me."

Cheung went suddenly pale. "I . . . I've never heard of them—"

"No!" Zhai interrupted. It was the first time he'd ever raised his voice to his father, and it felt like a floodgate opening. A raging torrent of emotion drove him on. "Stop lying to me! The men in derby hats marked me. Your guests, Father. They tattooed my hands and made me their slave. The only way I could be free was to do this to myself—to burn the marks off. Now their leader is in town—and he almost killed Master Chin. I need you to tell me what's going on, and how to stop them."

Cheung shook his head. "I . . . I don't know. I don't know anything about them."

"Yes, you do," Zhai insisted. "They told me that they own you, that they're in business with you somehow. Just admit that it's true! Admit you're working with them!"

Zhai's father stared back at him, his face as still as a death mask. Filled with a sudden frustration, Zhai slammed both his fists down on the desk. "At least tell me why the evictions in the Flats are still going on. My friend and his family just got thrown out of their apartment—he's homeless now, because of your company!"

Cheung sniffed and then wiped his nose with a handkerchief. "My work in the Flats is done," he said calmly. "I've sold my share of all those properties to Jack Banfield. He has a ten-year redevelopment plan for the area—outlet malls and condos, mixed-use properties. An office park. If your friend has a problem, he should take it up with Banfield."

Zhai stared at his father in disbelief. All these years he'd felt so empty, so devoid of emotion, so careful not to let himself feel anything. The only emotion he had allowed in was love for his sister, until he met Kate—and he couldn't help but love Kate. But now he was feeling something new and unfamiliar, an emotion so powerful that it scared him.

He was truly, genuinely angry.

"You can deny it, Father. You can lie to me. You can lie to Lotus and Li. You can even lie to yourself. But I know you work for the Order. And even now, now that I'm begging you to tell me the truth, to help me, to help my friends—you're protecting them, the men who branded your son. All the long hours you locked yourself away from me I thought it was your obsession with work, but now I know the real reason behind it. You can pretend it was for us—for your family. You can pretend to be a perfect, moral, disciplined person all you want, but I know the truth." Zhai's last words came out in something between a sob and a snarl. "The truth is, Father, you're nothing but a slave." And he wheeled around and stormed away.

The moment his hand touched the doorknob, however, he heard a sound from behind him, a pitiful groan, and he turned back to find his father standing now, tears streaming down his face.

"Zhai—my son." Cheung's voice trembled. "You're right."

Cheung Shao unbuttoned his shirt, exposing his bare chest. There, two familiar Chinese symbols were tattooed—the same symbols that Zhai had on his hands. The magical marks the Obies had used to control him.

And this tattoo was directly over his father's heart.

"The Order used their mark to control your fists, so you would fight for them," Cheung said, struggling to keep his voice steady. "But my mark is upon my heart, and it is that which they control. I disobey them, and they will break it by destroying all that I love. And then they will make it stop beating. Now do you understand?"

℘

With one swipe of his forearm, Raphael wiped the dripping blood and sweat from his brow. Already, his wounds were too numerous to count. So far, he'd defeated an ape-like humanoid, a caveman with a wooden spear, a bronze-age warrior with a sword, a barbarian wearing nothing but a fur tunic and brandishing a wicked, spiked club, and a Comanche warrior with a tomahawk. Now, his eyes flicked back and forth amid the swirling mist, searching for his next adversary. His new enemy's appearance happened so fast that Raph could barely register who he was.

This combatant wore nothing but a linen loincloth and a steel helmet with a large, brush-like flourish on top. He held a steel short sword in one hand and a spear in the other. Raph glimpsed his chiseled abs and bulging biceps an instant before the man's sword whistled toward his head, and all he could do was throw himself backward, out of range of the deadly blade. He landed on his back and then kicked his legs over his head and somersaulted over and back up to his feet, just in time to see the next blow coming. Somewhere amid the tumult, it registered in Raphael's mind who it was he was fighting—one of the most elite warriors of the ancient Greeks, a man who'd likely spent his entire life training for warfare. A Spartan. But Raph was already too exhausted to experience anything like fear. All he did was react to the blade when it whooshed toward him again.

But instead of retreating, Raphael stepped toward the Spartan as he swung, moving inside the radius of the blade and blocking the man's sword arm with a *Bong Sau*. He transitioned instantly into a *Lap Sau*, grabbing the meaty part of the man's forearm and using his own momentum to jerk him forward, off balance. At the same time, he stepped forward into a stomp kick, snapping the Spartan's knee sideways. The seasoned warrior didn't emit a single sound of pain, even as his tendons snapped. He did, however, drop his sword, and Raphael snatched it up and beheaded him with it in one swift motion.

There was not a second to acknowledge his victory. Already, an ancient Chinese warrior was charging him, swinging a *guan dao*—a weapon that looked like a broadsword affixed to the end of a pole—and it was whirling like a deadly helicopter blade.

Raphael watched the wide arc of the blade speeding toward his legs as if to cut him off at the knees. He managed to leap the blade and then he charged its owner. As his enemy tried to reverse the momentum of the pole to swing it back at Raphael, Raph pinned his elbow against his body with one hand and swung his sword with the other. The blade landed solidly in his enemy's gut, and Raphael yanked it through.

The Chinese warrior fell to his knees and slumped to the ground, dead.

But already the clatter of armor announced the arrival of Raphael's next opponents: a trio of Roman legionnaires. They formed up in a miniature phalanx, hiding behind their broad shields as they charged Raphael with their spears.

Reacting fast, Raphael parried two spear tips with his sword, then dove and rolled beneath the wall of shields. He sprang to his feet on the other side, bringing his blade up beneath the armor of the forward most legionnaire as he did. The man groaned and collapsed, but Raph had already pulled his blade free. He spun and beheaded the Roman behind him. Now, only one remained. Twice he feigned at Raphael with his spear and then he threw it directly at Raphael's heart. There was an instant of paralyzing panic as Raphael watched the deadly projectile speeding toward him, but he deflected it with a *Tan Sau* movement of his Spartan sword. The legionnaire was now drawing his own sword, but Raphael shot forward with a spring attack. With one hand, he blocked his enemy's arm so he couldn't draw his blade, and with the other hand, he swung his own weapon at his opponent's face and split his head in two.

For the first time in what had to be at least an hour, the battlefield was clear of enemies, and Raphael exhaled, releasing a sound that was half triumph and half exhaustion. His mind gave birth to two thoughts at once.

One was: *How many warriors can there be out here? I can't keep going like this.*

And the second: *I don't care how many there are; I'll never stop fighting until I win.*

But there was no time for a third thought or even to take another breath. Already, the thunder of more footsteps came toward him through the heavy fog, and another enemy was upon him.

CHAPTER 11

ZHAI FELT WEIGHTLESS AS HE LEFT HIS FATHER'S STUDY, hurried down the steps, and went out the back door of the house. The sickening revelation he'd just experienced filled him with fear—fear most of all for his father, but also for his family, and for the rest of Middleburg, too. Because if the Obies were capable of completely controlling a man as dutiful as his father, then how could the rest of them even stand a chance? But Zhai thrust these thoughts from his mind. He had other things to worry about now; his wasn't the only crisis happening in Middleburg.

He passed the pool and the pool house and followed the path through a row of stately fir trees. Behind them, at the rear of the property and out of sight of the main house, the old guest house came into view. Although Lotus sometimes talked about turning it into a photo studio or a greenhouse, she hadn't mentioned it lately and it hadn't been used in ages. Zhai didn't think his stepmother or his sister would notice that the Torrez family had moved in, and his father never came here. A tall young man was laboring in the doorway, sweat dripping down his face as he tried to move a heavy chest of drawers that seemed to be wedged in the entry.

"Dang . . . thing . . . is stuck . . ." Beet Ingram said, grunting out every word.

Whoever was holding the other end of the dresser moved, changing the angle, and Beet stumbled through the doorway, his thick, white-knuckled fingers still clutching the heavy piece of furniture.

Inside, Nass was setting the other end of the dresser down and wiping the sweat from his forehead with the bottom of his T-shirt. The rest of his family was there, too—his mom, Amelia; his dad, Raul; and Clarisse, Nass's friend from L.A. Benji was also there, stacking boxes in one corner of the room. They all beamed at Zhai as he came in.

"Oh, Zhai, we are so grateful!" Amelia Torrez said, charging Zhai with her arms wide, ready for a tearful embrace. "You are a hero, you know that? A heroic person. When they talk about doing to your neighbors how you want to be treated, they're talking about you! We just thank you so much!"

She grabbed Zhai in a big bear hug. He patted her on the back for a moment and then gently pulled away. Raul Torrez was already shaking his hand.

"Thank you," he said. "Don't worry, Zhai. We'll pay you rent, and we'll be out as soon as we find a place. And thank your mom and dad for us."

Zhai forced himself to smile. "No need to pay rent, and stay as long as you want, okay? I'm just glad to help," he said, hoping that by the time he had to mention it to his dad and Lotus, he'd have figured out what to tell them. He wished he'd been able to tell his father, but their conversation hadn't exactly gone as planned, and telling Lotus was out of the question. He'd just have to keep it a secret for as long as possible and hope Nass and his family would find a place soon.

He glanced at Nass and saw something like pride in his face. And it made sense, Zhai realized suddenly. Six months ago, who could have imagined a family from the Flats living on the Shao property? But it was the right thing to do, Zhai knew, the natural thing. And that was all because he and Nass had put their egos aside to look for Raphael together. Their friendship hadn't come easily and it had taken work, but they had achieved it. It was something they could both be proud of.

"Just make sure you go in and out through the back gate," Zhai said. "My stepmom doesn't want people walking around in the backyard. She's kind of militant about her plants."

Everyone nodded in agreement including Beet, who was still red-faced from moving the dresser. Looking around, Zhai ran through his mental roster of Flatliners. Someone was missing, besides Emory.

"Where's Josh?" he asked.

The remaining Flatliners exchanged a glance before Nass answered. "With Emory, at the hospital," he said. "Can I talk to you outside for a minute while these guys unpack?"

"Sure."

Zhai led the way out to the back gate, where Beet's dad's borrowed pickup truck sat half unloaded.

"Thanks again," Nass began, but Zhai waved his words away.

"Forget it," he said.

Nass took a small cardboard box out of his pocket. "What should we do with the shards?" he asked. "Should we each keep our own stash or put them all in one place for safekeeping?"

Zhai looked down at the box in Nass's hand. This was another example of the trust that had grown between them, that Nass would trust him enough to keep all their ring shards together.

"I think it's best if we each keep our own for now," he said. "That way if the Obies come looking for them, they aren't all together."

"Cool," Nass said. "I agree. You talk to the Toppers about theirs yet?"

Zhai nodded. "Yeah—but it didn't go too well. I've got five pieces—mine, Maggie's, Dax's, Mike's, and Master Chin's, but that's it. There's a chance I might be able to get the rest, but . . ."

"But?" Nass prompted.

"But I'm going to have to fight Rick for leadership of the Toppers—and for the shards."

Nass nodded slowly, taking in Zhai's ominous words. "Things didn't go too well with our guys, either," he said. "Josh is furious about what happened to Emory, and he wants revenge. He wants to fight Rick, too. The other guys gave me their pieces of the ring, but he wouldn't give me his. So—you gonna fight Rick?"

"I don't see any other choice."

"When?"

"Saturday," Zhai said.

"Don't worry—you can take him," Nass said. But Zhai could tell from the look on his face that he was worried. And, Zhai realized, it was probably the first time in his life that he, too, was worried about a fight. More than worried, in fact. He was downright scared.

❧

Orias Morrow lay floundering in a murky swamp of foul, black dreams. His father was there as he was every night, badgering and belittling him.

Foolish boy! Weak, pathetic half-breed! You had the ring! You had the key to making this world ours! You let it slip through your fingers, and you will pay for that! When I am free, I will reach inside you, grab your intestines, and drag you down to the Pit, where you will scream for all eternity! Then you will know why no one has ever dared to deceive me! Then you will know the true cost of your betrayal!

As he did every night, Orias relived the moment when the ring had shattered. In maddening slow motion, he saw the oncoming locomotive. It wasn't really a train, of course—Orias knew enough about the nature of things to understand that. It was a transport, a beam of energy like an arc of electricity, emanating from and returning to the All.

But the mortal apparatus of the human brain is a funny thing. Its main function is to process everything it takes in and repackage it in such a way as to be comprehended—thus, to the mortals present, and even to Orias with his half-human brain, the pure vibratory energy they had witnessed had manifested not as a nebulous blast of transcendent radiance, but as something familiar, something expected: a train.

Why had it struck that miserable ghetto urchin, Raphael Kain? And why, when it struck him, had the ring shattered? The artifact was supposed to be a pure relic of the All and thus incorruptible, indestructible. How, then, when everything was within Orias's grasp, had it all slipped away?

Next, his dreams turned to his future, to his fate. He saw himself growing old, but not as humans age. Each year for him was like a generation for the mortals around him. And yet, his perception of time was tied to his life span, not to a mortal's. Thus, in what seemed to him like a minute, two mortal days passed. In what seemed like a week, more than half a year would plunge irretrievably into the past. By the time he had experienced the equivalent of a human year, sweet, perfect Aimee would already be past the flower of her youth, entering the wilt of old age and the approaching decay of death.

He had not told her of his conundrum—this cruel quirk of relative perception was too much for most mortal minds to comprehend—but it haunted him day and night. He faced the prospect that before he knew it, everyone around him would have died of old age. From one week to the next, new friends would become old, and old friends would die. He had been through it all, eon after eon, but that was before he'd met Aimee and fallen in love with her. And yes, he loved her with a love he'd never thought possible. He could admit it in his dreams.

Of course, he had lied to Aimee about his age, as he was lying to her about everything except his feelings for her. He was hundreds of years old and still had hundreds more to go. In his current persona, he had chosen to be nineteen in order to establish a relationship with her. Now he felt like the world around him was made of sand. It was slipping through an hourglass before his eyes, and there was nothing he could do to stop it.

Nothing, unless he had the ring. With the ring came the power not only to move through time, but to manipulate it. With practice (he saw in his dream) he would be able to narrow the gap between his aging and Aimee's, stretching out her life span, conferring a measure of immortality on her. Then, once he knew he could keep her by his side forever, he would use the ring to open the gates to the Dark Territory.

He would lead his kin, the Irin, the Watchers, the mighty fallen angels, out of the darkness below and set them free to ravish and pillage the earth with neither human nor divine obstruction. With the power of the ring he would also control the Wheel and the celestial staircase, so that not even the exalted angels could come through to interfere with his rule. The Irin masses would adore him as their savior, and he would reign for a blissful near-eternity with Aimee at his side.

He stirred in his sleep, waking enough to remember that the ring was broken, lost forever, and without it the door to the Dark Territory would remain firmly closed. Orias would be damned to face the millennia alone, watching as everything he came to love slipped away.

As he drifted back to sleep his father's voice cut into his dreams again, echoing with vicious mockery. *Oh no, my son. You will not have millennia to suffer in this place. I will see to that. I will be free sooner than you think. Then you will waste away in the blackest, hottest, vilest corner of the Pit. Soon, my boy. Soon...*

With a start Orias came fully awake, his hands lashing out as if his father was hovering above him, Oberon's handsome yet eyeless face inches from his own. He sat up, terrified, but found he was alone in his bedroom, a room shrouded in shadows. Exhaling in relief, he looked to his left, at the bed he'd had moved into his room for Aimee, to make sure she was safe and well. It was empty.

Instantly he was on his feet. "Aimee?" he called. "Aimee!" He hurried into the hall and headed toward the bathroom. As he expected, a yellow light glowed from beneath the door. She was locking herself in his damned bathroom more and more lately, and he had no idea what to make of it. He had used his energy to bind her to him, but to break her connection with the Kain boy something stronger had been needed: the waters of the River Lethe, which flowed through the Dark Territory. All the angels—both exalted and fallen—knew it as the River of Forgetfulness. Orias added a drop of water from it to her tea each day, and it worked. She had forgotten Raphael Kain altogether.

Lethe Water had been used for eons in the Valley of Light when the exalted angels gave humans a cup full of the stuff, a dose large enough to wipe away all their memories of a previous life before the soul's reincarnation, or before their journey further into the light. Orias didn't want Aimee to forget her entire identity—the innocence of her soul, her logical way of looking at things and her sweet, steadfast hope that she could somehow help him find redemption—all the attributes that made her who she was. He just wanted to make sure she forgot the Kain boy. But he had to be careful. Too much of it over an extended period of time had been known to make humans go crazy. So he put only one drop of the water in each beverage or fruit cup he made for her, but already she seemed to be experiencing some undesired side effects. This bathroom thing was particularly concerning, given her ability to slip. What if she locked herself in there, then suddenly remembered that Raphael was lost somewhere in time and space? What if she decided to slip away and look for him? She could get lost, and Orias might never see her again.

"Aimee, you have to stop this." He reached for the door, surprised to find that it wasn't closed and locked as usual. This time when he pushed on it, it drifted open easily.

It was just as he had feared. The room was empty.

"Aimee?" he called with rising desperation. "AIMEE!"

After the echo of his shouts died away he paused, took a deep breath, and focused his energy, using his superior Nephilim senses to search out her whereabouts. What he heard was the faint *screek* of metal twisting against metal. The turning of a doorknob.

A trumpet blast of terror rang through his brain, and he shot down the hall—not running across the floorboards or even hovering above them, but rocketing in midair, down the hall and up the spiral staircase, up to the candlelit anteroom that stood outside the tower bedroom where he had imprisoned his father.

Aimee stood before the heavy wooden door in a thin white nightgown, her eyes closed. Her delicate white hand rested on the doorknob and she was slowly, slowly twisting it. The door itself made no sound—Orias's magic had ensured that—but it was twitching, bowing, shuddering violently in its frame as the furious fallen angel trapped inside battered against it, desperate to be let out.

"AIMEE, NO!" Orias bellowed, and he shot forward through the air and shoved her away from the door, so hard that she hit the wall beside it with enough force to crack the plaster. He got to the door just in time. As it came unlatched he managed to slam it shut again. Instantly, the tumult behind it subsided.

He should have realized that Aimee would have the power to break through his spell and open the door. Clearly, Oberon did, Orias thought as he snapped the deadbolt back into place.

A soft moaning sound drew his attention, and he saw Aimee was slumped against the wall, blinking in pain and confusion.

"Orias, what . . . what happened?" she asked. There were tears in her eyes, and when she reached up and touched the back of her head, her fingers came away bloody.

Orias hurried to her and helped her up.

"You were walking in your sleep, I think," he told her. "Aimee, you must never open that door. Never. Do you understand me? *Never!*"

"You . . . you hurt me!" she said with childlike indignation, struggling to get away from him. He scooped her up into his arms and held her closer.

"I'm sorry. I'm sorry, okay? I never want to hurt you. That's the last thing I want to do."

"Let me go. Put me down or I'm going to slip home!"

Hastily, Orias set Aimee back on her feet. She looked at the door to the tower room, then back at him.

"What's in there?" she asked quietly. "What's behind that door?"

"Nothing," he said. "Nothing important."

"Then why is it locked?" When he didn't answer she added, "Please tell me what's in there. I don't want any secrets between us."

He sighed. "Okay, I'll tell you," he said, gently taking her hand. "Let's go down to the kitchen, my sweet. I'll make you a nice cup of tea, and I'll tell you everything."

෨

Early Wednesday morning, Zhai held Kate's hand as they walked up the steps of Middleburg High with Dalton, Maggie, and Lily Rose. They all went through the doors, down the hall, and into the attendance office, to the desk where the principal's secretary sat.

"Hello there, Darleen," said Lily Rose. Mrs. Burns looked up from a stack of files, but the harried expression on her face disappeared as soon as she saw the small, sweet woman in the fancy lavender hat standing before her. Lily Rose was wearing her church clothes this morning, which, Zhai knew, meant that she considered this an important event.

"Morning, Lily Rose," Mrs. Burns replied. "What can I do for you?"

"I'd like to introduce you to a friend of mine," Lily Rose told her as she took Kate's hand and pulled her forward. "Darleen Burns, this is Miss Kate Dineen. Kate, this is Mrs. Burns. Kate is new in the area, recently moved here from Ireland, and she needs to sign up for classes." Lily Rose looked at Kate. "Isn't that right, dear?"

But Kate was completely distracted. Amanda, one of Li's friends, was working as student office assistant that morning, and she was standing at a big, outdated dinosaur of a Xerox machine, copying permission slips for some upcoming event. Kate was staring at the machine in wide-eyed wonder as it rattled and hummed and spat out more and more identical sheets of paper while the light from the machine's scanner flashed back and forth beneath the closed copier lid.

"Kate?" Lily Rose repeated, but the girl remained mesmerized.

"Kate," Zhai said, squeezing her hand.

At last they got her attention. "Oh, I'm sorry!" she said. "I was tryin' to count how many pages that printing press is puttin' out—one hundred and seventeen, and it's still going!"

Mrs. Burns looked at the copier, then back to Kate and cleared her throat. "Yes, well, that's what it's there for. Welcome to Middleburg, Kate. Are your parents with you?"

Kate shook her head. "No ma'am."

"I assume you have all the necessary documentation you'll need to enroll. Student visa? Birth certificate?" Mrs. Burns asked.

Kate looked uncertainly at Lily Rose.

"Darleen, you see—Kate is a dear family friend," Lily Rose said with a smile. "She's a stranger in a strange land, as they say, and all she wants is to learn. Now, if I'm not mistaken there are laws that say all children must be in school. There must be some way to get her signed up while she's waiting for her paperwork to get here—isn't there?"

As Lily Rose spoke, she reached out and placed her hand gently over the secretary's. Mrs. Burns hesitated for a moment, then blinked and looked at Kate as if seeing her anew. Sighing heavily, she opened the top drawer of her desk, pulled out a sheet of paper and a pen, and set them on the counter just as the first bell rang.

"Well . . . I guess so," she said uncertainly. Lily Rose patted her hand again, and she passed the paper and pen to Kate. "Fill out this form to the best of your ability," she instructed Kate. "I'll get you set up to take the placement test, then I'll get with Mr. Innis to decide what classes you'll be taking."

Kate beamed with happiness as she picked up the pen. "Oh, aye—indeed I will, and I thank you."

Zhai watched over her shoulder as she began, and he was amazed at her perfect, ornate penmanship.

"All right, Lily Rose," said Mrs. Burns. "I'll take it from here. The rest of you kids need to get on to class. I'm not writing late passes for all of you."

"Bye, Kate," Dalton said, eyeing her curiously. "We'll see you at lunch."

"Good luck on the placement test," Maggie added.

Zhai quickly put a hand on Kate's waist and gave her a small, sideways hug as she continued to fill out the form. "Have a good first day," he whispered. "If you need me, I'll be right down the hall." He headed for the door but hesitated in the threshold to look back at her. It was always so hard to tear himself away from Kate.

He saw Lily Rose smile at Mrs. Burns. "Thank you so much, Darleen. You always were such a helpful girl. We haven't seen you in church in a long time, you know. The choir sure could use that big alto voice of yours."

Mrs. Burns smiled back at her. "I'll drop in one of these Sundays."

Lily Rose nodded, satisfied, and headed for the door, but she paused to look at the old railroad map and the admonition that hung on the wall next to it:

Keep out of the railroad tunnels

And stay off the tracks

Don't go into the train graveyard

Zhai was caught by the look of dread that settled on her face, which turned ashen. Small beads of perspiration formed in a thin line across her brow.

"What is it, Lily Rose?" he asked. "Are you okay? Is it Master Chin?"

She shook her head as if to dispel whatever thought was troubling her. "No, he's still the same," she said. "One of my ladies from the missionary society is sitting with him this morning. It's nothing, son. Don't you worry about it." The old woman's strange mismatched eyes seemed to stare through the tattered, framed map and into other worlds. "You know, my grandfather was a conductor on that railroad. When I was a little girl, we used to play around those tracks, even though we weren't supposed to. I know all you kids do the same. You can learn a lot by exploring those tunnels. Just be careful, you hear?"

"Yes, ma'am. We will."

Mrs. Burns had already gone back to her files, and Kate was still focused on filling out her form. Lily Rose smiled at Zhai once more, and he held the door open for her as she left the office. In spite of her smile, she still looked worried.

℘

Nass crossed the lunchroom at Josh's side, a little light-headed. Although he was tired, the feeling didn't come from spending an uncomfortable night on the sofa in Zhai's guest house and it wasn't his concern for Emory, either. What he was feeling was anxiety, which had started when Josh had taken him aside at his locker before school.

"I called Emory's mom this morning," he'd said. "He's still not awake." Josh was pale and tense. His eyes were bloodshot and his voice had no expression. Nass thought he looked like he was about to snap. "I know we haven't exactly gotten along lately, but . . . me and the guys are going to Benton after school to see him. You in?"

"Of course," Nass said.

Josh nodded. He seemed relieved. That, at least, was a good sign. Maybe they could put their differences aside after all. "I'm going to challenge Rick at lunch today," Josh said. A tiny glimmer of fear surfaced in his eyes, but it disappeared immediately, replaced by icy resolve.

Nass wanted to try to persuade him not to go up against Rick, but the knowing kicked in, telling him that nothing he could say would talk Josh out of it. Instead, he gave him an encouraging slap on the shoulder. "You can take him. Just remember the stuff Raph taught us."

Josh didn't look convinced, but Nass knew he wasn't going to back down. "Will you go with me?" he asked.

Nass smiled. "You know I will, man. 'Even unto death,' right?"

And so it happened that ten minutes into the lunch period Josh crossed the room with Nass at his side. Their Flatliner brothers stood near their table, waiting for the summit that was about to take place, ready to charge into the melee if a fight erupted.

Josh's pace was quick and steady as he marched to the head of the Topper table and stopped to look down at Rick, who took another bite of

℘ 161 ℘

his quesadilla, slowly chewed it and swallowed it before acknowledging Josh's presence.

"Can I help you?" Rick asked at last, mockingly polite.

"Yeah," Josh said. "You can help me by joining Emory in the hospital in Benton."

"Oh, and let me guess, you're going to send me there, right?" Rick said, and a few of the Toppers snickered. Nass noticed that only Bran Goheen remained silent.

"That's right," Josh said. "You and me, after school, down by the tracks."

Rick's guttural laughter came out in a series of low grunts. "I don't know. The last time I fought someone as pitiful as you, it wasn't much of a challenge."

Josh rocked forward onto the balls of his feet as if to strike out at Rick, but Nass quickly grabbed his arm.

"You know the Wu-de, Rick," Josh said through clenched teeth. "This is an official challenge. You don't fight me, your honor is ruined. And believe me, I'll tell everyone in school you were a coward. I'll make posters. I'll put it on the damn morning announcements."

Rick laughed again. Nass had never seen him so non-confrontational, but he suspected it was only because his passive mockery was pissing Josh off more than a thousand insults could have.

Bran rose to his feet. "Fight me," he said and then looked at Rick. "You already have the thing with Zhai coming up, Rick. You can't be wasting energy on this." He turned to Josh again. "I'll fight you."

Josh was already shaking his head. "You weren't there the night Emory got hurt. Rick was. He's the one I want."

Rick sneered. "Bran's right. Why should I waste my time beating up a loser like you?"

It happened so fast Nass didn't have a chance to stop him. Josh slapped Rick across the face—hard—and the sound of the blow echoed through the lunchroom like a gunshot. What followed was pure chaos. Rick sprang to his feet as Bran tried to hold him back.

"Rick—no!" Bran shouted. "This isn't the time, man! Not here! Not at school!"

Nass was also trying to pull Josh away as Rick's backup of Toppers rose, getting ready to jump in. He knew from experience that if Principal Innis got into the situation, things would go much worse for the Flatliners than for the Toppers. But only a few seconds later, he heard the voice he'd dreaded.

"Break it up, boys! Down to my office—now!" From the scowl on Innis's round, normally happy face it was clear he was fed up.

It didn't take the knowing to tell him what was in his future, Nass thought as he shuffled out with Josh, Rick, and Bran. He was in for another miserable suspension and his mom was going to be plenty pissed.

As they walked, Rick sidled up to Josh. "Saturday night—the tracks outside the North tunnel," Rick hissed. "Eight o'clock. You can be my warm-up before I break your buddy Zhai."

Nass repressed a groan, and the refrain that had rung through his mind so often over the last few months repeated itself once more.

Where is Raphael?

CHAPTER 12

AFTER SCHOOL, DALTON WALKED DOWN THE HALL with Maggie and Kate, on the way to Miss Pembrook's history club meeting, and she continued to steal glances at Kate. The cheerful girl seemed so excited about everything and so eager to learn that Dalton's curiosity about her was growing every minute. As they walked, Kate recapped all her favorite parts of the day—which mostly seemed to revolve around various pieces of technology that everyone else took for granted, but that she found amazing.

"And the computer—'tis like a magical typewriting machine!" Kate exclaimed. "And that interweb thing—why, you can go to any library in the world, just like that!" She snapped her fingers. "Who could imagine such a thing?"

"Come on, Kate," Dalton said, amused. "You can't tell me they don't have computers in Ireland."

"Well, perhaps they do," Kate replied quietly, suddenly subdued. "But I'd never seen one up close before today." Kate was in Dalton's computer class, and she'd been completely baffled when she sat down in front of her monitor. Dalton had to show her everything, starting with how to turn it on and how to use the keyboard. When Kate had asked where the paper was rolled in for the typing, Dalton had pointed to the other side of the room and explained that when the document was finished, it would come out of the printer. When Dalton had shown her how to look things up on the Internet, Kate was ecstatic. Dalton couldn't believe how quickly she learned. The first search term Kate typed in was, IRELAND IN THE EARLY 20TH CENTURY.

Puzzled, Dalton was still looking dubiously at her, but they had reached their destination. They all filed into Miss Pembrook's room to find her sitting on her desk with a coffee cup in her hand. Mr. Brighton was with her, sitting at one of the student desks.

"Hi, Miss Pembrook. Hi, Mr. Brighton," they all said, not exactly in unison. Dalton noticed that the teachers seemed close and maybe a little embarrassed, like they were engaged in some kind of intimate conversation.

"Hi, guys," Mr. Brighton said, quickly standing and moving away from Miss Pembrook, who had a slight blush on her cheeks. The idea that her two favorite teachers might have a secret romance going on made Dalton smile.

"And what are you ladies up to?" Miss Pembrook asked. "Oh yeah, shoot. History club—I completely forgot." Yes, Dalton thought. She was definitely blushing and a little flustered as she turned to Mr. Brighton and told him, "Sorry, I'll have to take a rain check. Next week?"

"Sure." He raised his coffee cup to the girls. "You ladies enjoy your meeting," he said and left quickly, careful not to look at Miss Pembrook again.

"Ooh, girl," Dalton teased Miss Pembrook when he was out of ear-shot. "We messed up your date!"

"It wasn't a date," the teacher said hastily. "It was just . . . we were just . . ."

"Um-*humm*," Dalton said smugly.

"Relax," Maggie added. "We love Mr. Brighton. We are *so* in favor of you hooking up with him."

"Okay, guys," Miss Pembrook said, joining in their laughter. "I can tell when I've been outed—but don't spread it around, all right?"

Dalton noticed that Kate hadn't been paying attention to their banter. Instead she was standing by the door, staring at a corkboard collage that

Miss Pembrook had made. Dalton went over to see what had captured her attention. Beneath the collage was a caption: THE MYSTERY OF THE 3 CHURCHES. It consisted of a map of the world, and on it were pinned the photos of the three mysterious, identical churches that Miss Pembrook had shown Dalton and Aimee in a previous history club meeting. The location of each church was pinned on the map. There was one in China, one in Israel, and of course, Middleburg United. Under the caption, in cutout construction-paper letters, Miss Pembrook had stapled the words: WHO BUILT THEM AND WHY?

"Weird, huh?" Dalton said to Kate.

Kate continued staring at it, as if entranced. "What about the fourth church?" she asked.

Miss Pembrook looked at her, surprised. "There's another one?" she asked, and Dalton heard her quick footstep as she and Maggie came up behind them. Slowly, Kate reached out and touched the picture of the church in Israel.

"Back home, in Ballymore," she said, her voice quiet with wonder. "There's a church just like this."

℘

Rick was sitting in the Banfield's living room, going into hour two of getting chewed out when the doorbell rang. He should have expected his dad to be pissed. First Rick had made it known in no uncertain terms that he didn't approve of the upcoming wedding, and then he'd gotten himself suspended. Worse, because of the trouble with Josh, Rick was barred from participating in the next basketball game. It was school policy that players who'd been suspended had to sit out one game, and his dad was so angry that he didn't even try to get Rick off the hook as he usually did. He'd just signed the suspension papers—without a word—and marched Rick out of the principal's office.

Well, Rick was equally pissed. It seemed to make no difference to his dad that the dumb-ass Flats punk Josh had attacked *him*. Jack was lecturing him about the upcoming wedding too—and as for that crap, Rick felt he was doing everyone a favor by telling them that he couldn't live with Raphael. Wouldn't it be worse if his dad's new stepson reappeared and moved into the house, and Rick had to kill him? By warning them ahead of time, Rick was saving everyone a lot of trouble. But did he get any credit for it? No. All he got was an endless, meaningless lecture followed by the promise that if he didn't shape up, Jack was going to break his will the way a trainer breaks a horse.

Rick could think of a few things he'd like to break, starting with the finger his dad kept jabbing at him. Lately, thoughts of violence came to him more and more, simmering strong and hot just beneath the surface of his rigid self-control—a control that was increasingly difficult to maintain. His soul longed for release, and he stared at his father now with an anger and contempt that was dangerously close to hatred.

Then, the doorbell rang.

"You'd better make damn sure you're still in that chair when I get back," his dad said ominously, then left the room.

∽

Jack opened the front door and found Aimee and Orias on the stoop. He greeted Orias with a hearty handshake.

"Thanks for giving Aimee a ride home from school, Orias. I'm sorry to deprive you of her company, but I need her here to help with wedding planning. I'm sure you undersand."

"Of course," Orias said. Aimee started to protest but Orias leaned close to her.

"It's only for a few days," he said. He bent to her and quickly kissed her cheek. "Be a good girl. Listen to your father and do as he asks. No slips, okay?"

"Okay."

"Promise me?" Orias asked, and she nodded. "Good. I'll see you soon. Why don't you head inside? I need to have a word with Jack."

"Okay." Aimee shrugged and entered the house.

Jack watched her go, amazed at how docile she was when she was with Orias. When she was out of earshot, he said to Orias, "You've worked a miracle with her. You've helped her more than they ever did at that . . . that boarding school. What's your secret?"

Jack didn't want to come right out and ask Orias if he was sleeping with his daughter because if he got the wrong answer he'd have to slug him—and that wouldn't be good for business.

"It's no secret," Orias said. "It's just a matter of sympathy, understanding, and some herbal tea to help her relax. Which reminds me—" He reached into his coat pocket and took out a small glass bottle with a silver top. "Put this in her tea or juice a couple of times a day and you'll have no problems with her—but just a drop."

Jack eyed it suspiciously. "What is it?"

"Don't worry. I told you—it's an herbal remedy for nerves. I don't believe in drugs. This is perfectly natural—not harmful like that stuff they were giving her at Mountain High Academy." He smiled at Jack's surprise. "Yes—she told me all about her treatment there. Pills and injections and straitjackets. Barbaric if you ask me. This is completely homeopathic and harmless. Have it analyzed if you don't trust me."

"Not necessary," Jack said. "You say it's natural?" Orias nodded. "Does she know you're giving it to her?"

"No," Orias said. "I saw no reason to trouble her with that information. But if you prefer having the old Aimee back—" he started to put the bottle away, but Jack reached out and took it.

"No," he said quickly. "I would not prefer that. Twice a day, you said? Just one drop?"

"Yes."

"All right then." Jack pocketed the vial.

"One more thing," Orias said. "I heard Rick got suspended for a couple of days. I thought he might like to use the time to make some money."

Jack grinned. "A job might be good for him right now. Come on in and ask him yourself."

℅

Rick looked up, scowling as his dad returned with a fake smile on his face and Orias at his side. "Well, it's your lucky day," Jack told Rick as he and his guest sat down. "You want to tell him?" he asked Orias.

"I have a small job I need done, Rick," Orias said. "I think you're just the man for it."

Rick looked at Orias. True, he liked and admired the guy, and he was grateful to him. Rick didn't know how he'd done it, but he'd somehow reformed Aimee. In the time they'd been dating, his sister had gone from a total embarrassment to a tame little mouse who did as she was told. There was also the fact that Orias had healed Rick's broken arm and saved his football season. The problem was, Rick remembered how Orias had healed him—the weird chanting, the levitation, the hundreds of invisible hands groping him, the chalky powder in his mouth that had turned into a hideous rat that he'd vomited out. The strange power Orias possessed had made Rick respect him—but he didn't trust him.

"What kind of job?" Rick asked.

"I need you to help me out with something. A personal assistant sort of thing. We'll have to take a little business trip." Then Orias turned to Jack. "But I promise—I'll have him back for your wedding on Saturday."

"Where do I have to go?" Rick asked, skeptical.

His father looked at him with contempt. "You're asking a lot of questions of someone who's trying to do you a favor, don't you think? Instead of sitting around the house getting bawled out by me, wouldn't you rather be helping a friend and making a little cash?"

The answer his dad was looking for was clear, but Rick still wasn't ready to give in. "How much cash?" he asked sullenly.

"You help me out, Rick, and I'll pay you a thousand dollars," Orias said.

He looked at Rick, and for a moment his focus was so intense that Rick felt like there was no one in the room except the two of them. Rick suddenly wondered why he'd been so hesitant to accept Orias's offer. How bad could it be? What was he afraid of?

"What do you say, Rick?" Orias's voice was soft, insistent. "You want to help me out?"

"Okay," Rick said. "Why not?"

Rick and Orias were halfway down the front walk when Rick stopped short. Moments before, he'd felt a strong urge to get out of the house and away from his father's wrath. But out here in the chill wind, beneath the bleached out, empty blue sky, his fear suddenly returned.

"Wait," Rick said. "Before we go any further, you gotta tell me what we're going to do."

Orias turned to look at him. "That's fair, I guess. We're going to your girl-friend's house. I want to have a look at those tapestries her mother weaves."

"Why?" Rick said. "I've seen them. They're bizarre. And Maggie's mom is a head case."

Orias smiled indulgently as if humoring a small, ignorant child. "Not at all," he said. "Maggie's mother happens to be a very powerful woman."

"Powerful?" Rick scoffed. "You gotta be kidding. She's so powerful she hardly ever leaves her house? Her husband ditched her because she's wacko. She has no connections, and she doesn't own anything except that house. How exactly is she powerful?"

"Maybe you'll find out. Maggie could be a problem, though. She doesn't seem to care for my company."

"Don't worry about Maggie," Rick said, resentment rising in him again like bitter bile. "She's cheerleading at the basketball game." It was a home game against Benton, and both he and Bran were missing it, thanks to those Flats rats.

"Good," said Orias. "Now we just need a reason for going over there. Any ideas?"

"Leave it to me," Rick said. He took out his cell phone and dialed Maggie's home number. "Hey, Mrs. A.," he said, his tone friendly and inviting. "How you doing?" He waited for her answer and then said, "Great. Listen, is it okay if I come by and pick up some stuff Maggie said we could have? It's for the team's rummage sale to raise money for new uniforms. She said there's some old tires and a bunch of tools that you guys never use, out in the garage." Another pause. "Thanks. That'd be great."

"Excellent," Orias said when Rick hung up. He reached into the inside pocket of his overcoat and pulled out a small scroll. The parchment looked like it was made of black leather, and the sticks used to roll it up looked like the bones of a small animal. "Now, while I'm keeping Mrs. Anderson busy, you're going down to the basement—with this," he continued, handing the scroll to Rick. "When you get to the bottom of the stairs—I mean the very bottom, and it's quite a long way down—ask whoever you see there to find Dr. Uphir. When he comes to you, give him the scroll. But don't open it. I'm warning you, Rick. If you break the seal you're risking your life—and mine. You understand?"

"Uh, no," Rick said truthfully. "You're saying the Andersons have a doctor living in their basement?"

Orias's features remained impassive. "It's not a just a basement," he said. "Now come along. Your dad wants you back in time for his wedding, so we'll have to hurry."

Rick was starting to get it. This was no ordinary errand. It was a *business trip* in the same way that Orias fixing his arm had been a *medical treatment*—which meant it was probably going to be a freak show. The prospect filled Rick with a pins-and-needles feeling of giddy fear, but there was something else he was worried about, too.

"Wait. You said I'll be gone a few days?" he asked.

"Probably. If it takes that long."

"Then I need to take my friend with me. Bran."

Orias looked at him, his eyes narrowing slightly. "That wasn't part of the deal."

"I can't leave him here alone," Rick said. "Not for days—not right now. He might—uh, he's kinda going through a rough time."

"I see." Orias moved closer to Rick, keeping his voice low. "So there was a witness."

Rick backed away. "What do you mean? Witness to what?"

"Don't try to play a player, my friend," Orias said. "You're the one who messed up that Flats kid. When I read about it in the paper I knew it was you. Rick . . . I know what you are, which makes you perfect for this job. I think you might even enjoy it."

"Well, I don't know what you think you know—" Rick began, but Orias raised a hand, silencing him.

"Never mind. It doesn't matter. You can take your friend along. But understand this. He's not like you. He will be in great danger where you're going. There's a good chance he won't make it back."

Rick nodded. "Yeah, whatever," he said, taking out his cell phone again. It would be a shame to lose his closest ally during whatever crazy mission this was. But at the same time, it might be a good idea to put someone between him and whatever was at the bottom of those basement stairs. And if Bran didn't make it back, Rick wouldn't have to worry about him running his mouth anymore.

Bran picked up on the first ring. "Hey, man," Rick told him, "I need your help with something. Meet me in front of Maggie's house, ASAP."

∞

Aimee looked around the room that had been her refuge, after her mom disappeared and she'd realized how difficult it was to get along with her dad and her brother without Emily Banfield running interference. With a flop, she laid down on the bed and tried to settle down but found it impossible. She couldn't believe her father was actually going to marry that woman from the Flats and that somehow, he'd managed to have her mother declared dead less than two years after her disappearance.

She missed her mom so much, and she needed her. Her father was selfish, cold, and calculating and Rick was turning into the ultimate bully—or something worse. With her mother gone, there was no gentleness, no sweetness in Aimee's life, except what she got from Orias.

But there had been, once. There had been someone . . . someone she cared about, who loved her as much as (or maybe even more than) Orias did. Every now and then she got a quick mind flash of the happiness she'd found with that person, whoever it was, but then it would vanish as quickly as it had come, like a cork bobbing on a fishing line and then dipping under water before she could see what she had caught. Sometimes it seemed her mind had broken and had somehow become fragmented, like the crystal ring that had been so important to Orias.

A nostalgic longing Aimee didn't understand abruptly awakened in her. She somehow knew that if she could remember the person who had once made her so happy, the fragments would join together. The missing pieces would fall into place and everything would be clear and good again.

Suddenly she felt suffocated. She wanted to get out of there and, surprisingly, she wanted to be with her friends, to be part of something again. She went downstairs to ask her dad if she could go over to Dalton's to study. She had promised Orias that she wouldn't slip this time, and she would be true to her word—unless it became absolutely necessary.

஧

Raphael fought on. He could no longer count the number of enemies he'd defeated, step by step, blow by blow, through endless desert and unrelenting fog. He had no idea how much time had passed; the light above that masqueraded as the sun had to be counterfeit, he knew, because he'd been battling for what felt like weeks, but it had not moved at all. He didn't know how many injuries he'd sustained, but every joint felt twisted, worn, and inflamed. Big drops of blood drizzled down his brow and the cracked, parched earth at his feet greedily soaked them up.

He'd gone from being energized to exhaustion, and then new reserves of energy would shoot through him again in a cycle that kept repeating. The same had happened with his Shen energy; he'd felt such bountiful power rising within him that when a Napoleonic soldier in a French uniform charged out of the roiling gray, his bayonet raised, Raphael simply reached out a hand and blasted him into oblivion. Other times he felt his strength wane, and when he tried to call on the power of Shen he felt nothing but his own outstretched hand and the faintest flicker of a spark on his fingertips. At those times, he heaved a sigh, lifted his hands in a guard position, and fought on.

In this strange place Shen seemed to fail more often than not, and he had a feeling that its power was somehow dimmed in the borderlands of the Dark Territory. But he didn't really have time to think about it—whenever one enemy died, a new one appeared to take its place.

In the beginning, which seemed like weeks ago now, there had been moments when Raphael felt he couldn't go on. *I'll just stop,* he thought. *I can't do this. I'm too tired. I'll just lie down and let them kill me.* But somehow he'd found the will to continue, and he'd come to understand that he really could go on forever. He seemed to possess reserves of strength he'd never known he had and his will was almost boundless. He would not lie down. He would not die. He would not give up. And he would not quit fighting until he came out safe on the other side of this desert or whatever it was—even if he had to fight every kind of ancient warrior he'd ever read about.

And it was beginning to look like that's exactly what he'd have to do.

He'd gone through the ranks of every kind of historical combatant he'd ever heard of until he worked his way up to present-day foes. A man who looked like a U.S. Navy Seal, but who wore a shirt with Russian letters on it, now appeared out of the fog and almost gutted him with a huge knife. Raphael managed to dodge the blow and then landed a lucky kick, hitting the pommel of the Russian's knife and jamming the blade into his shoulder. He fell to one knee with an agonized scream, and Raphael blasted him with a head kick, sending him spiraling out of sight, into the drifting gray.

There was not a moment to rest. His next assailant stormed into sight wearing full Kevlar body armor. He also had some kind of headset and goggles that blinked with digital bits of information, like it was collecting battle data. Raphael's new enemy wielded a short, compact machine gun. He turned it on Raph, fired, and missed. The gun's report was like a cannon. Desperate, Raphael somehow summoned a surge of Shen from the soles of his feet and up through his body. He let it burst out of the palm of his hand, just before the tungsten bar the gun had fired streaked toward him (he didn't know how he knew what sort of ammo the gun used, he just knew it, in the same way that he knew he could go on fighting forever). The Shen blast split through the projectile like a hot blade slicing through a soft stick of butter, and the two halves shot harmlessly past Raphael on either side as he went into a spring attack, shot forward, disarmed the enemy with a *Bong Sau,* and then slammed the butt of his gun back into his face. The info-goggles shattered, sending streaks of blood down the futuristic soldier's cheeks. Raphael turned the gun on him and fired.

He didn't bother to look at the mess it made of his enemy's head; he stepped over his body, moving further into the fog, claiming the one extra yard of territory he'd gained. Already the next enemy drew near. Raph couldn't see him but a red laser light sweeping through the waste heralded his approach. Raph felt heat when the beam settled on him, and he threw himself backward into the dust as a pulse of energy blasted forth from his enemy. It missed him but caught the gun he was holding, and as Raphael landed on his back on the ground, the liquefied plastic of the gun's body melted onto his hands, scalding them. He cried out in pain and managed to dislodge his fingers from the steaming wreckage just in time to roll out of the way of another blast.

He looked up just as the fog parted and was able to make out what looked like a half-person, half-robot. A laser beam flowed from the single eyespot on its helmet, scanning for Raph. It looked a little like the guy in those old *Robocop* movies, he thought—except this was the real thing. A real cyborg commando, a warrior of the future, was coming at him.

He reached out to send a Shen blast its way, but came up empty and was forced to roll out of the way of another sonic blast. Raph didn't know what kind of gun it was, but it emitted a shot like a wave of distortion flowing through the air. It looked kind of like a heat mirage rising from the blacktop on a hot summer day.

Diving behind a boulder, he dodged another blast as the laser sight scanned past him. With no other weapons and no way to get close to the enemy without getting liquefied, Raph grabbed the only thing he could—the large stone he was hiding behind. His muscles protested, quivering as he lifted the heavy rock above his head with both hands and cocked back to throw it. As the laser scanner zeroed in on him, he chucked the rock at his enemy's head, then dove to the side to avoid the blast he knew was coming. The shot liquefied the rock in mid air, and something that looked like freshly mixed cement splashed onto the visor of the cyborg. It cooled instantly, leaving his laser sight covered by a crust of solidifying rock. Shrieking with fury, the creature fired but the shots went wild. As Raphael charged, they liquefied the ground right in front of him, turning it into a pit of simmering quicksand. Raph jumped over it as his blinded adversary blasted away, hitting nothing. Somehow Raph managed to avoid the deadly shots until he was close enough to touch his enemy.

"Hey R2D2, I'm right here," he said, and the cyborg jerked his gun toward the sound of Raphael's voice. As he did, Raph grabbed his forearm and, using his enemy's own momentum, swung him into the pit of molten sand. The cyborg hit feetfirst then lost his footing and fell on his back, sinking down with a cry of anguish until only his groping, metallic hands were visible above the quickly congealing quicksand.

Raphael grabbed the discarded energy gun and took another few steps into the fog. He was on the top of a low rise now, and he could see several more cyborgs coming toward him through the haze. He vaporized one, then another, then another with the gun he'd captured, demolishing thirteen of them by the time the gun's charge finally gave out. He was moving down the rise when the fog parted again. This time he saw that he was atop a slope that led down into a valley filled with futuristic warriors—hundreds of them, or thousands, or maybe hundreds of thousands. He stared at the sea of enmity and violence for a moment and then closed his eyes. He'd done this before, during slight pauses in the battle, just taking an instant to replenish his inner store of energy with a little micro-meditation. Now as he did so, he felt Shen filling him as never before, and within it, there was a message.

It wasn't a message from some outside source, from Master Chin or from the All or from the Magician, even. It was from within himself, maybe his subconscious or his higher self, maybe even his soul—whatever that was.

As long as you are willing to fight, enemies will come. There will always be another opponent, another confrontation, another injustice to right, another insult to avenge, another reason to go to war. You can keep fighting forever.

It was true. Raphael understood that instantly. He could keep on going like this for all eternity, and it would never stop. But that wasn't what he wanted.

The only way to stop fighting, he thought, *is to refuse to fight.* The epiphany struck him with such weight that it made him dizzy, and giddy excitement replaced his exhaustion.

Raphael looked down at the gun in his hand and cast it aside, and then he fell to his knees. The new wave of opponents was grinding its way toward him now. They were monstrosities of flesh and robotics, drone-like death machines, small, bizarre tanks that seemed to breathe. He saw these horrors approaching and opened his arms wide, as if to embrace them. He saw the gun barrels pointed at him, the titanium teeth, the steel blades, the missile tips.

He took a breath and shouted across the desolate plains with all the power his voice could muster: "I will not fight!" he yelled. Then, even louder, "*I WILL NOT FIGHT!*"

For an instant, he was overcome with the terrifying thought that this was the end. His enemies would now destroy him, and he would die. Then, in a crunching of gears and a clink of armor, their advance stopped. All his mighty futuristic opponents stood before him, gloriously power-ful, ominously deadly—and completely, totally still.

Raphael was still, too, except for his chest, which was heaving with exertion and fear. Then the wind shifted, the fog swept fast across the val-ley, and his enemies vanished. For a moment, there was nothing but the roiling mist. Then, through the fog, he heard footsteps, and he saw the silhouette of a tall, thin man approaching through the eerie half-light. It was the Magician.

At the sight of him, all the weariness Raphael had somehow miracu-lously held at bay during his battles hit him at once with such crushing force he could hardly stand upright or keep his eyes open. He had no energy and no patience for the Magician's mockery now.

"All I wanted was to get back to Middleburg," Raphael said.

The Magician nodded approvingly. "But now you understand."

"Yeah, I think so," Raph replied. "If I keep fighting, it'll never stop. It's like a cycle. Like . . . a wheel. I attack them, they attack me, I attack them. It just keeps going around and around. The only way to stop it is to quit fighting. Is that what I was supposed to figure out?"

"There is no '*supposed to,*'" the Magician said, his voice deep and strangely grating. "You either learn, or you do not learn." He turned and inhaled, as if sniffing the damp, slightly acerbic scent of the fog. "Some have spent eons lost here on the battlefields that border the Dark

Territory. And you are correct; you can remain here fighting for all of eternity. Or you can simply . . . stop."

The thought of being damned to an eternity of fighting terrified Raphael. He wondered how much time he had already wasted. "So what now?" he asked.

"What is it that you want?" asked the Magician. "You can go to any time and place you wish, now that you've learned what you needed to know."

"I want to go home—to Middleburg. I've got to get back to Aimee."

"Ah, yes—Aimee. Are you sure?"

"I'm sure. How do I get to her from here?"

"The journey will be arduous and fraught with danger," the Magician warned.

"Fine," Raph said. "Been there, done that. Bring it on."

"Reach into your right pocket and take out that piece of crystal."

Raphael took out the ring shard and held it in the palm of his hand. At first nothing happened. Then, after a moment, the shard began to glow. He stared down at it, mesmerized by the depth of its brilliance. When he looked closely, he saw that it was not just a glowing piece of crystal. The light inside it looked like photos he'd seen of nebulae in space, vast, multicolored, many-faceted clouds of swirling illumination, infinitely beautiful.

When he looked up, the train had appeared behind the Magician. The fog that haunted the landscape seemed to be pouring from its high, broad smoke stack. The door to its cab stood open, waiting for him, and the Magician gestured toward it.

Raphael closed his hand on the ring shard.

"Can the train take me anywhere I want to go? Any time, any place?" he asked.

The Magician smiled. For once, his expression wasn't mocking or creepy, but kind. "Some say that if you board the train with an open heart, it will take you not where you want to go, but where you *need* to go. Do you have the faith to try it?"

Raphael looked at the Magician, then at the glowing piece of the ring in his hand, then at the waiting train. "Go ahead," the Magician told him. "Make your wish. It will take you where you want to go . . . eventually."

"What do you mean by that?" Raph asked suspiciously.

Again, the Magician smiled his mysterious, enigmatic smile. "Only that you may have other stops to make along the way."

CHAPTER 13

STANDING BEHIND RICK AND BRAN as they waited for Violet Anderson to come to the door, Orias noticed what a nice day it was. It was unseasonably pleasant for this time of year and the steel-gray skies of winter had given way to a pale blue that was filled with the twitter of robins and sparrows. Though he usually dreaded the whiplash of endless adjustments that marked his life of near immortality, this time he would welcome the change of seasons. Because, he knew, the changes coming to Middleburg with the arrival of spring would be more than warmer days, tender new buds and flower blossoms. If all went well, this would be the season he and Aimee would be bound together forever.

But there were still hurdles to overcome. Aimee's sleepwalking incident had made that clear. If she had twisted that doorknob a little further she would have released Orias's father, and once freed, Oberon would first vent his rage on his traitorous son and send him to a place worse than hell. After that, who could guess where his vengeance would end? He might very well decide to destroy all of Middleburg, or all of humankind. Even in the Dark Territory, there were few who understood the full extent of Oberon's power. Before Orias had locked his father in the tower room, he'd done his research, and he knew that releasing Oberon now would have devastating repercussions.

Aimee's dreams were proof that despite the protections Orias had put in place, his father's power was beginning to seep out. She was probably susceptible to his psychic pleas because she was close by, and because the Lethe tea had weakened her judgment. Orias should have realized long before that Aimee would have the power to break the imprisoning spell he had cast on the tower room.

Something had to be done. He had to silence his father completely, forever, and he knew that Uphir was the only one who might know how to make that happen. He had to contact the doctor, but to venture below before he had the shards of the crystal ring in his possession was too risky. Oberon's Irin brothers despised those like Orias. They considered the race of half-human, half-angel Nephilim lower than mongrels—and if any of the Fallen spotted him, they would make him pay. They would imprison him and torture him for eons, simply for being what he was.

He needed a messenger, and who could be better than Rick? Anyway, it was about time Rick started getting acquainted with the Dark Territory.

At last, they heard the sound of footsteps from inside and then, within the tiny, convex window of the peephole, the light changed almost imperceptibly.

"Hi, Mrs. Anderson," Rick called out. "It's Rick."

There was a slight pause, and then, "What do you want?"

"I called," Rick said pleasantly. "Remember—about the stuff for the rummage sale."

Another pause. "Who are those people with you?"

"My friend, Bran—he's on the team, too. And Orias. He's a friend of my dad's. They're in business together. He'd like to meet you, if that's okay."

Silence. Orias repressed a sigh and summoned his patience.

"Why?" asked the voice.

Orias pushed past Rick and said through the closed door, "Because I'm a great admirer of art, and I've heard about your wonderful tapestries. I'd love to see them."

"Who told you about them?"

"We have the same framer," Orias told her. Of course they did—

Vivian Gonzalez was the only framer in town, and in truth, she'd told Orias about Violet's unusual designs weeks ago, when Orias had shipped some of his paintings from New York to hang in Elixir. But Orias didn't have time to go into all that now. He needed her to open the door. He would do it himself but that was impossible. The magic that protected this place was more powerful even than the spell he'd placed on the tower room. There was no way that any Irin, Nephilim, or demon could penetrate it unless its owner invited him in.

He focused all his powers of persuasion on her, bringing his energy into a fine point, like the focus of a flashlight beam shining through the little peephole and into Violet Anderson's brain. He felt his skin begin to warm up, almost igniting with the heat of the energy coursing through his veins. "Please," he entreated gently. "Let me come in."

He held his breath, waiting, and then he heard the sounds of locks being released and bolts sliding back. He sighed in relief as Violet opened the door. For a moment, she eyed him warily, but when her gaze moved to Rick and Bran a big smile lit her face, recapturing for a moment the great beauty she'd once had.

"Rick ... so good to see you," she said, opening the door a little wider and standing aside so they could enter. "Sorry for the delay. I don't get many visitors these days. One can't be too careful, you know. Come in, boys, come in." After Rick introduced her to Orias she said, "So nice to meet you. You're a friend of Jack's?"

"I am," Orias replied, noticing that the color rose in her cheeks a little as she said Jack's name, and he knew that they'd once been sweethearts. "He sends his regards."

A dreamy look came into her eyes for a moment. "He was my escort the last year I was Middleburg High's homecoming queen. Did you know I was homecoming queen for three years in a row?" She took them into the sitting room, invited them to sit, and offered them coffee. "It's all ready," she said. "I got it all ready—with some cookies too—right after

Rick called. They're store bought, but they're really good. I don't do much baking anymore."

"No thanks, Mrs. A," said Rick. "We're kind of in a hurry. Got to get the stuff back to the school. If you don't mind, we'll just let ourselves out the back door, grab it, and be on our way."

"Oh . . . I guess that's all right," said Violet.

"You guys go ahead," Orias told Rick. "I'll catch up with you later." He turned to Violet. "I'd love a cup of coffee," he said. "And those cookies look delicious. Chocolate chip?"

While Orias continued charming Violet, Rick and Bran left and quietly made their way down the hall. Violet poured the coffee and put two cookies on a little plate that she passed to Orias.

"It has been so long since I've entertained a handsome young man in my living room," she said. "Do you know my daughter, Maggie?"

"We've met," said Orias. "She's a lovely girl."

After he'd suffered through half an hour listening to Violet's insipid stories of her glory days at Middleburg High, she finally said, "All right. You can see the tapestries. Come right this way." She led him through the little foyer and into a long hallway with an impossibly high ceiling. Huge, colorful tapestries hung on the walls on both sides.

Slowly, he walked the length of the gallery, gazing at each one in turn. When the framer had told him about them and she'd mentioned that their creator had been homecoming queen three times, Orias had known exactly what they were—the prophetic works he'd read about in his mother's books.

It was fascinating now for Orias to see them for himself. They were more engaging and interesting than he'd imagined them. The figures depicted in them seemed almost alive and several times, when he looked away, his peripheral vision caught movement within the scenes, as if they were changing all the time—but in a way that was difficult to perceive if he was looking directly at them.

As he walked down the hall, the story of Middleburg played out before his eyes. It was a tale that few living mortals would understand, but it was one Orias knew well, not from his father who shared almost nothing with him, but from the secret books his mother had hidden away in the basement of their home in Manhattan before she did.

He saw the founding of Middleburg by the Order of the All, in a time now forgotten by human history. He witnessed an ancient queen's coronation, when the Harvest Crown, now Middleburg High's homecoming crown, was first placed upon her head. He saw the construction of the Wheel of Illusion, a massive undertaking completed by the angels, when they were all exalted, before any of them fell.

In the beginning, there had been four Wheels of Illusion, created by the All so that humans, when they were ready, could move forward in their spiritual journey and join the glory of the Light. During the most recent celestial war the fallen angels had battled against those that remained in the service of the All—and the spoils were the souls of humans. The exalted angels had prevailed in that last final battle and the fallen ones had gone into hiding. During the fighting, three of the Wheels—those located in what were now China, Israel, and Ireland—were destroyed, and the four staircases that led from the Wheels up into the heavenly realms were sealed to prevent the fallen from ascending to conquer the Heavens.

Now that the ring had been destroyed and the Wheel in Middleburg was inert, that portal, too, had closed, and Orias's dream of leading the Irin out of their underground stronghold had been shattered. If the story the tapestry told was true, he saw, the Wheel was destined to be opened again—and perhaps the staircase, too. But in what way, at what cost, and with what result? All these things were unclear.

The only thing he saw clearly in the tapestries was strife. He saw two boys he recognized as Zhai Shao and Raphael Kain, and the war between their two factions. High up, in one corner, almost at the edge of the cloth were the figures of five women inside the tunnel gazing at the Wheel of Illusion.

He saw himself, depicted shirtless and with a black halo, and the image sent a shock through him. In the tapestry, he had one hand reaching upward and the other downward, as demons and Irin below and exalted angels above clambered for him, threatening to tear him in two. He turned quickly away from the sight.

"They're magnificent," he said at last. "Are there any more?"

"Yes . . ." Violet replied slowly, glancing toward her workroom. "But it's not finished."

"May I see it?"

Silently, she led him into her little studio. The last tapestry was larger than the others and contained a number of scenes that all blended together. Instinctively, Orias realized that the proper way to view it was not to look at each element separately, but to take them all in and let them soak into his subconscious all at once. As he did, the various images seemed to wash over him—the spiritual brothers, Raphael and Zhai, the rival armies with their clacking swords and fluttering banners, and the Wheel. There was one element that Orias recognized—it was repeated from one of the tapestries hanging in the hall outside—and he knew it was gravely important. It was an image of a beautiful young woman, who the tapestry labeled "the Princess of the Wind."

He recognized this blond-haired beauty instantly as Aimee, and his mind snapped back to a piece of text, the ancient scroll his father had preserved in his study all these years: the Scroll of the Wheel. In it, there was a passage about a princess who had ne'er lain with a man and who walks with the winds, transcending the bonds of the earth. This, he knew, was *La Princesa del Viento,* the Princess of the Wind.

Aimee.

That's why he'd instinctively known to be careful with her—and it had not been easy. He had merely desired her at first but as he fell in love with her, that desire increased to a level he'd found difficult to control. But he'd had no choice. He'd known that to take her, even if she wanted him to, would weaken her powers or destroy them altogether. Now, because of Violet's tapestry, he saw that his instinct had been right. Her unusual abilities were connected to—no, they actually depended on—her purity. He had to protect her until his work in Middleburg was complete, and they could be married. Then, the future he envisioned for them would become a glorious reality.

All else in the tapestry confirmed what he'd suspected: war was coming, and it would be truly horrific. He also saw in it the image of the crystal ring, the cracks in its surface clearly visible. Orias couldn't tell if it was still broken or if it had been repaired—but it sent a startling jolt of hope through his mind.

He was about to turn away when something at the very top of the image gave him pause. There, Violet Anderson had stitched the figure of a dark angel. He was flying upward as powerful shafts of black radiance flowed from him, and broken shackles and chains fell from his wrists. It was an imprisoned Irin, breaking free.

Orias stared at the image for a full minute, until he felt sick. This was the one prophecy he couldn't allow to come true.

"Well," Violet broke into his thoughts. "Now you've seen everything. What do you think?"

"I think . . . you are very gifted, Mrs. Anderson. What you have here are masterpieces." He wondered if she had any idea what they meant. Her reaction to his next statement told him she did. "They should be hanging in a big gallery for the world to enjoy."

"Oh, no," she said. "They have to stay right here in Middleburg. I . . . I wouldn't want that kind of attention." She turned pale and fear crept into her eyes. "I'm sorry—I feel a headache coming on. This has been lovely. Let me show you out."

As they walked back into the hallway, Orias glanced at the basement door and saw that the bolt was no longer securing it. Violet saw it too. She hurried to it and quickly slid the bolt back in place, firmly locking the door. But, Orias knew, Rick and his friend had gotten in.

"These old houses," she explained. "They get so drafty if you don't keep things buttoned up tight."

"Indeed." He studied her a moment. She reminded him a little of his mother, and he felt as much compassion for her as he was capable of feeling for any human. "Thank you for showing me your work. If you ever decide to exhibit, I would be honored to sponsor you. Goodbye."

She closed the front door behind him, and he heard locks clicking shut and bolts sliding into place. As he continued down the walk, Maggie came around the corner. She was trudging up the street, her head down as if depressed or deep in thought. When she looked up and saw Orias, she froze for a moment and then hurried to him.

"What are you doing here?" she demanded. "My mother didn't let you in, did she?"

"Yes, Maggie—she did," he said complacently. "We had a lovely afternoon. She gave me coffee and showed me her beautiful tapestries."

"You leave my mother alone," she said. "And don't ever come back here."

"Or what?" He couldn't resist taunting her. "I've told you before, Maggie, and I'll tell you again. Stay out of my way."

&

Savana Kain unbuttoned her jacket as she stood on Lily Rose's porch, waiting for the dear old woman to come to the door. What had been a frigid, brutal winter seemed to be fading into an unusually early spring, and the pleasant afternoon sun warmed the air enough that she felt like stripping off a layer or two and basking in it. Besides, her massive belly was straining at the buttons of her coat, making the already constricted feeling of pregnancy even worse.

There was a bustling from within, and Lily Rose peeked out the window at her from behind a lace curtain. After another moment, the door swung open.

"Savana!" Lily Rose said sweetly. "What a nice surprise. Come on in, sugar!"

Savana entered the living room and found three girls sitting around the coffee table, doing their homework. With Dalton were an adorable redheaded girl she didn't know and Aimee.

"Hi, Mrs. Kain," Dalton said, and the other girl waved. Aimee just looked up at her a moment and then back down at her books.

"We've got quite a full house these days," Lily Rose observed. "It's right nice!"

Savana was surprised to see Aimee there. Jack had told her that his daughter spent most of her time with her boyfriend Orias. When Savana wanted to know if that concerned him, he'd waved the question off.

"Not really," he'd said. "This is the first time in a year and a half that I *haven't* been worried about her. She's dressing like her old self again, her grades are up, she's not having any more emotional outbursts, and she's finally making some decent choices in life, Orias among them. As long as she's back on track, she can hang out with him all she wants."

Although Savana didn't agree, there had been a note of finality in his voice so she had dropped the subject. But she was still worried about Aimee. From what Raphael had told her before he disappeared, he and Aimee had been pretty serious. It was strange that she had forgotten about him overnight and jumped into a new relationship that seemed to be even more serious. But, Savana knew, teenage girls were like that, changing their allegiances often. And they weren't the only ones. She wasn't proud to remember that for a long while after Raphael's dad died, she had been so grief stricken that she sought comfort wherever she could find it.

"Hi, Aimee," she ventured. "It's good to see you."

Aimee smiled politely. "Thank you," she said vaguely.

Savana nodded. "I was hoping to get to know you a little better before the wedding." Aimee didn't respond. She just kept thumbing through her history book. "Well, I'm glad you're here, hanging out with your friends," Savana finished weakly.

"That's just because her beau is off taking care of business," Dalton said. "When he's around, she's off the grid. But that's okay. We take her when we can get her."

Before Savana had time to worry about what to say next, Lily Rose spoke again. "Come on out to the kitchen with me, honey," she said. "Let's leave the girls to their studies."

"Sure," Savana replied. When they reached the kitchen, she added, "You're a saint, you know—letting the kids hang out here. You really do have a full house!"

"I'm glad to have them. Truth be told, it's my other guest who's worrying me the most."

"Other guest?" Savana asked.

Lily Rose told her how Zhai had brought Master Chin to her several days before, saying only that the kung fu teacher had been injured in a fight. "But that's my lookout, Savana," she said. "Nothing for you to worry about. Now tell me—how are you and that new little one getting on?"

"Oh . . . fine, I guess," Savana responded quietly. "I'm just so worried about Raphael."

"No need for that," Lily Rose told her. "Raphael is a strong and resourceful boy. Wherever he is, he'll find his way back."

In spite of her efforts not to cry, Savana was suddenly swept up in a monsoon of tears. "I just wish . . . he could be here for . . . for the wedding," she said, giving way to soft little sobs. Lily Rose patted her shoulder comfortingly. "But—I know he wouldn't approve, you know? He'd be so angry, with me, and with Jack. But he doesn't realize what it takes to raise a baby. I can't do it on my own. And Jack—he may not be perfect, but he loves me. I mean, he really loves me. A sixteen-year-old kid can't understand how rare that is. But when Raph comes back, he'll be so mad—and he'll be devastated when he sees Aimee with her new boyfriend. He'll be crushed. I miss him, Lily Rose. He was—*is*—my best friend. I just miss him so much!"

Lily Rose embraced Savana as she wept, hugging her with more strength than Savana would have thought that frail old body could muster. A few minutes passed as Lily Rose waited for Savana's tears to ebb.

Savana sniffed and regained control of her emotions. "I didn't mean to do that," she said. "Sorry."

"Don't be. I'm glad you came to see me," Lily Rose said, arching one eyebrow. "But that wasn't all you came to tell me, was it?"

Savana shook her head. "No. It's—look, I know Jack is against it, but I need you to deliver the baby, Lily Rose—no matter what he says. *I can't* go to the hospital."

Lily Rose looked at Savana, perfect peace and calmness radiating from her beautiful, mismatched eyes. "And why is that?"

Savana reached down and pulled her shirt up, exposing her bulbous abdomen. As she did, she felt movement beneath her skin, and they both watched as her belly roiled unnaturally. The movement was so forceful it almost took Savana's breath away.

"It wasn't like this with Raphael," Savana whispered when the baby quieted again. "I've read dozens of pregnancy books. It's never like this. And sometimes—"

As if on cue, a white light flared to life, glowing just beneath her skin.

Lily Rose came forward, gazing intensely at the light that moved inside Savana, like a flashlight beam shifting inside a nylon tent. Slowly, she reached out and placed both hands on Savana's belly. Then she closed her eyes, concentrating all her attention on whatever was in there.

After a moment, her amazing eyes snapped open and fastened on Savana's. "This is not a normal child," she declared, a new gravity in her voice.

"I know." Savana's whisper was scarcely audible.

Lily Rose stared at her with those magical eyes. Beneath their gaze no one could tell a lie.

"It's very important that you tell me the truth now, Savana Kain," Lily Rose said, her voice low. "Is this Jack Banfield's child?"

Savana opened her mouth to speak, but instead of words, only a choked sob came out, and again, she wept.

ဆ

Bran knew the minute he saw the staircase in Mrs. Anderson's basement that something was terribly wrong. The steps were made of ancient-looking, rough-hewn wood and the walls seemed to be dirt and stone carved out of the raw earth. Worst of all, from where he stood at the top he could see no end to it. Orias had given him and Rick a pair of powerful little flashlights before they set off, but the deep blackness below swallowed up their beams, and Bran got the distinct feeling that there was no landing waiting for them just a little way out of sight. As he gazed downward, he was sure the staircase went on forever.

As a kid living in Alabama, he'd witnessed a horrible motorcycle accident one summer. As he'd stared out the window of his family's minivan, his mother had told him to look away but it was too late. He'd already seen the rider—a shirtless middle-aged man without a helmet—who was now lying face down in a pool of his own blood.

If he closed his eyes, Bran could still see the long, red scrapes on the man's body, the gouged out flesh, the awkward angle of his arm, and most of all his total, unnatural stillness—the final indication that had made Bran understand that the man was completely and irrevocably dead.

The situations were different, but the feeling they gave him was the same and it was this: something that, once seen, can never be unseen. He would never pass Maggie Anderson's house again without knowing that this nightmare staircase lay beneath it. *What was it?* he wondered. *An old Cold War–Era bomb shelter? One of those pre-Civil War places for hiding runaway slaves—part of the underground railroad? The entrance to an old mine?*

Or, some deep and terrified part of him whispered, was it something worse? Something unnatural?

As Bran hesitated on the top step trying to figure it out, Rick thundered past him at full speed.

"Come on, man!" Rick said.

A frisson of fear shot down Bran's spine at the thought of being left behind so, hesitantly, he started after Rick. With each downward step, the temperature increased. Soon Bran's clothes were soaked through with sweat, and the heat seemed to consume all the oxygen. It was like breathing the scalding fumes from a car's exhaust pipe. Bran realized he was panting, and he was feeling lightheaded and sleepy—but Rick wasn't slowing down. If anything, he doubled his pace, taking the steps two at a time. Struggling forward, his legs trembling, Bran tried to keep up.

A long time passed that way—Bran didn't know how long, but it seemed like hours. When he looked at Rick again, he saw a change so subtle he almost hadn't noticed it. And when he did, he thought it was only a trick of light and shadow. Rick seemed taller somehow, and it looked like his shoulders were getting broader. And—although Bran knew it was impossible—the shape of his head was changing, too.

Finally, after lurching down the steps in that crematory heat for what seemed an eternity, Bran's legs simply gave out. He fell to one knee and skidded down a few steps, groaning with pain, before coming to a stop. Rick didn't notice. He was already leaving Bran behind.

"Rick," Bran called desperately, gasping for air. "Wait, man . . . I need . . . a break."

Rick turned back to him, and Bran screamed. His best friend was gone, and Bran was having trouble getting his head around the thing that was standing there in Rick's clothes.

"Dude, man up," it said, its voice low and guttural. "What the hell's wrong with you?"

Its shoulders were hulking and misshapen, bulging with sinewy muscle. Its face was that of a hideous beast—a deformed wolf, maybe, crossed with an alligator, and it had ram's horns protruding from each side of its head. Knifelike claws formed the tips of its powerful hands and one of its arms looked like it was made entirely of some sort of burnished, rusty metal. The creature's eyes, though, were the worst. The whites were now black, and the pupils were a starburst of faintly glowing crimson that reminded Bran of the roiling heart of a volcano.

"Hey," the beast said, and its voice was a little more like Rick's. "If you're this out of shape, you're gonna die when coach starts us up on two-a-days this fall." The thing grinned, revealing a mouth full of teeth that looked like razor-sharp scissors.

"Rick? Is that you, man?" Bran asked, fighting the panic that threatened to steal his mind.

"Who else would it be, asshole?"

"You—you changed," Bran said. "Look at your hands."

With a snort of contempt, Rick looked—and his demonic eyes widened, the red in them deepening as they flashed with fear and shock.

"What the hell?" Rick stammered. He reached up and touched his face and his eyes got even wider. "What do I look like?" he asked.

"Like . . . like . . ." Bran couldn't figure out what to say.

"WHAT DO I LOOK LIKE?" Rick screamed, his voice blasting so powerfully that it unleashed a shower of dirt from the ceiling above them. Bran looked up, terrified that the staircase would collapse and bury them alive. He looked back at Rick.

"You look like a monster," he said quietly.

Rick shook his head. "No. No—something's wrong. I gotta find a mirror." He started walking down the stairs again. Bran rose and followed him.

They had gone only about ten steps when Bran noticed that his flashlight was reflecting back at him. He moved it around and saw that the walls of the staircase were now lined with mirrors. Everything around them was made of mirrors—the steps, the walls, the ceiling, everything.

Rick noticed, too. He stared at himself in one of them, moving slowly toward it.

"No . . ." he whispered, reaching out to touch his reflection. "I'm not a monster," he yelled. "I'm not!" And he punched the mirror with his iron fist, trying to smash it, but it remained intact. He struck it again and again and again, then wheeled around and attacked the other wall. He kicked at his image in the mirrored steps, like a child throwing a temper tantrum. No matter what he did the glass would not break.

Bran was afraid to look at his own reflection, terrified that he'd turned into a monster too. When he finally got up the courage, he was relieved to see that he looked like himself, just scared and exhausted.

Rick, still in full freak-out mode, charged up the steps, surging past him.

"This place is messed up!" he yelled. "I'm done. Orias—Orias! I'm done with this crap!"

Bran followed with a groan, his legs aching at the thought of retracing their steps. He was both relieved and disturbed when, only thirty seconds later, the door that led back into the Anderson house came into sight. It was absolutely, completely impossible, Bran knew; there was no way they could have jogged downward for hours, only to make it back up in under a minute. But possible or not, the door was there, and Bran felt a wave of joy at the thought that he would soon be back in Maggie Anderson's hallway.

But when Rick tried the door, it was locked.

"Come on . . ." he grumbled and yanked the door harder. "Come ON! Orias! ORIAS!"

He pounded on the door with his iron fist for what seemed like forever, then slammed into it with his shoulder, then tried to kick it down with his big, muscular leg. Even though the wood trembled against his assault, it did not crack, and the latch did not break. Wherever they were, Bran thought, they were trapped.

"I knew I shouldn't have trusted him," the Rick thing snarled. "Damn you, Orias! Damn you to hell!" He finally turned away from the door.

The response seemed to echo from the ether around them. *Now, now, Rick. That's hardly fair—and there's no going back on our bargain.* Bran couldn't be sure, but the voice sounded like Orias's.

The Rick thing looked up at the ceiling and growled. "Let me out!" it screamed. "Open the damn door and let me out of here!"

Sorry. I can't do that. I'm calling in the favor you promised me when I fixed your arm.

"No. No way!" Rick shouted. "You didn't just fix my arm—you turned me into this! This wasn't part of the deal!"

Orias's laughter filled the stairwell. *I didn't turn you into anything, Rick. You made yourself what you are.*

"Go to hell, you liar! Let me out of here!"

You want to get out? Orias continued. *Then do what I asked. Take that scroll down the stairs and deliver it to Dr. Uphir.*

"How? We've been going down that staircase for hours! It never ends."

Of course it does. Look—the entrance to the Dark Territory is just ahead.

Bran turned his flashlight back down the steps. Sure enough, perhaps fifty yards away, he saw the landing. He knew it hadn't been there only moments before but that didn't matter. It was there now.

"I ought to shove this scroll down your lying throat," Rick shouted. There was no response.

"Okay—great," Bran said. "Whatever. Let's just get this done so we can get out of here." He hurried down and the Rick thing, still grumbling, followed him.

The landing was about forty feet long, and at the end of it, they found a massive wrought-iron gate. Although it was rusted and clearly ancient, it looked solid, too. Judging from its big rivets, thick bars, and heavy industrial construction, it looked like it had been made strong enough to stop a speeding semi-truck. It had decorative flourishes—fleur-de-lis and starbursts—also made of black wrought iron. In thick, Old English letters of burnished brass, two words were affixed to the gates:

𝔇ark 𝔗erritory

Bran and Rick stood together, staring at the entrance before them.

"What is this place?" Bran asked in childlike wonder.

"I guess we'll find out," Rick said.

The moment they stepped forward, the gates swung open by themselves, moving slowly with a biting screech of iron on iron.

Side by side, Bran and Rick entered the Dark Territory.

CHAPTER 14

Clarisse had been looking for Rick all afternoon. She was sure he would be at the basketball game, but he didn't show and she'd overheard a couple of the cheerleaders talking about how he got suspended. Thinking that he would probably meet his Topper girlfriend after the game, she had followed Maggie to her house, turning away only when she saw Maggie stop and talk to the weird rich guy—Orias—who was opening Elixir, the cool new coffee shop where Clarisse intended to get a job as a barista.

It would be a lot better than the job she had now—bus girl at Rosa's Trattoria. She had taken it out of desperation, just to get Nass's mom off her back. Ever since she'd gone out with Rick after the big fight the night Raphael disappeared—and hadn't made it home until the next morning—Amelia Torrez had been on her case. Rosa's wasn't so bad. Clarisse had found it easy to bully her coworkers into trading shifts with her whenever she wanted so that she could have more freedom and some kind of private life, but at Elixir she would make a ton of money in tips.

After Orias split and Maggie went inside, Clarisse waited for a while but Rick didn't show. She felt a small surge of triumph. *It's about time he dumped the stuck-up homecoming bitch,* she thought. She headed back down to the gate and made sure to smile and wave at Mike as she went through. Flirting with that goofball guard got her into Hilltop Haven every time.

She was halfway back to the Flats when her phone chimed. She figured it was probably Amelia Torrez or Nass, texting to ask where she was.

But it was her Facebook app, alerting her to a new message. She opened up the program and the text that appeared there was so terrifying she had to stop and sit down on the curb. It was from Oscar Salazar, and it was just one sentence:

I know where U are & I'm coming 4 you

Well, that's just fine, she said to herself, remembering her secret weapon. She thought of how Rick's eyes glinted with red sparks and his shoulders broadened when they made out and she got that breathless, excited feeling again, like she always got when she knew she was going to see him. She texted Oscar back:

I can hardly wait. I'll have something special waiting for you.

⚭

The Dark Territory was by far the strangest and worst place Bran Goheen had ever ventured into in his life. The landscape was barren, covered with powdery reddish soil, and its desolate expanse was dotted here and there with jutting rock formations, many of which looked like very old statues of humans or horses that had been effaced by the elements. Or perhaps—and Bran didn't know where this disturbing thought came from—like people turned to stone. He'd looked back after he and Rick had passed through the gate and was horrified to see that the staircase had disappeared. A featureless haze hung above them, the same shade of purple as a winter sky just before it fades to the blackness of night. In the distance, Bran thought he saw the red glow of a setting sun, but as he and Rick walked toward it, he noticed that it wasn't going down. It didn't move at all, in fact, but sat resolutely on the horizon, sending its flickering rays across the wasteland.

After an hour or so of walking toward it, Bran realized that it wasn't the sun at all, but some sort of a conflagration, like the most massive bonfire he'd ever seen. The quivering red light he'd mistaken for the sun was more rectangular than round, and as they got closer he saw that it was a wall of red fire stretching across the blasted earth. Since there was no other feature in sight on the dead landscape, they headed toward it and walked for what seemed like an eternity. Though he was exhausted and becoming increasingly concerned, Bran drew hope from the fact that, whatever it was, they were, indeed, getting closer.

There were other things that worried him, too. For one, it was even hotter here than in the stairwell. The wind at their backs was like the airflow in a convection oven, and it seemed to be pushing them toward the distant wall of flame. He saw no living creatures but occasionally, when he glanced to his left or right, he glimpsed in his peripheral vision a flutter, like the undulating black wings of a massive bat. When he'd try to look directly at whatever it was, it invariably disappeared, sometimes with the eerie sound of fast-fading laughter.

The other thing Bran found disconcerting was the path they were following. At first he'd thought it was made of white stones that had been exposed by the erosion of many passing footsteps, but several times he saw features in the stones: knobs that looked like the ends of human leg bones, rows of teeth, and the parallel lines of ribs—once, even the little splayed bones of a human hand. After that, he stopped looking at the trail.

If the place they'd wandered into concerned the monster Rick had morphed into, he didn't show it. After his outburst in the stairwell, he seemed to have settled into his new body and this bizarre environment quite nicely. Bran even caught him flexing his iron claw, testing it out, with a look of smug pride on his deformed face.

Bran had no way of marking the passage of time. He didn't wear a watch and, not surprisingly, his cell phone had gone out the minute they passed through the gate. But after what seemed like about two hours, the macabre stone path led them between two hills, and then a crossroads came into view. There was a road sign of ancient black wood with arrows pointing down each of the four roads, like some kind of perverted gothic cartoon. Bran noticed that the squiggles and hieroglyphs on the sign were not remotely close to English. He glanced at Rick to see how he was taking all the weirdness, but he was oblivious. He was holding up his clawed arm and staring at it, fascinated. Ahead, beyond the crossroads, a black river cut a serpentine swath through the empty land, its flow so torpid that it hardly seemed to be moving at all.

Trying to get his head around the whole twisted scene, Bran looked around. The road that stretched off to the left promised nothing but more of what they'd seen so far: another path cutting across a vacant wasteland. To the right, however, the landscape changed. Perhaps twenty yards down the road, there was a big, dilapidated silver gate. Beyond that, Bran saw a vista of rolling hills covered with low plants that had lush leaves of such a dark shade of green they were almost black. Mixed in with them were a series of three-foot-tall flowers, with ghostly white, opalescent petals, their blossoms as wide as a dessert plate. There was a massive chain and a padlock on the gate and above it in wrought iron was one word: MORROW.

"Ho, ho! What have we here?" asked a raspy voice.

Startled, Bran turned at the sound and saw a small-statured man trotting up the side of a ditch. When he topped the ridge, he headed straight for them. His eyes were small and squinty, like the eyes of a mole, and milky with cataracts, and his skin was the color of ash. His misshapen face seemed to be frozen in a distorted grimace of haughty disgust, like he smelled someone's revolting fart. His clothes were filthy, tattered rags, but he wore several necklaces of gold and silver around his neck, and rings sparkled on each hand. He waggled his fingers at the boys as he approached, just as two other little men who looked like they could be his brothers joined him.

"Travelers, travelers! How long since we've seen travelers about these parts!" The man's voice contained, simultaneously, the sounds of a cooing bird and a hissing snake. He moved closer and stared up at Bran and Rick, and his friends sidled up behind him and followed suit.

"Welcome to our crossroads," he said. "I am Steel. These are my friends, Burrow and Begg. We are the guardians here and all who pass must pay us homage."

Rick started laughing, but Bran spoke up before his friend's ego could get them in trouble. "Hey there, buddy. What kind of homage you looking for?" he asked.

"Why, the kind that sparkles or shines or jingles in a coin purse, my friend. A toll."

"Look, you little freak. We're not giving you sh—" Rick began, but Bran interrupted, taking out his wallet.

"Here, twenty bucks," he said, and the small man's eyes widened, but Rick grabbed the money and held it out of his reach.

"Okay," he said. "We'll give you the cash, but first you give us some information. We're looking for someone. Dr. Uphir. You know him?"

The man frowned. "Certainly. He's in the city. Everyone knows that."

"Can you tell us how to get there?"

The man's expression darkened. "That's a long ways away. Across three rivers and the lake. And that money is just paper, with no sparkle or shine to it."

Bran dug into his pockets, trying to think of what else they could offer. "How about this?" He raised his left hand and displayed his new Middleburg High football state championship runner-up ring.

The little man's eyes widened. "And your demon friend's, too?" he said.

"Hey!" Rick said. "Who you calling a demon, you freaking sideshow attraction?"

The man chuckled. "Well, if it looks like a demon and walks like a demon and *quacks* like a demon—I'd say it's a demon! A very rude demon, at that!"

But it's true, Bran thought. That's exactly what Rick was. *A demon.* He didn't know how he knew; he just did. And the strange part was, something told Bran that Rick had been a demon for a while. Maybe always.

"You take us to Uphir and show us how to get back home, you can have my ring and Bran's," Rick said.

"All right." Steel's eyes narrowed shrewdly as he took the rings and examined them. "You got yourself a deal. Right this way," he said, gesturing toward the path that led straight ahead, toward the river.

Bran started after him but Rick held back.

"Wait," he said, and Bran and their guide turned to look at him. "What's that place?" he asked, pointing to the gate with *Morrow* written above it.

"Ah," Steel said with dark glee. "That is the entrance to Asphodel Meadows—the Morrow Estate. Produces the most sublime tea in all of creation, yet they don't sell much these days. Long has it been since the master of the house returned to open the gate."

"Who is the master?" Rick asked.

"Oberon Morrow, of course. I've heard rumblings that he might return one day soon," Steel confided with an evil little giggle. "But there are always rumblings." More quietly, he added, "Some say it will be the master; others that it will be his heir. He's just a half-breed, you know—but one of exceptional power, I've heard."

"Orias," Rick whispered.

It was strange, Bran thought, to hear a whisper coming from the mouth of a creature that looked like it was born to utter only war cries.

Steel looked at Rick, wide-eyed. "Few here know that name, and fewer still dare speak it aloud." He gave another throaty giggle. "The master has forbidden anyone to say it."

Rick shrugged. "Yeah, well I know Oberon and Orias, and I'm not scared of either one of them. Now are you going to take us to Uphir or what?"

Their guide glanced at his two companions, who remained by the roadside. Their eyes were so thick with cataracts that Bran guessed they had to be blind and couldn't go even if they wanted to. Steel spoke to them in an unknown language, in a series of grunts and clipped consonants. They both nodded but remained rooted in place. Steel gave Rick a big fake-looking smile.

"All right, then. Follow me."

As they walked with him down a short rise toward a warped, sagging, rusted steel bridge that spanned a black river, Steel gestured toward it.

"That is the River Lethe," he said with the pleasant inflection of a professional tour guide. "If you're thirsty, this is the last place to get a drink—and it will be a long, hot journey to the Flaming City. Are you thirsty?"

Bran hurried toward the riverbank but Rick hung back, watching. Steel's two companions were still at the top of the rise, gazing down on them, each holding an ancient-looking crossbow.

"You don't have to drink," Steel told Rick as Bran knelt beside the gently flowing river. "But don't complain to me when your tongue swells and your brain is boiling inside your skull."

Bran was already leaning toward the water. He'd never been so thirsty in his life—not at football or baseball practice, not at Spike Ferrington's MMA gym—never. His mouth was painfully dry. His clothes were soaked with sweat and the sharp ache in his head was throbbing in time with his heartbeat. It had to be at least a hundred and twenty degrees, and he'd read articles about kids dying of heatstroke on football practice fields in weather cooler than that. It might be a long journey and he knew if he didn't drink now, he might actually die.

He took a scoop of the black water in his cupped hands and lifted it to his lips. It barely moistened them before Rick rushed to his side, knocking his hands away from his mouth.

"You don't want to drink that," Rick said and his voice came out like a growl. From behind them, Bran could hear Steel and his friends laughing with hysterical glee.

Perhaps Rick was right to be cautious, Bran thought, but his thirst was too much. He licked his lips hungrily and slurped a few drops of water from his moist palms before he could stop himself.

Almost instantly he realized the mistake he'd made, and he experienced a moment of panic as he felt his awareness slipping away. He tried to spit the water out, but it was too late.

Soon, there was nothing but blackness.

CHAPTER 15

WHEN HIS EYES OPENED, THE FIRST THING he saw was a pole above his head, bobbing along parallel to a dark purplish, opalescent sky. After a few moments of mental groping he understood that his hands and feet were bound above the pole and he was hanging down from it like a pig ready for roasting. His vision was blurry, but he blinked and looked around. At every glance, what he saw grew more improbable. To his left, another person was hogtied as he was, except that it wasn't exactly a person. It looked like the love child of one of the beasts from *Where the Wild Things Are* and *Conan the Barbarian*. One of its arms seemed to be made out of some sort of metal. Two very short men held on their shoulders the pole from which this monster hung, and they labored forward under its oppressive weight, grunting and sweating and cursing with every herculean step.

He saw two more little men hauling, with equal effort, the pole he was tied to and he felt his backside dragging against the dark, powdery earth. As they trudged forward, a nightmare menagerie of strange, deformed creatures surrounded them, seeming to watch their passage, and occasionally emitting mocking howls of glee. There were other things, too: fluttering black birds, snarling mangy dogs, and a few dirty, ragged children with pointy teeth that looked as if they'd been filed sharp. There were even a few slowly moving figures that seemed to be animated skeletons.

Beyond the figures he saw arched entryways on a series of decrepit, creepy old buildings, some made of cracking adobe, others of ancient black stone or dark, tarry-looking lumber. Most had sagging roofs of slate or reddish thatch.

He also saw shops and a wheeled vending cart where a fat-faced boy with batlike wings was selling what looked like a kebob of roasted monkey heads. Nearby a couple of tall, filthy buskers with long, greasy hair were playing music. One had a flute that looked like it was made of a cow's horn, and the percussionist beat out a rhythm on what looked a bit like an ivory xylophone. As they drew closer he could see that it was really the bleached bones of a human ribcage. A man with a lizard's face stood beneath a leather tent selling all sorts of twisted, wicked-looking metal weapons, and a hideous old woman with a face like a rotten tomato sat on a stool next to three wooden barrels with taps on their sides. Above her a sign read, simply, *BLOOD*. Beyond all these sights ran a line of one-hundred-foot-high flames that quivered and flickered against the strange, otherworldly sky. The city, it seemed, was surrounded by a great wall of fire.

As bizarre as all this was, none of it disturbed him as much as the fact that he could not remember his own name. He was sure he had one and he thought that it started with a B.

Barney? Blake? Brad? Brice?

He didn't have a clue—and he was fairly certain that wasn't normal. People didn't forget their names. But then, he realized, he didn't remember a lot of things. Where did he live? Who were his parents? And, more importantly, how had he become the prisoner of these foul-smelling little guys?

He wanted to choke one of them until they told him, and he struggled against his bonds. He soon found that the more he struggled, the more they cut into his wrists, so he stopped, deciding instead to let his body go limp until the men reached wherever they were going. Judging from their grunting and groaning, he didn't think they'd make it much further and when they let him down, he'd get free and demand some answers. Until then, he would try to remember his name.

Bill? Brady? Bart?

He must have blacked out again, because the next thing he knew he was sprawled on a cold stone floor with the heavy pole lying on top of him, his head and shoulders aching. A large man with a strange, expressionless face stooped over him and loosed his bonds and then, with one impossibly large, strong hand, grabbed him by the back of his shirt and pulled him to his feet.

The other prisoner, the monster, was also being lifted to his feet—by a *stone statue*. There was no other way to describe it. All of it—its muscular limbs, flowing robes, perfectly masculine face, dead eyes, broad sword, and oval shield—were all the color and texture of gray sandstone. When it had the beast standing, it stepped back and froze in place, motionless like the statue it seemed to be. He looked at the guard that had helped him up. It also stood at attention, frozen like a statue.

He rubbed his wrists and glanced around. The room was a huge round hall with a gigantic dome for a ceiling. The dome was painted midnight blue and lit only by pinprick lights that looked like constellations. It was almost like he was outdoors, camping under the stars. The room was bounded with columns and arches, and the floor was made of obsidian-like stone, so shiny it seemed he was standing on the black liquid of a frozen midnight sea. In the center of the floor was a round firepit bounded with a ring of stone, and in it a blue fire burned, casting the room in an eerie and tenuous light. Despite the almost unbearable heat, the lighting gave the room a feeling of cold emptiness.

Ahead, the three little men were kneeling before a throne, facedown on the ground, prostrate before the creature sitting there.

The being was huge. Its skin was Crayola black, perfectly smooth, and hairless, like a shark's. Black feathered wings arched grandly out of its back, and it wore a glittering black chainmail body suit beneath a cloak of royal purple. One huge, perfectly formed hand drummed on the stone armrest of the throne with long, black, talon-like fingernails.

It was an angel—but not the good kind and he knew, instinctively, that it was evil.

The young man who couldn't remember his name also knew he should be skeptical at the sight of such a creature. He knew he shouldn't believe it could really exist. However, he found upon reflection that he was not surprised at all. Suddenly, one horrifying memory sprang to his mind. Such scary winged men had often populated his childhood dreams—especially the ones he forgot by the time he awakened.

"Rise and explain!" the dark angel bellowed, and the little short guys got quickly to their feet.

"We caught them on the edge of the Territory, my lord," one of them said. "Asking for Uphir."

The winged giant stood, rising to its full height—which had to be nine or ten feet. Slowly, it descended the steps of its throne and approached Bryan or Bob or whoever he was and his malformed companion, looking from one to the other with soulful, brown eyes that were strangely, almost heartbreakingly human.

"Who are you?" it asked, and though it spoke in a low murmur, a shock went through the young man's body, like when a fighter jet passed overhead during an air show. He wondered if he'd ever seen an air show.

"I . . . I don't know," he replied.

The angel's eyes narrowed. "Steel," it said with an air of subdued irritation. "Did you bid them drink of the Lethe?"

A look of contrite terror spread over the short man's face. "No! Oh—no, your glorious, beautiful lordship! He had but a drop, Azaziel—just one small drop, that's all!"

Azaziel moved with incredible speed, reaching out and grabbing the man by the neck. In a few long strides, he was standing above the fire, holding the squirming, squealing man over it.

"What information can I gain from them if you've wiped their minds clean?" he asked calmly.

"We didn't! We didn't—I swear! That one tried to drink but his demon companion prevented him. Only one drop touched his lips, merciful lord. Only one!" Acrid smoke began to rise from the squirming man's feet. "Mercy, mercy my lord, my master! Please!" he shrieked.

Azaziel seemed to consider his request for a moment, then sighed and cast him away. He thudded to the ground and skidded across the floor, finally slamming into one of the columns and coming to rest against it with a groan of pain or relief—or both.

Now, Azaziel turned his attention to the demon. "You stopped him from drinking. Perhaps you have wisdom as well as beauty." He reached out to place one hand on the demon's hideous head, but it shied away. "Do not be afraid—I'll not hurt you. Do you know your name, or have these fools erased your mind?"

"I'm Rick," the demon said. "That's Bran. And I'm pissed!"

Bran fell to his knees, trembling. *Bran!* Yes, that was it! His name was Bran!

"I have no doubt you're angry," Azaziel replied to Rick. "But that is not the information I seek." He reached out again to touch Rick's head.

"Whoa, there," Rick said. "Who the hell are you?" He backed away a little. "Before I give you any information, how about you give me some?"

"Rick," Azaziel said. "You're right to be careful. I can access your mind with but one touch. But," he added distastefully, "it is such a polluted tangle of thoughts, I doubt it can give me the information I seek. Let us try the other."

As the angel approached, Bran fought the urge to cry out or run. It smelled like sour wine and incense, and upon its head there was something that looked like a crown—or a halo—made of swirling, writhing black smoke with tiny, flying creatures swarming inside. They looked like black hornets with eyes that glowed red, like embers. Azaziel seemed even larger and more terrifying up close.

The angel reached for him and Bran closed his eyes. The palm of Azaziel's hand was strangely cool against his skin, and then a sudden, unbearable heat pierced his brain. In that instant all his memories came back, falling in on him all at once, like the crashing debris of a building undergoing demolition.

He grew up in Alabama, lived in Middleburg now. His name was Bran, he was a student, and he played football. And the demon—Rick—was his best friend. They had gone down into Maggie Anderson's basement and somehow ended up here. And it was all because of Orias.

Azaziel's eyes narrowed with shrewd understanding.

"Orias—that filthy half-breed bastard of Oberon," Azaziel sneered. "I might have known." He reached into one of Rick's pockets, pulled out the black leather scroll, and unrolled it. His eyes scanned the page impatiently and then he cast it violently to the ground.

"UPHIR!" he bellowed furiously, his voice so loud that Bran winced and covered his ears.

Instantly, the bluish bonfire sputtered, and a thick swirl of black smoke rose from it. As they all watched, the smoke drifted to the ground and coalesced into the human shape of a stoop-shouldered man with a thin moustache and a pair of goat horns on his forehead. Even when he was fully formed, he looked more like the hologram of a person than a person in the flesh. Bran guessed that this was Uphir, who looked around for a moment, confused—but as soon as he saw Azaziel glaring at him, he fell to the ground as the other men had done.

"Your gloriousness!" Uphir's voice was sickly sweet and his tone fawning. "To what do I owe the honor of this privileged audience?"

"Get up and look at me," Azaziel commanded, and Uphir quickly got to his feet. He stood before the dark angel with his head bowed and his eyes averted.

"Tell me, good doctor," Azaziel said slowly. "I have not seen Orias in eons. Do you have news of him? When last did you see him?"

Uphir blinked and a shudder seemed to run down his spine. "Me?

What makes you think I'd have anything to do with Orias?" he asked with mild indignation. "A *Nephilim*?"

"You didn't answer my question," Azaziel said. "There have been rumblings that Oberon took his abomination back to his bosom. Have you reason to believe that this is true?"

Dr. Uphir hesitated, wringing his hands for a moment. "Sire . . . there are always rumblings," he said.

"Don't think for a moment, doctor, that just because you lack a body I cannot punish you," Azaziel told him. "As Lord Regent of Dark Territory, I have authority to disperse you into oblivion—or worse, to banish you for a thousand years in the Pit, without consulting the tribunal. Do not lie to me again."

The little men who had brought Rick and Bran to Azaziel tittered wickedly, and Uphir glared at them. He finally looked at Azaziel and cleared his throat, yet he still lacked the courage to speak.

"Let me press you further, Uphir," Azaziel said. "You know I sent Oberon, my finest soldier, on a mission to locate the crystal ring. You know also that he has not lived among us for quite some time and that he did not attend the last two meetings of the council. I am aware that he has been seduced by the human way of life, but this is unlike him. A peculiar coincidence was that his disappearance happened at the same time his Nephilim *git* returned to him. Now, I ask you again—what do you know about it?"

Uphir shook his head. "Nothing, my lord! I swear!"

"Indeed," Azaziel said darkly. "My patience wears thin." He held out one huge clawed hand, and the scroll he'd thrown aside now flew out of the shadows to settle in it. He opened it and read aloud:

Uphir,

You remember the affair you helped me with last time you were in Middleburg.

I need your help again. My prisoner is restless and you know as well as I what it will mean for both of us if he escapes. We must put this matter to rest soon, and for good. I know if anyone knows how to do that, it will be you. I implore you, come with all haste, for which I will pay you one hundred times your normal fee.

Orias

Azaziel lowered the scroll and calmly gazed at Uphir. "Last chance," he said.

"All right!" Uphir shrieked. "I was going to tell you. I was on my way here to do exactly that when you summoned me. Orias has imprisoned his father with a spell of his own creation. And now . . . it sounds like he intends to kill him! But I had nothing to do with his terrible plot, my lord—I swear!"

The mighty angel paced, agitated. "Then how did you come by this knowledge?" he demanded.

"Well, I . . . it was . . . that house call I made. You remember, sire. Oberon was injured and he needed me to tend him—and you told me to remind him about the council meeting. I had no idea what his Nephilim abomination was up to, until it was done."

"And you chose not to tell me?" Azaziel asked coldly and held up the scroll. "It sounds like you were in on it. Did it not occur to you that with Oberon trapped, I would get no news of the crystal? You know how long I have wanted to possess it. With its power I can open the Wheel and my army can cross into the Light and vanquish the Exalted Ones at last—then we can wipe out the humans, and the earth will be ours. The last communiqué I had from Oberon informed me that he had located it. And you helped a Nephilim imprison him?"

"No—no! But I can help *you*," Uphir argued with a weak smile. "The boy—the mongrel—he trusts me. I can help you get Oberon back."

"No," Azaziel said. "You are not to be trusted." He reached out one hand, wrapped his shiny black talons around the wispy smoke-neck of the doctor, and lifted him up. Uphir wriggled violently, trying to get free.

"No! Lord! Almighty one! Azaziel, NO!" he screamed, but the angel's countenance, terrible its beauty, was as immobile as those of his stone guards as he crossed the room with the spectral doctor in his grasp. To the left of the throne, a set of massive steel doors swung slowly open. Instantly, the room was filled with a gush of strong wind and searing heat.

"Behold!" Azaziel commanded. "Few are those who look upon the Pit and forget the sight!" He released Uphir, who drifted out over the edge of the balcony, suspended as if by an invisible hand.

The three bounty hunters scrambled along behind Azaziel. Rick and Bran exchanged a glance and followed, too. To Bran's surprise a series of angelic figures emerged from the shadows around them. They were clothed in black robes and had black wings but their skin, not as dark as Azaziel's, was a pale, silvery gray. Some had long raven hair and perfect features, like terrifying china dolls. Others looked like mannequins come to life, their exquisitely chiseled faces expressionless. The shortest of them was over six feet tall. Bran and Rick were swept up in the crowd as the fallen angels filed out onto a broad balcony.

At first Bran thought it looked out over a massive canyon, but on second glance, he decided it was an ocean. The shuffling crowd pushed him closer to the stone railing that bounded the balcony, and Bran understood that it was neither a canyon nor an ocean.

It was more like a black hole.

Below them was a pit that seemed to be miles wide and edged not with earth and stone but with the roiling black wind of a funnel cloud. It was as if someone had dug a huge crater and a tornado had fallen into it. At the center of the swirling hole, so far below that he could hardly make it out, there was a single spot of red, and Bran imagined that it might be the earth's molten core. From the pit there rose an endless wind that bore with it almost impossible heat.

The dark angels crowded around him and Rick, making their way to the edge of the railing, all of them gazing placidly at Dr. Uphir, who hovered above the swirling black pit, struggling harder against whatever invisible hand was holding him.

"Uphir!" Azaziel roared. "You are a betrayer, a purveyor of deceit. Even among the cursed inhabitants of the Dark Territory, you are a cancer that must be cut out. What say you?"

"P-p-please!" Uphir sobbed.

Bran looked at Azaziel's face; it was horrible in its serenity.

"Justice is inescapable," Azaziel pronounced. "Your disobedience will be burned away in the Pit, Uphir. And when you have climbed up that long, long staircase, you will once again be worthy to serve me. If you make it back to the top."

Bran looked over the edge of the balcony. There was indeed a staircase that wound downward in a great spiral, along the edge of the Pit. He wondered how far it was from that tiny red point back up to the top. A hundred miles? A thousand?

"NOOOOOOOOOOOOOOOOO!" Uphir shrieked.

"Yes," Azaziel said quietly, and he lowered his hand.

Uphir plummeted downward into the Pit. After a few moments, his scream was lost in the sound of the wind and his flailing body vanished in the haze and the black, swirling clouds. Wordlessly, the angel congregation turned and went back inside. Bran now saw that there were stone bleachers along the edge of the room, and there the angels seated themselves. Azaziel took his throne and the ugly little bounty hunters arrayed themselves near the foot of it and knelt. The huge, steel doors swung shut again with a deep clunk, and Azaziel turned his gaze on Rick and Bran.

"What to do with the two of you, now . . ." he mused.

"Hey, look," Rick spoke up. "You've heard the saying 'don't shoot the messenger,' right? Orias sent us to deliver the scroll to some guy named Uphir. We had no idea we were going to end up in this place. The truth is, we don't even know what this place is, or what you are. I don't know how you guys decide your justice around here, but I can tell you for certain, we've got no idea what's going on."

"That I can believe," Azaziel said. "The sons of man, as usual, are eager to wrap themselves in ignorance. I'll give you a lesson, boy. Remember it: ignorance is among the worst of sins, especially when you have the means of understanding, yet choose to ignore it. Take yourself, for instance. Do you have any idea what you are? What you truly are?"

Rick considered, then shrugged. "Those little guys called me a demon."

"What do you think?" Azaziel asked.

"I don't know why I look like this, but I'm not a freakin' demon. My dad is a human. My mom is a human. I'm a human," Rick reasoned.

Azaziel laughed bitterly. "Forget your parents; you made yourself what you are. You have embraced the darkness, and now it's overtaking you. You delight in causing pain to others and sowing chaos wherever you go. What do you think it has made you?"

Rick didn't say anything for a moment. Then slowly he said, "I'm a demon?"

"One of the finest I've ever seen," Azaziel assured him. "Now, approach my throne."

As Rick obeyed, Azaziel held out his hand again and the black scroll obediently flew into it. The angel wrapped his talons around it and closed his eyes and a strange purplish glow emanated from his grip. After a moment, he opened his eyes and handed the scroll to Rick.

"Give that message to Orias for me," he said, looking Rick in the eye. "And one more thing . . ." Azaziel leaned forward, cupped his hands, and whispered something into Rick's ear. Rick's eyes glazed over and, for a moment, a pulse of purplish light glowed in them. When he was finished speaking, Azaziel stepped back.

"You understand your task?" he asked. "When Oberon calls to you, you will go to him."

"Yes. I will go to him." Rick's voice was a strange monotone.

"But remember—not until he calls," Azaziel said, and he smiled. "Keep thinking those wonderful, dark thoughts of yours, my boy. Do that, and you'll be quite a useful beastie."

Rick smiled proudly and stuck the small scroll in the back pocket of his jeans. Azaziel waved his hand, and when the massive steel doors swung open once more, Bran couldn't believe what he saw.

This time, they opened not onto a balcony, but onto the foot of a small staircase encased in earth, in a room that looked for all the world like the one in Maggie Anderson's basement.

"Go!" Azaziel commanded.

Bran bounded toward the steps before the angel could change his mind. Rick followed closely behind him. Bran was exhausted and dehydrated and his legs felt like Play-Doh, but there was nothing he wanted more at that moment than to reach the top of those stairs and get out of Maggie's house.

CHAPTER 16

IT WAS FRIDAY EVENING AND WESTON DARLING sat in an oversized chair in the Goheens' family room, gazing at the little tan knees that peeked out from the bottom of Li Shao's skirt. She was crammed next to him in the chair, so close that he could smell her intoxicating floral perfume, and the scent made him almost dizzy with longing. All the Toppers except Zhai were there, watching the Kansas Jayhawks play the North Carolina Tar Heels.

The year they had moved to Middleburg, the Goheens had thrown a basketball party when the Jayhawks played the Tar Heels, and they invited every family they knew in Hilltop Haven. They had done it every year since, and it had become a tradition. Today, while the adults were gathered in the great room and the little kids ran around like maniacs in the basement, the teens had congregated here in the family room, watching the game on a smaller (but still respectably large) TV.

Kansas was down by nine points and the exuberance the party guests had felt at the beginning of the game had dwindled. But D'von Cunningham and his brother had a policy, just to keep things interesting, never to root for the same team and D'von, who had chosen the Tar Heels, was mocking his brother and talking smack, clapping loudly and taunting Cle'von every time his team made a shot.

Weston, however, had little interest in basketball. He'd realized early on that he would never be tall enough to play, and he had no interest in pursuing activities in which he had no future. He'd come to the party because, A) his parents had come, and B) Li was coming, and it was a good opportunity to spend time with her, especially since it was public. He had a conviction that if he spent enough time with her in public, they would become a couple by popular consensus. He used the same principle that if one person claimed they saw Bigfoot or a UFO, nobody would believe them—but if a hundred people said they saw it, it had to be real.

There was a C, too: he hoped to find a piece of the crystal ring. Ever since he'd gotten his commission from Agent Hackett, he'd been eager to make progress on the case, but he'd been so busy with homework and an extra-credit science project that he hadn't had time for sleuthing. Besides, he really had no idea where to look. He couldn't very well break into the houses of kids older and bigger than him and rifle through their dresser drawers.

Finally, he'd realized he had an advantage. They all underestimated him. Ergo, they would never imagine that he'd actually have the nerve to steal from them. Once he had that epiphany, he walked right up to Dax.

"Hey, um, Dax . . . excuse me, but . . ."

Dax's eyes were glued to the game. "Bathroom's down the hall on the left," he said.

Weston cleared his throat. "No. What I was going to ask you was if you have a piece of the crystal ring. From the train tracks. You know—from the night Raphael Kain disappeared."

At this, Dax had looked away from the TV. "Why you wanna know?"

"I . . . well, I'd just like to see it. Everyone's been talking about that night, and the ring and . . . I just want to see it, that's all. I'm just curious."

Dax glanced around to make sure no one else was paying attention to them. "Don't tell Rick or Bran, but I let Zhai borrow mine," he said. "Back when he was still the leader of the Toppers. I mean he still is, technically, but . . . anyway, he has it. You want to see it, ask him."

Dax turned back to the game, and Weston went back to his chair and his spot next to Li, feeling mildly frustrated. She looked at him with a question in her eyes, but before he had a chance to explain her phone rang.

"Hello, Mother," she answered. "Yes, the party is nice."

Her mom, Li had told Weston earlier, hadn't been feeling well, so she and Li's dad had decided to skip the party this year. Weston suspected they weren't really the sports-party-type anyway—a point of view that he sympathized with immensely.

"Yes, Weston is here. He says hello. Kansas is losing. What?" she paused, listening. "Yeah, everybody's here—except I haven't seen Bran yet. Or Rick and Maggie, which is kind of weird." She listened again. "Uh-huh . . . Okay, let me know if you need anything else. Bye." She ended the call and looked at Weston. "No luck with Dax?" she asked quietly.

"He said he gave his shard to your brother," Weston whispered.

"I'll take care of my brother," Li said. She seemed so sweet and delicate, but when she made a declaration like that, it almost gave Weston the shivers—and that made her even more attractive.

"I wonder why Bran isn't here," she said. "His mom told me he's off doing something with Rick. Want to go up and poke around in his room?"

Weston felt a sudden burst of panic. "What if someone catches us?" he whispered.

"Don't worry about that," Li said. "Just follow my lead." And she took his hand, dragged him out of the chair, and led him down the hallway.

"I don't know . . ." he began, but she put her finger to her perfect lips, silencing him, and led him up the stairs and into a long hallway lined with doors, which were all shut. Weston didn't know whether to be relieved or disappointed. There were too many doors, and he didn't know which one opened onto Bran's room. It would take time to try them all, and if they lingered, they would likely be discovered. It was better to go back down and think of another plan.

But Li was already charging forward and pulling him along. She hesitated at the first door and then walked on down the carpeted hall, slowly, like a member of a bridal party walking down the aisle. She passed three doors and stopped at the fourth.

"Here," she said, and reached for the knob. But Weston grabbed her wrist.

"How do you know?" he hissed. "What if it's the wrong room? What if someone's in there!"

She smiled at him gently, as if pitying his ignorance. "He's an athlete," she explained calmly. "His dirty clothes smell like sweat."

She pulled out of his grasp, opened the door, and pulled him inside.

It was clearly Bran's room, Weston thought as the door clicked shut behind them. There were shelves full of trophies, walls full of Alabama Crimson Tide football posters, a dusty stereo, and a frayed wicker clothes hamper. The floor was a minefield of athletic shoes, balls of various kinds, a dog-chewed Frisbee, a cellophane-wrapped case of a drink called Muscle Milk, and a stack of magazines with the *Sports Illustrated* swimsuit issue on top. There was also a desk, a chest of drawers, and a set of accordion doors that, he guessed, concealed a large closet.

"This is going to take forever," he whispered. "We'll never find it in this chaos."

Li took the room in at a glance. She walked directly up to the dresser and opened a wooden box that sat on top of it. That's when Weston heard footsteps in the hallway.

"Do you think he's asleep? He'd never miss the party," A voice was saying.

"He's either napping or he's off with Rick somewhere," another voice said.

"Which one is his room?"

"This one."

Weston gave Li a look of wide-eyed desperation. "What do we do?" he breathed.

The footsteps were at the door and the knob was turning. But Li was perfectly calm. She grabbed the front of Weston's shirt, pushed him down on the messy, unmade bed, fell on top of him, and started kissing him. He almost fainted with shock as she jammed her tongue into his mouth.

The door opened, and Weston glanced over to find Dax, Michael, D'von, and Cle'von all gathered in the doorway. The Cunningham brothers snickered, and Dax and Michael looked stunned, as if they were staring at a pair of ghosts.

Li giggled as if embarrassed, stood up, and smoothed her skirt. "Whoopsie!" she said and scampered out of the room. The guys turned their attention to Weston.

"Nice work, little man!" Michael said with a grin.

D'von started chanting, "Wes, Wes, Wes!"

The other guys picked it up and, trying to act cool, Weston exited the room in a flurry of high-fives, hair mussing, and slaps on the back. He found Li waiting for him at the foot of the stairs.

"What—that was—why did you—?" he stammered, but Li simply held the ring shard up in front of his face. He snatched it and stuck it in his pocket before anyone else could see it. "You . . . you're brilliant," he managed to say.

Her only answer was a cold smile as she took his hand and led him back to the family room.

so

The thing in the dark was coming for them. Bran and Rick had gone up no more than one hundred steps before the massive doors leading to Azaziel's chamber had swung shut, leaving them in darkness. On the way down those crazy stairs some strange ambient light from an unknown source, along with their flashlights, had lit their way, but now the illumination was gone and they had lost their flashlights. They climbed for another ten minutes or so in static, empty blackness before they heard it—the scratch and shuffle of movement beneath them.

Simultaneously, Rick and Bran stopped to listen and it came again—more insistently—followed by the clear echo of heavy footsteps. Whatever it was, it was coming up the stairs toward them. They ran then, pitching headlong into the unseen space above until, with an epic thud, Rick crashed into something. It had to be the door, Bran thought.

Please, God—let it be the door!

He raised his hands to pound on it and opened his mouth to scream for someone—anyone—to come and open it. He was already trying to tell himself that what he'd seen and heard down below had just been part of some bad, weird dream. That's what it had to be—a nightmare—but he was ready to wake up now. He wanted out of the dream and out of the basement. He took a deep breath, forming the name Maggie on his lips when suddenly a broad hand slammed across his mouth.

"Shut up," Rick said. "Don't scream. We don't want to wake Maggie and her mom."

"We've gotta get out of here, Rick—come on!"

"We're getting out," Rick said calmly and something chimed in his pocket. His cell phone powering on. He grabbed it and lifted it to his ear, and in its glow, Bran could see that the monster was gone. He was Rick again.

"See—what did I tell you?" Rick said triumphantly, and he quickly punched in a number.

From somewhere in the darkness, Bran heard a growl. Whatever stalked them from below was coming closer. Bran smelled it, too, and the smell was hard to describe. It had the musky tang of a hog farm mingled with the dizzying reek of turpentine. And it was getting stronger.

"Rick . . ." Bran said uneasily.

"Don't be such a baby," Rick said. "Whatever it is, we'll kick its ass." And then he called down into the abyss below, "You hear that? Bring it on!"

The growling grew louder. It was hard to tell, but it seemed to Bran like it couldn't be more than a few feet away.

"How close are you to Hilltop Haven?" Rick was saying into the phone. "Great—I'm at Maggie's house. We're trapped in the basement.

You gotta come and open the door." He paused to listen and then he chuckled. "You *would* know a window. You're my kinda girl." He hung up and said to Bran, "She's close by—already at the back gate. Five minutes."

It was the longest five minutes of Bran's life as he listened in the dark for the shuffling and that low growl. Exhausted, he sat down on a step and cradled his head in his hands. And heard it again—the scratching, shuffling sound. Rick got out his cell phone again, switched it on, and turned its faint beam down the stairs.

What Bran saw confirmed that he was having a nightmare. It couldn't possibly be real. It was a scorpion the size of a Fiat, with a dark, sleek exoskeleton that was like body armor. But its head, its face, was that of a woman. Only she had the domed, multifaceted eyes of an insect, and where her mouth should have been, there was a set of black pincers that opened and shut continuously, endlessly . . . insatiably.

"Oh my God," Bran whispered, scrambling to his feet. He'd accepted everything he'd seen so far with amazing calm, but now, he was completely overcome with terror. Heedless of Rick's order to stay quiet, he began pounding on the door. "Maggie!" he yelled as loudly as he could. "Mrs. Anderson! Maggie! Help!"

He glanced back once and saw the arachnid slowly climbing the stairs, getting closer. Its strange, carnivorous mouth was only a few feet away from them when somehow it spoke.

"Dead end," it said, its voice buzzing like a bee, and it lurched forward.

Bran was bracing himself for the agony of those pincers tearing into his flesh when the door he was leaning against fell open and he found himself lying on his back in the Anderson's hallway, with Maggie standing over him. She was holding a very big frying pan and had it poised to come right down on his face.

"Bran?" She lowered the frying pan. "What are you doing in my basement?" she demanded—and then she saw Rick. "Never mind," she said. "If he's involved it can't be good."

Rick shoved past Maggie, into the hallway, with Bran right behind. When Maggie saw the giant scorpion on the stairs, she slammed the door—but it was too late. The monster already had its front legs jammed in the doorway.

"Wait—what about Maggie? We have to help her!" Bran protested, but Rick had already grabbed his shirt and started dragging him down the hall. It took Rick only seconds to unlock, unbolt, and unchain the front door.

Bran glanced back to find Maggie retreating as the giant scorpion with the woman's face advanced on her, its pincers chomping and chomping and chomping.

"Run, you idiots!" Maggie shouted at Rick and Bran. She didn't have to ask him twice.

Rick swung the front door open, and he and Bran dashed out into Maggie's front yard, running so fast that Bran crashed into a tall bush and rolled onto the grass on the other side of it. Lying on his back on the Anderson's lawn, seeing how normal everything looked in that beautiful, moonlit front yard, Bran was more positive than ever that it had all been a dream or a delusion, some kind of a waking nightmare.

"Maggie! What's going on?" Mrs. Anderson's voice called from inside the house. "What's all that noise?"

As Maggie slammed the door, Clarisse came around the side of the house.

"Where the hell were you?" Rick asked her. "I thought you were coming in the window."

"I tried," she said. "It wouldn't budge. What happened to you guys?"

"Never mind," Rick said. "You wouldn't believe it anyway."

"You ready to roll?" Clarisse asked.

Bran was more than ready, but suddenly they heard the sound of breaking furniture, shattering glass, and shouting.

"Wait in the car," Rick ordered, tossing her the keys. His car was still parked in the Anderson's driveway, where he'd left it.

"All right," she said with a pretty little pout. "But I'm not waiting all night."

Rick went back to the window and pulled himself up to look in. As scared as Bran was, he was curious, too, so he followed—and he thought he must still be dreaming. What they saw inside Maggie Anderson's house defied all logic. The huge scorpion was standing at the top of the stairs and Maggie's mom was facing off with it—and she was *glowing*. Bran couldn't believe it. Her whole body looked like it was filled with light.

As they watched, the beast slapped Mrs. Anderson with one of its long, slender legs and then struck at her with its deadly tail. Dodging the attack, she held one arm out and pointed at the scorpion, and a beam of light blasted out of her outstretched hand and sliced off two of the scorpion's front legs. They fell to the hardwood floor in a splat of brownish blood, still twitching.

The beast made another lunge at Mrs. Anderson, but she yelled and pointed at it with her other hand, sending another bolt of energy into the monster, knocking it back into the basement and down the stairs. And then she slammed the door and locked it.

Rick dropped from the window, and Bran dropped beside him. "Don't tell anyone about this," Rick said. "This stays between us—you got it?"

"I got it," Bran said, and together they ran to the car. Rick didn't have to tell him to keep his mouth shut about Maggie's basement or her super-hero mom. If he tried to describe it to his parents, they'd be shipping him off to a military school version of Mountain High Academy.

CHAPTER 17

AFTER WATCHING THE BASKETBALL GAME at Bran's, D'von and Cle'von returned home to a dark and empty house. The Tar Heels had won the game, much to the disgust of everyone at the party except D'von. When North Carolina made that last three-pointer, the outcome of the bet he'd made with his brother was clear: Cle'von would have to make D'von a roast-beef sandwich when they got home.

They had made their first sandwich bet on the first day of football tryouts freshman year, when Cle'von had bragged that he was going to beat D'von in the 40-yard dash. Cle'von had gotten the better time, and D'von had reluctantly made the sandwich. At that moment, a tradition was born. So far, Cle'von had won a turkey on rye, three pastrami and swisses, and a deluxe P, B and J. D'von had won two sloppy joes, five Italian subs, and a Thanksgiving Day leftover special with all the fixings—and now, a roast beef, cheddar, and horseradish on Texas toast.

But it wasn't just the sandwich that was important; it was the tradition, with the winner taunting the loser as he made the sandwich. That was part of the fun.

The result was always a lot of laughter, some good-natured cursing, and one amazing sandwich that the winner would eat in front of the loser, consuming it with a series of appreciative groans designed to make the loser feel *really* bad.

Cle'von was gathering the necessary ingredients from the fridge and setting them out on the kitchen counter while D'von ramped up his smack talk. "Come on now, make it snappy. I expect some service up in here."

Cle'von chuckled and shook his head. "I'll give you service..." he said, as he dug around the fridge looking for the Dijon mustard. That's when they heard the sound of breaking glass from upstairs. They exchanged a glance. Their parents had gone out to a movie so whoever was upstairs had to be an intruder.

The brothers moved toward the stairs as quickly and as quietly as they could, with Cle'von pausing at the hall closet long enough to grab a wooden baseball bat. They stopped together at the foot of the steps, exchanging a silent question—sneak attack or charge? Silently, in the intuitive language of twins, they decided to charge, and a moment later they were stomping up the steps, shouting threats at whoever had invaded their home. In the upstairs hallway, however, they each found themselves with a dagger at their throats. The Asian men in the derby hats had been waiting for them. The Cunninghams recognized them from the battle on the tracks—these were the men Zhai had called Obies.

Cle'von hesitated for a second and then, deciding that he was probably dead anyway, swung his bat at the nearest intruder. The man struck the speeding weapon, using the edge of his hand like a blade, and the bat shattered like an icicle on a concrete driveway, the end of it skittering away down the hall.

Cle'von dropped the stump of the shattered bat and raised his hands meekly in surrender; D'von did the same.

"Hey, man. Take whatever you want," said D'von. "My wallet's in my back pocket. I got eighty bucks in there—"

"The ring shards," the taller Obie interrupted. "We searched your rooms. They are not there."

The brothers exchanged a glance once again, and once again came to a wordless agreement. If they fought these guys they would get themselves killed. What did they need those broken pieces of glass for anyway? Neither of them understood why they were so attached to mementos of a night full of fear and pain, a night that had defied their understanding of all they knew as reality. They saw no reason to risk their lives for them.

"No," D'von said. "We been keepin' them with us. Here."

He took his shard out of his pocket and handed it to the nearest Obie, and Cle'von did the same. The men disappeared into the shadows then, so fast that if it weren't for the broken window in Cle'von's room and the shattered baseball bat in the hallway it would have been hard to believe they were ever really there.

&

Orias opened the door to find Rick and Bran standing on the steps, looking exhausted, disheveled, and scared, *and they both stank of fear*. Under other circumstances, he would have slammed the door in their bedraggled faces, but he needed to know how their errand had gone. Even now, he could feel his father's power growing stronger from behind the tower door.

"Tell me what happened," Orias said quickly, ushering them inside and leading them into the parlor. "Well?" he asked Rick. "Did you find Uphir? Is he coming?"

"Um . . ." Rick stalled, and in that moment of hesitation, Orias felt despair rip through him like a gunshot.

"He isn't coming?" Orias demanded. "Why not? What did he say?"

Rick couldn't suppress a low chuckle. "He said, 'please don't throw me in the Pit!'"

Orias glared at him. "Just tell me what happened," he repeated.

"Azaziel," Rick said, and it seemed that any moment he would lose all self-control and burst into hysterical laughter. "He grabbed Uphir and tossed him right in."

"How did you get mixed up with Azaziel?" Orias was having trouble with his own self-control. He wanted to release the full force of his rage on these two ineffectual boys—but then Bran stepped in, and he was a better communicator than Rick.

"See, here's what happened," Bran said. And he told Orias how he and

Rick had been captured by a trio of cutthroats who took them to Azaziel, and how Azaziel had summoned Uphir and then banished him to the Pit. "And he gave us a scroll to bring to you," Bran finished.

Orias held out his hand. "Give it to me and get out."

Bran looked at Rick, who took the scroll out of his back pocket.

Orias grabbed it, broke the seal, and hurriedly unrolled it. He took it over to the fireplace and as he stared down at the words, his human side took over. His heart was pounding and his hands trembling.

Orias,

It has come to my attention that you, with a bold impertinence that defies precedent, have imprisoned your father Oberon, who is also my finest soldier. Worse, you have sought the help of that miserable wretch Doctor Uphir to murder him. Do you think that the law of the Prefects and the rule of the Tribunal do not extend to you? You will find that they do, and that your impudent machinations will not go unpunished. Therefore, I issue you this command and warning with the full authority of my office as the head of the Council of the Seven Prefects:

Release Oberon at once.

If you comply I will consider forgiving your offense. If you fail to comply, however, I shall have you arrested and dragged down to the Dark Territory for trial. You have twenty-four human hours in which to decide.

Azaziel

He crushed the scroll and threw it into the fireplace as hard as he could, and then he turned to face Rick and Bran who started backing away. "What are you still doing here?" he asked harshly.

"Waiting to collect my fee," said Rick.

Taking a roll of money out of his pocket Orias hurriedly peeled off a few bills. "Get out," he said, thrusting them at Rick. When they hesitated too long to do his bidding, he roared, "NOW!"

As the door slammed shut behind them, Orias sank into an easy chair and stared into the fireplace. The scroll was now burning, and a cloud of thick, sparkling purple smoke that looked like a swirling, twilit sky was rising from it. As Orias watched, the smoke then sank to the floor.

"No . . ." Orias said, his voice a hoarse whisper.

The smoke was now slipping down through the cracks in the wood floor, as if a massive vacuum in the basement were sucking it downward.

"NO!" Orias said, falling to his knees as if he would scoop the smoke up in his hands. But it was no use. It slipped downward and disappeared. The message was clear. Azaziel knew he had burned the scroll.

He knows my answer, Orias thought. *And his minions will be coming for me.*

❧

Clarisse and Rick were in the backseat of Rick's Audi SUV, making out. It had taken some convincing from her to get him out here. First, after they'd escaped Maggie Anderson's house, Rick had insisted on leaving her in the car while he delivered some message to Orias. Then they'd had to drop Bran off at home. After that, Rick said he was exhausted and just wanted to go home and sleep. It took only a few heated kisses for Clarisse to convince him otherwise.

They took off in his car and the closer they got to Macomb Lake, the more energized Rick became. When he'd found a good, secluded spot and parked, he leaned close and grabbed her by the hair, and the pain sent a scattering of goose bumps over her skin. Suddenly, his lips were just an inch from hers. His eyelids lowered with desire, and the intoxicated, lust-filled grin she loved spread across his face. He started to pull her close but her phone chimed, alerting her that she had a text.

"Don't answer," he said huskily.

"I should," she said, teasing him.

"Who is it?"

"Why—you jealous?" she asked and then added nonchalantly, "It's just this guy I knew back in L.A."

"Who? What guy?"

"My ex-boyfriend," she said, pouring it on. "He says he's coming to Middleburg."

"Why?"

"To find me and take me back to California—after he kills you."

"The hell he is," Rick said. Fury flared in his eyes.

"He says he's bringing friends, and they're going to kick your ass."

"Let him try it," Rick said, his face going a little red and his knuckles white as he squeezed the steering wheel.

Clarisse smiled and tapped out a text to Oscar S. "That's what I just told him," she said as she hit the *SEND* button.

Rick pulled her into his arms and she reveled in his big, powerful body as he moved against her, his hands tearing at her clothes.

"Yes," she whispered as his fingers, now turning to claws, raked against her bare skin.

Already halfway to being a demon, he pressed her back against the folded-down seat of the SUV, a low growl in his throat as if he would devour her—*really* devour her—and she had never felt so turned on. It was amazing, she thought, how his arousal unleashed a sort of primal, animal lust in him. Part of the thrill was not knowing if he would be able to stop before he really did some damage.

Maggie prowled her house like a restless lion, making a circuit. She checked the basement door, then the other doors and windows on the ground floor of the house to make sure everything was locked, and then she climbed the stairs and checked on her mother, who was in her own bed now, dozing fitfully.

Maggie had watched in awe as her mother had battled the giant scorpion, aware for the first time how truly powerful she was. But it had left her drained, and Maggie had insisted she lie down and get some rest.

She'd dozed off immediately. That was when Maggie began her frenetic circuit: down to the basement door, around the perimeter of the house, and back up the stairs to check on her mother, over and over again.

Logically, she knew that she shouldn't worry so much. Her mother had dealt with the monster that had come out of the basement. But what if there were others? And that wasn't the only thing bothering Maggie. What had Rick been doing down there? Why had Orias wanted to see her mom's tapestries?

In the middle of her fourth circuit around the house, she stopped dead. The uncanny realization that she was acting eerily like her mother hit her with a hurricane-force blast of fear and revulsion.

"No," she said aloud. "That's *not* my destiny. I reject it. I will *not* give my life to guarding that *stupid basement door!*"

CHAPTER 18

THE CLOCK TOWER ON THE TOP OF MIDDLEBURG'S city hall bonged out the hour, and its sonorous clangor seemed to rattle every brick of the large historical structure. But Savana Kain hardly noticed. She was sitting on a toilet in the first floor of the building, wearing a white dress, weeping endlessly, and blowing her nose until it was so red and disgusting she couldn't fix it with makeup, which made her cry harder.

Her dress made her cry harder, too. It was white. Whoever heard of a pregnant ex-stripper with a sixteen-year-old kid wearing, to her second wedding, a color that was supposed to denote purity and innocence? It was like a sick joke—but Jack had insisted on it, so here she was.

"And that's not even the worst part, is it?" she said aloud, cradling her stomach. The child inside her kicked, it seemed, in agreement. Over the last few months, she'd taken to talking to the baby. He—she already knew it was *he*—had become her silent sounding board, her confidant, her understanding best friend. Normally, she would have shared her thoughts with Raphael. He was often harsh with her, but that was probably because he held her to a higher standard than she was able to hold herself. For a moment, she was almost glad he wasn't here to see what she was about to do.

"He wouldn't understand," she crooned to her belly. "I'm doing this for him, for both of you. How else are we going to get out of the Flats? How else am I going to support a baby and a teenage son, never mind coming up with the money for college? And Jack is good to me. He really is . . ."

There was a rap at the door that echoed wildly in the cramped, tiled bathroom.

"Coming!" Savana said brightly, then sniffed violently, yanking a huge wad from the oversized toilet-paper roll, and scrubbing her face with it. She stood and stepped out of the stall, smoothing her absurd white dress as she went. At least, she consoled herself, it was a simple silk sheath with a roomy jacket that almost hid her condition—not some puffy princess gown with a ten-foot train.

She stared at herself in the mirror, her face a miserable wreck of smeared mascara, her eyes swollen from crying.

"You okay?" She could hear the tension in Jack's voice, a seesaw balance with sweet concern on one side and impatience on the other. "Orias just got here—he's with Aimee—and we've decided not to wait for Maggie."

"Yes, fine, honey. I'll be out in a second. Just fixing my makeup," she called as she dug her compact out of her purse.

"Make it snappy, okay? It looks like rain out there."

"Okay, baby. Sure." She was digging into her bag for a makeup removal wipe, when the bag slipped off the edge of the sink. Its contents exploded across the floor like shrapnel from a grenade.

"Dammit . . ." she muttered, stooping with great effort to pick up the items. She could hear Jack outside the bathroom door as he gave a frustrated sigh. Then, his footsteps receded, and she knew he was walking away, across the lobby.

ॐ

Orias waited until Aimee was distracted in her conversation with Dalton before he went to talk to Jack. Fighting resentment that he had to waste time with this wedding when he needed to be putting an escape plan into action, he reached out to shake Jack's hand. "Congratulations," he said.

"Thanks," Jack said. "How'd your trip go? Rick didn't have much to say about it."

"It was fine," Orias said. "Better than expected, in fact. I may be looking to liquidate some of my holdings in the next couple of days."

"Really? Why?"

"I'm relocating—a business deal. An offer I can't refuse."

"Well, I'll be sorry to see you go. I'm sure Aimee will, too."

Jack's phony smile didn't convince Orias of his sincerity. "The herbal drops I gave you," he said. "Did you remember to put them in Aimee's tea?"

"Actually—no," Jack said. "She hasn't needed them. She's been happy and cooperative—more like her old self. Even asked permission to go hang out with her friends the other night instead of just disappearing like she does."

Orias should have known better than to trust him. The stupid man had not given her the Lethe water. At any moment she could remember Raphael Kain—and then Orias would lose her. The realization had a profound effect on him.

He had never loved another creature—not angel or demon, human or Nephilim—as much as he loved Aimee, and he fully intended to take her with him when he fled from Middleburg. More important than anything, even more important than escaping from Azaziel, was that he did not lose Aimee.

❧

Savana looked up from her scattered belongings and saw her reflection in the mirror on the back of the door. She looked sad, miserable . . . and pathetic.

She could almost hear Raphael chastising her. *It's bad enough to deceive everyone around you, including your new husband. It's worse to lie to yourself.*

Then she remembered what Lily Rose had told her. *Ain't no medicine like truth, sugar. Remember that. There aren't too many problems it can't fix, even those that seem unfixable.*

She stared at herself in the mirror for a moment, and before she knew she'd intended to speak, she was shouting.

"JACK!" In the echo chamber of the bathroom, it sounded like someone yelling from inside a tomb. A moment passed and then she heard his footsteps returning.

"What is it?" he asked from the other side of the door.

"Jack," Savana said, her voice tremulous. "I need to talk to you."

"Yeah. You want to come out? You want me to come in?"

"No," she said quickly, then added, "It's bad luck."

The truth was, she was afraid. Afraid she'd look into his eyes and lose her nerve. Afraid of what his reaction would be—and knowing that it would be the end of their relationship.

"Okay, then," he said, annoyed. "So talk."

"I have to tell you something. About the baby," she said.

"Yes?" Jack said slowly, with exaggerated patience.

She took the deepest breath she could. "Jack, the baby is—" she stopped abruptly and winced.

"The baby is *what?*" Jack said, his patience eroding at last.

Savana's mouth was open, but no sound was coming out. Finally, a strangled groan escaped her, and she fell to her knees, holding her belly with both hands.

"The baby is . . . coming," she managed to say.

"Lily Rose!" she heard Jack shout. She heard the door opening, and then everything fell away from her, like the ending of a movie, fading to black.

Moments later, she found herself blinking up at the ceiling, cradled in Lily Rose's arms. Aimee and Dalton were standing in the doorway, watching her with concern.

"Am I . . . is the baby . . . ?" Savana whispered, confused.

"You're fine, and so is the baby," Lily Rose said patiently. "And don't worry—he's not coming quite yet. I'll bet my hat it was just false labor brought on by the stress of the day."

Savana glanced up at Lily Rose's hat. It was a jaunty little lavender number covered with fake flowers—daisies and baby's breath—and it had an organza frill accent. As much as Lily Rose loved her hats, Savana knew, there was no way she would bet one if it wasn't a sure thing. Feeling better, she sat up, but it took a huge effort. It really felt like the baby was doubling in size every day.

She looked up at Lily Rose and the two frightened girls in the doorway. "I'm getting married today," she said softly.

The girls probably thought it was just an affirmation of the obvious, but Savana knew Lily Rose understood what she meant.

"We all got our path to walk, don't we?" Lily Rose said. "Come on, girls, help me get her on her feet and let's get her makeup done."

❧

Ten minutes later, Aimee stood on the courthouse steps, hand in hand with Orias, as her dad and Mrs. Kain faced each other and the justice of the peace started the ceremony.

"We're gathered here today to join Jack Banfield and Savana Kain together as man and wife . . ."

It was a small party. The only people there were herself and Orias, a mildly disgruntled Rick, the Shaos, Dalton, and Lily Rose. Aimee wasn't surprised that Maggie hadn't shown up. She didn't think her former best friend had much interest in Rick anymore.

"I do," said Savana.

But more important than the people who were there, Aimee thought as the justice's voice droned on, were the people who were not there. Emily Banfield and . . . someone else. Someone Aimee had once cared about very much. Since she'd been staying at her dad's, she'd started getting quick little memory flashes of things she used to do with her friends . . . that boy Tyler, who had died . . . and another boy, after Tyler. Someone she had really liked. Her mind grappled for more information during those brief flashes, trying to remember, and just as she almost had it, it faded away. The one recollection that stayed with her now was her burning need to find her mother and bring her home. Somehow, she'd gotten so comfortable in her life with Orias that she had forgotten.

"I do," said her father.

"Do you have the rings?"

Aimee's mind wandered throughout the ceremony, jarred back to reality only by the sound of applause as the justice said, "I now pronounce you man and wife."

And that was it. They were really married. The truth was Aimee had expected something to stop it—some grand catastrophe, maybe, or someone speaking up to object to the proceedings. But no—it was done. She and Orias followed as Jack and Savana descended the courthouse steps, smiling while the Shaos showered them with handfuls of rice. Her dad was shaking Orias's hand and then hugging Rick. Savana was giving out hugs, too, first to Lily Rose, then Dalton, and then scooping Aimee into an awkward embrace.

She watched in bemusement as her father helped her new stepmother down the steps to the waiting white limousine, and then the car took off, on its way to the nicest hotel in Topeka for a mini honeymoon. Jack had promised Savana the real thing in an exotic location after the baby was born. Just like that, they were gone. The whole ceremony had taken less than fifteen minutes.

A fat, cold raindrop plunked down on Aimee's face, then another and another, and suddenly she felt the insistent swell of an encroaching panic attack. With it came the overwhelming need to be someplace else. Before could stop herself, she slipped.

Almost instantly she was standing in front of the perpetually burning fire in Orias's living room hearth. She moved closer and warmed her hands, allowing the heat to evaporate the rain from her skin and her hair. She watched the flames quiver and intertwine for several minutes before she heard Orias come in.

"What the hell was that?" he asked angrily.

"I had to get out of there. I couldn't breathe."

"We've been over this, Aimee," Orias admonished. "You can't slip in front of others—you know the problems it could cause. Lily Rose is pretty savvy, but most humans are not advanced enough to understand your gift."

Her eyes locked onto his, and she felt the sting of tears. She fought to hold them back.

"I know," she said. "But during that farce of a wedding, it hit me."

"What?" His tone was warmer now, less angry.

"Don't get me wrong," she said. "I've loved spending all this time with you. I loved it so much that I forgot about some other things I want to do. I forgot how badly I need to find my mom. All this time—we were supposed to be looking for her. How could I just forget about that?"

"You're not ready," he said.

"Yes, I am."

"Did you remember anything else—staying at your dad's?" he asked quietly.

"Just . . . I don't know. Some disjointed things I can't quite put together. But I remembered the most important thing—I've got to go and get my mom."

"You can't go alone—"

"I'll be fine," she said. "If anything gets too weird, I'll just slip. Anyway, I won't go unprepared. This time I'm taking supplies. A flashlight, for one thing, and—you're going to help me, right?"

Orias put his hands on her shoulders, and she loved the strength she felt in them. "This has to wait, Aimee—just a little while. There are other factors at work now," he said. "I can't stay in Middleburg any longer, not even eighteen-seventy-seven Middleburg. I have to leave—maybe forever—and I want you to come with me."

"Where are you going?" she asked. "Why? What's happened?"

He sighed, a darkness she hadn't seen in a while returning to his eyes. "I've explained to you the relationship—or lack thereof—between Nephilim and the fallen angels?" he said.

"Yes. No love lost. Enemies for centuries and all that. I got it—and?"

"And it seems I've somehow offended a very angry—and very powerful—fallen angel named Azaziel."

"How?"

"Who knows?" he said, shrugging slightly and giving her a little smile. "Maybe I got too rich." He leaned over and lightly pressed his lips to hers. "Or maybe I became too happy. With a Nephilim there doesn't have to be a reason. They despise us."

"But what's the problem?" she asked. "If you can't die, how can he hurt you?"

"He can make the rest of my existence—many thousand more years—a living hell. He wants to arrest me and take me to trial in the Dark Territory."

"Maybe a trial would be good," she ventured. "I mean, if you didn't do anything. Maybe it's an opportunity for us to find out how to save your mortal soul."

"Half soul," he reminded her. "Even if there was a way and Azaziel knew it, he wouldn't tell me. And he doesn't have the authority to grant anyone's redemption. He's a cold, jealous Irin who hates all humans and all Nephilim."

"Why does he hate humans?" she asked.

"Jealousy. Because Irin are banished from the light of the All, and humans are not," he said. "It's that simple."

She thought about that for a moment. "Okay," she said. "All the more reason to go and find my mom. I don't think I ever told you but she studied angels for years—read everything she could get her hands on. She'll know what to do."

"Aimee," he was pleading now. "You have to listen to me. It's wonderful that you want to help me—but Azaziel is coming, and I cannot stay here. Don't you want to be with me, as we planned?"

"Of course I do," she said—and she did. She didn't remember ever being as happy as Orias had made her. "Just call or text me when you get to wherever you're going, and I'll come to you. In the meantime, I'm going back to 1877 Middleburg and bringing my mother home."

"No," he said softly. "You're coming with me." He took her in his arms and kissed her then, and his kiss was full of longing. So full, in fact, that she knew if she didn't get out of there she would give in to him.

෨

And suddenly, Orias was holding only empty air. Aimee was gone.

He uttered a curse and sank into the easy chair to stare again into the dancing flames in his fireplace. He had to find her—but it would have to wait until after he had arranged his departure. And he would have to go soon. It wasn't death that frightened him. It was the kind of judgment Azaziel would pass on him.

Azaziel could add eons to his Nephilim curse. He could torture and mutilate Orias, make him so repulsive that no one would want to look at him, so that he would go through all those lifetimes completely and utterly alone. He could throw Orias into the Pit and keep him there indefinitely while Aimee grew old—and then release him on the eve of her death.

Orias knew he had to take evasive action. He had to stay a few steps ahead of Azaziel, to escape and hide until the Lord of the Prefects moved on to other business and forgot about him for a while.

There was only one thing he could do. An explosion would distract anyone who might be looking for him as he made his getaway. It had worked for him before, a couple of times. Orias had everything he needed to make the bomb—he'd been gathering it for a while, just in case, and he knew how to build it. It wouldn't kill Oberon, Azaziel or their minions, but if he was lucky it might slow them down a little and give him the precious time he needed to escape.

After he had placed it and set the timer, he would find Aimee and convince her to come away with him.

෨

On Saturday morning, Agent Hackett lounged in a chair inside his room at the Solomon Motel on the outskirts of Middleburg, chewing on a plastic coffee stirring stick—a bad habit he'd picked up since he quit smoking. The remains of a fast-food lunch were scattered on the bed and his feet were propped up there too, atop a luridly colored duvet made from some kind of stiff synthetic fabric. Judge Judy was on TV, berating some young kid for failing to pay his child support. Hackett chuckled. No one could eviscerate people like ol' Judy.

His phone chirped then, and he was still grinning when he answered it. It took him a second or two to recognize the voice on the other end—it was the Darling kid.

"Weston. I thought you'd fallen off the face of the earth. What have you got for me?"

What he had, he said, was a piece of the ring. Finally.

"Good work," Hackett said. "Sit tight. I'll send a car for you."

He rallied his team, and on the way to the police station, he felt more energized than he had in days. When he was first assigned this mission, the prospect of bringing in a high-level target like Feng Xu had him salivating, and the particulars of the case were interesting. Hell—Feng Xu wasn't just high level, he was almost legendary in the counterespionage field.

Mounting his head in my trophy room, Hackett had thought, *will make my career.* He would be able to write a ticket to whatever cushy, high-level job he wanted. But as the Middleburg mission wore on, he grew increasingly frustrated. He'd kept the recon team on point—they had half the town wired up for surveillance by now—but the surveillance had turned up nothing. He had some ideas for flushing Feng Xu out of hiding, but every time he called his superior in Washington, his orders were the same.

Be patient. Sit tight and wait. Let the target make the first move. Well, Hackett was getting sick of waiting. There was only so much fast food and daytime TV a man could endure.

Today, however, all that had changed. The Darling kid had finally turned something up. And he learned when he got to the station, there had been another development.

"Agent Hackett, you need to see this," the desk officer on duty said as he handed Hackett a file.

"Thanks, Johnny." Hackett scanned the documents inside and then looked up at the officer. "Anyone check this out?"

"I did," Johnny said. "There wasn't much to see except a broken window, but look at the description of the perps—two Asian men with black hats and daggers."

Hackett was already nodding,

"And the only thing missing was the ring shards. These are our guys," Johnny finished.

Hackett gave the report back to Johnny. "Make copies of this for everyone on the team. Is there any surveillance footage for that area for the time frame?"

"Already looking into it, sir," Johnny assured him.

"Good. The snake has slithered out of his hole. It's time to find it."

That's when Weston Darling entered, with his cute little Chinese girlfriend at his side. Hackett glared at Li, then at Weston.

"This is how you keep a mission secret? You bring your girlfriend along?" he demanded.

"But I never would have gotten the shard without her help," Weston protested.

Hackett cursed and grumbled for a moment before finally letting the matter drop. The younger Darling would never be half the man his father was, but that wasn't Hackett's concern. All that mattered was the glistening piece of crystal the boy was now pulling out of his pants pocket.

Hackett put a thick rubber glove on before examining the ring fragment. If it generated as much power as everyone claimed, there was no way in hell he was going to touch it bare-handed. God only knew what kind of radiation might be coming off the thing.

When he was finished he called in his science officer, Rom Blipton, who placed it in a lead-lined box and walked away with it.

"Where's he taking it?" Weston asked.

"We've got a mobile lab set up out back," Hackett said dismissively. "Come on, let's sit down over here. I want to go over this list with you one more time."

He led the kids into a back room and sat down with them. He took a document out of the file and handed it to Weston. "This is the list you gave me—of people who might have a piece of that crystal ring."

"Yeah?" Weston said.

"Take another look. Is there anyone else you can get to? To try to find pieces?"

Weston scanned the list. "I don't think so," he said. "We got lucky with this one. We just happened to be in the right place at the right time. We don't have many opportunities to go wandering around in other people's houses, you know."

"I guess that's true." A plan was fast taking shape in Hackett's mind, and he wanted to make sure he had his facts straight before he took any action. If the Order of the Black Snake was planning to go around breaking into houses and collecting ring shards, he might be able to work it so that they would play right into his hands.

The plan was simple: Hackett and his men would collect the ring shards from all the kids who lived in the Flats. If they resisted, his men would ransack their homes until they found what they were looking for. That was one of the perks of being a Black-Ops agent—normal rules didn't apply. Once Hackett had all the shards from the Flats kids, the Snakes' only option would be to get the rest from the kids in Hilltop

Haven—and that was where Hackett would catch them. It was gated, guarded, and already outfitted with a top-of-the-line video surveillance system, and he'd already found a vacant house where he could set up his command center. The minute the Snakes set foot in Hilltop Haven, he'd clamp down on them like a bear trap. All he had to do was catch one of their foot soldiers. Hackett was confident he could make him spill his guts about where Feng Xu was hiding. That was another perk of being off the books. He didn't have to worry about pesky things like human rights violations. And torture was a tactic that Agent Hackett rather enjoyed.

"Thanks, Weston. We appreciate your help," Hackett said. He shook the boy's hand and then looked at the lovely young girl there with him. "And you too, miss. Thanks."

Hackett reached for the girl's delicate hand, but she was momentarily distracted, glancing out the back window of the station, where Blipton was standing on the steps of the mobile lab, talking on his cell phone.

It was only for an instant, though, and then the girl's sharp eyes flicked back to Hackett. She took his hand and squeezed it and her strength surprised him.

"I'm Li, nice to meet you," she said and smiled.

ℴ

Saturday morning Zhai was in the basement of the Shao house. He had just run through some attack sequences on his *Mook Jong* in preparation for his battle with Rick that night and had finished his cool down. Now he was anxious to get to his violin. Master Chin would have advised him to spend the day of a fight in silent, relaxed meditation—or better yet, trying to find a way to avert the battle. He missed his sifu's wise counsel, and as the appointed time of the confrontation drew nearer, Zhai felt increasingly nervous. It wasn't his own abilities that worried him. He was confident that he could, if not defeat Rick outright, at least survive the fight and teach his former second-in-command a lesson in humility. He wasn't worried that his honor or his body would receive injury today. He was concerned that the feeling with which Shen was filling him—a jittery, buzzing sensation of uncontainable electricity—meant what it did when he'd felt it before: major events would soon come to pass in Middleburg. Last time he'd felt this way, his *sidai* Raphael had disappeared. Zhai wondered if tonight it might be his turn.

There was another possibility, too. What if Rick didn't show? He and Bran had been suspended from school for the last three days, and no one had seen them outside of school, either. But Rick never missed an opportunity for a fight. Zhai was sure that, wherever he was, he would make it back in time for their face-off.

He picked up his violin, took a few deep, relaxing breaths and began to play, eager to lose himself in the music. He'd only managed a few bars when his father entered.

"I'm sorry to interrupt, Zhai," he said, and Zhai noticed that he was more subdued than ever. "I heard you playing. Would you be so kind as to honor a request? *Brahms concerto in D major?*"

Zhai eyed his father warily. "It's such a sad piece. Are you sure?"

"If you please."

"Of course, Father."

He began, the bow slithering across the strings as smoothly as a feather moving across a tabletop. It was a gentle, serene melody, and Zhai felt his apprehension, his anger, and his nervousness drifting away on the wings of the glorious, soaring strains.

When he was finished, he let the violin slip from beneath his chin. His father was smiling warmly at him, and in the simplicity of his happiness, he almost seemed childlike. The sight gave Zhai pause. He'd never once seen his father shrug off the black mantle of tension and rectitude he wrapped himself in day and night. Now, he seemed utterly fallible, flawed, human, and Zhai wondered if the fact that he knew about the tattoo over his father's heart, and hence his mortality, had made the revelation possible.

"Lovely," his father pronounced. "Such a sweet, calming piece. Thank you. It was just what I needed."

Zhai smiled. "I'm glad, Father." He started putting the instrument away.

"And . . . I have another request," his father said. "Li wants to go down to Macomb Lake this afternoon, to meet with some friends from school. Something about selecting a site for the spring break party. Bob is driving Lotus today. Will you take her?"

"Sure," Zhai said. "But I can't stay too long. I have plans later."

"Ah . . . Kate?" his father asked. The inflection of his words betrayed interest, but his face remained passive.

"No," Zhai said truthfully. "With Rick."

His father nodded. "Well, I'll tell Li you'll take her." He turned to leave but paused in the doorway and turned back. "It has come to my attention that there are people staying in the guesthouse. Some of your friends, I believe."

Zhai felt as if all the air had been sucked out of his lungs. He'd known it was only a matter of time before his father and Lotus found out.

"Yes," Zhai said, facing his father squarely, a hint of accusation in his tone. "They were thrown out of their home by Jack Banfield's redevelopment project. They have nowhere to go."

Cheung nodded slowly. "You have your mother's heart," he said. "A giving heart. Still, that guesthouse belongs to me, Zhai, and to Lotus. It is not yours to give. You should have asked me first. Lotus will not be pleased."

Zhai sighed heavily. "Yes, sir."

"So—please do not tell her," his father finished, and Zhai saw the hint of a smile.

Zhai gaped at him. "They can stay?"

"For a while," Cheung Shao said, and he left the room.

∽

When Aimee had slipped out of Orias's grasp, she'd teleported to the top of the tunnel mountain, to a spot that overlooked the town. It was peaceful up there, and beautiful. The storm that had blown through during the wedding had dissipated as fast as it had come, sweeping the sky clear except for a few crisp, fast-moving clouds set against a pale-blue firmament. She sat there for a while, collecting her thoughts and making a plan.

Orias was right, of course. She shouldn't go slipping in and out of public places just because she could or because it was easier than asking for a ride or dealing with a situation. All that would do was complicate her life. He was right about something else, too. She shouldn't go after her mother alone, but she couldn't ask him to go with her again, either—he would just try to talk her out of it. Her dad was on his honeymoon and, like Rick, he would be no help anyway. She didn't want a confrontation with her brother so she decided against going home.

She didn't need much—just a couple of bottles of water, a flashlight, matches, and some food, and she could get all that from Dalton. And she knew that she should tell someone—a grownup, like Lily Rose—where she was going. She had one shard from the crystal ring, and she thought Dalton would give her the one she carried. And maybe, just maybe, those two pieces, combined with her ability, would be enough to get the Wheel of Illusion working again, so she could teleport back to Middleburg in 1877.

Before the ring had shattered, the Wheel had taken her—and *someone*—to other realms, other times. As she made her way to Lily Rose's house, she tried to remember who it was.

Dalton answered the door and led her into the living room where Lily Rose, Maggie, and Miss Pembrook were waiting—like they were having a meeting or something, Aimee thought.

"What's going on?" she asked.

"Well," Dalton began. "We were just—"

"Praying for you," Lily Rose finished, a serene smile wrinkling her features. "So good to see you here, my dear. And it's good to see you walking on the two good legs God gave you."

Aimee glanced from one face to the other. "What do you mean?"

Dalton hesitated and then confessed. "We were sort of talking about you, Aimee. We've been worried about you. You've been kind of out of it since you hooked up with Orias."

"And there's that little matter of how you just up and disappeared from the courthouse today," Lily Rose put in. "We decided to get together and try to figure it out."

"So this is some kind of intervention?" Aimee asked.

"I guess you could call it that," said Lily Rose. Dalton and Miss Pembrook nodded in agreement. "So . . . what's been going on, little girl?"

Aimee was confused—and touched—by their concern. "I don't know," she said. "Okay—I guess I have been spending a lot of time with Orias and not enough with my friends." She knew they all thought him cold and unapproachable. How could she make them understand that he was a kind, loving, patient guy who had helped her more than all the shrinks at Mountain High Academy? "Orias is good for me," she said, louder than she'd intended. "All he's done is care for me when no one else has."

"We all care about you," Miss Pembrook said gently.

Aimee had a sudden feeling of panic, like the world would collapse around her at any moment. Lily Rose moved quickly to her side and put one age-gnarled hand on her arm.

"Sit a spell with us, child, and have some of my lemonade."

Looking into the old woman's two different colored eyes, Aimee saw in them what she was longing for: peace. But she still felt afraid—not for herself, but for Orias. What if something happened to him when she wasn't there to help him? What if he couldn't get away from Azaziel?

Not that she could protect a mighty Nephilim from the wrath of an even mightier fallen angel, of course, but she still felt a need to be with him. It hit her suddenly and hard that she could lose him, and it felt like a thorn lodged deep in her lungs, pricking her with every breath.

She couldn't lose him.

She wanted to pull away, to slip back to Orias, into his arms, his house, his bed. But Lily Rose's hand was on her arm like an anchor, gently tethering her to the earth. Those kind bright eyes were still upon her.

"Orias can take care of himself, Aimee," she said calmly. "It's time for you to go find your mama. And you know what? I betcha we can find a way."

Lily Rose led her into the kitchen and sat her down at the table. Dalton and the others followed. Aimee was so moved by the love surrounding her that she couldn't speak, and her vision was blurred by tears. When she blinked them away, she saw a glass of lemonade sitting in front of her, the white, flowered pattern on it bristling with water droplets.

The fear, sadness, and loss she felt threatened to dislodge her, to break her tenuous grip on time and space. In the beginning, it had been hard to slip. Now, it was almost too easy—and she could escape any situation, any fear, any moment of sadness with a single twist of her thoughts. She almost did it now, almost slipped out of Lily Rose's kitchen, but when she wrapped her hand around the cool glass, it seemed to hold her in place. And when she took that first sip of lemonade, it was like a blast of sunlight shining into the darkened recesses of her brain, chasing the shadows away.

"It's fresh-squeezed," Lily Rose said. "Grew the lemons myself in a tree out back. You drink deep now, my dear."

And Aimee did.

CHAPTER 19

IT WAS THE FIRST REALLY NICE DAY THEY'D HAD in weeks, now that the rain had cleared up. The temperature was climbing toward sixty and Zhai was standing at the edge of the inky-dark waters of Macomb Lake, holding Kate's hand. It had been a tradition among Middleburg High students to congregate on this sad little patch of beach on the first nice day of the year for as long as anyone could remember. Of course, not everyone was there since the "first nice day" was a pretty subjective thing.

Li, Weston, and Li's friend Amanda sat on the end of an ancient, rickety dock that jutted out into the reed-choked water. A few kids were sitting on blankets and looking out at the water while others walked along the shoreline, trying to skip stones on the lake's surface. Zhai glanced down at Kate, and she smiled at him and moved closer. He put his arm around her, and she snuggled against him.

"'Tis a beautiful spot they've chosen for the party," Kate said.

Zhai nodded. "Yeah," he agreed.

"You're worried," Kate observed. "About your fight with Rick, is it?"

Zhai shrugged. "Not . . . worried exactly," he hedged. "Okay, maybe I'm a little worried. Josh wants to fight Rick, too. And the way Rick has been acting lately, I'm afraid someone might get killed."

Kate gazed at the water pensively. It shone with little glints, like bright light reflecting off a diamond set in black onyx. "So why fight?" she asked.

"Because, if I don't, he'll be the leader of the Toppers. And then the feud with the Flatliners will never end. Plus, we'll never get enough of the ring shards together to bring Raphael back."

A piercing scream made them look around. Some of the kids had found the knotted old rope that was attached to a massive willow tree that rose from one edge of the lake and they were taking turns swinging on it, out over the water and back again.

As Zhai watched, Li's friend Amanda flew out over the water in a high arc before swinging gracefully back to shore. Li would be next.

"You want to try it?" Kate asked. "It looks like fun."

Zhai looked at her. "And what if I fell in? The water is freezing!"

"But you only live once!" Kate laughed and tugged at his hand, leading him toward the tree.

"That's not what the Buddhists think . . ."

"Sometimes, we should dive in first and think about the water later," she said. "Otherwise, what is life but an endless bit of drudgery?" Zhai's eyes locked on Kate's and the magnetism between them was so strong he couldn't look away. She leaned closer to him. "It's easy," she whispered. "You take the rope, you hold on tight, and you just go."

As she pronounced this last word, her lips brushed against his. A shiver of desire rustled through Zhai and he closed his eyes, ready for her kiss, but a shout from Weston broke the spell.

"Be careful, Li!"

Li was standing next to the tree holding the rope. "Watch this!" she yelled.

She backed all the way up the grassy incline that sloped uphill next to the tree, and Zhai saw what she was going to do. If she got a running start, she could launch herself from there and gain more thrust, which would take her farther out over the water than any of them had gone. From the dock below Amanda was cheering her on, while Weston looked worried. She gave them a big smile.

"Woooo!" she yelled.

She raced downward toward the dark, glistening water, gripping the rope as she swung out over it, speeding through the air in a broad arc. Just as she reached the apex of her swing, there was a loud cracking sound, and the huge branch above her—the branch the rope was tied to—broke off the tree and fell. Li hit the water first, landing flat on her back with a huge splash and a loud *smack*. Then the two-foot thick bough hit the water, on top of her.

Zhai was already leaving Kate behind, sprinting across the beach and down the dock, shoving past Weston and Amanda, and diving into the water.

The chill hit him instantly, causing all his muscles to convulse at once in a massive spasm. He felt his heart pounding. As he thrashed his way to the spot where Li had gone in, his limbs ached with the cold. There was an uncomfortable tingling sensation, as if they were about to go numb.

Still, Li had not surfaced.

At last he reached the spot where she'd disappeared. Ripples still radiated out from where the branch had hit. His only consolation came when his feet found the mucky, sucking bottom waiting for him about five feet down—at least the water wasn't too deep. He took a huge gulp of air and went under, and the rushing white noise of the water in his ears swallowed up the shouts of alarm from the shore.

He opened his eyes but could see nothing at all through the thick, drifting silt, so he closed them again, relying on his sense of touch as he groped around the muddy lake bottom for any trace of his sister. He found the smooth surface of the dead willow limb, and moved along its length, groping in the blackness for any sign of Li. There was none.

Out of air, he returned to the surface, took a huge breath, and then shot back to the bottom again. This time, he felt his sister's small, smooth leg almost immediately. His fingers traced blindly up it, to her arm. He yanked, pulling her toward the surface, but she didn't move. She was stuck, pinned somehow. His hands traced up her arm now, to her shoulder and down to her back. Thrashing wildly, she almost knocked out one of his teeth before he could find the problem. The sleeve of her sweater was caught on one of the branches of the willow bough that was jammed into the muck. Quickly, he pulled her out of the sweater and an instant later he broke the surface, hauling his gasping, thrashing sister up with him.

Everyone on the beach cheered as Zhai and Li swam over to the dock and pulled themselves up onto the warped wooden planks. Then they both flopped down on their backs, gasping up at the sapphire spring sky.

Kate was at Zhai's side, throwing a blanket around his shoulders, and Weston was with Li. Everyone else gathered around, too. They were all talking excitedly, but between his own heartbeat pounding in his ears, the shock of the cold water, and the oxygen deprivation, Zhai had trouble picking out one person's words from another's. Finally, he sat up and tilted his head to get the water out of his ears. Kate had also found a blanket for Li and was about to put it around her.

"Wait," he said, and everyone went quiet. Under her sweater, Li had worn a pink cotton tank top and beneath the right strap Zhai spotted a dark discoloration on her skin. He came up on his knees and pulled the strap aside. It was a tattoo—of a Chinese symbol.

"What are you doing?" she demanded, squirming out of his grasp.

"What is that?" he asked.

"What is *what*?"

"The tattoo, on your back?"

Li's eyes met his, and there was an instant of hesitation where he could see the wheels of thought turning in her mind. There were several thoughts moving through his, too.

Could the Snakes have somehow captured his sister and marked her, just as they'd marked him to enslave him, and as they'd marked his father so many years before? The possibility filled him with a chill much worse than Macomb Lake's icy waters. But it couldn't be—Li hadn't disappeared, as he had. She hadn't been acting strangely at all.

The second thought was that if Li had gone out and gotten a tattoo, Lotus was going to kill her, then him for not looking after her.

"Your mom is gonna be so pissed," he said, and she erupted in merry girlish laughter.

"You should see the look on your face, brother mine. You're as white as a ghost!" she teased. "Relax, it's just henna! It'll be gone in a couple of days."

ℴ

"Hey, guys?" Josh rattled his keys then yanked them free from the lock in his apartment door (they always stuck in the crappy old lock). "Anyone home?"

Outside, the afternoon sun was beginning to wane, and the living room was strewn with thickening shadows. As he went through he turned on a floor lamp to ward them off. Clearly, his family wasn't at home. They'd mentioned earlier that they might head down to the Starlite to check out the latest superhero movie.

Josh had run home on his break from bagging groceries at Ban-Waggon supermarket to snag his wallet. Normally, he would have just grabbed a cheap, prepackaged sandwich at the market and hung out in the cramped little break room, eating, zoning out, and staring at the time clock until he had to go back to work. When he realized he'd forgotten his cash, he asked the manager if he could hook him up with a sandwich, promising to pay for it at the start of his next shift. But the manager wasn't having it, so Josh had been forced to jog all the way back to the Flats from downtown, and as soon as he found his wallet he'd have to jog all the way back. His white polo shirt embroidered with the Ban-Waggon logo was already pitted-out with sweat. The whole thing irritated him, but he was starving. There was no way he could finish his shift on an empty stomach.

He was in his room now, which he shared with his little brother, Beau. LEGO blocks, Nerf swords, plastic G.I. Joe vehicles, half-transformed Transformers, and stuffed animals of every color and variety littered the floor. Josh tended to think the kid was a bit spoiled, but he couldn't hold Beau's stockpile of playthings against him. Half of them were Josh's hand-me-downs and most of the rest came from Goodwill and garage sales.

The wallet wasn't on the bedside table where he expected it to be, nor was it sitting on the top bunk of the bed he shared with his brother—the spot he called his penthouse.

Finally, he found it in the top drawer of his dresser, grabbed it, and stuck it in his pocket. With a sigh, he glanced at his watch. It was almost five. At this rate, even if he ran all the way, he'd be late getting back and he wouldn't have time to eat—which was completely unacceptable. He was fighting Rick tonight, and he knew it would be the battle of his life. There was no way he could go into it on an empty stomach. He needed to carb up, build up some energy. Maybe there was a piece of cold pizza in the fridge he could gnaw on while he jogged, he thought. But before he got to the kitchen, he stopped. He heard something in the living room. Footsteps, low voices, then a crash.

It took only a moment to realize the voices didn't belong to his parents. He glanced around the room looking for a weapon and settled on a hockey stick standing in the corner next to the bed. He was creeping back toward the door when a series of rapid footsteps came toward him. The door burst open and he found the barrel of a pistol in his face. A man in a black, long-sleeved shirt bulked up with a bulletproof vest was holding a gun on him. Two men dressed the same way were right behind him.

"Drop it," the guy barked at him.

Josh retreated until his back was against the bunk beds, but he continued holding the hockey stick out in front of him.

"You deaf? I said drop it," his captor said. This time, Josh processed the request and let the stick fall from his hands.

The man lowered his gun but watched him closely as his companions ransacked the room.

"What . . . what's going on?" Josh asked. "Are you guys here from

Banfield Real Estate? 'Cause we didn't get an eviction notice yet." He added defiantly, "And even if we did, we aren't going anywhere."

The man with the gun snorted. "Do I look like I'm in real estate?" he asked.

He didn't. He looked more like a Navy Seal who'd gone over to the Dark Side. But that wasn't what concerned Josh now. They were tearing his room apart!

One of the guys yanked every piece of clothing from his closet, checked the pockets, then chucked them on the ground. Another guy was jerking out his dresser drawers and dumping the contents onto the rug.

"Stop it!" Josh yelled. "What the hell do you want?"

The guy with the gun moved closer. "You're Josh, right? You were there when Raphael Kain disappeared? Don't bother denying it—we know you were there. We're looking for pieces of the crystal ring that shattered during the event. Any chance you have one?"

Josh hesitated. Certainly, he had a piece of the ring. And the truth was, he didn't care if these guys took it or not. What use did he have for it? Raphael was gone, Emory was barely alive and the Flatliners were drifting apart. What was the use of hanging on to a piece of broken glass? And yet he did want to hang on to it. For some reason he couldn't explain even to himself, he couldn't imagine parting with it. More than that, with every object these guys tossed onto the floor and every piece of furniture they overturned, his anger grew. Maybe they weren't from Banfield Real Estate or Shao Construction, but they were part of the same corrupt system. They thought they could come in here and push Josh around and steal from him because he was a poor kid from the Flats. *Well to hell with that,* he thought. They could tear the place apart. They could torture him, but he wasn't going to tell them where the shard was. Nothing could make him tell.

From the other room there came a bang and the sound of broken glass.

"You better not be breaking my mom's stuff in there!" he shouted.

"Just calm down," the man with the pistol said. He put it away, but he was just as intimidating without it. Josh thought he was six-feet-two at least, and he had arms like a pair of fire hoses. When Josh tried to slip past him again, the man pushed him back on the bed and held him down, twisting one of his arms behind his back—hard—and sending a jab of hot pain through his wrist.

There was a *screek* of springs, and Josh saw the top bunk bow above him. A second later a voice came from up there.

"Got it."

Before Josh knew what was happening, he'd been released and all three men were heading for the door—and he knew they had his piece of the ring. He'd been keeping it under his pillow, inside his pillowcase. Now, it was gone.

Two seconds later, he heard the front door of the apartment slam. There was a clatter of booted steps on the stairs, then silence. Josh wandered through the wreckage of his bedroom, then his parents' room, then the living room, all the while clenching and unclenching his hand. His wrist still ached, but the pain was going away fast, and he was pretty sure that the guy, whoever he was, hadn't done any permanent damage. The apartment, however, was demolished. His mother was going to go ballistic when she saw the carnage, he thought, and the vision of her spending hours cleaning up what those guys had wrecked in only minutes made him feel sad and a little empty.

And that reminded him that he was hungry and his break was pretty much over. He looked at his watch. He should have clocked in two minutes ago. If he didn't get back there soon, he'd lose his job.

He didn't know why—he didn't even know he'd been planning it—but he walked into his parents' bedroom, went into their closet, and took a small cardboard box off the top shelf. Inside, wrapped in an old T-shirt, was his father's small revolver. He stared at the gun, feeling its cold, dead weight in his hands, and almost put it back in the box. Why take a gun?

He didn't want to kill anyone. But suppose the men who broke into the apartment decided they didn't want any witnesses and came back to kill him? Was he supposed to just let them do it? What about Rick? Was Josh just supposed to roll over and let Rick beat him into a coma, like he'd done to Emory? The answer that came within him was a primal shout of triumph: *No—I will not go down without a fight.*

But he wouldn't use the gun, he amended. Not unless he had to. He put the empty box back on the shelf, grabbed a backpack from his bedroom, and zipped the revolver into one of its pockets. Then he rushed out the door, slammed it, and hurried down the stairs.

He ran all the way back to the supermarket, all the way back to the break room, where he shoved his backpack into his locker and clocked back in. The manager was there, talking to the head stocker, and he tapped his watch and shook his head at Josh as he came out of the break room.

"Josh, you're late."

"I know. I'm sorry. I was just—"

"I don't care. Just get out front and start bagging," the manager said and went back to his conversation with the stocker.

Clenching his teeth together, wiping sweat from his brow with one sleeve, Josh walked to the front of the store and finished his shift on an empty stomach.

☙

Nass was in the middle of his Saturday evening shift delivering pizza for Little Geno's when his cell phone beeped. It was a message from Beet. His dad had been in the process of closing the body shop for the evening when some men with guns had shown up and demanded to see where Emory's family was staying. They had ransacked the garage that was the Van Buren family's makeshift home, found Emory's piece of the ring, climbed back into their black SUVs and left without another word. From the descriptions, they seemed to be the same government agents who had interrogated Nass on Valentine's Day.

He should have collected those other ring shards sooner, Nass realized, but Zhai hadn't finished collecting the pieces from his crew yet, and it didn't seem appropriate to ask Emory's family if they could go through his stuff while he was in the hospital in a coma. Now the chances of restoring the ring and getting Raphael back seemed more remote than ever.

"What should we do?" Beet asked when Nass called him back.

Nass cursed under his breath. "It's all right, man. We'll figure something out." But he had no idea what he was going to do or how it was going to work out. He wondered if the ring shards Beet and the others had entrusted to him were still safe at home, where he'd hidden them.

"When do you get off?" Beet asked. "Benji and I were going to head down to Rack 'Em to have a good dinner and gear up for the fight."

"Couple of hours," Nass said. "I'll meet you guys there." He ended the call and glanced at the clock on the cracked, discolored dash of the car—his father's old beat-up Honda Civic.

He'd just completed a delivery out in the country north of town, and the place had been hard to find. By the time he got back to Geno's, there would probably be five pizzas waiting to go out. But he was about to pass the entrance to Hilltop Haven, and there was no way he could just breeze by without checking on the shards he'd put together so far. He was pretty sure Clarisse or his parents would have given him a heads up if a pack of government thugs came by and robbed them, but it would make him feel better to know they were safe. And, he decided, he should keep the shards with him, hide them in the car someplace. If the agents found out where Nass and his family were staying, it would be easy for them to show up and do a search. But if the pieces were in the car, at least they'd be dealing with a moving target.

He waved to Mike the security guard, who buzzed the gate open and nodded at him as he passed, and Nass thought about how different it was before, when he'd first come to town, when the Haven security viewed him and his buddies as public-enemy number one. All it had taken was a few words from Zhai, and they treated him as well as their wealthy residents.

His tires screeched slightly as he shot around a curve and came to a stop next to the back of the Shao property. He jogged to the metal walking gate, entered the five-digit security code, and went inside. Footlights glowed dimly among the new landscaping, which had just been planted, a harbinger of spring.

He was a little breathless when he entered the house, but he didn't find the scene of chaos he had feared. His parents sat in front of the TV with a bowl of popcorn between them, looking surprised to see him.

"'Nacio, what are you doing home?" his mom asked. "I thought you didn't get off until ten?"

"No, I just came home because . . . I have to check on something. In my room," he said awkwardly, then shot past them, headed toward the hall that led to the bedrooms. The hall light was on, as was his bedroom light, which was odd. His father was pretty militant about wasting electricity.

He was about to step into his room when he found himself face to face with Lotus Shao, and for a moment, the thick floral scent of her perfume made him a little light-headed. The jade-colored eyes she leveled at him were arrestingly beautiful.

The sight of her gave Nass a jolt. *Ah, crap,* he thought. Zhai had told him they could stay only until his stepmother found out they were there, that she didn't want anyone living in her guesthouse. Nass had not relayed that information to his parents who would have refused to stay under those conditions. Now what the heck were they going to do?

Lotus gazed at Nass now, eerily calm. "Excuse me," she said evenly. She was holding a thick book and she had a fancy purse slung over her shoulder.

"Oh. Sorry, excuse me," Nass said, and stepped aside to let her pass. He held his breath, waiting for her to lambast him and his family for being there.

But she didn't say anything. She just made a quick exit. Nass watched her go and then he hurried into his room. He went straight to the vase that sat on the bookshelf and tipped it upside down so that the shards hidden inside would fall into his outstretched hand. They didn't.

"Mrs. Shao just wanted to grab one of her books on flower arranging," Amelia Torrez said from the doorway. "She was very nice."

Nass stared at his empty palm, his heart pounding.

"Mom, I had something hidden in this vase. Some, like, pieces of crystal. Have you seen them?"

His mom shook her head.

"Did anyone come in here today? Men in black outfits. Men from the government?"

His mother frowned. "'Nacio, I've told you about staying up late and watching those violent movies. This is what happens. You get paranoid. Video games, too. Everything is a conspiracy!"

Nass sighed heavily and set the vase back on the shelf.

"No one came in here today?" he asked. "When you got back from the store it didn't look like anyone had torn the place apart searching for stuff or anything?"

"No," Amelia said, looking at him like he was a little bit nuts.

Nass groaned and glanced at the alarm clock.

"I gotta get back, or Geno is gonna rip me a new one," he said, and he planted a kiss on his mother's cheek as he hurried out the door.

∽

Lily Rose took a few minutes to check on Master Chin while Maggie called Kate on the new cell phone Zhai had given her and asked if she could come over. Ten minutes later she showed up, her nose a little pink with sunburn. She told them what had happened to Li out at the lake, and that Zhai would be over as soon as he'd dropped her off at home.

Aimee held fast to her lemonade glass the whole time, until Lily Rose came back into the kitchen.

"How does Chin look?" Dalton asked her grandma.

"The same," Lily Rose said. She explained to Aimee that Master Chin had been wounded in a fight, with a poison-tipped weapon. "I've done everything I know to do and he's not getting any better." She smiled mysteriously. "But I think that's about to change."

"What do you mean?" Aimee asked.

"First things first," said Lily Rose. "Let's get down to business. You want to go and find your mama. Isn't that right?"

"I know where she is," Aimee said. "I've just got to go and get her."

Lily Rose looked at all the women gathered around her table. "The time has come for us to speak openly," she said. "I think by now everyone here has witnessed some of Middleburg's peculiarities firsthand so let's not waste time pretending that magic is impossible. Middleburg is an unusual place, and we're all unusual women. Here, with us, nothing is impossible and nothing is foolish so none of us should be afraid the rest of us won't believe what we have to say. We *will* believe. Agreed?"

They all nodded.

"Aimee, have you ever seen the tapestries Maggie's mother has been working on?" asked Lily Rose.

"No—I mean, maybe—a couple of years ago."

"Well, I've seen 'em all," said Lily Rose. "They're all about Middleburg's history. The images in them depict our town's past—and its future. I'm here to tell you that they are no ordinary tapestries. And Aimee—you're in them." She paused and looked at the others. "You're all in them, in one way or another. The tapestries suggest that Aimee has some rather special powers that will be useful in reaching her mother. Do you?" she asked Aimee.

Aimee hesitated. Her gaze drifted to Maggie Anderson. Her former best friend had snubbed her when she'd returned to Middleburg from boarding school, and it had almost broken Aimee's heart. But Maggie was different now—she was a lot nicer. Even Dalton, who had once hated her, was now treating Maggie like a friend, but Aimee still wasn't sure she could trust her.

She stared down at the tabletop in front of her, unsure what to say, and was surprised when Maggie spoke first.

"I can see auras," Maggie said, looking at Aimee. "And I can move objects with my mind—for real. Sometimes I can even create this crazy pink fire. And the wall that collapsed at the homecoming dance—it was an accident, but it was me. And that's not all. The basement door in my house leads to hell. My mom guards it with magic—that's her job. She can't leave it unattended for long. That's why she never goes anywhere—not because she's crazy."

There was a brief silence as the girls all took in Maggie's revelations.

"I've been healing folks' bodies with my hands since I was a girl," Lily Rose said warmly. "And healing their souls with words. My garden grows in all seasons. And I got a few other tricks up my sleeve, too."

"I can put people into trances—or put them right to sleep—when I sing," Dalton said sadly, as if it hurt her to admit it. "It's only one song. It's from Grandma's *Good Book*, and I don't know how it works. I'm not even sure I want to sing it, but I can." Once her confession was out, she smiled and she looked relieved.

Anne Pembrook, who sat next to Aimee, put a gentle hand on her arm. "I don't have any abilities like theirs, Aimee," she said. "But I was entrusted with some information that brought me to Middleburg this year and made me part of this whole thing—whatever it is. And I've seen enough since I came to this town that I promise I'll believe anything you say to me. And whatever you say, your secret is safe with me. We're all sisters here."

"Aye, we're all sisters," Kate agreed. Aimee wondered what abilities she might have, but Kate said no more.

Aimee cleared her throat and hesitated for another moment before she said, "I can slip." She spoke so quietly she could hardly hear herself. No one responded, so she said it again. "I can slip. Through space. You know, teleporting or whatever."

Maggie frowned. "You mean like . . .?"

"Like this," Aimee said. She let go of the room she was in and allowed herself to fall into Dalton's bedroom. There was hardly any sensation, just a slight twitch, like the feeling someone got if they were nodding off in class and suddenly jerked awake. She walked out of Dalton's room and back into the kitchen. There was a moment of silence as she sat back down, and then Lily Rose's laughter rang out heartily.

"That was beautiful, child," she said. "Only I don't think your daddy's gonna like it. It's hard to control something that won't stay put."

"Maybe. But I'm not sure it's developed enough for me to go back in time and get my mom," Aimee said.

"Back in time?" Kate asked.

"Yeah. She's in Middleburg in 1877." Aimee looked at Lily Rose. "What do you think? Is there any way I can do it?"

Lily Rose pursed her lips, pondering the question. "I don't know much about your particular brand of magic, Aimee," she said. "But I know of a book that might." She got up, went to her bedroom, and came back with a large black leather-bound volume. Aimee remembered seeing her with it before, when she was just a little girl and Lily Rose had come to babysit her. Now she set the book in front of Aimee and opened it.

Aimee looked down at the page and was surprised to find that it was blank. Or not blank exactly—it wasn't merely an empty piece of paper. It was a three-dimensional, swirling world of drifting white, like a billowing cumulus cloud.

"It's beautiful," she whispered.

"Open your mind, and let the words come," Lily Rose advised.

Aimee did, going into the same meditative state that someone, not so long ago, had taught her to achieve. After a moment, words began to form on the page.

All time is one in the mind of the All
If space is North, South, East and West
Then time is rise or fall
Its gravity pulls us to all our tomorrows
But to climb against gravity requires some power

Aimee read the passage aloud and then looked around the table. "What do you think it means?" she asked.

"Power," Dalton said. "Maybe you need all the pieces of the ring. The guys are thinking they need it to get Raphael back, too."

At the name—Raphael—something tugged at Aimee's heart. He was the boy they said she'd gone to the dance with, but she couldn't remember him clearly. And she didn't have time to worry about it. She'd figure it out after she got to her mom.

"The pieces of the ring are scattered all over," she said. "I have one and I know Dalton has one—"

"And I have one," put in Miss Pembrook.

"Okay, so that's three," said Aimee. "How are we going to gather the rest of them up?"

"I don't know—yet," said Lily Rose. "It may be that you don't need all of them to get where you got to go. While we're trying to figure it out, I think there's one good service you might be able to perform that would greatly benefit someone very special. Are you able to take things with you when you—what did you call it? Slip? Besides your clothes, I mean?"

Aimee nodded. "Yes. I've taken Orias. And the ring. I'm the one who got it out of its underground vault. What else? I brought some luggage along when we went to Paris. Just a couple of small suitcases."

Lily Rose was smiling.

"That will do just fine," she said. "Why don't you ladies come with me? We're going to watch Miss Aimee perform a miracle."

CHAPTER 20

IT WAS ALMOST NINE THIRTY WHEN NASS walked into Rack 'Em Billiards Hall. Out of habit, he looked around the place, expecting to see Raphael wiping down tables or hauling buckets of ice behind the bar. When he remembered his friend wasn't there, the realization left him feeling even more bereft than he had a moment before. The crowd was sparser than usual, and Nass guessed that the evictions and layoffs that had been plaguing the Flats didn't leave the residents any extra cash to spend on eating out.

He found his friends back near the pinball machine at what had become the Flatliners table. Josh was still wearing his polo shirt from the Ban-Waggon. There was a mostly empty plate in front of him, populated only by a few straggling fries. He stared into the dark liquid in the mug in front of him—probably root beer, Nass guessed—as if it were a crystal ball that held the solution to all the Flatliner's problems, and he'd be able to see it if he could just stare hard enough. Beet and Benji sat across from him with a deck of cards playing *Speed*.

None of them noticed Nass until he'd sat down heavily next to Josh. Beet and Benji looked at him, and Benji began gathering up the cards.

"Why you guys look so depressed?" Nass asked. "I mean, other than the fact that one of us Davids is going to have to take on Goliath tonight?" As he said the words he got an image of Rick as he had looked during their last fight, in the snowstorm, viciously beating down everyone who tried to get in his way—except Raphael.

"Should I tell him, or do you want to?" Beet asked Josh. Josh shrugged.

"The government guys got Josh's ring shard, too." Beet said.

Nass swore and pounded his fist on the table, rattling the metal basket full of condiments that sat on it. "They got mine, too—and I can't figure out how they did it. The shards were there this morning—I checked. And my mom was home all day, but when I went to check on them a little while ago, they were gone."

"So how are we going to get Raph back now?" Benji asked. "Snagging them from the Toppers was going to be bad enough—we'll never get the shards back from those government guys."

No one said anything for a moment. Benji had voiced the question they were all thinking, Nass knew, and none of them had an answer.

"Well," Nass said with a sigh. "There's nothing we can do about it now. We have to get Josh ready for his duel with Rick tonight. We all have to be ready. If the rest of the Toppers jump in, we'll all be fighting."

Everyone nodded, somber, and Nass felt his hope slipping away. There was no way any of them could win a fight against Rick with morale this low.

There was a beeping sound. It was Josh's phone. He dug it out of his pocket and answered it. Then there was a pause as he listened to the caller, and Nass saw the color drain from his face.

"Okay. I'm with the guys. We're coming now," he said, ending the call. He looked around at his friends. "It's Emory," he told them. "We have to get to the hospital, now."

☙

The girls and Miss Pembrook followed as Lily Rose led Aimee to the edge of Master Chin's bed. The sight of him lying there gave Aimee a shiver of fear. Lily Rose had said he was ill, but she hadn't been prepared for this. He was so gaunt—much thinner than she remembered. His skin was sallow, his mouth gaped open, his breathing was labored and his hands were twisted into rigid claws as if his muscles, contorted in pain, had frozen in that position. He looked like a man who was dying, Aimee thought. She didn't know what Lily Rose wanted her to do, but she was certain she couldn't do it. All she could do was move things from place to place.

Before she could protest, Lily Rose gently squeezed her hand. "Mister Chin has had a rough time," she said, her voice sympathetic. "The poison of the Black Snake is far more persistent than anything I've ever seen. That's what's killing him. A very potent poison, running through his veins. Using my compresses, I've managed to draw it out of his brain and his kidneys—enough to keep him alive, anyway. But he's losing the battle. Unless we get the poison out of him, Aimee, Chin is going to die."

And then Aimee understood. "That's what you want me to do, isn't it? You want me to slip and take the poison with me?"

Lily Rose smiled, her strange eyes almost glowing in the lamplight. "I think it'll work, Aimee, but you have to be careful," Lily Rose warned. "You must visualize the poison and make sure you take only that. It's a sickly, deep green color. When you place your hands on him, you will feel its presence. You can also smell it on his skin; it's in his sweat and on his breath. Focus in on that, and move only the poison. Because if you accidentally take the blood that it's mingled with, he won't make it."

Aimee looked again at Chin's gaunt, rigid form. She was scared, and suddenly wished that Orias was there with her. He'd be able to tell her if what Lily Rose suggested was possible or not; he would be able to tell her how to do it. He would even hold her hand as she tried, bolstering her fear with his unwavering confidence. She had never imagined she would have the ability to save a person's life. What would it feel like, she wondered, to have that kind of power? She thought it was way too much responsibility.

But there was no way she would let Master Chin die if there was any chance she could save him.

"Okay," she said. "I'll try."

Aimee went to Master Chin's bedside, forcing herself to breathe very slowly through her nose until her heart quit pounding and she felt calm. To her surprise, as she neared him, Chin started mumbling.

"Yut, yee, sarm," he said in a dry, throaty whisper. "Say, ng, look, chut."

He was counting, she realized—and then she knew. All those times, standing in front of the mirror and practicing her kung fu moves, those words had come into her head and she'd repeated them. Somehow, it had been Chin all along, teaching her, coaching her, encouraging her. For some reason, the knowledge gave her courage.

She bent over him and let her hands hover above his body for a moment. Then, she closed her eyes and inhaled, taking in the putrid stink of the venom rising through his pores. Finally, her hands drifted down, settling on either side of his neck. She could feel his labored pulse beating within his carotid artery as the blood flowed through it, and within that blood, she imagined she could feel the yellow-green line of the poison tracing through his body, sickening it and strangling it cell by cell. She felt the poison, each drop of it, each molecule, each atom . . . and she slipped.

She didn't go far. When she opened her eyes, she was standing only three feet away from Chin's bed—but that wasn't the extraordinary part. Extending from her hands was what looked like the framework of a man, made entirely of strings or wires of dark greenish-yellow and they were arranged in the exact shape of his sleeping, contorted form. It was a liquid map of his system of blood vessels that was so exquisite in its detail that it looked like an extraordinary work of art. The others gasped, and Aimee's breath caught in her chest. Then, in a fraction of an instant, the liquid sculpture collapsed, falling with a faint spat, leaving a foul-smelling, man-shaped mess on the hardwood floor of Lily Rose's guest bedroom.

"I'll get a mop and bucket," Dalton said softly, her voice filled with quiet wonder.

The rest of them just stared, looking from Aimee to the puddle of poison she'd slipped out of Master Chin's body, and back to Aimee again.

"Wow, Aimee," Maggie said. "That was awesome."

Lily Rose went to Master Chin and passed her hand over his forehead—and his eyes snapped open.

He sat up quickly, like he'd only meant to rest his eyes for a moment and now thought he'd overslept. He looked up at Lily Rose.

"Hello, Chin," she said.

Chin lifted his hand and absently touched his neck. The two wounds Feng Xu's strike had inflicted were now scabbed over. Color was already flooding back into his cheeks and the yellowish tinge had disappeared from his complexion.

"Aimee removed the poison from your body," Lily Rose continued. "You've been asleep for a while. How do you feel?"

A slow smile spread across Chin's face. "I feel . . . hungry."

∽

The Beetmobile jittered into a parking space outside the Benton Hospital, and the crew got out and headed for the front doors. Even though it was dark out it was surprisingly warm, and the air hung still around them. Above, a handful of stars stood out against the night sky.

I can relate to those stars, Nass thought as he wove his way through the maze of parked cars. He, too, felt like a lone glimmer of light about to be swallowed up in a sea of chaotic blackness.

It wasn't the knowing that told him this—it was more mundane than that, and he'd felt it ever since Josh had gotten the phone call. *It's Emory. We have to get to the hospital, now.*

The memory stoked the urgency already burning in his chest, and Nass redoubled his pace. A moment later, he and the rest of the Flatliners were inside the hospital. There was an old man ahead of them at the information desk where they were supposed to check in, but Josh blew past him and hurried toward a set of double doors at the far end of the lobby. Beet and Benji exchanged a glance with Nass, and they all stepped out of line and followed Josh, ignoring the protests from the help-desk lady.

Josh went through the double doors and then down a long hallway, and on into the intensive-care unit beyond. He had been to visit Emory the most, so he knew the way through the confusing network of hallways, doorways, and elevators. At last, he led them through a final set of double doors and into the ICU, past workstations populated by nurses in bright-colored scrubs who scowled at them as they hurried past. They finally arrived at Emory's hospital room and they all stopped running at once, their shoes squeaking against the tiled floor. They stared, bewildered, around the room.

The bed was empty.

From somewhere down the hall there was a piercing scream, and Josh spun around and shoved his way past Beet. Again, Nass and the others gave chase. They didn't have to run far. There was a waiting area on one end of the ICU, outside a set of doors with a sign above it that said *SURGERY*.

A tall doctor wearing a hairnet, with a surgical mask still dangling from his neck, was standing with Emory's parents, and Mrs. Van Buren was sobbing quietly. Myka was there, holding on to Emory's sister Haylee, who had her face buried against Myka's stomach. She was screaming, and Myka was trying to comfort her.

The knowing was not with Nass now. All he experienced in that moment was a vast emptiness that felt like the wind sweeping across a frigid, silent landscape. Then, he and the rest of the Flatliners were walking forward, going to Emory's family, although he hadn't even realized they'd begun to move.

"A nurse will be in soon with some paperwork," the doctor said to Emory's dad. "I'm sorry for your loss." And he turned and walked away.

Mr. Van Buren turned to Nass and the crew, his eyes red-rimmed and vacant. "Thanks, guys," he said. "Thanks for making the drive. Emory would have appreciated it."

"Mr. Van Buren—what?" Josh was shaking and his voice was trembling. He couldn't go on.

Nass glanced at little Haylee, whose life he had once saved. She was sitting quietly now, holding a stuffed rabbit while Myka whispered gently to her and stroked her hair. He looked at Emory's mom, who was clutching her husband's shirt so hard that it was beginning to rip at the shoulder as she continued to sob. Finally, his gaze returned to Emory's dad, whose face was as expressionless as that of a carved Egyptian pharaoh.

Nass put a steadying hand on Josh's shoulder and stepped forward. "Mr. Van Buren, what's going on?" he asked, forcing himself to stay calm.

Mr. Van Buren finally looked at Nass and their eyes locked.

"He's gone," he said. "They tried, but—Emory's gone." His voice broke then, and he turned to his wife for comfort.

∽

Another Saturday night, Clarisse thought, and she was parked with Rick out at the lake. She was getting pretty sick and tired of going with him to secluded areas where no one would see them—and as soon as her deal with Oscar S. was settled she was going to let Rick know that she wouldn't stand for being his secret fling anymore. It wouldn't be much longer, she thought, as Rick kissed her again, and she couldn't wait to see Oscar's reaction when her football jock turned into something worse than an animal and beat him up. Once that low-life drug dealer saw what Rick was capable of, she was sure he'd hightail it back to Los Angeles and never bother her again. She'd had a text from Oscar the night before last telling her that he was on his way, and then another one tonight, just before she met Rick in the alley behind the Starlite Cinema.

She'd texted him back, saying that he could meet her at Macomb Lake—he could Google it for directions—and that her new boyfriend would take care of her debt to him.

At that moment a pair of headlights pierced the tinted windows of Rick's car and his head snapped up. Their caresses were just getting steamy, and he was starting to change into that otherworldly thing that got her really turned on. Now his wild red eyes stared out at the intrud-

∽ 275 ∾

ers with the look of a hungry wolf whose meal had been interrupted. She recognized Oscar in the driver's seat. He parked his tricked-out Escalade and left the motor running as he got out. Four car doors slammed as three other men got out with him.

"Clarisse, come out," he called. "You better have my money, you crazy bitch, or you're going to be real sorry I drove all the way out here!"

Clarisse felt a twin shock of fear and anticipation. So far, her plan was working perfectly. Right on time, here he was: Oscar Salazar, her sadistic, drug-dealing boyfriend from South Central. But Oscar was smart and she knew how his mind worked. He was hanging back, close to his car, until he could make out who was with her.

She looked up at Rick, thrilled to see that he was still transforming into her beastie boy, and he was clearly taking the bait. With a snarl, he opened the door of the SUV, but she grabbed his arm.

"Wait," she said. "Let me go first. I'll get him to come closer. Can you handle them all?"

Rick laughed. "What do you think?"

She gave him a quick kiss and reached over and turned on the Audi's headlights before she got out on the passenger side. "Calm down, Oscar," she said. "Don't worry—I'm gonna take care of it. Come on over."

"Who you got with you?" he asked.

"Just my new boyfriend," she said. "Better be careful. He's a football player, and he's pretty big and pretty mean."

"You think I'm worried about some punk-ass high school *gabacho*? Where's my money?"

"Oh, come on, papi," she cajoled. "Be nice. Come and say hello to Rick. He's rich. He's going to take care of it for me." She turned and signaled to Rick, and he got out of the car. The look on Oscar's face when he moved into the headlights was everything Clarisse had expected—and more.

Oscar's three thugs were all sporting gang tats, baggy jeans, and side-

cocked baseball hats, and they were holding Louisville sluggers and trying to look tough. But the moment they saw the crouching monstrosity
Rick had become their eyes grew huge with childlike terror.

"*Ay dios mio,*" one of them said. He looked like he wanted to run, but
he seemed frozen to the spot where he was standing. "Oscar—what the
hell is that, man?" he asked, backing away.

Only Oscar stood his ground, raising his baseball bat as Rick
approached. "Stay cool, Manny," he said "Don't be stupid. It's just some
kind of leftover Halloween costume—"

At that instant, the Rick thing sprang at Manny. He didn't even get a
chance to swing his bat before Rick had ripped out his throat with gnashing, razor-like teeth. Oscar's other two soldiers squealed like little girls
and tried to run, but Rick pounced on them with the grace and power of
a lion after prey, tackling them both at once. In a matter of seconds, he'd
torn them apart.

Filled with bloodlust he raised his head, sniffing the air, and the
ring of glistening gore that surrounded his mouth looked like the red of
a clown's makeup. He took a few quick steps in Oscar's direction, and
Oscar reared back with his bat and swung it at him as hard as he could.
Rick blocked it with his iron arm, and it splintered at the impact. Rick
then picked him up by the throat and beat him against a tree until he was
as limp as a rag doll.

Trembling, Clarisse stared at Rick in horror, not quite believing what
had just happened. A crazy adrenaline rush shot through her veins, and
she moved toward Rick slowly, cautiously, as if she were approaching a
dangerous animal in the wild. When he saw her, the feral look in his eyes
softened. "You like that?" he asked.

"Oh . . . yes. Thank you, baby," she said. "You helped me more than
you know tonight, *corazon*. No one has ever done something like that for
me."

But it shook her to the core. The first time she'd seen him morph into a monster, she'd had a weird thought that they would become some kind of power couple, like that *Beauty and the Beast* fairy tale, but now she knew that could never happen. She was terrified of him, but she knew better than to let him see that.

"Okay," she said. "We gotta clean this up—somehow. Maybe we could push them—what's left of them—into the lake."

Rick nodded and with a low growl, he grabbed Manny and one of the other guys and started dragging them toward the water. While he was busy with that, Clarisse ran to Oscar's body and searched through his pockets until she found the wad of cash she knew he always carried. She grabbed it, jumped into his car, and took off.

As soon as she got to the main highway, she pulled over for a minute and typed *Greyhound Bus Station, Topeka, KS,* into her phone's navigator, and then she drove away as fast as she could. She didn't stop until she got to Topeka. A few blocks from Greyhound, she ditched the car, after wiping her fingerprints off the steering wheel, gear shift, and door handles.

She was aware of the strange looks people gave her as she bought her ticket—one way—to L.A. But she paid no attention. All she cared about was getting as far away from Middleburg—and Rick—as she could. What she'd seen that night would haunt her for the rest of her life, and it would affect her deeply—body, mind, and soul. It wouldn't be until several hours later, however, when she went into the bathroom in Denver where she had to change buses, that she glanced in the mirror over the sink and saw that her hair had turned completely white.

❧

While Lily Rose made a big pot of spaghetti and a sauce with the tomatoes from her garden, Kate called Zhai and gave him the good news about Master Chin.

Lily Rose asked Aimee and Maggie to go and set the table. The two girls worked silently, a little shy with each other, and Aimee realized that this was their first moment alone together since she'd come back to Middleburg from boarding school, when Maggie had been so cruel to her.

"Aimee . . ." Maggie began, and then hesitated for so long Aimee thought she wasn't going to speak at all, before she plunged ahead. "I'm sorry. I wasn't a very good friend to you when you got back from Montana. The truth is, I was afraid. Everyone said you went crazy, and I felt like I was on the edge of going crazy myself, taking care of my mom and trying to live up to some stupid image. I felt like I was hanging on by a thread and I was afraid that thread would snap. I was afraid of you. But we were friends once, weren't we?"

"Best friends," Aimee agreed. "I thought we always would be."

"I haven't been a very good friend, though," Maggie said. "Even when I saw you falling for Orias I didn't say anything, and that was wrong because he's dangerous."

"He isn't dangerous," Aimee told her. "You just don't know him like I do. But yeah—it really sucked when I came back from boarding school and it seemed like you hated me."

"I don't hate you."

"I don't hate you either," Aimee said and smiled. Her smile turned into a soft chuckle, and her chuckle turned into a loud laugh.

"What?" Maggie said.

"I just remembered the way you looked with that homecoming crown on your head—after you yelled and the wall came tumbling down," Aimee said. "It was priceless!"

Maggie started laughing, too, and soon they were hugging. They were friends again.

As they ate, Lily Rose advised Aimee to wait until morning to start on her journey.

"I can't," Aimee said. "I've already lost too much time, and I have this feeling inside me that I have to go now."

"Then that's just what you ought to do," the old woman agreed. "Now tell me—what do you need from us?"

Aimee explained that she didn't want to venture back into the past without a couple of modern conveniences—like a flashlight, bottled water, some matches, and her cell phone. Maybe some bread and cheese, in case it took a while for her to get to her mom. Aside from that, she needed all the shards of the ring that she could get her hands on.

"And then I'm going into the tunnel," she finished. "If I can get to the Wheel of Illusion with a few pieces of the ring, it might generate just enough power, combined with my ability, to get me back to the right year—1877."

"It might," said Lily Rose. She looked pointedly at Dalton, and then at Maggie and added, "But I don't like to think of you going alone."

"She's not going alone," Maggie said. "I'm going with her." She looked at Dalton. "You in?"

"I'm in," said Dalton. She looked at her grandmother. "Is that okay, Grandma?"

"It's more than okay," said Lily Rose. "It was meant to be."

Zhai arrived as they were finishing dessert—Lily Rose's homemade apple pie—and he was overjoyed to see Master Chin sitting on Lily Rose's old couch, one of her handmade quilts around his shoulders. When he embraced his kung fu teacher, he seemed moved almost to tears. Aimee had never seen him get so emotional about anything and somehow it gave her a feeling of hope.

"I should go with them," Chin said.

"Over my dead body," Lily Rose told him. "You need rest—and these girls are more than capable. And this is a task best left to women." She turned to their history teacher. "What about you, Miss Pembrook?"

Miss Pembrook grinned. "I wouldn't miss it," she said. "But . . . you really think you can get us back to 1877, Aimee? I mean—yeah, I've seen some weird things since I've been here—but time travel?"

"Oh, aye—'tis possible," said Kate, who had been uncharacteristically quiet. She dabbed at her mouth with the paper towel Lily Rose had provided as a napkin and looked seriously at Zhai. "Lily Rose said the time's come when we should talk openly about everything," she told him. "It's time for me, too. There's somethin' I've been holdin' back—from all of you. I'm not from around these parts, you see."

"We know," Zhai said. "You're from Ireland."

"But I never told you how I came to be here. Maybe it's better to say I'm not from this *time*." She glanced at Miss Pembrook. "I don't have any special gifts either. And I didn't come by any information that brought me here, lookin' for answers. But I've traveled through time. And I don't even know how I got from there to here. All I can tell you is that I was on a train on my way to Dublin to talk my little brother out of signing himself into the army—he's determined to go and fight Germans. I was there, in Ireland, on that train. And it was nineteen fifteen. There was a bright flash of light—and then I was here, in Middleburg. I was in the old locomotive graveyard, in that little car I've made my home, with no idea how to get back to my own time."

"Well, that explains a lot!" exclaimed Dalton. "And you never said a word about it."

"How could I?" said Kate. "You'd have all thought me daft. For a while I thought it myself." She turned to Lily Rose. "Do you think there's any chance, if Aimee can get that Wheel thing goin', I'll be able to get back home?"

Zhai grabbed her hand. "No," he said. "Why do you want to go back? Stay with me."

She looked at him tenderly. "There's nothin' I'd like better," she said. "But I've got to make sure my little brother doesn't do anything so foolish as to put himself in a war. I've been readin' about that war in Miss Pembrooks' books, and on the Internet. World War One, they call it, and it's horrible. I never imagined how horrible it would be! And my little brother . . . you see, our ma's not well and he's the baby of the family. She would never survive if anything happened to him."

"Nothing is certain, Kate," Lily Rose said gently. "There may be only enough power in those crystal pieces to make one slip. But I suppose you want to go along, just in case?"

⁘

Zhai sat in the comfortable old swing on Lily Rose's front porch, holding Kate's hand. Usually her beauty, her fresh, lively attitude and view of the world—and yes, her hand in his—made him feel renewed, but not tonight. He glanced at his watch, a Movado that his father had given him for Christmas, and it told him it was time to get moving.

"I have to go . . ." he said quietly.

Kate's bright-green eyes glistened softly in the moonlight as she looked up at him. "To fight Rick," she said. He nodded. "You know, one of my favorite books was always *Ivanhoe*," she continued. "And like the fine ladies who gave the knights a token of their favor before they went into battle, I want to give you one. Here's my token."

And before Zhai knew what was happening, she gently pulled his face down to hers and gave him a long, sensuous kiss. For a second he froze, and he couldn't yield to the infinite pleasure of it. His lips felt wooden against hers. But after a moment, he relaxed, pulled her close, and kissed her more deeply. When the kiss ended, they were both trembling.

"Wow," Zhai said softly. "I definitely feel braver now."

"You know this is the silliest thing I've ever heard of," Kate declared. "You're going to bash each other's brains in, for what? It makes no sense a'tall!"

He brushed her cheek with his fingertips. "I can understand why you think so," he said. "Believe me, I don't want to go. But I have to." She nodded, and he kissed her once more. If he survived the fight with Rick, he thought, he would kiss her every chance he got. "You've got to promise me something, Kate," he said.

"I will if I can."

"If Aimee can get you back home—if it works—promise me that once you make sure your brother is safe, you'll come back. You have to come back. Now that you're in my life, Kate, I can't get along without you. I love you." There. He'd said it, and it felt good.

Her eyes lit with joy, she said, "And I love you, Zhai. Of course I'll come back to you, if there's any way I can."

"If you guys could wait—let me get this thing with Rick over with—then I could go with you," he suggested, but Kate shook her head.

"No. Miss Lily Rose is right. Bringing Aimee's mom back is a task best left to us women."

Zhai nodded. "Yeah—I get it. More Middleburg mystery. Just promise me you'll be careful."

"You too. Come back to me safe," she said, and drew him close for another kiss. And he knew that would have to be enough for now. They both had their paths to walk.

∽

An hour later, Aimee, Maggie, Kate, Anne Pembrook, and Dalton stood reverently in a circle in Lily Rose's living room, holding hands. Lily Rose and Master Chin held hands, their arms around the girls, forming a circle within a circle.

"You know I'm sending good wishes along with you," Lily Rose said. "Just be careful and keep a sharp lookout. We don't know who or what sent your mother back in time, and if you get there and it's too dangerous, you come right on back and we'll make another plan, you hear?"

They murmured their assent, and Aimee thought Lily Rose had a lot more confidence in them than they had in themselves. Her heart was beating so hard she felt like it might explode. But it didn't matter. She had three pieces of the crystal ring—hers, Dalton's, and Miss Pembrook's. She wouldn't let anything stop her.

"Okay, everybody. Ready?" Aimee said, and Miss Pembrook and the girls all nodded and closed their eyes.

Aimee felt for the three shards in her pocket, making sure they were still there. Then, as they stood in a circle holding hands, she took a deep breath, closed her eyes and focused on her mother's face, and on the Wheel of Illusion inside the tunnel. And suddenly they were falling, gliding, slipping through space.

CHAPTER 21

Z<small>HAI WAS TROMPING THROUGH THE WOODS</small> at the foot of the tunnel mound, the mountain that contained Middleburg's abandoned rail tunnels. He was to meet Rick outside the north tunnel—which meant hiking through a few miles of thick woods with only the faintest hint of a trail to ease the journey. As he pushed his way through the underbrush, he focused on the battle ahead, clearing his mind of all else.

Rick would be more filled with rage than ever; that was certain. His father had married Savana Kain this morning, and Rick had made it no secret that their union disgusted him. He hated everyone from the Flats, and the Kain family especially. Rage would make him strong, but it might make him reckless, too. How would a fury-blinded Rick attack? With a flurry of overhead punches? Zhai could block them with pair of *Biu Saus* and give him a stomp kick to the knee to halt his charge, then follow up with a kick to his gut. But what if he came in gunning for a takedown? Zhai would be ready for it and catch him with a knee to the chin as he came in.

And if he hurt Zhai, really hurt him in that first attack? Then Zhai would use Shen. He was hesitant to use the power of the All—and he wasn't sure he could use it on someone who had been his friend as long as Rick had. But if all else failed, that's what he would do. He could already feel the energy building in his lower abdomen, rising up through his chest and into his limbs, bristling into his forehead, like a tree made of crackling, fizzing electricity.

Ahead, an orange light shone through the trees, and Zhai slowed his advance, creeping forward like a commando sneaking up on an enemy encampment. When he got to the edge of the treeline, he saw that he'd reached his destination. The Toppers had built a bonfire in the center of the tracks. Rick was standing in front of it, his hands on his hips, gazing into the flames. He looked dirty and disheveled, as if he'd already been in a fight and his expression seemed kind of vague and dreamy. Somehow, he seemed bigger than usual. The other Toppers were gathered around, too. Cle'von and D'von sat on opposite rails, talking, while Dax and Michael, sitting on the stone railroad bed, glanced uneasily out into the darkness that surrounded them. Zhai spotted Bran a moment later. His shadowy shape moved back and forth on the far side of the fire, as if he were pacing in agitation.

Apparently, the Flatliners hadn't shown up yet, which was good. Zhai was hoping he could defeat Rick before they arrived—because he was sure that if Rick ended up fighting Josh, the Flatliner didn't stand a chance.

So far, none of the Toppers had seen Zhai. Closing his eyes, he took a slow step back, allowing himself to slip once more into the cool embrace of a meditative state. No thoughts of kung fu moves or battle tactics disturbed his serenity now. It was just him and the faint sound of insects newly born and freed from the bonds of winter's frost, the rustle of trees in the wind, and the warm glimmer of firelight that painted shapes on the back of his closed eyelids.

Something bad was about to happen, he now understood, because nothing good could come from the animosity that had built up over the preceding months. The gangs had abandoned the Wu-de, and there was nothing leading them forward now but fury, loathing, fear, and disgust. It was like a farmer planting a crop of thorn bushes—one could not expect to reap a harvest of corn from them, only a harvest of blood. That's what Rick wanted, and it's exactly what he would get tonight.

But the thought did not exactly fill Zhai with terror, as it should have. What he felt was a sense of inevitability, like a person who's slipped off the edge of a cliff might feel as he plummets toward the ground. All Zhai could do was accept what was happening and step into the firelight.

Rick spotted him and shouted when he was still twenty yards away. "Here he comes, boys. Get ready to see a show," he said, cracking his knuckles.

Zhai climbed up onto the tracks and stood in the center of them, as still as the trees around them, silent wooden witnesses.

"All right, Rick. You've wanted this for a long time," Zhai said. "Come and get it." He assumed a ready position.

Rick grinned, his features distorted by the firelight. With a laugh of wicked pleasure, he walked forward. Zhai was watching his elbows for the first sign of an attack when a sound broke the stillness of the clearing. It was the beating of footsteps on railroad ties—not just one set, but several. Zhai tried to ignore it, to remain focused on the enemy, but Rick was already looking over his shoulder, peering down the tracks.

"RICK!" a voice rang out in the darkness, and Zhai could no longer refrain from turning around to see who was coming.

It was the Flatliners—or what was left of them. Nass, Beet, Benji, and Josh sprinted toward them up the tracks with Josh in the lead, and Zhai could see that his eyes held a wild look that seemed like the first spark of insanity.

"Josh!" Nass yelled. "Josh, don't!"

Zhai moved off the tracks to let the newcomers pass, and as he did he was able to see more clearly. Josh was charging at Rick.

Nass grabbed the back of Josh's sweatshirt as if trying to pull him back, but Josh ripped free and continued toward Rick, who actually retreated a step or two.

Now, Zhai understood. Nass and the other Flatliners, who he had thought were attacking with Josh, were actually trying to stop him. That's when he caught sight of the gun in Josh's hand.

All was eerily silent as Orias stalked Middleburg's darkened streets, moving in and out of the shadows carved by massive, ancient Oak trees and the yellow-white gleam of the sporadic streetlights. Sometimes he moved along the pavement on long, jerky strides, sometimes he drifted above it for several yards before settling back to the earth. His thoughts were like a team of horses that had broken free from their tackle and now stampeded through his mind, with no order or reason to their motion.

Half an hour before, he had packed his bags and loaded them into his car, but when he reached for the car's ignition button, he had stopped, unable to press it. Everything he had, everything he'd built in Middleburg was slipping away from him and the choices that lay before him were impossible. Could he run away and abandon everything he'd come to love—especially Aimee? No. Could he free Oberon and face his wrath? Or refuse to free him and face Azaziel's reprisal? No. None of the choices before him were acceptable.

Agitated, he'd gotten out of the car, intent on taking a walk to clear his mind. Now, he glanced at his watch. Time was ticking down to the deadline Azaziel had given him—only a few more hours to go.

The bizarre truth was that Aimee's defection bothered him most of all. He should be happy to be rid of her. She should have been nothing more to him than an amusing little pet, and here he was deluding himself that he was in love with her. Only he knew it wasn't a delusion. He would give his soul for her if he had one. But love made him weak, and she was his Achilles' heel.

Orias knew that his enemies—his father and Azaziel—would abduct, torture, and kill her if they thought it would bring him pain. All this time, he had told himself that Aimee might still be useful because of her abilities, and because she had some special role to play in Middleburg's fate, and that was why he kept her around. But now that she was gone, now that he felt her loss like a gaping wound in his chest, there was no denying the truth. He'd kept her around because he loved her. An existence without her would be meaningless—and time was growing short. He glanced at his watch again.

He couldn't possibly stand against Azaziel, with all the power—and all the soldiers—of the Irin Council behind him. Orias's only option was to run. Fallen angels were incredibly intelligent, but they were neither psychic nor omnipotent. He had business interests and money put away in a network of other countries, so hiding out for a while in luxurious but secluded accommodations would be no problem. He'd spent most of the afternoon and evening working intently to get the device ready and put it in place. Even Oberon, locked away in the tower, was quiet as if listening, as if trying to figure out what he was up to. Now all was done. The bomb was in place. The timer was set. But Orias could not leave without Aimee. He had to find her, and he had to find her soon.

&

Nass watched helplessly as, just a few steps in front of him, Josh charged at Rick with the gun clasped in his clenched fist. Josh gave an earsplitting battle cry and took aim. Rick didn't even flinch, and Nass wondered if, in the dark, he could see the pistol that was coming ever closer to him. Instead of running the other way, Rick charged straight toward Josh, as if he would face down the bullet by sheer force of will.

"This is for Emory!" Josh screamed, and he stopped and set his feet to better his aim. As he slowed, Nass caught him from behind and Rick sandwiched him from the front. Zhai, off to one side, yelled one word: "No!"

Suddenly Nass was blasted sideways with the giddy-painful sizzle of a Shen energy discharge. He recognized the feeling from his sparring with Raphael, but the sound it made wasn't the normal bang of a Shen explosion—it was the sharp crack of a gunshot. When he opened his eyes, he found himself lying on his side in the ditch that ran parallel to the track bed with his feet higher up the embankment than his body. The rush of blood to his head left him momentarily dizzy. It took him a moment to realize that the thick, sticky liquid he felt was blood, and then another moment to find its source. There was a sickening feeling in his stomach as he thought he might have been shot. Wincing with pain, he rolled onto his back and sat up.

I moved to this damn town to get away from gang violence, he thought. *Look at me now!*

But after a moment he discovered he had banged his head on a jagged chunk of concrete during the fall. The blood was from a small gash on the side of his head. He hadn't been shot at all.

Above, up the hill, he heard the sounds of a fight: shouting, grunting, and cursing. Wincing again, he rose and stumbled up the embankment.

Josh and Rick had clambered to their feet, too. Nass didn't see the gun and hoped that it been lost in Zhai's Shen attack, but Josh and Rick were trying their best to kill each other without it. They were fighting with everything they had. The rest of the guys, Nass included, looked on, paralyzed, too weary or scared to take any action to stop what was unfolding.

Josh put up a good fight, bloodying Rick's nose and ripping his expensive T-shirt, until Rick got him in a clench like the MMA star Anderson Silva, and began cracking him in the head with a series of elbows, punctuated by the occasional knee to his face.

"That's enough, Rick," Zhai was saying, but Rick ignored him. He seemed to be lost in a haze of bloodlust. The grin on his face was like the serene, satisfied smile of a Buddha under a Bodhi tree.

"You asked for it, you got it, Flats rat," Rick said, landing another vicious blow with a sickening thud.

Beet charged forward. "Back off, Rick," he snarled, ready to jump into the mix, but Michael stepped in front of him.

"Let them go. It's a fair fight," he said, and Beet shoved him.

Behind them, Rick landed another savage punch to Josh's temple, and he crumpled to the ground. Rick towered over him, and as Nass and the others watched, he seemed to grow even larger. His face twisted into a beastly grimace, and his thick, powerful hands warped into claws. He was becoming a monster.

Nass didn't understand what this transformation meant exactly, but the knowing told him that it wasn't something new. It was the completion of a process that had begun a long time ago, the completion of what Rick was, and not so much a transformation as a blossoming. Whatever it was, Rick was a monster, a savage beast who was about to kill another of Nass's friends, and he wasn't going to let that happen.

With a deft capoeira move, Nass cartwheeled around Beet and Michael, who were grappling with one another, and shot in between Rick and Josh, surprising Rick and felling him with a quick leg sweep. Only a second passed before Rick was on his feet again, charging Nass like the bull that he now sort of resembled.

Nass caught him in the face with a cartwheel that transitioned into a kick, and managed to spin out of the way of two of Rick's haymaker punches. The third caught Nass square in the side. It was like getting slammed in the ribs with a sledgehammer, and Nass felt his legs go to jelly beneath him.

Somehow he stayed on his feet and he parried Rick's next two jabs with the *Pak Sau* move Raphael had taught him. He even managed to land a couple of glancing punches, one striking Rick's rock-hard stomach and the other banging off his steely forehead.

Benji jumped on Rick's back, but Rick grabbed him with one hand and chucked him off easily.

"Rick—my turn!" Zhai shouted, but Rick ignored him and continued advancing on Nass.

Nass cartwheeled out of the way of two overhead rights and landed a kick to the knee that almost buckled Rick's tree-trunk of a leg, but when Rick caught him with an overhead right, Nass's world went dark.

When he opened his eyes again his face was throbbing, as if someone had removed his nose and forehead and replaced them with a couple of aching, beating hearts. For a moment, he wanted to cry—not because of the pain he was feeling (although he did hurt all over) but because of the stupidity, the futility of the situation. They had come here to avenge Emory; now they would all probably end up mangled, beaten, or even dead. And for what? What good would come out of it? Emory was still dead. Raph was still gone. The ring was still shattered. What had they accomplished with all their fighting, all their hate, and all their impotent anger? Nothing. Nothing but pain.

Zhai was now in the middle of the tracks between Nass and Rick, facing Rick down with an eerie calm. It reminded Nass of something, and it took a moment to figure out what it was: it was the image he'd seen in social studies class of a lone, unarmed Chinese activist in Tiananmen Square, facing off against a column of massive tanks. And it was like Raphael standing still as the ghost train struck him.

All around, the wind was picking up until it howled, the trees were waving and trembling, the distant otherworldly drums and battle cries that Nass had heard during other battles between the Toppers and the Flatliners had come again, and now they were louder than ever.

"What do you say, Rick?" Nass heard Zhai speak calmly. "Let's find out who's the best, once and for all."

The maniacal grin on Rick's face was like the leer of a flaming jack-o'-lantern.

"Yes," he replied hungrily. "Once and for all."

∽

Between one heartbeat and the next, Rick was on him, a one-man melee of slashing claws, hammering fists, and gnashing teeth. Zhai worked systematically to defend himself, retreating from the first lunge, blocking the groping claw with a *Tan Sau*, stepping to the side and blocking his low hook with a *Guan Sau*, while simultaneously striking out with his opposite fist. It was no use. Rick's normally long reach had grown by another foot, and if Zhai fought him close in, he'd open himself up for a bear hug that could crush the life out of him. So, he retreated a few steps and started circling. His only chance was to get outside of Rick's arms and attack him from his blind side, *Wing Chun* style. But it wouldn't be easy. Rick knew his game and was turning as fast as Zhai circled, lobbing a series of powerful overhead punches every few seconds.

Zhai fought to bring up his Shen power, but the sight of Rick in his transformed state filled him with a fear that seemed to freeze the blood in his veins. In that state of tension, he knew, Shen energy would not flow. Rick caught him with a leg kick that almost made Zhai's knee give out. In that moment's distraction, Rick lashed out, clapping him with two thunderous blows to the head and clawing his chest before Zhai was finally able to retreat out of range.

His head ringing, his chest drizzling blood, Zhai hung on to his composure, trying to rationally analyze the situation. And he heard Master Chin's voice, speaking to him as if he were really there: *You're in your head, Zhai. Now is the time to let go and fight with your spirit.*

But Zhai couldn't do that. He'd always had trouble letting go enough to feel any kind of emotion. He had barely been able to kiss Kate. His inexplicable reserve had always held him back in friendships, in relationships, and in his training. Now, he would have to overcome it if he wanted to live. But how?

He stepped forward and tried for a stomp kick, but Rick batted his leg aside and blasted him in the face with a punch that left him lying face down on the train tracks, spitting up blood.

As he tried to get to his feet he felt a kick wrack his ribs, sending him facedown on the tracks again. When he looked up, he saw Nass cartwheeling toward Rick, but Rick slapped at him and sent him flying.

Rick kicked him again, and Zhai felt his vision swimming. Another kick sent a lightning bolt of pain down his right arm and shoulder. Another flipped him over, leaving him staring up at the spinning, drifting stars. He was falling toward unconsciousness, and he fought it with all his might. Another kick sent him tumbling to the bottom of the ravine next to the tracks, and he spit some dirt from his mouth and groaned. This was it, he thought: the end of peace, the end of the Wu-de, maybe the end of his life.

He had always feared death, he realized suddenly, feared it with a desperation that was so powerful, so all consuming, that sometimes he had to quit feeling altogether in order to block it out. But now that death was in front of him, it somehow seemed less scary—and he thought he knew why.

He wasn't afraid to die, because he had lived.

His right hand, now aching and trembling, snaked down and reached into the pocket of his pants. His fingers fumbled for a moment, then found what they were looking for and brought it up to his face.

It was the locket that contained the thick copper curl he'd snipped from Kate's hair the night he met her. He'd told her that he carried it with him always.

"Do you find that creepy?" he'd asked her.

She'd smiled up at him, everything she felt for him shining in her eyes. "Oh, no, 'tis the sweetest thing I've ever heard," she'd said. "I hope you'll carry it with you forever."

And, he had vowed to himself, he would. He touched it to his face now, as he gazed out at the formless blackness of the nighttime forest. Strangely, it still held her scent, and he let it wash over him as he brushed it across his cheek. And for one extraordinary moment, for perhaps the first time in his life, *Zhai felt*. He felt so much that his body trembled, so much that tears poured down his cheeks. And he was no longer afraid to die.

"Sorry, my friend, but this is the end," said Rick.

Zhai rolled over and saw him standing on the tracks—only he wasn't Rick anymore. The other combatants noticed it too. They all stopped pounding each other and stared at the Toppers' new leader in awe. As they watched, the beast that was Rick grew taller. The seams in his clothing gave way with a loud rip as he grew larger and more fearsome, until his hulking form eclipsed the moon. Beneath his shredded shirt, his human flesh turned leathery and sharp spikes started popping out of his crusty skin. He'd gotten a battered two-by-four from somewhere and it was stuck through with a half dozen nails that glinted wickedly in the moonlight. Rick was hideous, and he was no longer smiling as he descended toward Zhai.

Zhai fought to get to his knees. His head throbbed as he tilted it back to look at the giant horror looming above him. But within the pain, within the heartache, within the fear, there was an all-powerful calm, an endlessly deep, vast store of peace and might that rose up through the earth and rained invisibly down from heaven, filling Zhai completely.

Rick was raising his club, ready to bring it down and crush Zhai's head.

Zhai merely reached one hand out, palm up.

Rick tilted his head and looked down at it, puzzled, and a blast of fire burst forth from Zhai's outstretched fingers like a powerful arc of lightning. Zhai's body convulsed with an ecstatic jolt as the Shen flowed through him, propelling Rick backward, a whirling windmill of arms, legs, and screams. He landed at the top of the rise, on the railroad tracks, and Zhai moved fearlessly toward him. Steam rose from Rick's leathery, demonic flesh, its plumes made silver by the moonlight—but he was still alive. He writhed and groaned as Zhai drew near.

"Do you yield, Rick?" Zhai said, his voice loud and strong. The others—Flatliners and Toppers—skidded to a halt behind him and watched in silent fascination.

Rick sat up fast and swung his club at Zhai, but Zhai snapped it with one sharp kick, sending it exploding into splinters. Then he hit Rick with a blizzard of lightning-fast punches and kicks that left the monster stunned, a stream of blood oozing from his fanged mouth.

"Do you yield?" Zhai repeated even more forcefully.

Rick grimaced as he rose. "Never," he snarled, and before anyone could react, he took off into the woods, disappearing with the speed of a spooked deer.

When he was gone, everyone seemed to exhale at once. Beet and D'von Cunningham exchanged a weary glance, as did Benji and Dax Avery, but no one seemed to have any desire to continue fighting. Ignacio cursed softly and then vomited and spat between a set of railroad ties.

"You okay?" Benji asked, and Nass nodded.

Zhai looked around. There was somebody missing.

"Bran!" Cle'von shouted, and he ran over to a tree at the edge of the clearing. Zhai and the others followed. Bran was sitting on the ground, leaning against a slender birch tree. His face—even his lips—were nearly as pale as the paper-white bark.

"Bran? What happened, man?" Michael Ponder asked, then his eyes traced down his friend's body and he said, "Oh."

The single syllable fell heavily from his lips.

Bran was trembling and his hands, clenched tightly together over his stomach, were covered in blood. He looked down and when he saw it, he passed out.

Zhai stared at him for a moment, trying to figure out what had happened. It wasn't until someone behind him said, "Oh, God," that he understood.

Josh had regained consciousness and recovered the gun. He limped up to the edge of the gathering and stared at Bran for a moment, and then the gun fell from his hand.

"I hit him," Josh said in stunned disbelief. "I didn't think I hit anything— *crap!*" He was suddenly frantic. "Well, don't just stand there!" he shouted. "We have to get him to the hospital—somebody call for an ambulance!"

And together the Flatliners and Toppers lifted Bran and carried him out of the woods.

CHAPTER 22

Rick ran through the moonlit forest, sometimes sprinting and dodging through trees like he was scrambling on the football field, sometimes galloping along the forest floor on all fours, his hands digging into the thick layers of leaves and earth beneath him and propelling him forward. As he blasted his way through the quivering shadows he struggled to identify what had happened to him. Something in him had changed—he'd known that since he ventured down Maggie's basement stairs. But the change was going deeper, and it felt more permanent.

It was strange. In some ways, he felt more himself than ever. He was a fuller version of himself, as if he'd now reached a state of ripeness, of completion.

He could still remember the night his father had found the note from his mother, saying that she'd left.

He remembered his father berating him, taking his anger out on him with a series of vicious verbal attacks, and feeling lost because neither his mother nor Aimee was there to bear the brunt of Jack Banfield's wrath. He remembered locking himself in his room and crying bitter, angry tears feeling as alone as a satellite drifting in the black, frigid reaches of space. Then, he'd gotten angry.

And, instead of diminishing over time, the anger had grown, until it was like another entity abiding within him, a living tumor with its own heartbeat, its own will, its own stubborn desire to exist, then to thrive and finally, to reign. He was angry with his mother for leaving, angry with his father for taking it out on him, angry with Aimee for being the cause of it all because maybe she killed Tyler, angry with Savana Kain for being the seductress who'd led his father astray. He was angry with Zhai for always wanting to keep the peace, angry with Bran for his slick-talking charm, angry with the other Toppers for not being as angry as he was.

He was angry with the Flatliners because no matter how bad his life was, they were there to make it worse. He was angry with them for being so resilient, for laughing and having fun even though they were such miserable losers. He was angry with them for meddling in his father's business and for trying to tip the normal order of the world in their own favor, and he was angry with Raphael Kain for—for *being*.

There was more. He could go on and on about all the things that pissed him off, that made him want to smash something or choke someone—or rip them apart like he'd decimated Clarisse's drug-dealing ex. But they were not individual issues anymore. They were all one, absorbed into the tumor of anger that had been growing inside him for so long. His body seemed to have turned inside out, and the tumor he'd felt swelling within him was now attached to his skin like a giant barnacle. It was a great relief, in a way, to finally look on the outside how he felt on the inside, but it was also mildly disturbing—because he knew he was not exactly one hundred percent human anymore.

He broke out of the woods onto Golden Avenue amid screeching tires and honking car horns and ran north, intending to head back to Hilltop Haven, but as soon as he passed Main Street, something pulled him to his left. It was like . . . a voice coming from within his body, as if the hate-tumor thing had developed the power of speech.

Come to me, Rick. Come now. Come fast.

And it was drawing him like a magnet, pulling him around the corner, off the well-lit main drag, and onto a tree-canopied side street.

My jailor is gone. His spell weakens. Now is the time. Come to me.

Rick ran harder, his muscles pumping beneath his sweat-soaked skin. He stopped suddenly, as if he had run into an invisible wall.

Yes. I'm here. Come to me. Release me.

Rick looked up. He was standing in front of Orias's house, a grand but dilapidated Victorian structure as beautiful as it was forbidding. The lights were all out, but he knew, somehow, that someone was inside. Not Orias. Not Aimee, who basically lived there now. But someone was there, calling him.

Come to me, Rick . . . Come and release me. Let me out. Now.

Up the steps he went. As he reached the door it creaked open by itself, revealing a foyer cloaked in impenetrable shadow. But since Rick had made darkness his home, he found that he could see. He went up the steps, down the hall, and all the way back to a smaller spiral staircase made of black wrought iron.

Come, Rick. Set me free.

Rick climbed those stairs, too, all the way to the top of the tower, and was soon in a tiny anteroom. Sickly, pale moonlight was spilling in from an oval window, revealing a door directly in front of him. It was bowed outward, as if some incredible force was pushing against it with enough strength to bend the wood. Large flecks of paint from the door's warped face littered the floor at his feet.

Open it. Do it, Rick. Now!

He was desperate to make the voice stop, and he understood that the only way to make that happen was to open the door. But he was suddenly afraid. Something was locked inside that room. It was calling him, and whatever it was, the last thing on earth Rick wanted was to see its face. He wanted to run down the stairs, maybe even to throw himself out the window, and keep on running until he was back in the woods. But it was too late for that. The magnetic power that drew him held him fast. He belonged to it—maybe had always belonged to it—and there was no use resisting.

Do it now. Rick Banfield, open this door!

Rick reached forward and with the hand that had become a claw he was somehow able to pull back the latch bar. The cool metal of the door-knob felt strangely normal against his skin. He expected some resistance as he turned it, but there was none. The knob turned easily, and the latch made a small grating click as it pulled free. The door creaked softly as he pushed it open and gazed into the darkened room beyond.

He had been terrified of what he would find, but there was nothing but impenetrable darkness. He was about to step into the room and grope for a light switch when he saw a form coalescing out of the blackness. He heard a boot step and the plaintive squeak of a floorboard as someone came toward him.

"H . . . hello?" Rick's voice was just a whisper.

"Hello, Rick."

The tone was friendly, but something made Rick back up a little. The figure moving toward him was tall, wispy thin, and as dark as the shadows surrounding it. It looked like a black skeleton, a tall man made of onyx who had been left to starve for months. Bones pressed against the creature's black skin, as if eager to be free of the flesh surrounding them. But it wasn't the thing's gauntness that was most horrifying, or even the luxurious, black wings that protruded from its back like a great cloak. It wasn't the stench of sewage that drifted from the room, or the feeling of vague, electric malevolence that seemed to radiate from the creature.

It was his eyes.

They were gone, and where they should be were just two scarred craters in the skull-like surface of his face. And hanging in front of the craters were what looked like quivering, reddish holograms of eyes. Their shape was bizarre and their stare unblinking. They looked like they had been borrowed from something that, like Rick, was inhuman.

Then something else struck Rick. He recognized his man. It was his father's enemy. The man who had kidnapped Aimee. The one everyone thought was dead.

"Oberon Morrow?" he asked in a tremulous whisper.

"That's right," the dark angel said. "But you can call me master."

"Master?" Rick said, recoiling. The last thing he wanted was to be anyone's servant.

Oberon was looking him up and down with his freaky ghost eyes. "Oh yes," Oberon said. "I always saw the seed of darkness in you—just look how it has bloomed. Follow me, help me, Rick, and I will teach you to use your newfound power. Follow me, and I will give you the strength to conquer your father, Middleburg, and the world."

෨

Orias pounded on Lily Rose's door and waited impatiently for her to answer. He had not been surprised to find no one at home at Jack Banfield's place. With Jack on his honeymoon, Rick—who'd gone almost completely over to his demon side—was probably out causing trouble for someone. Aimee had mentioned getting supplies for her journey so Orias assumed she would go home—but she wasn't there. Logically, Lily Rose's house was the only other place she was likely to go. But it had taken him longer than he'd hoped to mix the explosives, build the timer, and place the detonator, and after so much delay, he had little hope that Aimee would still be here.

Aimee had always said she knew where her mother was and all she had to do to retrieve her was learn how to teleport back in time. What Aimee didn't know was that she already had that ability. Her gift was special, growing exponentially more powerful every day. All she had to do, really, was visualize where and when she wanted to be and she would go there. But it could be to his advantage if it took her a while to figure that out.

Lily Rose opened the door then and when she saw Orias standing there, she smiled. The moonlight, slanting in sharply, cast her in a silvery shadow. "Figured you'd be showing up sooner or later," she said.

"I'd like to see Aimee, please," he said politely and made himself unclench his fists.

"She's not here."

He looked over the old woman's shoulder, but all he saw was the Chinese man who taught kung fu, standing in the hall behind her.

"Please," Orias said. "It's important. "Tell me where she's gone."

"You know where," said Lily Rose. "She's gone to get her mama. It's all happening, son—just like it's supposed to."

"What do you know about what's supposed to happen?" he asked her. This old soul, he realized, wasn't like everyone else in Middleburg. She wasn't like any human he'd ever met.

"I know you got a choice to make," she said.

"What do you mean?"

"It's closing in on you, boy," she told him gently. "You got to find your way."

"My way is preordained." He couldn't keep the contempt and the bitterness from his tone. "I have no choice."

"You always got a choice," she said. "Like now. You can walk away from all this and leave Aimee behind—or you can go and help her. No telling who or what she might run into where's she's going."

There was a moment of heavy silence, broken only by the ticking of the grandfather clock in Lily Rose's den. Orias looked at her, deep into her different colored eyes, and he knew what he had to do.

"Yeah," he said. And then he turned and walked away.

☙

The Flatliners and the Toppers rode in a caravan, following the ambulance as it bore Bran to the hospital in Benton. Zhai rode shotgun in Michael Ponder's car, staring out the window at the barren expanse of moonlit fields and the hulking shadows of big trees as they swooped past. He kept running his tongue over his slit lip, tasting the blood. His whole body ached from the fight with Rick. A car length ahead, Beet's old beat-up Impala chugged along, looking like it had escaped from a junkyard. In front of him was the ambulance, its flashing lights cutting wide red swaths through the starless night.

"I can't believe this," D'von said pensively. "Bran didn't even want to fight tonight."

"I know, right?" Cle'von agreed.

"That Flats rat is going to rot in jail for this," Dax said, his anger momentarily overcoming his fear. "They're going to lock his ass up—fifty to life."

There was a moment of silence filled only with the shush of the tires on the road.

"You guys see what happened to Rick?" asked D'von.

"You mean like he morphed into some kind of monster and ran off into the woods like an animal?" asked Dax. "What the hell was that?"

"We all saw it," said Zhai. "And we saw Josh aiming at Rick, not Bran."

"If I'd had a gun, I'd have taken a shot at Rick myself," Cle'von admitted.

There was another moment of silence, and then D'von said, "I'm gonna tell the police it was an accident."

"Me too," said Cle'von.

"Me too," said Michael, after a pause.

"Yeah. I guess I'll say it was an accident, too," Dax said.

They all nodded in solemn agreement.

Zhai smiled wanly out the window. It hurt his swollen lip.

∽

Nass and the Flatliners entered the ER limping and shuffling, ragged and bloody. A young nurse behind the reception desk frowned at them, but when they said they were with the kid in the ambulance, she directed them to the waiting area. They all settled into the vinyl seats and glanced at one another, and Nass knew they were all thinking the same thing. They had been here only hours before, for Emory. Now, it looked like they might have to bury another student from Middleburg High.

Nass didn't like Bran Goheen much. He had always equated Bran's

Southern charm with huckster evangelists, smooth-talking car salesmen, and crooked politicians. But Nass respected him. Bran had always abided by the Wu-de, behaving honorably when the Flatliners and Toppers fought. He was a great athlete, and word around school was that he was a straight-A student. The thought that he might die tonight from a bullet that should have hit Rick was hard to take.

The Toppers came in, then, and were passing the nurse's station when a police officer walked in and called them back. Nass groaned. It was Johnny the Cop.

Josh's eyes were shut, his body slouched, and his head tilted back against the chair next to Nass. Nass elbowed him now and pointed across the room to the spot where Johnny stood talking to the Toppers. Josh followed his gaze and the color drained from his face.

"They're telling him I'm a killer, Nass. They're going to lock me up, man," he said, his voice rising. "What's my family going to do? My little brother? My job pays for his clothes. I can't go to prison—"

Nass put a hand on Josh's shoulder. "You need to calm down," he said, serious and quiet. "It's going to be okay, you hear me? But you gotta stay cool—and stop talking."

Across the room, Johnny the Cop was glancing over at the Flatliners.

"We'd better go and give them our side of the story," Beet said.

"Yeah," Nass agreed. "Let's go." When they got within earshot, however, he couldn't believe what the Toppers were telling Johnny.

"It was an accident," D'von said.

"He didn't mean to shoot anybody," Dax Avery put in.

"He was just showing us the gun, and it went off," Cle'von added.

"Yeah," Michael Ponder agreed. "It wasn't Josh's fault."

Johnny looked at Zhai.

"It was an accident," Zhai said.

Nass heard Josh draw in a quick breath and glanced over at him. He was struggling to contain his emotions.

"Josh," Johnny the Cop said. "Let's step outside and have a little talk."

Josh nodded and followed him out the automatic doors that led into the parking lot, leaving the Toppers and the Flatliners alone together. Nass went weak with relief. The last thing he'd expected was for the enemy to protect Josh.

"Thank you," he said. "Josh has been through so much. He really didn't mean to—"

"We know," Zhai interrupted. And he reached out a hand. Nass clasped it and shook it, and the Flatliners and the Toppers all sat down together to wait for news on Bran.

❧

They were in total darkness. Aimee switched the flashlight on and saw that they had landed right where she'd hoped. They were standing on the X of the crossed railroad tracks, at the center of the Wheel of Illusion. The Wheel was a massive round platform made of age-darkened brass with railroad tracks running across it. Directly in front of them stood the Wheel's wooden control panel.

"Everybody okay?" she asked.

"That was awesome," said Maggie.

"Incredible," agreed Miss Pembrook. "Where are we?"

"Inside the tunnels," Aimee said. "We're right in the middle, where the tracks cross."

They all turned, looking around at the massive dome above them.

"In the tunnels to be sure," said Kate. "But what is this place?"

"In the olden days when the trains were still running, it was a switching station. The big metal plate we're standing on was once used to turn the locomotives around," Aimee explained, and she had a quick spark of memory. She had come here before—with that boy they were always talking about, Raphael—but she couldn't remember why. "It's called the Wheel of Illusion."

"What's it for?" asked Dalton.

"For one thing, it sort of controls time," Aimee said. "Or at least the layers between times. I don't know what else it's supposed to do."

Miss Pembrook and the other girls were staring down at it. Aimee saw that its control panel, once lit with an amber glow, was now dark. Attached to one side was a lever that looked like it belonged on an old-fashioned slot machine.

"Okay, so what now?" Dalton asked. Aimee noticed that she didn't look impressed like Maggie or intrigued like Kate and Miss Pembrook. She looked worried. "How is this going to work?"

"I'm not sure," said Aimee. She had another quick memory flash. The first time she'd been here someone—she thought it was that Raphael guy—had fitted an old pocket watch into a circle that was molded into the Wheel's console. Moving closer so she could get a better look at the control panel, she spotted the concave circle. She took the three pieces of the shattered ring out of her jeans pocket and looked at them in her open palm.

"When I first found the ring, it was underground, in the middle of a bunch of machinery that's right beneath us. Its energy was used to power the Wheel," she said. "When it blew apart, the Wheel stopped working."

Orias had told her that. He knew a lot about this stuff, and she wished with all her heart that he was here now. The last time she'd been in the tunnels, she'd had his voice directing her, which had made her feel safe, and suddenly she longed to be with him, to run back to him, and hide in his house, in his arms. She missed him like crazy, but she had to keep her mind on her mission. Fixating on Orias was what had made her forget about finding her mom in the first place, and she wasn't going to let that happen again.

"We only have three shards," she continued. "If we can somehow connect them to the Wheel, that might power it up enough for me to teleport us all to 1877." She thought all she'd have to do was keep the shards closed in her fist and then put her fist in the circle. And then, when they were ready, use her other hand to pull the lever.

It was as if Miss Pembrook could read her mind. "I think you're the conduit, Aimee," she said.

"Let's hope," Aimee replied. "Grab hands and somebody hang on to me. And it's really, really important that we all think about where we want to go. Like, we have to visualize Middleburg in 1877 and my mom there in that time. We get that fixed in our minds and then I pull the lever. I think it'll work."

"And how do we get back if the Wheel stays here, in this time?" asked Dalton.

Aimee was about to say she didn't know when Miss Pembrook spoke up again. "No—it'll be okay," she said. "The Wheel was there in 1877, just like it is now."

"Okay, then," Aimee said. "Everybody ready?" They all assured her they were, and Maggie and Dalton each put an arm around her waist. Miss Pembrook held Maggie's hand and Kate took Dalton's hand.

Aimee clutched the crystal pieces and placed the hand holding them against the circular indentation on the Wheel's console. As she reached for the lever she reminded them all, "Think about Middleburg in 1877. Think of my mom. Try to imagine the old town, the way it was then, but with her trapped there. . . ."

But when she pulled the lever, she was still thinking about Orias, wanting to be with him, and wondering what he'd done to make Azaziel so angry. She tried to force her thoughts back to her mother as they slipped through a whirling, multicolored vortex of light, falling . . . falling . . . falling . . .

∽

And landing with a thud on a sawdust-covered floor. Honky-tonk music was playing, and the only thing louder than the piano was the raucous laughter of the dance-hall girls.

Dalton opened her eyes. They were in a bar—or rather, a saloon that looked like it belonged in a movie about the old west. It was complete with spittoons and a long counter where a few cowboys were slugging back mugs of beer and shots of whiskey—and at the entryway, it had the same kind of swinging doors that Rack 'Em Billiards had.

"Wow," Maggie said. "I think we did it."

"Indeed we did," said Kate. "But where's Aimee?"

෨

An hour and a half after they'd gotten Bran to the hospital a doctor came through the set of double doors and into the waiting area. Zhai had called Bran's family, and they had wasted no time in getting there.

Zhai glanced at the faces of the guys around him. The Toppers looked miserable, inwardly freaking out as they wondered if their friend was alive or dead. The Flatliners looked equally tense, and Josh was as pale as the moon outside.

The doctor nodded and shook Bran's father's hand and walked away as Mr. Goheen fiercely embraced his wife. She was crying, but Zhai couldn't tell if they were tears of joy or tears of grief.

"What happened?" Dax whispered. Zhai only shook his head.

After a moment, Bran's father noticed them watching, and he walked over to them.

"Hey, kids," he said, his warm Southern drawl even more pronounced than Bran's. "The doctor said he'll be okay. The bullet didn't hit any major organs or anything, and they were able to patch him up pretty easily. He lost a good bit of blood, but they have him on a transfusion now, so he should be feeling better in no time. He's gonna have to stay on the bench for basketball this season, but he'll be okay."

In unison, it seemed, every Topper and every Flatliner released the collective breath they had been holding and relaxed. Zhai didn't know if he wanted to laugh or shout or just go home and go to sleep, but he was relieved and it felt amazing.

"Now, how did this happen, anyway?" Mr. Goheen asked, his hands on his hips.

The guys all exchanged a quick look, and then Zhai spoke up. "It was just an accident, Mr. Goheen," he said. "Josh was showing us the gun. We didn't know it was loaded. It was a stupid mistake, and it won't happen again."

Mr. Goheen looked at them, Zhai thought, as if he was trying to figure out if they were telling the truth. "You boys weren't fighting?" he asked.

"We were messing around. Wrestling and stuff—but we weren't really fighting," Nass said quickly.

"No," D'von Cunningham agreed. "We're all friends."

"That's good. Life is too damn short for fighting." Mr. Goheen's eyes swept over them all once more, coming to rest on Nass's forehead. "You better have that looked at, son," he said.

"I'm okay," Nass told him. "It's just a scratch."

Mr. Goheen nodded, satisfied.

Nass added, "Did Bran say anything—about what happened?"

"He says he doesn't remember. The doctor said that's not unusual with a traumatic injury. That cop wants to talk to Bran and then he's going to rest for a while. You kids should go home now and come back tomorrow to visit him."

઼

Kate was right. There was no sign of Aimee. "Maybe she landed outside," said Dalton.

"Let's go out and see," said Miss Pembrook. "We're already attracting too much attention in here." She gave a slight nod toward the bar where a rough-looking cowboy eyed them suspiciously. He had a gun on each hip and his right hand rested lightly on one of them. "Come on," she finished and led them through the swinging doors, out into the moonlit night.

"Okay, I'm gonna say it," Dalton warned them.

"What?" Maggie asked.

"Something tells me we're not in Kansas anymore."

"Yeah, we are," said Maggie. "Like . . . about a hundred and forty years ago."

Amazed, Miss Pembrook added, "Not a telephone pole in sight—and no paved roads. I think it worked. I think we really did go back in time."

"I hope Aimee came with us," said Dalton.

"Maybe we got separated when we slipped," offered Maggie.

"So now what should we do?" asked Kate. "How will we get back?"

"Okay—look," said Dalton. "We'll find her—or she'll find us. She wants to get to her mom. Aimee's here somewhere or she will be soon. We've just got to keep the faith. In the meantime, we should lay low and try to blend in. And we need to stay out of sight until we can find some other clothes."

"Dalton's right," said Miss Pembrook, and then she spotted a boarding house across the rutted dirt road. The sign out front read ROOMS TO LET and beneath that a smaller sign swinging on two hooks declared there was a vacancy. With Miss Pembrook leading the way, they hurried to it and the teacher knocked on the front door. When there was no answer, she turned the knob and found it unlocked and they stepped into the foyer, which seemed to serve as the reception area. There was a desk with a registry book on it. Beside it were a little silver bell and a sign: PLEASE RING FOR SERVICE.

Dalton picked up the bell and shook it.

"I'm back here!" a voice called. "Please come through!"

They walked into a pleasant sitting room furnished with a tall corner cabinet and a writing desk that both looked like they were made of oak, and a beautiful sofa with a mahogany frame and green cut-velvet uphol-stery. The fireplace was broad and the mantle was stained black at the top from constant use.

From there they went through a lovely dining room, and they could hear a rhythmic sound: *scrape, whack, scrape, whack.* Dalton moved cau-tiously, as quietly as she could, in that direction. "Hello?" she called out, and the sound stopped.

"Constance—is that you?"

Dalton thought she recognized the voice. "Mrs. Banfield?" she said and peered through the door, into the big, old-fashioned kitchen. A woman sat on a wooden chair in the middle of the room. She was wearing an ankle-length dress topped with an apron almost as long, and she was plunging a wooden paddle up and down into a long, thin barrel. Maggie and the others came in quietly to join Dalton.

"She's churning butter," said Miss Pembrook, her voice a whisper.

The woman had beautiful youthful features, bright playful eyes, and long blond hair she wore pulled back in a bun.

"Mrs. Banfield?" Dalton said again. "It is you!"

Emily Banfield looked up, surprised, and then she rose and hurried to them. "Dalton? My goodness!" she exclaimed. "How did you get here—and Maggie?" She sounded stunned. "Oh, I am so glad to see you girls—but I don't understand."

"We don't either—not really," said Miss Pembrook. "It seems your daughter has a rare gift for travel. She brought us here—and she can get us back—but she can explain it better than we can. I'm Anne Pembrook, Aimee's history teacher."

"Aimee brought you here?" asked Emily.

"That's right," said Maggie. "We came to get you and take you back home, to Middleburg. *Our* Middleburg, in the twenty-first century."

"But—where is she?" asked Emily.

"We got separated somehow," Kate explained. "But we think she'll be here soon. I'm Kate, a friend of hers. Pleased to meet you, ma'am."

"And I you," said Emily. "Please make yourselves at home. As soon as I wrap this butter and put it in the icebox I'll get you something to eat and you can tell me everything that's been going on in Middleburg."

At that moment there was a loud knock on the back door, and Dalton noticed the sudden look of dread that clouded Mrs. Banfield's eyes. Silently, Emily motioned for them to go into the dining room. "Wait in there," she whispered. "Don't make a sound."

She closed the swinging kitchen door, but Dalton managed to catch the bottom of it with her toe, leaving it slightly ajar so they could hear Mrs. Banfield's greeting.

"Good evening," she said. "It's late, Mr. Crawford. What do you want?"

A rough male voice asked, "You get any new boarders tonight?"

"How is that possible?" countered Emily. "Don't you and your men have the entire town on lockdown?"

"Someone coulda slipped in," he said. "I'm going to ask you again, ma'am. Anybody new show up here tonight?"

"As a matter of fact, yes," she told him. "Some ladies looking for a room—a teacher and three of her young charges. With all the armed guards you have posted around the town, I'd think you'd already know that. They're just a few inconsequential females. What's the problem?"

"If they can get in, someone else could get out."

"Well, maybe you should have a word with your men," said Emily. "Perhaps they're imbibing a lot more spirits than is good for them—or you."

"I'd like to have a word with the ladies."

"I'm sorry," Emily said. "They're getting ready for bed. Surely a gentleman such as yourself wouldn't interrupt their toilette."

There was a moment of silence and then he said, "Make sure they're at the counting tomorrow morning. And there better not be anyone missing."

When they heard Emily close the back door, they ventured into the kitchen again.

"What's going on?" asked Dalton. "Why are guards posted around the whole town?"

"Maggie, please go and lock the front door," Emily said as she checked the back door. When Maggie returned she continued, "It's a long story." She invited them to take seats around the big kitchen table and then opened a cabinet and took out a huge pie. "It's apple," she said. "Freshly made, with all fresh ingredients. That's one of the only good things about living back in this time. No preservatives—the food tastes amazing."

She cut them generous slices and took a big pitcher of milk out of the icebox. "We get the ice from Macomb Lake," she explained. "It's plentiful in the winter—but I sure miss my big Kenmore side-by-side." She poured a mug full for each of them and then she sat down to tell them about the outlaws.

"They rode into town about two weeks ago," she said. "The first thing they did was take the sheriff and his family hostage—they're holding them all at the jail. Then, at gunpoint, they herded everyone into Middleburg United Church—it's the biggest building in town, in this time—and they counted everyone. Every morning when they ring the church bells, we have to go stand in a lineup in the town square and be counted again to make sure no one has tried to sneak away and get help. If anyone is missing, they'll start killing us—a dozen at a time."

"What do they want?" asked Miss Pembrook.

"They're waiting for the train," said Emily. "They say it's carrying the payroll for all the railroad workers from here to California. For some reason, it has been delayed. They've told us if we just stay calm and cooperate, they'll be out of here as soon as they get that payroll."

"And if something's happened to the train?" asked Maggie. "What if it doesn't come?"

"I don't know," said Emily. "I think they'll just line us up and shoot us all—after they've taken everything of value that these people have."

"That's awful," said Dalton.

Emily nodded. "At first, some of the men talked about trying to sneak away, to try to get to Topeka and bring back help. But I got their womenfolk to talk them out of it."

"Why?" asked Dalton.

"Don't you see? It's not just these people who are in danger. Dalton, your great-great-great grandparents are here. So are Aimee's and Maggie's—

and the ancestors of hundreds of people who live in *our* Middleburg. If people get killed here—then you might not even be born."

"Wow," said Dalton. "That's twisted." She was having trouble getting her head around the idea that she wouldn't even exist.

"What are we going to do?" asked Anne Pembrook. "We're kinda stuck until Aimee gets here."

"There's only one thing we can do," Maggie suggested. "We have to get rid of them."

"Like I said before," Dalton told them. "We've got to sit tight and wait for Aimee and then we'll figure out what to do. Mrs. Banfield—can you get us some old-timey clothes so we can blend in?"

"Indeed I can," said Emily. "Constance—she owns the boarding house—is also the town seamstress and she has a trunk full of samples. I'm sure I can find something for everyone."

"Is she here now?" asked Maggie.

"No. She went to visit her sister in Topeka a few days before the outlaws arrived. She's not due back for another week. I'm worried about what they'll do if a stagecoach shows up before the train gets here." By now they'd all finished their pie and milk. "Let's get you all settled in for the night," Emily said. "We'll have to get up early to get to the counting."

⁊

Aimee still had the ring shards and the flashlight, but she was no longer on the Wheel of Illusion. Instead, she was in a strange barren world with a stifling hot climate, standing in the middle of a dirt road, a few hundred yards from a desolate crossroads. And she was alone.

Why, she wondered, hadn't she ended up in the same place as her friends (which she hoped was 1877 Middleburg)? Then, she remembered that she'd been thinking about Orias as she'd pulled the lever. Was it possible that he was here, somewhere in this strange place?

She could try again to slip to her mom, but she didn't think she could go back in time that far without the Wheel. So, she walked up the path she was standing on, toward the crossroads. Off to her left over the horizon was a strange reddish glow. As she reached the crossroads, she saw something else: a big, ramshackle silver gate that was chained and padlocked and looked like it hadn't been used in ages. The sign on it read: *MORROW*

"Well, well, well—what have we here?"

Aimee looked around but saw no one—and then someone tugged on her sleeve.

"Down here," said the voice and when she looked, she saw a little guy who was too tall to be a child but too short to be a grownup. He smiled up at her. "And behold—she's a pretty, pretty one," he said over his shoulder.

Another small guy stepped out of the shadows. He gave Aimee a careful appraisal and then turned to his friend. They exchanged a few words in a language she didn't understand and then the first little man spoke again. "What's a pretty-pretty like you doing here?" he asked. "What do you want?"

"I'm looking for someone," she said. "Orias Morrow. Is this his place?"

"Oooh! *Orias!* What do you want with *him*?"

"Sorry, it's kind of personal. Is he here?"

But he didn't reply to that. "I'm Steel and this is Begg," he said. "Who are you?"

"Aimee Banfield."

"And what is Orias Morrow to you?"

She gave an aggravated sigh. This was wasting time. "Not that it's any of your business but he's my boyfriend, okay? Now, come on—is he here or not?"

"We can't tell you that," Steel said. "But Azaziel can. We can take you to him."

Of course, she realized. *I had Orias's problem with Azaziel on my mind when I slipped. That's why I ended up here.* "Let's go," she said. "I'd really like to talk to him."

Steel and Begg led her down a stone pathway that ran parallel to the Morrow Estate. It felt to Aimee like they walked forever. They passed bizarre rock formations, half-buried skeletons of huge, strange animals, and a few slowly turning black windmills that gave Aimee the creeps.

All the while, the red light that Aimee had seen earlier loomed in the distance, and she soon understood that the glow came from flames and that somehow, the massive conflagration was their destination. As they approached it, however, the place's true nature became apparent. It was no massive bonfire, as she'd imagined. Instead, the flames made of the walls and ramparts a huge fortification. The heat that rose from it was so much that Aimee could scarcely breathe.

"Behold," Steele said as they drew nearer. "The Burning City!"

They passed through a broad gate, running quickly as their clothes and hair began to smoke from the heat. Aimee was surprised to find on the other side a bizarre, ancient-looking city made mostly of black stone. The peculiar beings that passed her on the street were too numerous and malformed for her to even guess what they could be. She rushed past them as fast as she could.

Finally, her small guides led her into a foreboding black castle and down a long staircase.

From there they went through another gate, deep into a cavern, until they came through an arched passageway lined with giant columns. And then, suddenly, they were in a wide, cold room with a domed ceiling and black, stone floors. On a platform several feet above the floor was a silver, jewel-encrusted throne. The creature sitting on it was astonishing and as black as obsidian. Its head was enormous and its shoulders broad and muscular. She wanted to shrink away from it, but for some reason she drew closer.

Steel and Begg bowed low before it, and then Steel ran behind Aimee and pushed her forward. "My Lord Prefect Azaziel," he said. "See what a pretty-pretty we have brought you."

Slowly, the creature rose from the throne to its full height. He stared haughtily down at them. He was the tallest man Aimee had ever seen— only he wasn't a man. Not exactly.

"I have no use for a human woman," Azaziel said with contempt.

"Not even if she's Orias's woman?" Steel asked slyly.

The being turned to Aimee and a pair of black, feathery wings unfurled from its back. Its skin was as sleek and black as a killer whale's and its eyes had sizzling red irises. His gaze raked over her, and she could feel disdain radiating from him.

"How fortuitous," he said. "Fortuitous, indeed. Why go after the prey when we can make him come to us?" He descended from his throne, never once taking his eyes off Aimee. Passing close to her, he moved gracefully to the edge of a balcony that seemed to look out over a wide chasm from which the red glow emanated. "Uphir!" he bellowed. "Come up from the Pit! I have a job for you!"

∞

Bran, in his hospital bed, stared groggily at the TV. A rerun of *Saturday Night Live* was on, but the volume was off. He was pretty sure he wouldn't be able to concentrate on the words even if he could hear them. With every breath, the wound in his side sent a jolt of pain through his body, but all in all, it wasn't too bad. Maybe it was because he was in shock or maybe it was because of all the pain meds they had him on, but he felt pretty good, given the fact that he'd almost died. Now, for the rest of his life, he'd be able to tell girls he got shot. If that didn't give him bragging rights as a bona-fide badass, nothing would.

The thought of bragging about it like some rap star made him laugh, and the laugh made his stomach hurt, which made him quit laughing. *It's a good thing SNL is on mute,* he thought. *If I was cracking up right now, I'd probably die.* He was still trying to keep from laughing when Johnny the Cop entered the curtained enclosure.

"Hey—Bran, isn't it?" Johnny asked. "How ya feeling?"

Bran shrugged. "Okay."

Johnny nodded sympathetically. "I know this might not be the best time, but I need to ask you a few questions about your injury. Can you tell me what happened tonight?" He had a little notebook in one hand and the tip of his pen hovered over it, ready to write. A long moment passed before Bran finally spoke.

"I don't really remember," he said.

"Yeah—the doc said you might not. Trauma and all that. But if you can remember anything, it would really help. We'd like to investigate this as an attempted murder case, but it's going to be tough."

"Why?" asked Bran.

"Because of the account your buddies gave—and those kids from the Flats backed them up."

"They did?" Bran couldn't hide his surprise.

Johnny nodded. "Yep. They all said it was an accident. That Josh was just showing off a gun."

Suddenly, it all came back to Bran. Josh, enraged, sprinting up the tracks toward Rick with a gun. Zhai shooting some sort of energy out of his hand at the last second, knocking Josh off the tracks. Bran remembered feeling a pain in his side, like a bee sting that kept getting worse and worse. He'd fallen to his knees and then he'd blacked out.

It was Josh, and he'd taken that gun out with the intention of taking a life with it; Bran knew that. But it wasn't Bran's life he was trying take, it was Rick's. In a way, it had been an accident. He decided to stall for time.

"Yeah. Like I said, I don't remember," he said slowly. "But if the Flatliners and the Toppers actually agree on anything, it must be true."

Johnny snorted. "But it's curious, don't you think? Two known gangs get together in a place where everyone knows they go to fight. You all come in here beat to hell. Somebody gets shot, and you're telling me it's an accident? Come on, Bran. What happened?"

But Bran wasn't thinking about what had happened to him anymore.

He was thinking about Emory, his body limp, as Rick continued pounding away at him. He was thinking about Emory's girlfriend screaming as she saw his body behind the Dumpster, broken and bloodied. Emory had been in this hospital. He might even have been in this bed. And Bran had lacked the courage to tell the truth about what had happened to him.

Bran remembered all the times he'd seen Josh and Emory hanging out together at school, sitting together in the lunch room, walking home together. They were best friends. It was understandable that Josh wanted revenge.

"You know, even without your testimony, whoever that gun belongs to could get charged with attempted murder. That's how it works," Johnny said. "Try to remember."

Bran looked Johnny in the eye. "Like the guys said—it was an accident."

Johnny's eyes narrowed. "So, you don't think that Flats kid—Josh—should be charged?"

"No," Bran replied. "He's not the one who should be behind bars."

"Then who should be?" Johnny asked.

Rick had been Bran's first friend in Middleburg, since the first day of football practice Bran's first year in town. Rick had watched him carry the football twice, and then he'd introduced himself. They had been allies, comrades on the football field, on the basketball court, and more recently in the octagon at Spike Ferrington's gym. But Rick wasn't Rick anymore. And he was more dangerous than ever.

"Is Rick here?" Bran asked.

"Rick Banfield?" Johnny was surprised. "No."

Bran nodded, his eyes drifting absently back to the TV.

"All right," Johnny said, flipping his notebook shut. "I can see you're tired. We'll pick this up tomorrow. Feel better, okay?" He headed for the door.

"It was Rick," Bran said.

"What?" Johnny turned around.

"Rick Banfield killed Emory Van Buren," Bran said, and it felt like a vault inside his chest clicked open, releasing a host of warming sun rays.

CHAPTER 23

On Sunday morning, Agent Wade Hackett woke to the deafening chirping of his cell phone. His first thought was that there could be nothing worse than the grating, high-pitched sound of that ring. He was wrong.

Ten minutes later, his teeth unbrushed, hair uncombed and tie askew, he stood at the door to the mobile lab unit where the three ring shards his men had collected so far were being kept and analyzed. It wasn't going to be easy to get inside, he saw. There were puddles of blood on the metal steps that led up to the door, and the lifeless body of Agent Whitehead was slumped across them. A gaping red slash had opened his throat from ear to ear.

"Cover him up," Hackett said. "Get him out of here."

"Detective Z said he's waiting for his crime scene team to—" Agent Brown started, but Hackett cut him off.

"I don't give a piss what Z said. I told you get him out of here!" Hackett barked, then stepped over his fallen comrade and into the mobile trailer. It was just as he thought. Two of his science officers lay butchered on the floor, and the door of the lead-lined safe where they'd been keeping the shards was standing open. He didn't bother to go over and look inside—he already knew it was empty. The shards were gone. He sat down heavily at the desk near the door, feeling like someone had stomped good and hard on his gut.

His cell phone chirped again and when he saw who it was, he silenced it. It was his commander in Washington D.C. The guys who had found the body had notified him as soon as they discovered the casualties, no doubt. It was protocol. Hackett would get reamed out for not answering the call, but he didn't care. He was getting a reaming either way, and he needed time—a few minutes anyway—to sort through what had gone wrong.

It was pretty clear. He didn't need Z's crappy CSI unit to tell him that the Order of the Snake had waltzed in here, slaughtered his men, and taken the ring shards. The question was, how? His own men were highly trained and the lab was wired up with all sorts of sensors, cameras, and alarms. The whole unit would have been alerted the minute someone approached the trailer. Furthermore, how had the Snakes known that the shards were in the trailer? Hackett wasn't an idiot. He'd set up a decoy lab across town and manned it with heavily armed, well-trained agents to create a perfect trap. *Well, obviously, not perfect,* he thought. Somehow, the Snakes knew the shards were there and they'd snagged them. They could be halfway back to China by now.

With a heavy sigh, he leaned his elbow on the table and heard a sound like the crinkling of paper. It was the science team's report. *Fresh off the printer when they were killed,* he thought and scanned it.

Hackett was no scientist. High school chemistry, for him, had been an exercise in boredom, and the rows of numbers and chemical symbols he was looking at now might as well have been Egyptian hieroglyphs. Fortunately, there was a section at the bottom that the team had written in layman's terms, a concession to Hackett's superiors in Washington, who didn't understand chemistry either.

The specimen's chemical composition does not match that of any known element, compound, or alloy, and its properties seem to be completely unique. There appears to be enough potential energy stored within a ten-gram sample to power the city of New York for three thousand years, and yet the compound is completely stable, emitting no more radiation than a common piece of glass. The potential for peaceful energy use, as well as weaponization of the material, is nearly infinite. The team recommends that all available resources be used to secure the remaining material and keep it out of the hands of the Chinese government. Priority: Alpha.

Hackett dropped the report back to the table, unable to suppress a groan. The morning had started out bad when he learned that three of his agents were killed and his security was breached. He hadn't thought it could get any worse, but his blunders might cost the United States its role as leader of the free world. A few minutes ago, he was concerned about his career. Now, it looked like the balance of world power was at stake.

"Connors!" he barked, and a husky agent with ruddy cheeks vaulted into the trailer.

"Yes, sir," Connors said, whipping the aviator sunglasses off his face and standing at attention.

Hackett fought the urge to roll his eyes. He hated when they sent him guys fresh out of the military. They were always stiff and by-the-book. But there was no way he was going to tell the kid to relax—not now, when Feng Xu was on the move. Hackett's phone chirped again.

"Scan this report and email it to headquarters now. Use the encrypted line," he said, handing the pages to Connors, and then he answered his phone.

"Hackett here." The tongue-lashing began immediately and lasted so long Hackett felt obliged to butt in. There would be plenty of time for him to get dressed down later, but now there were more important matters at stake. "Sir," he broke into his superior's tirade. "I'm sending the science team's report to you now . . . Yes, they finished it . . . You'll see when you get it, sir, but I think you'll want to send your strike teams in now. I recommend six units, at least. . . . Yes, six. The urgency of this situation can't be overstated. If Feng Xu gets the materials back to China, it might tip the balance of global power forever. It might be the end of us, sir. . . . No, I'm not out of my freakin' mind, sir. You'll see when you get the report. Just read it—and send me the units *now*. We need to form a perimeter around the city immediately, order a media blackout, and bring in every damned asset we've got. If we don't find a way to stop it, Middleburg, Kansas, is going to be a war zone."

ℂ

Dawn was breaking as Orias parked his car on Golden Avenue and headed north, toward the wooded path that would lead him to the Middleburg Tunnels. If Aimee had gone to bring back her mother, Orias was sure she would try to use the Wheel. And that, he now realized, would be very, very dangerous. The Wheel was a portal. And a portal could lead to all sorts of places—good places and bad ones, too. It was also the place in Middleburg where the power of the Irin was the greatest. His only hope was to find Aimee before Azaziel did.

Orias picked up his pace. He was floating weightlessly a couple of inches above the sidewalk when a little way ahead he noticed a strange glow. Streams of reddish light were shining up from around the edges of a manhole cover in the center of the street. Orias froze, staring at the heavy circle of steel as it slowly rose into the air like the roof of an invisible elevator.

His feet hit the sidewalk as a shape emerged from the round opening. Was it possible that the mighty Azaziel would choose such an undignified route to the surface? Although he thought not, anything was possible. But the creature that emerged from Middleburg's sewer system was not the Lord Prefect of the fallen Irin.

"Uphir?" Orias said.

"None other." This time the demon doctor had not bothered with a human disguise. "I have a message for you—from Azaziel."

"I don't answer to Azaziel."

Uphir reached out an arm that was little more than wispy smoke and opened a skeletal hand to reveal a scroll. "You might today," he hissed. "I'm in a lot of trouble because of you, Orias. Your friend Aimee is, too. He has her."

Orias snatched the scroll from the demon, broke the seal, and unrolled it to see that a vivid image had been burned into the leather. Azaziel, his hand clamped around Aimee's neck, was holding her over a smoldering chasm. Beneath the picture, the fallen Irin had inscribed,

Orias,

Your presence is requested. Come at once or Aimee will bear the brunt of my displeasure.

—Azaziel

෨

Aimee forced herself to stay calm, which was a lot easier said than done since she was locked in a cage right next to the doors that led to the Pit, and Azaziel's soldiers or disciples or whatever they were continued to stare at her from the shadows.

The throne room, lit only by the eerie glow, was constructed of dark stone with huge marble columns set around its outer circumference. She'd caught glimpses of the creatures hiding between them, and she could sense their malice. Their lord prefect lounged on his throne, sipping from a crystal goblet filled with wine. Azaziel's eyes were closed as if he was listening to the whispers coming from the figures in the shadows. The murmurings were vaguely ominous, going on and on like some kind of chant, like they were reciting some kind of perverted rosary, and the sound made Aimee shiver. She watched Azaziel for a few moments, until his eyes snapped open. He looked at her and grinned.

"They're coming," he said.

A set of jeweled doors at the far end of the room slid open and Orias stepped out, as if he were getting off some kind of elevator. With him was the strangest being Aimee had ever seen. It had the shape of a man but no substance. It was like a person made of smoke. It ran around Orias and bowed low before Azaziel.

"My Lord Prefect," it said. "As you have decreed, I deliver the prisoner into your mighty hands. It is my proud privilege to be of some small service to your bountiful majesty—"

"Shut up, Uphir," Azaziel ordered. "Unless you want to go back into the Pit."

Without another word, Uphir scurried into the shadows.

"Orias," said Azaziel. "I must say I'm surprised to see you. I never thought you'd have the courage to stand before me just for the sake of one pitiful human girl."

Ignoring him, Orias walked toward the cage where Aimee was waiting.

"Stay where you are, Nephilim!" Azaziel thundered. "Or she will suffer." He waved one grotesquely taloned hand and said, "Release her."

Instantly, the cage door sprang open.

"Orias!" Aimee exclaimed and ran into his arms.

"Aimee, I'm so sorry," he whispered.

"Oh, do spare me your tiresome human emotions, half-breed," said Azaziel. "And there will be no more physical contact, Orias, or you will watch as my Sacred Guard beheads her."

Dark faces with enormous sorrowful eyes peered out from between the ring of marble columns as Orias moved away from Aimee.

"What do you want, Azaziel?" he asked, turning to the terrible fallen Irin. "You never bother with us lowly Nephilim."

"Unless you interfere with my plans," was the reply. "What I want is to put you on trial."

"Fine," Orias said. "You got me here so you have no more use for Aimee. Let her go."

"I'm not going anywhere," Aimee said. "I can speak for you, like a character witness."

Azaziel rose and strode gracefully to her. Towering over her, he looked at her with so much evil she was tempted to try to slip—but she knew better than to run from a bully. If high school had taught her anything, it was that. She stared up at him defiantly. Azaziel smiled.

"Aimee, no," said Orias. "You need to go."

"She stays," said Azaziel. "I would be greatly intrigued to hear her testimony."

"Why?" Orias challenged. "We both know how this is going to turn out."

"Have you any other witness to speak for you?" asked the Lord Prefect of the fallen. Orias said nothing. "Very well, then. Let us begin." He took his throne again and continued, "This royal court is now in session. Orias Morrow, you are hereby charged with imprisoning an Irin and trying to enlist the aid of a demon to kill him. How do you answer these charges?"

Meeting his gaze Orias replied, "We both know what my true crime is—the unforgivable crime of existing."

Smug and amused, Azaziel responded, "Be that as it may, we shall proceed." Aimee could hear a stirring in the darkness between the columns as he continued, "The Nephilim before us stands accused of trying to end the life of my finest soldier, Oberon, to whom I assigned a most important mission."

"Wait," Aimee interrupted. "Aren't you guys immortal or something? How can Orias kill someone who's immortal?"

Azaziel looked at Aimee, as if mildly amused. "Oh, angels can die if you know how to kill them. But unlike His precious humans, God did not see fit to give us souls. So if we are destroyed, that's it for us."

"What about Nephilim?" Aimee asked. "Orias's human half has a soul."

"It hardly matters—he is a mongrel, as repulsive to those above as he is to those below," Azaziel told her. "Now approach the throne. What say you in his defense? Do you have any proof that he is not guilty of these charges?"

"I don't know anything about that," Aimee said. "All I know of Orias is what he has shown me, which has been nothing but good. Sure, he's probably made some mistakes, but if he'd been treated better all these years maybe he would have made better choices. We all make mistakes— that's what humans do."

"Answer the question, please. Can you prove that he did not conspire to kill his father, Oberon?"

Aimee hesitated. She remembered Orias waking her up in front of that locked tower door and chastising her for nearly opening it. She hadn't thought much about it at the moment—in fact, her memory of the event seemed to have faded almost instantly. She remembered it now, but she had no way of knowing if Oberon had been behind that door.

"I don't know," she said. "But if he did I can't say that I blame him. Oberon is a creep. He kidnapped me once and killed a boy for no reason, right in front of me. What about *his* crimes?"

"Oberon is not on trial here," Azaziel retorted. "Answer the question. Have you any evidence that the accused did not hatch a plot to imprison and assassinate his father?"

"No. I don't."

"The witness is dismissed. We will hear next from Dr. Uphir, whose help the accused tried to enlist."

Another fallen angel, onyx-skinned and eerily beautiful, approached Azaziel and whispered in his ear.

"Indeed?" Azaziel responded. He looked at Orias. "It seems we have a surprise witness."

The double doors behind him slid open again and a murmur rustled through the crowd of Irin hidden in the shadows. A lone figure strode boldly into the room with a beast—a warped, misshapen demon thing—

beside him. Silhouetted as he was against the firelight from the Pit, he looked like a black shadow at first, but when the doors shut behind him, the dim ambient light shone on his face and the whole assembly uttered a collective gasp.

"Hello, Oberon," Azaziel said coldly. "It's high time you honored us with your presence. You have been away long from your true home."

Orias stared at his father, the great fallen angel, the mighty Irin soldier, but Aimee's gaze traveled from the monster who'd abducted her to the one standing beside him.

"Rick?" she said. "What the hell happened to you?"

That thing couldn't be her brother, she thought—and yet it was. And suddenly she realized that Rick—the real Rick—was gone and there was no hope for whatever he had become. He was beyond help—hers or anyone else's. He looked at her and laughed—a kind of snuffling, chortling sound.

"Silence!" Azaziel roared. "I will have order in this court! Oberon—tell me. Who has kept you from me for so long?"

Oberon bowed slightly from the waist, giving Azaziel, it seemed, only the minimal obeisance necessary. "The accused who stands before you now is the one who prevented it," he said. "But for him I would have saved the ring and brought it to you."

"Saved the ring?" Azaziel sat up a little straighter on his throne. "Has something happened to it?"

"Yes, my lord," replied Oberon. "There was a great battle on the fields of Middleburg as several factions tried to take it. It exploded—shattered into many pieces. Although I was locked away, my demon servant Rick has reported it to me exactly as it happened." The Rick monster shuffled closer to the throne and bowed, careful not to look directly at Azaziel. Oberon continued, "If we retrieve all the pieces and put them back together we can still accomplish our goal."

"What goal?" asked Aimee. She couldn't imagine what would

transpire if the wrong people—or the wrong creatures—got hold of the ring. She prayed that the three shards in her pocket wouldn't suddenly start to glow and reveal that she had them.

Azaziel gave her a scathing look. "Be quiet. You do not ask the questions here."

"If I may be permitted, my lord, I would like to answer her. My objective should be a part of the court record, don't you agree?" said Oberon.

"Indeed," said Azaziel. "Continue."

"Many eons ago, when we Irin were still among the exalted ones, we were the caretakers of the humans. We were angelic missionaries who appeared as teachers, leaders, and friends to the new beings the All had created. The Four Gates were open in those days, and when human lives ended, it was our task to escort their souls through one of the gates so they could travel onward and become one with the light.

"But then the lowly human women seduced us with their charms and we were cast out of the light forever and forbidden, for all time, to be in the presence of God."

Right, Aimee thought. *Blame women for your mistakes, you low-life.* But she knew better than to speak. As twisted as it was, this was supposed to be a court hearing, and she didn't think Azaziel would tolerate any more interruptions from her. If she had any hope of helping Orias, she had to keep silent.

"With the blessing of the Lord Prefect and the Irin High Council," Oberon continued, "I ventured up onto the earth, bent on accomplishing a single task—to retrieve the ring, the last one remaining with the power to open the gate to the higher realm. If we gather the pieces and put them back together we can open the gate and transport our army there to defeat the exalted angels. Without their protection, the human race will be at our mercy. We can destroy them all, until there are none left. God wants their worthless souls—I say let Him have them. We shall inherit and inhabit the earth. We shall live in darkness no more!"

Azaziel had been listening intently. "And how do you suggest we recover the shards of the ring?" he asked.

"We must hone our swords and ready our armor," Oberon replied. "Several of the humans have been collecting the shards. We go to war—and we take them!"

Ecstatic shouts rose from the crowd, but a gesture from Azaziel silenced them.

"Let it be as you say. We must prepare," he said. "In the meantime, we will hold the accused as a prisoner, in case we need to torture him for more information. When we return with all the pieces of the ring, I will ask for a verdict and render my sentence."

With one elegant gesture from Azaziel, four dark angels came out of the shadows, grabbed Orias, and threw him into the cage Aimee had just left. She went to him and reached out for him, through the bars.

"No," he said, backing away from her. "Go now. Save yourself—and your friends, if you can."

She moved closer and whispered to him, "If they see that I have the shards—"

"You don't need them, Aimee," he told her. "You never did. You can do it on your own. You have to forget about me. But always remember—I love you."

Tears misted her eyes, but she knew now was not the time to give in to emotion. "I will remember," she said. "And I will find a way to help you."

She turned to Azaziel. "This isn't over," she declared. "I'll be back—with help."

And she slipped.

CHAPTER 24

ON SUNDAY MORNING, ZHAI AND LI were still in the family room, watching some lame show on MTV before they started their normal weekend regimen of homework and exercise.

"So," he said to his sister. "What's up with Weston?"

She looked at him placidly. "Nothing. Can't a girl be friends with a boy without it turning into a Nicholas Sparks novel?"

Zhai shrugged. "Sure, I guess. But the way he looks at you doesn't exactly scream *friend*."

"So?"

"If you don't really like him, why do you spend so much time with him?"

Li stretched and yawned, like a lazy, graceful cat. "He amuses me," she said.

Zhai's smile disappeared. He hated it when Li acted as selfish and uncaring as her mother. It didn't happen often, but when it did it gave Zhai the creeps.

"And what about that henna tattoo?"

"What about it?"

"You couldn't have put in on yourself—you can't reach that part of your back. Did Weston do it for you?"

Li laughed. "Brother mine, you're getting protective in your old age! I don't ask you questions when you come home in the wee hours of the morning, all filthy, and with your clothes torn from fighting, do I? Besides, I *can* reach the middle of my back, you know," she said, and she reached one of her graceful arms over her head, brought the other one up behind her back, and linked her fingers. She was indeed very flexible.

"Happy now?" she asked.

Zhai laughed at himself. Truthfully, he didn't care if Li went out with Weston. He seemed like a nice enough kid. It was the tattoo that worried him. The fact that the Obies had once used tattoos to make him their slave was bad enough, but the memory that really bothered him was that of his father, unbuttoning his shirt in his office, revealing the tattoo that rested over his heart. He hadn't told Li about it yet, and he wasn't going to. Knowing that his father could die if he disobeyed the Snakes was hard enough for Zhai to process; there was no need to burden Li with the knowledge.

"I guess . . . you're right," Zhai said. "I am protective—of Weston. I can already tell that poor kid is going to get his heart broken!"

"Shut up!" Li laughed and socked her brother in the shoulder. The sound of someone approaching in the hallway cut their conversation short.

"Excuse me, Mr. Zhai," the maid said as she appeared in the doorway. "You have a visitor."

Zhai wondered who it was—Nass, maybe, or one of the Toppers— but he was completely unprepared for the sight of Master Chin standing in the foyer, waiting for him.

"Chin!" He ran to his teacher and grabbed him in a fierce embrace. "Wow—you look great!"

Chin laughed. "If it weren't for Lily Rose's Shen keeping me stable until Aimee could get that poison out of me, I wouldn't have made it. But I'm much better now."

He was thinner and paler, but the light in his eyes was as bright as ever. "I'm so glad to see you out of that bed," said Zhai.

"I'm glad to be out of it. But we don't have time to celebrate. As soon as Lily Rose was convinced I could leave, I went over to Violet Anderson's house to examine the tapestry she's working on. It's nearly finished."

"What did it show you?" Zhai asked.

"That the battle for this world will soon reach its climax. Time is short. We need to reunite the shards of the ring as soon as we can and bring Raphael back. Do you still have them?"

Zhai nodded. "Yes—in my room. Come on."

Student and master hurried up the stairs and into Zhai's bedroom. Near the head of his bed, Zhai stooped and pulled the grate out of the air-conditioning register that his bed skirt obscured. He took a small wooden box out of the duct and then he grabbed a notepad from his desk. They hurried back downstairs, out the back door, across the lawn, and to the guesthouse.

Zhai knocked on the door and Nass opened it, yawning. He was wearing his pajamas—a T-shirt and boxers. "Master Chin. Whoa—you're looking better!" Nass said.

"I am—much better, thank you," Chin answered.

"Sorry if we woke you," Zhai said. "But we need to figure out who still has pieces of the ring. We need your help making a list." He held up the notepad.

"Yeah, come in," Nass said, ushering them inside and leading them over to the glass-topped kitchen table. "I don't know—it's not gonna be easy. The government guys snagged all the shards we had."

"And the Obies stole some of the pieces the Toppers had," said Zhai. "Let's start with those. We'll list what shards are where, and then we'll make a plan to get them back."

He clicked his pen and started writing. First they listed everyone who had been on the tracks the night the ring shattered. Then they listed how many shards they thought each person had now.

"Okay," Zhai said. "I have five. Aimee has one, Dalton has one, and Miss Pembrook has one. From what we know, it looks like Agent Hackett and the Obies combined have about eight. Have we forgotten any?"

The three of them gazed at the list thoughtfully. "So," Nass said. "Out of sixteen, we've got eight."

"Yeah. Maybe we should each hang on to a couple, in case—" Zhai took the shard he always carried with him out of his pocket, then opened the box he'd taken from the AC unit and looked inside, and the words died in his throat. Nass and Chin craned their necks to look inside, too.

The box was empty. Zhai's four shards were gone.

so

It was just after dawn when Emily woke her guests and told them breakfast was ready. She'd brought them all the same kind of ankle-length dresses that she wore and told them to hurry. When they joined her at the big kitchen table and tasted the ham, eggs, grits, and biscuits she'd made, Maggie thought she would die of sheer pleasure. Emily Banfield was right about one thing—the food was delicious. But it was hard to enjoy the feast she'd placed before them knowing what they were about to face.

"You all look adorable in those frocks," Emily said.

"I hope you have one for me."

Maggie would have found it almost impossible to describe the look on Emily's face when she heard that familiar, beloved voice.

"Aimee?" said Emily, and they all watched as Aimee materialized, like a character out of *Star Trek*, right in front of the icebox.

"Mom!"

They ran to each other and Aimee fell into her mother's arms. In an avalanche of tears and laughter they hugged, pulled back to look at each other, and hugged again. Maggie was almost overcome with emotion herself, and she looked around at Miss Pembrook, Dalton, and Kate. They were having the same reaction.

When at last their joy subsided enough for them to speak, Emily said, "How did you do that, Aimee—and how did you get here?"

"Mom, since you left, a lot of weird things have been happening in Middleburg. What you just saw—me teleporting—is one of them. I call it slipping. That's what got us here and that's what will get us home. But how did *you* get here?"

"I'm afraid you won't believe me."

"Dad said you left us, that you didn't love us, and you didn't want us anymore. But then, when Dalton and I were helping Miss Pembrook with some research, I found an old photo of you here in Middleburg—taken over a hundred years ago. Trust me. I'll believe you."

"Well, first, you know that I'd never leave you and your brother and just go away."

"I know. But after what happened with Tyler—"

Emily held a hand up to stop her. "I should have been stronger," she said. "I should have stood up to your father. He told me that sending you to Mountain High Academy was the only way we could keep the police out of our lives and make sure you'd never go to trial."

"Mom, I didn't kill Tyler."

"Sweetheart, I know that. And after we sent you to that . . . school . . . I was trying to figure out how it happened, which is why I ended up here."

"I don't understand," said Aimee.

"I went to the tunnel. I wanted to see for myself where they found his body."

"Why?" Maggie asked.

"I don't know," Emily replied. "I was just trying to understand."

"What happened in the tunnel?" asked Aimee. "Did you go inside?"

"I was about to when I saw one of your father's business associates coming out of it. You remember Oberon Morrow?"

"Do I ever," said Aimee. "Go on."

"Well—and I know this will sound strange—but something was happening to him. Something weird. He was becoming someone else. He was changing."

"Yeah, I've seen that act," Aimee told her. "I had a front-row seat, in fact. He morphed into his true self—a fallen angel."

"That's right," Emily said. "I knew right away what he was. You remember all those books I'd read about angels—and I believed in them, both the good and the bad kind, but I never thought I'd actually see one. I gasped. I'd never seen anything so beautiful and so frightening."

"And he heard you," Dalton surmised.

Emily nodded. "Yes. I'd seen what he was and there was no way he was going to let me tell anyone. I tried to get away. I ran but these great black wings came out of his back and he flew right over me and landed in front of me to block my way. He could have killed me, but he sent me here instead. He said it was better than killing me. It would be a living death, knowing that I'd never see you and Rick again."

"Ah . . . Mom?" Aimee said. "About Rick. He's . . . he's not himself these days. He's changed—and not in a good way."

"Yeah," Maggie interjected. She looked at Aimee. "You've seen it too?"

Aimee nodded.

"Mrs. Banfield, I don't mean to be rude," Dalton said. "But I never could figure out how a nice person like you could have two such different kids."

Emily smiled. "Yes. Aimee was always so sweet, cooperative, cheerful—until Tyler died. But Rick—I could never reach him. I saw a cruel streak in him when he was just a toddler. I tried to stop it but over the years he became such a bully."

"It's more than that," said Aimee. "It's like something dark has seeped into him somehow."

"Oh, God," Emily whispered. "My poor boy."

"He's not your boy anymore, Mrs. Banfield," Maggie told her sadly. "I know it sounds weird, but he's turned into some kind of demon or something."

"All the more reason to get home as soon as possible," said Emily. "Aimee, are you sure you can do it?"

"Yes, I can," Aimee assured her. "Don't worry, Mom. I'll get you home."

Emily hugged Aimee close again and then caught her up on what was going on in 1877 Middleburg, what the outlaws wanted and how much they were all in danger.

"Okay," Aimee said. "So . . . we have to make a plan. We've got to figure out how I'm going to teleport us all back to our Middleburg without those outlaws noticing you're gone and starting to shoot everybody."

"Not just your mom," said Anne Pembrook. "They know we're here now, too."

"We've got to take them out," Maggie said. "We've got no other choice."

Before any of them could react to that, the church bells started ringing. "They're starting the counting. Come with me, darling. I'll get you a dress to wear. We have to hurry."

"Wait," said Aimee. "They don't know I'm here. That could work to our advantage."

CHAPTER 25

The moment he opened the box and found the ring shards missing, the neurons in Zhai's brain started firing overtime. The shards were gone, taken from his house despite Hilltop Haven's robust security detail, despite the community's cameras, despite the state-of-the-art security system that supposedly protected the Shao house, and despite the endless array of house staff and family members who were constantly parading in and out of the place. Was it possible that the Obies or government agents had somehow been able to enter the house undetected and take the shards from Zhai's hiding place?

Maybe. But there was a simpler explanation.

Since his father had always been reliable and honest, Zhai had somehow failed to fully comprehend that he *really* belonged to the Obies. They held sway over his father's life or his death—and they could get him to do anything. Why had Zhai thought the ring shards would be safe in his house?

"My father," he said grimly. "If he doesn't have them he may know where they are. Wait here," he told Chin and Nass and hurried across the lawn toward the back entrance of the main house. He charged up the steps and down the hall, calling for his father, and blasting through the study door almost hard enough to knock it off its hinges.

Cheung Shao was standing by the window and he turned, surprised when Zhai ran in.

"Zhai, what is it?"

Zhai grabbed him by the front of his shirt and shook him. "The shards," he demanded. "Where are they?"

"I don't know. What shards?" Cheung Shao asked. "What are you talking about?" He was either baffled by the question, Zhai thought, or pretending to be.

"Don't lie to me!" Zhai yelled. "You've lied about everything. Why we came to America, how we got here, where your money came from. All of it—lies! I'm warning you, Father. If you lie to me about this, I'm done with you!"

Sadness crossed Cheung's face. "You do not understand," he said. "I have nothing to do with the shards or the treasure. I have nothing to do with any of it. I am a businessman, Zhai, not a fighter. I conducted the Order's businesses—their legitimate businesses—not their dirty work."

"Then who took the shards?" Zhai demanded.

"I took them," a voice behind Zhai said, and he turned around.

It was Li.

ဆ

As Nass and Chin followed Zhai toward the back door of the main house, Chin warned him, "It's slipping away, Nass. We're running out of time."

"It'll be okay," Nass said hopefully. "We just have to get the shards back. Zhai will talk to his dad. He'll—"

Chin was still recovering from his illness and was moving a little slower than usual, but they were almost to the back door when it opened. Lotus Shao, wearing a jade-colored turtleneck sweater, black pants, and tall black riding boots stood there, blocking their path. Her hair was tied back into a sleek black ponytail that reached halfway down her back. If there was an award for hot moms of Middleburg, Nass figured, she'd win it hands down. If there was an award for scary moms, she'd win that, too.

"Let us pass," Chin said.

Lotus shook her head slowly, and she was smiling. "Not this time, Chin," she said. "It's over."

They eyed each other silently, and then Nass spoke up. "Look, we don't want to make any problems," he said quickly. "We're with Zhai. He just went inside." He tried to slip past her, but she stopped him with one small hand pushing firmly against his chest.

"No," she said.

"Well," Chin said mildly. "I always wondered why the Order would send Cheung on such an important mission without a handler. That's your job, Lotus—isn't it?"

She bowed slightly, giving Chin an icy smile. "How clever of you to finally figure it out," she said. "But I'm afraid it's a little too late for it to do you any good."

Chin nodded. "Your husband's trust—and his heart—were misplaced," he said.

"My husband is a fool whose mind is distorted by love."

"I'm afraid I must disagree with you," retorted Chin. "Love cannot distort. Even the most misguided love is more productive than a rational hatred."

"Ever the philosopher." Lotus's voice was low and sarcastic. "Go now. Leave—at once," she commanded.

"Not without Zhai," said Nass.

It all happened in a split second. Nass decided to bolt past Lotus and charge into the house to get Zhai. He even lifted his foot to take the first step. Lotus reacted in a blur of motion, and suddenly Nass was upended, his body parallel to the ground, legs in the air, hands windmilling. He hit the stone patio in a back-smacker of epic proportions, and at the moment of bone-jarring impact, his whole world went black.

∞

As Zhai stood staring at his sister, Weston entered the room behind her—and he seemed completely befuddled. He was looking at Li as if hoping her actions would give him some clue about what was going on.

Zhai released his father and quickly stepped away from him. It was an unwritten rule in the Shao household to keep Li away from anything ugly or unpleasant, and this situation certainly qualified. But he was still having trouble processing what she'd just said.

"Li, this is a private conversation," Cheung Shao said as he smoothed his shirt, but Li continued to walk purposefully toward Zhai.

"I'll need those ring shards you've been collecting," she said evenly, as if she were asking to look at his homework assignment.

"What?" Zhai said.

"The shards. You still have one. Give it to me," she said.

Zhai stared at her, confused. Behind her, Weston said, "Li, thanks— but you don't have to do this for me. It's really not necessary. I mean, unless you *want* to give it to us, Zhai?"

Zhai glanced at Weston, then back to Li. "What's he talking about?" She merely held out her hand. Neither sibling moved.

"Okay, look, so . . . here's the deal," Weston began with a heavy, confessional sigh. "I've been working for the federal government. I know, I don't seem like the secret-agent type, but you know what they say. You can't always judge a book by its cover, right? I mean look at you, Zhai. You look like a normal kid, and you're a martial arts master. Which I respect. Which is why I would never *demand* that you give us the shards. But we're acting on behalf of the United States government so we're requesting, respectfully, that you—"

"No, you're not," Zhai said, still looking at his sister.

"Um . . . what?" Weston said.

"You're not working for the government," he said. "I can't believe I've been so blind."

Li smiled, but it was not her normal schoolgirl grin; it looked eerily like her mother's smile—tight and frigid.

"I'm sorry, Zhai, but yes we are," Weston assured him. "Aren't we, Li? Tell him."

Zhai and Li stood facing each other, their eyes locked. A thousand childhood scenes flashed through his mind: playing on the backyard swing set, riding bikes together in the afternoons, back and forth to music lessons, playing endless childhood games like Go Fish, War, Monopoly—and Li's favorite, Risk.

"I should have known," Zhai said.

"Yes, you should have," Li said simply. "But you've always been so . . . inside yourself. I bet you didn't even know that I'm an expert at Venom of the Fang, did you?" She laughed at his surprise. "You can't possibly beat me in a fight, and I don't really want to hurt you, Brother. Just hand over the shard and everything can still be okay."

"Venom of the what?" Weston asked, and Zhai felt sorry for the kid.

He felt sorry for his father, too. He could see Cheung Shao's reflection in the mirror on the wall behind Li. He had gone completely pale, like he was about to faint. But he was telling the truth. He hadn't taken the shards. He had no idea what was happening. He really was just a lackey, a glorified accountant. It was Li—and if Li worked for the Obies, then so did her mother.

Suddenly, Weston seemed to get it. "You weren't helping me," he said to Li. "You were working for *them*. For the Chinese agents! Oh, God, I've been such an idiot. My dad is gonna kill me."

"Don't feel so bad, Weston," Zhai said. "She tricked me, too. She doesn't even seem to remember that in the last few months, I saved her life—twice."

"Oh—didn't I remember to thank you?" Li said with a sarcastic little smirk, and Zhai understood that there was nothing he could say, nothing born of logic or of love, that would change her course now. Her mother had been grooming her, brainwashing her for as long as Zhai could remember. He had always dismissed it as the love of a devoted, overbearing parent. Now he saw it for what it was: the conditioning of a soldier.

Still watching Li, Zhai reached into his pocket, took out the shard, and held it up in front of his face. Perhaps ten feet separated him and his sister now. "Okay, Li," he said. "If you want the shard that badly you'll have to come and take it from me."

The girlish grin that had been missing earlier rose to her face now. She sprang forward with the grace of a young puma, and attacked.

જી

As they left the boarding house, Maggie went over the plan again in her head. It would utilize every skill they had, but it would also require a bit of luck. Dalton nudged her and nodded at the man on horseback posted on the corner.

"That's Crawford," said Aimee's mom. "He's in charge of this street. He escorts us over to the town hall, and after the count, he brings us all back."

When they passed him, Maggie saw his eyes following them. His hand rested on the six-shooter on his hip and his gaze shifted as one by one the townspeople—men, women, and children—came out of their shops and homes and joined the line. They all looked so tired and anxious, Maggie thought, and she knew they wouldn't be able to depend on them for much help. The stress they were under showed in their faces. She wondered how much longer they could take it. She couldn't help noticing that in their old-fashioned clothes they all looked like extras in some amazing period movie—but she had more urgent concerns at the moment. The number of men keeping guard over them had grown from a couple to about a dozen, and they were all heavily armed.

"Get in line!" one of the outlaws barked, planting a boot in the back of a man wearing dingy work clothes and shoving him into place as the last few stragglers came out to join them. By now they were in front of the town hall, lined up before a long watering trough.

The desperado who seemed to be their leader dismounted and stalked down the column of frightened people. "Which are the new arrivals?" he asked.

"Right here, boss," said Crawford. He walked to where Emily was standing with Anne and the girls.

"I've seen pictures of him," Anne Pembrook whispered excitedly, staring at the leader of the gang. "That's the outlaw Sam Bass!"

"Shut up," Crawford ordered. "Step out. The boss wants to have a look at you."

Calmly, Anne and her students did as they were told. The boss was taller, more broad-shouldered, and uglier than the rest of them, and Maggie didn't like the look he was giving them, especially the one directed at her.

"Well, ain't you a pretty little thing," he said when he stopped in front of her. There was a lecherous gleam in his eye. "I think I could have some fun with you."

"Not really," she said and pointed at Dalton. "She's a lot more fun than I am."

"Oh, yeah?" he replied and sauntered over to where Dalton was standing. "Why do you say that?"

"She's an entertainer," said Maggie. "She sings like an angel. Really—you ought to hear her."

He chuckled. "Been a while since we had any entertainment," he said. "Go ahead. Show me what you can do."

"Right now?" asked Dalton.

"Sure," he said. "Go on—give us a song."

"Okay, then. If you insist." She turned to her friends. "You guys ready to hear a song?" They all assured her that they were.

Maggie felt the energy she'd learned to harness, the power that Raphael called Shen, boiling up within her. She pressed her hands tightly against her ears, like a petulant child trying to block out a reprimand. Emily, Miss Pembrook, and Kate also covered their ears as Dalton opened her mouth and the crystal clear strains of the song from *The Good Book* rang out clearly. The faces of the outlaws and the townspeople turned toward her, curious at first, then smiling, and then drowsy, and then their eyelids drifted shut. What happened next reminded Maggie of a YouTube video she'd seen of a bunch of goats that fainted whenever they got excited. One by one villagers and outlaws dropped to their knees and then slumped to the ground as they fell fast asleep. It was amazing.

When they'd been enemies, Maggie had felt jealous of Dalton's pure, perfect voice, but she was thankful for it now as Crawford wavered in his saddle and then fell off his horse, hitting the ground hard.

When the last of them were down and out, Aimee ran out of an alleyway where she'd been hiding, pulling cotton plugs out of her ears. She was carrying a huge picnic basket that she flipped open, revealing ropes, horse tackle, hair ribbons, belts, and scarves—anything that could be used to tie a person up.

"Quick!" Dalton shouted. "The spell doesn't last forever!"

Miss Pembrook and Aimee's mom helped Maggie and Kate tie up the outlaws while Aimee collected their guns and threw them into the watering trough. They had restrained most of the bandits by the time a thunder of hooves announced the arrival of the sentries who'd been posted around the outer perimeter of the town.

"More of them?" Miss Pembrook said with a groan.

"Keep going!" Maggie shouted. "I'll handle them." She strode confidently into the center of the street, standing her ground, and glaring at the oncoming outlaws, like an old-west gunfighter at high noon.

As they drew nearer, the man in the lead saw that something was wrong and he reached for his gun. Maggie raised her hand and let go with a Shen blast, giving it everything she had. The energy exploded through her body with so much force that for a second she thought it would rip her apart. A pinkish-white cyclone made of pure fire tore down the middle of the road, cutting through the riders like a buzz saw, blasting them off their horses and leaving them stunned.

"They've got dynamite!" one of the bandits yelled. "Shoot 'em— shoot 'em all!"

Maggie felt the world waver and she fell to her knees. Never before had so much Shen flowed through her and it left her depleted, barely able to stay upright. Crawford woke up and struggled to his feet, and then he started ominously toward them. Dalton took a deep breath, preparing to sing again but from behind her a gloved hand snaked around and clapped over her mouth. Crawford's cohorts were also waking up and those that weren't tied up were moving in quickly, forming a ring around her and the others.

With an incredible kung fu sweep, Aimee swept the legs out from under one of the bandits and then brought her heel down on his face with a sickening crunch that left him limp. Another man was coming toward her now, already drawing his gun. Reacting purely from instinct, she kicked it out of his hand. He reached for her, and without even thinking about it, she brought her arms up inside his, forming a triangle with her fingertips. She shot her hands toward his face, the movement hard, fast, and stiff, as if her arms were a couple of switchblades, deflecting groping hands as her outstretched fingers jabbed right into his eyes, blinding him. He fell to his knees with a muffled scream, and Aimee grabbed his head and brought her knee up into it. It sounded like a coconut getting hit with a hammer. Reeling, his head flopped back and he fixed his bloodshot eyes on her. With a smooth motion, she brought her elbow up to shoulder level and smashed it into his face. He biffed into the sand facedown. After that, he didn't move.

Aimee pushed the hair out of her face and looked down at the man she'd just demolished, and then she reached down, rolled him over, and unbuckled his gun belt.

"That'll be enough!" bellowed the boss, and when they all looked in his direction, they saw that he was holding a gun to Kate's head. "Crawford—you and Waylon go untie those men," he ordered. He looked at Maggie, Anne, Dalton, and Aimee. "Get over here—or I'll spray her brains all over the street."

When they were all standing in front of him, he lowered his pistol and looked at Aimee. Unflinching, she returned his stare. "Crawford said those other girls came in last night. Where the hell did you come from?" he demanded.

"From your worst nightmare," she said.

"Oh—that's how you want to play it?" he asked. "Well, maybe I'll blow her head off anyway, just to teach you a lesson."

As he raised his gun again, a shot rang out and he collapsed in a spray of blood. The outlaws looked around wildly, swinging their guns this way and that, searching for the source of the shot. And then they all heard a sound that made them freeze—the shrill whistle of a train in the distance, getting closer and closer.

"Forget about them," yelled Crawford, taking charge. "The train's coming. Waylon and John—keep your guns on these people while we grab that payroll. Then we can get the hell out of here!"

The train rolled into the station in the middle of town, and Maggie, Aimee, and the others watched as the outlaws rushed it and clambered aboard. It was the biggest, blackest train Aimee had ever seen.

"Don't try anything," warned one of the men covering them. "First one makes a move gets it right between the eyes."

"Where'd that gunshot come from, John?" asked the other man, Waylon. "The one that got the boss?"

Before he could answer, Crawford and the other men came running off the train. "There's nobody on board!" Crawford called out as he hurried over to Aimee and the girls. "And there's no safe and no payroll." He looked at them suspiciously. "This is some kinda trick, and I reckon you got something to do with it."

"I don't know what you're talking about," said Aimee.

"Maybe you ought to have our Western Union man send a wire to Topeka and find out what happened to it," suggested Emily.

"You'd like that, wouldn't you," said Crawford. "Somethin' funny's going on here. What kind of train rolls into a station without a soul on board?"

"It's . . . maybe it's some kinda ghost train," ventured Waylon.

"So what do we do now?" asked John.

"We do what the boss told us to do as soon as we got what we came for. We line 'em all up and shoot 'em. Then we take whatever they have that's worth anything and skedaddle—after we set the town on fire." He pointed at the girls. "And we start with these newcomers. They gotta be behind this."

Waylon and John held their rifles on the townsfolk, and Crawford pointed his gun at Aimee. "And we're going to waste this one first," he said, aiming his six-shooter at her. But by the time he'd leveled it, she was already gone, watching him from twenty feet away, at the far end of the churchyard.

"What in the hell is going on here?" Crawford shouted as he looked around, clearly spooked.

At that moment, the bells in the church tower began ringing, and everyone looked up in that direction. A man with a bandana covering his face stepped out of an arched opening in the bell tower. He was holding a huge rope (the pull for the bells, Aimee guessed), and as she watched, he let it fall down the side of the building. He then used it to rappel, first down the steep pitch of the slate roof, then over the side and down to the street below, moving with incredible grace. He was dressed in the same garb as their enemies, like an old-west cowboy.

"It's okay!" Crawford yelled. "He's one of ours."

The mystery man headed toward them through the drifting dust and gun smoke, and suddenly he started shooting with the expertise of a gun-slinger. It took a moment for Aimee to realize he was coming toward her. There was something vaguely familiar about his amazing blue-green eyes but before she could figure out what, she felt rough hands grab her from behind.

"Well, we got us a slippery one, didn't we!" Waylon said triumphantly as he pulled out his gun and pressed it to Aimee's temple.

"One down, four to go!" John yelled gleefully.

Aimee heard the shot, so close that it was deafening, and for an instant she thought the outlaw's gun had gone off, and that she would soon be dead. But then she saw that Waylon now lay motionless on the ground several feet away.

Crawford turned his six-shooter on the enigmatic gunslinger. "Stay back!" he shouted.

"No," the masked man responded simply, and he ran forward with incredible speed. Before Crawford could pull the trigger, the stranger deflected the gun with one hand and shoved it upward, slamming the enemy in the face with his own weapon. Crawford fell to his back, blood drizzling out of his nose, unconscious.

"Thank you," Aimee said to him, little breathlessly.

The gunslinger's eyes glinted as he tipped his hat to her and then continued the battle. Two minutes and a few gunshots later, it was all over. A cheer went up from the citizens of Middleburg. Someone ran to the jail to release the sheriff, who the bandits had locked up, and he quickly took control. He ordered several men to round up the surviving outlaws and lock them up.

Aimee and Maggie looked at each other wearily. "Great job, Aimes," said Maggie.

"You too," Aimee replied.

Everyone nodded except Dalton, who seemed distracted. She was looking at a tall man coming out of the crowd, and he was looking back at her, too. Slowly, they began to move toward one another. As he approached, Aimee noticed that his skin was the same caramel shade as Dalton's and his eyes were two different colors—one amber and the other blue, just like Lily Rose's. He put a gentle hand on Dalton's shoulder.

"I heard your song, child," he said. "It was beautiful."

"Thank you," Dalton responded softly.

"The world needs songs like that," he added, his voice resonant and warm. "I hope you'll keep on singing it."

"I will," Dalton promised, gazing up at him in awe.

He smiled brightly, squeezed her shoulder, and pulled a gold watch out of his vest pocket. After glancing at it, he headed off into the crowd, whistling Dalton's song as he went.

Emily was also smiling. "I think it's safe to leave now," she said to Aimee. "You really think you can get us back home?"

"I do," Aimee replied confidently. "But I wanted to thank him."

"Who?" Dalton asked.

"The man who came down from the church tower. The . . . gunslinger. He saved us!"

"Then turn around," Kate said. "He's right behind you."

Aimee turned and looked into that awesome pair of beautiful blue-green eyes, staring down at her from beneath the brim of a cowboy hat. As the young man came closer he pulled the bandana down from his face and smiled at her.

She offered him her hand. "We can't thank you enough," she said. "My friends and I will be eternally grateful. I'm Aimee."

His smile faded. "My pleasure, ma'am," he said quietly. She shook his hand and then went to join her mom and the others.

∽

Maggie couldn't believe it. "Raphael?" she said, moving quickly to his side. "How . . . we all thought you were dead. Where have you been all this time?"

"I've been traveling," Raphael told her. And she could see that he had. His face was sunburned, crisscrossed with cuts, and mottled with bruises. There was a scab and a bump on his nose, as if it had been broken. He also looked as if he'd grown an inch or so since she'd last seen him.

Without thinking, she hurled herself into his arms and pressed her face against his chest. After a moment, he gently moved her away and she saw the pain in his eyes.

"She still doesn't know me," he said.

Maggie felt a familiar ache of sadness rising within her. So many things had changed, but apparently one thing hadn't: Raphael was still hung up on Aimee. "You really love her, don't you?" asked Maggie.

"I really do."

"Give her time. She's . . . things are starting to come back to her. Maybe when we get back to our Middleburg—"

But Raphael was shaking his head. There was a hardness in him now that broke her heart.

"I'm not going with you," he told her. "I've got one more stop to make." He glanced at the other girls and tilted his hat to them and then he turned away and walked quickly to the eerie black train. He didn't look back as he boarded it.

&

In all his years of martial arts training and practice, Zhai had never experienced an assault like this. Li's fists slipped through his defenses like water through a strainer, and the resulting blows came faster than Zhai could block or counter them. It seemed that by the time one strike ended the next had already begun. With great effort, he managed to jam the ring shard into his pocket and land one glancing strike before Li forced his retreat.

He threw himself backward over his father's desk and hit the floor behind it with a thud. He rolled away as fast as he could, heading for the window. Li hopped effortlessly onto the desk and looked down at him, calm and amused.

Zhai's father shouted for them to stop fighting, while Weston backed into a corner and stayed there, his hands clasped nervously together.

Li laughed and kicked a coffee cup off the desktop, toward Zhai, who smashed it with a quick blow that sent the broken pieces exploding across the room. But it was only a distraction, and Li leaped after it, barraging Zhai with an unending series of kicks and punches. Zhai watched her elbows and her knees and managed to block most of her attacks. He was even able to land a blow to her chin that split her lip. She paused and put a finger to her mouth and when it came away bloody, a pouty little-girl look crossed her face. It reminded Zhai of their childhood together, and he almost turned and walked away. Then, with a savage snarl, she was on him again, her assault more furious than before.

Zhai fought on: moving, retreating, circling, getting in a quick punch here or a leg kick there, and then retreating again. Finally, Li got a little too reckless, and he managed to catch her with a kick to the knee. She groaned with pain as her leg buckled beneath her. Instinct took over, and for an instant, the person before Zhai was not his sister, not a girl, just a deadly adversary he had to overcome. He lunged forward and caught her in the side of the head with an elbow. She collapsed to the carpet instantly.

Panting, Zhai looked down at her and passed his hand across his face. He had no idea if he was wiping away sweat or blood, and it didn't matter. He understood that she had betrayed him and that she was the enemy. He still had the ring shard—that was all that mattered now.

He glanced at his father and then at Weston. Then he headed for the door.

"Zhai, look out!" Weston shouted and pointed behind him.

Zhai turned to find that Li had sprung to her feet and grabbed a wooden chair, and she was charging him with it. He barely managed to throw up a *Bong Sau* in time to block it and keep from getting his head bashed in. The chair shattered against his arms and pieces of it skittered across the carpet. In each hand, Li still held two jagged pieces of the chair like two deadly vampire-slaying stakes, and she advanced on Zhai.

She stabbed at him with one stake while swinging at his head with the other. He managed to block both strikes at once, and then to block two more after that.

"Leave him alone, you liar!" Weston said, and he shuffled toward Li with all the ferocity of a librarian. She swept his legs out from under him, and he landed on his backside with a thump.

Zhai was about to make use of her distraction when the double doors behind him burst open. *What now?* he thought. Before he could turn, someone grabbed his arms from behind.

"Get the shard, now!" It was Lotus's voice, sharp and brittle—and she had a strength he never would have believed. Li rushed forward and thrust her hand into Zhai's pocket as he struggled to get free.

"Take it to them," Lotus commanded. "Go! I'll take care of Zhai."

Li looked at Zhai, a flicker of concern clouding her eyes for a moment. And then she dashed out the door and down the hall. Weston charged after her.

Zhai bucked, trying to break free of Lotus's grip.

"And as for you, stepson," Lotus said softly, "you have been a nuisance for far too long,"

Zhai finally managed to jerk away, and he spun to face her. She had already picked up one of the sharp stakes that Li had discarded. With a wicked gleam in her eye, she advanced on Zhai.

"Lotus—enough!" Cheung shouted, moving toward her. "I will not let you harm my son."

"Shut up," she ordered him. "You have quite outlived your usefulness!"

The words seemed to strike Zhai's father like a slap to the face. He stopped in his tracks as Lotus advanced on Zhai. When Zhai tried to get past her she feigned a sweep, then spun and hit him with a crescent kick to the face. It brought him to his knees and knocked him back against the wall. She advanced, the stake in her hand. He tried to throw up a *Bong Sau,* but in one deft move she trapped his arms and brought the sharp wooden point up to his throat. Just a little pressure was all it would take to drive it up into Zhai's brain.

"It's really too bad," Lotus whispered. "If you hadn't been corrupted by Chin you might have made a good Snake—instead of just a mediocre stepson. And now, you must die."

Zhai lashed out with all his strength, but her arms were as powerful as a pair of constricting pythons. Just as the stake broke the skin of his neck, however, someone pulled Lotus off him.

It was his father. Zhai coughed, the pressure on his neck finally released.

"Go! Stop, Li!" Cheung shouted. He was holding Lotus in a bear hug from behind, and smoke was rising from their struggling bodies. "Go!" he shouted again.

Slowly, Zhai backed toward the doorway. As he watched, Lotus shook Cheung off, catching his arm in a lock. Zhai heard the bone crack as she broke it and Cheung fell to his knees. Zhai hesitated, ready to go back and help his father, when something else caught his eye.

The front of Cheung's white dress shirt had burned away revealing his bare chest. His tattoo was glowing red. Smoke rose from it as if it were searing his flesh, burning into him like a hot coal.

"Father," Zhai shouted. "Dad!"

Lotus tried to go after Zhai again, but Cheung grabbed her leg. "Run!" he yelled, his voice strangled with agony. "Don't let the Snakes have the shards, Zhai! Don't let them win."

Zhai understood. By helping him his father was disobeying the Obies—and the Obies were cashing in on their ownership of him. He'd told Zhai that if he disobeyed them they would kill him.

"Go!" his father yelled once more. The burning mark on his chest was no longer just a glowing spot on the surface of his skin—it was a ball of fire consuming his heart. His shirt was now aflame, and Lotus's clothes were catching fire, too.

Zhai realized that there was no saving his father. He would never be able to extinguish the flame that was burning Cheung Shao's heart.

"Do not let me die in vain," his father said. "Go now—stop them."

Engulfed in flame now, Lotus was struggling. Cheung's face was contorted into a mask of agony as flames rose around him. "Go, Zhai—do what you must," his father said with his last breath.

Zhai ran.

He sprinted down the steps, grabbed the keys from the door by the kitchen, and tore out into the garage. As the door went up, he caught a glimpse of Li in her mother's BMW backing out of the driveway, and he jumped into the driver's seat of his dad's big Maybach. He started the car and shot out of the driveway in reverse, in time to see Li tearing off down the street. He looked around for Chin and Nass, but they weren't there and he couldn't wait for them. He snapped the car into drive, hit the gas, and felt the surge as the massive V12 engine revved up and shot him forward, down the hill. Li had just passed the gate and it was about to close. He hit the accelerator and blasted through, losing a rearview mirror as he went.

He registered a movement off to his left and saw that it was Nass, stepping out into the road and waving at him. Master Chin was there, too. Zhai hit the brakes and stopped a few yards ahead of them in a squeal of tires and a haze of rubber smoke.

"Hurry! Li has the shard!" Zhai shouted.

Master Chin and Nass piled into the back. Glancing in the rearview mirror, Zhai saw that they were both beaten and bruised.

"What happened to you?" he asked.

"Lotus," Nass grumbled. "She jumped us and then called security and had them escort us out of Hilltop Haven."

"She got me, too. And so did Li," Zhai said.

"Your sister . . . she's one of them," Chin said. It was not a question, but a dark realization. "What depravity, bending a little girl to their cause. We have to stop them. They must not come to possess the completed ring."

"We will," Zhai said. They were flying down River Road now, heading out of town at warp speed.

"But we can't face Feng Xu's gang alone," Chin said, and he turned to Nass. "Do you have your cell phone?"

Nass took it out. "Right here," he said. "What are we going to do?"

"We are going to call in the cavalry," Master Chin replied.

CHAPTER 26

RAPHAEL FOUND THE MAGICIAN waiting for him when he returned to the train after his raid on old-west Middleburg. It felt good to have helped Aimee's mom and the crew of girls defeat the outlaws—but the fact that Aimee still didn't recognize him had burned him deeply. He was so devastated by the empty stare he received from her, he was almost glad to return to the train and to ride it once more into the featureless fog that marked the world between times and places. At least here, in oblivion, there was nothing as painful as love.

There was only one time and place in the universe that could possibly be more terrible than his encounter with Aimee had been—and ironically, that's exactly where he hoped to go next.

"I believe there was another stop you wanted to make in your journey?" the Magician said.

Raphael hesitated. It was no surprise that the Dark Teacher had looked into Raphael's heart and read his deepest desire. But the thought of what he might now face if the Magician were to grant his wish was so frightening, he could barely find the courage to voice it aloud.

"I want to go to the Middleburg Materials Factory," he said finally. "I want to know how my father died."

"Vengeance makes for a bitter feast," the Magician warned.

"He was my *dad*," said Raphael. "And he was a good man—the best. I deserve to know what happened—and whoever was responsible deserves to pay for it."

The Magician nodded, no trace of mirth in his dark eyes now. "Very well," he said. "Sleep now, for you are weary. The train will take you to the place you seek."

❧

After Raphael left and old Middleburg settled back to normal, Maggie suggested that they return to the boarding house and change back into their own modern clothes before they headed home. They were all surprised when Emily opened a drawer on the bottom of the tall corner cabinet in the living room and took out a carefully wrapped package. She opened it to reveal the slacks, shirt, and sneakers she'd been wearing when Oberon had banished her to the past.

"I saved everything, just in case," she explained. She pulled something out of the pocket of her jeans and showed them. "I even have my car keys!"

Aimee laughed, and Maggie was so happy for her and her mom. "Are you ready to go home?" Aimee asked.

"More than ready," said Emily. "As soon as I write a note to Constance and thank her for her hospitality and all her help. I can't wait to get home and take a shower in an indoor bathroom that has hot and cold running water."

Maggie saw a shadow cross Aimee's face. "Uh . . . Mom, there's something else I have to tell you," she said, and she explained about Jack marrying Savana Kain.

Clearly shaken, Emily had to sit down. "How long have I been gone?" she asked. "I mean, in your time frame?"

"Almost two years," Aimee said. "Somehow, Dad managed to have you declared dead."

Emily laughed bitterly. "Well, won't he be surprised! And the woman he married—what's her story?"

Maggie spoke up then. "Don't blame her," she said. "None of it was her idea, I'm sure. I—I know her son and I think she's . . . you know, nice. But there's one more thing you should know." She paused and looked at Aimee.

"Oh, yeah," Aimee said. "She's going to have a baby—like, any minute."

"I see," Emily said. "I guess I'll have to find someplace to stay then—until after the divorce." She turned to Aimee, and Maggie could see the sadness in her eyes. "What about you, Aimee? Are you comfortable at home, living with your dad and his new wife?"

"Not exactly," Aimee said, and Maggie wondered how she was going to explain about staying all that time with Orias.

"You know what?" Maggie jumped in. "You could stay with us—both of you—until everything is settled. I think my mom would be happy to have you. What do you think?"

Emily was silent for a moment, and then she said, "I think that's a great idea. But first, I'd like to give Jack the surprise of his life."

"We should get back," Maggie said. "We need to get the shards to Zhai. So what do we do now, Aimes?" she asked. "Hike back to the tunnel and find the Wheel?"

Aimee smiled and shook her head. "No," she said. "That won't be necessary. I can teleport us from here."

∽

The train had stopped. That's what woke Raphael. Everything was shrouded in half-light, like predawn gloom, just before the sun bursts forth. He rose and stretched and went to look out the cab window. At first he had trouble taking in what he saw. When he finally did, his breath caught in his throat.

He was in front of a vast brick building. The sign in front identified it as Middleburg Materials, Inc.

I'm here. It really happened, he thought with fascination and a kind of sick excitement. The Magician had come through after all, and he had no idea how to feel about it, other than terrified.

He reached into his pocket to make sure the ring shard was still there, then, wishing desperately for something to eat—or at least some Red Bull—he left the train.

No one seemed to notice him as he went inside through the front entrance. He walked through reception, past the executive offices, and into the manufacturing area, not drawing so much as a glance from anyone.

The interior walls of the factory were high and caked with black soot. The expansive space was filled with great, looming pieces of chugging steel machinery, churning conveyer belts, and soaring catwalks. A huge bucket suspended from the ceiling poured a thick stream of some kind of brightly glowing orange, liquid metal into a receptacle. Then a mechanical track in the ceiling sent it jerking away toward some other part of the factory, and another bucket as tall as Raphael took its place.

He stared, wide-eyed, taking in the immensity of the place, hearing the droning, banging, and grinding sounds of the machinery, smelling and nearly tasting the vaguely sweet, acerbic tang of metal in the air. It was steel, Raphael recalled vaguely: that was the primary metal Middleburg Materials used in its products. He felt nervous, nauseous, and giddy all at once. He had never been inside Middleburg Materials before, not even when his dad was alive.

"All right, keep her coming," a man said into a walkie-talkie. He stood on a low catwalk that ran along the side of one of the machines, and as he talked he gazed up at one of the big buckets of molten metal drifting along over his head. He held up a hand and the big bucket jerked to a halt.

"Clear," he called out. "Dump her!" He gave the thumbs up to a man in a glassed-in booth up on another catwalk. After a pause, the bucket tilted and poured its load of deadly hot liquid steel into the machine below. The man on the catwalk watched until the pour was finished, then nodded and went back up the catwalk, looking up at the next bucket that was already moving slowly toward him.

He pushed back his yellow hard hat, pulled his safety goggles down around his neck, and swiped a red bandana across his face. It came away dark with sweat and soot, and Raphael stared at him.

He had a lean, tan face with crow's feet creasing the outer corners of his blue eyes, from years of squinting into sparks from the hot metal. His face was also eerily, wonderfully, like Raphael's own. It was his father.

The breath left Raphael's lungs in a sharp huff, and he did not breathe again for a long moment. He stared up at his dad in a state of suspension, as if the slightest movement on his part might make the vision cease to exist. He took his piece of the crystal ring out of his pocket and ventured a glance at it, partly to give it a silent prayer of thanks, and partly to confirm that it wasn't flashing, getting ready to whisk him away. This time, it showed only faint illumination.

On the catwalk, his father jammed the bandana back into his pocket, righted his goggles, and got back to work, following another bucket of molten metal as it moved along its track in the ceiling. He hadn't seen his son—the factory was dimly lit and Raphael was standing in the shadows next to the big, whirring machine. Or maybe, Raph thought, he was invisible in this version of the past.

He almost hoped he was invisible. When the possibility of coming back to this crucial time and place had become a reality, he'd told himself that he would not—could not—interfere in any way. He'd seen plenty of sci-fi movies and read lots of books on time travel, string theory, and black holes, and he knew well enough that if you went messing around with the past you could change the entire course of history. And besides, dead was dead. There was no way he could bring his father back. He just wanted to find out how it had happened, to see the truth for himself, once and for all—and if someone had done something to his dad, he wanted to find a way to prove it. If he could find some damning piece of evidence, he could finally exact justice for his father, and his crusade against the Toppers could end.

But now that he was actually here, the desire to avert the accident rose inside him, from a match-lit flicker to a blazing conflagration. He almost stepped out of the shadows and called out to his father to come down, to watch out, leave the factory now and live.

But then a voice came over the PA system. "Foreman Kain—please report to Mr. Banfield's office." There was a pause, and it repeated.

Raph watched as his dad signaled to another man to take his place and then headed for the front office. Careful to keep a discreet distance, just in case, Raph followed. He stood outside the door as Jack greeted his father.

"Come in, Marcus."

"What's up, Jack?"

"Sit down, please." Jack was trying to make his voice friendly, but Raphael didn't buy it.

"Thanks—I'll stand," Raph's dad said. "I'm hoping this won't take long. I don't want my crew to get behind. Is there a problem?"

"That's something you'll have to tell me," Jack said. "You were at Cheung Shao's house yesterday?"

"Yes—I went to pick up my boy, Raphael. He and Zhai take kung fu lessons together. They were over there practicing for a match that's coming up."

"Cheung believes you might have overheard something . . . of a private nature. Something you weren't supposed to hear."

"Maybe. He was having a meeting about a real estate deal. With all due respect, Jack, I don't see how this concerns you."

"It concerns me," said Jack, leaning across the desk and dropping his voice, "because I will be his partner in that deal. And for now we don't want word getting around. That could make other interested parties swoop in ahead of us and try to grab the land."

"Oh, you don't have to worry about that."

Jack smiled his barracuda smile. "That's good to know—"

Marcus Kain cut him off. "Because I'm going to stop it—or at least make it more difficult. A development deal like Cheung was talking about will wipe out the Flats and leave a lot of people homeless. I can't let that happen. I'm taking the story to the newspaper."

"The hell you say?"

"What's really going on, Jack?" he asked. "A development deal in the Flats, of all places, when Middleburg is dying? There's more to it than that, and I'm going to find out what."

"You've got nerve, Kain—I'll give you that," said Jack. "You know if you stir up trouble it'll cost you your job."

"Yeah—but sometimes a man just has to do what's right. I can't stand by and let you and Cheung Shao put innocent people out of their homes for the sake of greed."

Tears started in Raphael's eyes, but he blinked them away. His dad was a hero—or would have been if he'd lived.

"So what's it going to be, Jack?" Marcus continued. "You want me to finish out the shift or just clear out now?"

"Oh, come on," Jack said. "Relax. We can work this out. Give me a few days—I'll talk to Cheung."

"One week. If you don't call off your plans to buy up the Flats I'll go to the paper. Hell—I'll even alert CNN. Maybe if enough big corporations are bidding, someone will come up with the money to help all these families relocate."

After his dad left the office, Raphael lingered to see what Jack would do. He made two phone calls. The first was to Cheung Shao.

"He's not going to back off," Jack told him, and there was a long pause before he spoke again. "Look—I told you. This is going to take some time to get set up. It's not going to happen overnight, if we want to get in there solid. I'm on it. Trust me—Kain won't be a problem."

With the second call, although he listened intently, Raph couldn't figure out who was on the other end. All he heard was, "I've got a little problem I'm going to need you to take care of—today. Here's what I want you to do—hold on a minute." Jack got up and closed the door to his office.

When Raphael turned around to head back to the workshop, he suddenly felt dizzy and unsteady on his feet. The world blurred for a moment, and when his vision cleared, he noticed that the shadows had lengthened on the floor and workers were punching their time cards and leaving the factory. It was as if someone—the Magician, maybe—had hit the world's fast-forward button, causing him to skip ahead to the end of the work-day. It was a disorienting feeling, but Raphael tried to keep steady as he walked back to the shop where his father was working.

He got there in time to hear his dad call out to the man in the glass control booth, "Let's pour this last one and we'll call it a day."

Raphael got a sick feeling in his stomach. He wanted to yell, "No—Dad! Just go. Get out of there—now!" But he couldn't move or speak.

The flicker of a shadow moving above his father caught Raph's eye and he looked up. It was Oberon—as he had looked before Raphael had destroyed his eyes in the fight to rescue Aimee. Carefully poised on the catwalk above Marcus Kain, Oberon followed the next huge bucket of molten steel. It was suspended by two metal arms from the ceiling track, and it was moving toward Raphael's father.

Horror flooded Raph as he understood the situation fully—but he was powerless to stop what was about to happen.

In a heartbeat, Oberon changed from his human form to that of a massive onyx-skinned angel. Raph tried to step forward to warn his father, but he couldn't move—it was like he was paralyzed. "Dad—look out!" he shouted, hoping that somehow, through the layers of time, his father would be able to hear him.

Marcus Kain glanced around for a moment, as if he thought he might have heard something, but an instant later his attention was once more on his work.

Raphael kept shouting as, above, the bucket continued on its path until it was directly over his father. Oberon pointed his index finger at the bolt that secured the bucket to the metal arm holding it. The bolt turned—and turned again—and turned faster and faster until it fell out of its curved anchor shackle and dropped to the floor at Marcus's feet. He looked up and the bucket swung downward, spilling the glowing load of molten metal as it fell. It struck Raph's dad and knocked off his hard hat. He collapsed against the side of a big machine and then slumped to the floor, unconscious. The boiling metal poured out onto his back and shoulders. For a moment everything was silent and still and then the place erupted in shouts and curses from some of the other workers. The man in the control booth came rushing down to the factory floor. Everyone was yelling.

Call 911! Get an ambulance out here! Kain's hurt! He's hurt real bad!

Raphael couldn't watch anymore. He already knew how this story played out. His father had died, and he hadn't been able to stop it. But now he'd seen how it had happened, and he knew who was responsible. The Magician's words came back to him.

Vengeance makes for a bitter feast.

Maybe so, Raph thought. But Jack and Oberon would pay for what they'd done. One way or another, they would pay.

CHAPTER 27

WESTON DARLING RAN INTO HIS HOUSE, slammed the door, and slumped onto the floor. His heart was pounding, he was out of breath, and his face was slick with sweat and streaked with tears.

"Weston, is that you?" his mother called from the living room.

Weston cursed under his breath. The world was collapsing around him; the last thing he wanted to do now was try to explain it all to his mother. If she saw him, she would demand to know why he'd been crying. Even though she'd never done any government work, she was a better spy than Weston had turned out to be.

"Just need to grab something from my room," he said, and he dashed up the stairs.

By the time he'd slammed his bedroom door shut, he'd already dug his cell phone out of his pocket and punched in the number.

"This is Hackett."

"We have a problem," Weston blurted out. "Li's a double agent."

There was a pause. "Who is this?"

"It's me—Weston. Li's my . . . my friend. You met her." He choked up for a moment; he'd almost said *my girlfriend*. "She's one of them. She has the shard."

"One of what?" Hackett asked impatiently.

"One of the Snake people!" exclaimed Weston. "She just raced out of Hilltop Haven in a black BMW. If you hurry, maybe she can lead you to them!"

જ

જ 367 ભ

"You can all get home okay from here?" Aimee asked Maggie and the others as they came out of the tunnel to present-day Middleburg. They all assured her they could.

"Yeah—and after what we just went through, that hot shower idea of your mom's sounds really good," said Maggie. "If you need a place to stay, Mrs. Banfield, just let us know."

Aimee turned to her mother. "Are you sure you want to go home?" she asked. "Maybe we should go with Maggie, and you can let your lawyer get in touch with Dad."

"Oh, no," Emily said adamantly. "This is one showdown that has been a long time coming." She looked at Miss Pembrook, Dalton, Kate, and Maggie. "Thank you all for your help," she said. "Maggie, tell your mom that I'll probably be seeing you soon—but make sure it's all right with her if Aimee and I bunk in with you guys for a couple of weeks."

"Okay, then," Aimee said when they'd gone. "Are you ready?"

Emily smiled and nodded.

"You'd better brace yourself," Aimee added. "Dad is not going to be too happy about this."

She took her mother's hand and they slipped—and appeared in the kitchen of the Banfield house in Hilltop Haven, right in front of the refrigerator. The room was dark; no lights were on, but from the den came flickering illumination and canned laughter from the TV. She could hear something else, too—soft voices belonging to her father and Savana. They were back from their mini honeymoon.

Before Aimee could say anything, Emily put her finger to her lips and she leaned over and whispered in her daughter's ear. "I'm going around front—I want to make an entrance." Aimee started to protest but Emily added, "Don't worry. It'll be okay. I'm a lot stronger than I used to be."

Soundlessly, her mother opened the back door and went out while Aimee tiptoed down the hall, past the dining room, and to the doorway of the den. She found them sitting close together on the couch, and her father was tenderly caressing Savana's huge baby bump. For the first time, it crossed her mind that her dad might actually truly love Savana. From her vantage point in the shadowed doorway, she could stand, unseen, and watch them. After a moment, she heard the sound of the front door opening and closing.

"I'm home!" a voice sang out from the living room.

"Oh, what the hell," Jack grumbled.

"Who is it?" Savana asked.

"How should I know?" Jack replied, getting to his feet, but in the next moment he found out. Emily Banfield came walking confidently into the den, and at the same time, Aimee came out of the kitchen.

There was a thick silence as Jack tried to take it in. Smiling as if she didn't have a care in the world, Emily looked up at him and asked calmly, "What's wrong, Jack? You look like somebody died. Who's your friend?"

"Emily!" Jack was stunned. "What—where the hell have you been?"

"Emily Banfield?" Savana asked, and she too rose to her feet.

"That's right," Emily said brightly, extending her hand. "And you are?"

"I'm Savana," the pregnant woman said quietly. "Jack's wife."

"But that's impossible," Emily said sweetly. "I'm Jack's wife."

"Look, I can explain everything," Jack said. "Just sit down and listen." He took Emily's arm, but she pulled away from him. He stared at her, clearly unable to take in her sudden reappearance.

"Surprised to see me?" Emily asked. "Never mind. Of course you are. You are a pathetic human being, Jack Banfield. All you do is take and take and take. You're like a human black hole—you suck everything into your darkness and keep it. I swear, if you could put a rope around the sun and drag it down here, you'd keep that, too—and charge people twenty bucks a pop to look at it. You're a selfish bastard, Jack—and you're a coward. I see it didn't take you long to replace me. I knew you were having an affair."

"Look," Jack tried again. "I told you—I can explain."

The contempt Emily felt for him showed in her face. "You always could," she said sadly. "And I used to be stupid enough to believe you. Not anymore." She looked at Savana sympathetically. "I hope you don't think you're the first," she told Jack's new wife, and then she faced Jack again. "You've always gotten what you wanted, haven't you? And you justify it because you think you're all powerful, because you're the richest guy in Middleburg. But the truth is, Jack, you're a failure. You failed as a husband, and you've failed as a father. You're going to drive your children away—and one day, this poor misguided woman and the baby she carries will leave, too. You'll be all alone with your big house and your cars and your money. You're going to die alone, and no one—not a soul on this earth—will even notice you're gone."

Her words finished, the silence echoed through the big house. Aimee wanted to applaud: it was exactly what she'd wanted to say to her father so many times in the past, but had never found the courage. He stood there, glancing from one wife to the other, speechless. Then he noticed Aimee.

"Aimee, honey," he began. "I hope you don't think—"

But an agonized groan from Savana interrupted him. Even in the dim light of the TV, Aimee could see that the sweatpants she wore were suddenly soaked with something.

"My water broke," she said.

"I'll call Dr. Rosenberg," Jack said. "We'll get you to Topeka in a couple of hours—or I'll get him here on a helicopter."

"No," Savana said firmly. "I want Lily Rose."

"Dammit, Savana!" Jack yelled. "I told you—I'm not having that old woman deliver my child." He already had his cell phone to his ear. "Yes, I need Dr. Rosenberg . . . I know this is his answering service. . . . I don't care if he's on duty or not. This is Jack Banfield. Get him on the line—now! I'll hold."

"Jack, please—take me to Lily Rose," Savana begged, her tone growing more desperate.

"No," Jack said flatly.

Savana started to cry. "Jack please. I need Lily Rose. Otherwise, the baby—"

"It's *my* baby!" Jack shouted. "And *you* are my wife. And *my* baby is going to be born in the hospital *I* choose, brought into the world by the best doctor in the state, the one *I* chose for him. Is that clear? So settle down, Savana. I will *not* have some ex-stripper making medical decisions about *my* child."

Aimee got a whole new respect for Savana when she looked at Jack, a strange serenity in her eyes. "It's not your baby, Jack," she said.

Jack looked at her. Without a word, he ended the call and put the phone back in his pocket.

"I wanted it to be yours," Savana continued. "But it's not. And I need you to take me to Lily Rose. *Now.*"

Jack stared at her for a long moment, and Aimee held her breath, bracing for whatever was going to happen next. Jack cleared his throat and said softly, "You're delusional, honey. I understand that you're mad because Emily is back, but there's no need for hysterics. I'm going upstairs to get our bags, and then I'll try to call the doctor again. I'll be right back."

When he was gone, Savana's face contorted as a contraction suddenly wracked her body. "Something's . . . wrong," she said. "The contractions shouldn't be this strong yet. It's happening too fast!" Aimee saw the sheen of sweat on her face, the glint of her bared teeth, heard the gut-twisting howl of pain that issued from her lips. When she could speak again, she said, "I've got to get to Lily Rose."

"I'll take you," Emily said quietly. She turned to Aimee. "At least your dad kept my car. I noticed it was still in the garage when I circled around. You coming, too?"

"Yeah," Aimee replied. "But there's a faster way to do this."

Emily smiled. "You're right," she said. "Let's go." And then she turned to Savana. "By the way—about Jack. You can have him, with my blessing."

"No thank you," said Savana. "I think I'll be better off on my own."

Aimee reached out and gently took Savana's hand. For some reason she didn't quite understand, she felt a sudden, overwhelming love for Mrs. Kain. "I'm going to help you," she said quietly. "I'm going to take you to Lily Rose, but you have to trust me, okay?" With her other hand she grabbed her mom's arm. "Okay, let's all close our eyes for a second, like we're saying a prayer, and relax. One . . ."

"What—why?" Savana asked, bewildered.

"Two . . . just close your eyes . . . *three.*"

And when they opened their eyes they were in Lily Rose's living room. Savana looked around for a moment, amazed.

"I don't know how you did that—or if maybe I'm in the middle of some weird dream—but thank you." She gave Aimee a big hug, and then she turned to Emily. "All I can say is that I'm sorry. If I'd thought for one moment that you were still alive, I would never have—"

"It's okay," Emily interrupted. "It doesn't matter. What you need to do right now is concentrate on having a healthy baby—right, Aimee?"

But Aimee was imagining the look on her father's face when he got downstairs and found that his wife—both his wives—were gone. It was all she could do to keep from laughing.

"Right," she said. "So . . . if you don't need me right now, there's someplace I have to be." She had to get the shards she still carried in her pocket to Zhai. Maggie and Dalton had said the Flatliners were going to put them all together to try to bring back that boy, Raphael. For some reason she didn't understand, she was as eager as they were for that to happen.

❧

The driveway was overgrown, hemmed in by trees and crisscrossed with cracks. Off to the right, a faded, half-fallen sign read *SOLOMON INDUSTRIES* Zhai pulled the car up next to the sign and put it in park as Nass looked doubtfully out at the thick forest surrounding them. Abandoned places always gave Nass the creeps, and this empty driveway was worse than most.

"You sure Li went this way?" he asked.

"Yeah, I'm sure," Zhai said. "The Obies kept me in an abandoned factory when I was their slave. This is it. It must be one of the places Middleburg Materials put out of business."

Nass glanced at Chin. "Maybe we should call the police," he said hopefully, but the old man shook his head.

"They'll alert the government agents—and if they get the shards they'll try to weaponize them. It will be just as bad as the Obies getting them. The tapestry is clear on this: the only hope for Middleburg is if we get the shards, reunite them, and use them to try to bring Raphael back. He is the ring's rightful guardian."

Nass could see Zhai in the front seat, texting his friends for reinforcements. Nass did the same. By the time their cars pulled in behind them, and Zhai put the Maybach in drive and started to roll, dusk was settling in.

"You think they're expecting us?" Zhai asked.

"Since it took us a while, maybe they'll think we lost her," Nass said.

"No," Chin said. "They know we're coming. They're waiting for us. Watching us. See?"

He gestured out the window. In the shadows of the forest floor, Nass noticed a barely visible black shape slithering along next to the car, just far enough away to remain indistinct.

"Look," Zhai said. Up ahead, Lotus's BMW was parked in front of a huge, brick warehouse along with several other large black sedans. Nass stared up at the building. It was at least six stories high, with four huge smokestacks reaching up toward the darkening sky. One of them had been damaged, probably by a storm, and the bricks from it lay scattered across the weed-tangled parking lot.

As Zhai stopped the car, the Flatliners and Toppers pulled up next to them. On their right was the Beetmobile, with Beet, Benji, and Josh in it. On their left was Michael Ponder's Lexus, with Dax in the passenger seat and the Cunningham brothers in the back.

They all climbed out of the cars and stood shoulder to shoulder, with Chin just ahead of them, gazing up at the massive factory. Nass felt a strange sense of pride at the sight of all these former enemies standing together. Just the fact that they were all finally on the same side was an accomplishment.

In the next moment, however, a prickling of fear replaced that warm fuzzy feeling. Sure, they were united, but if they didn't defeat the Obies now, none of it would mean anything.

"Whatever happens, we've got to get the shards back," said Zhai. "If the Obies get them, then the apocalyptic vision the Magician gave me and Raphael will come to pass. Middleburg will be destroyed."

"So we won't let that happen," said a feminine voice behind them. They whirled about to see Aimee standing there, smiling at them. "I've got three shards—mine, Dalton's, and Miss Pembrook's. What do we do now?"

"We have to try to get back the ones Li took from Zhai," said Nass. "And then figure out how to get the others from those government guys."

They all looked over at the abandoned factory, but there was no movement visible through the dusty windows and no sounds coming from the place. Chin took the lead.

"Don't pretend you don't see us, Feng Xu," he shouted. "Come out."

After a moment of heavy silence the large, rusted steel doors of the factory rattled upward, revealing a man Nass recognized from Agent Hackett's picture—Feng Xu. He wore an expensive-looking black suit and his dark hair was slicked back. Five Obies stood behind him in their familiar black suits and derby hats. And behind the Obies, in the factory's dim interior, a shaped moved. Nass recognized it.

The Black Snake God.

"Hey, guys," he said quietly. "The odds do not look good."

"Chin. I know you are stubborn, but this is bold, even for you," Feng Xu said in a deep, strangely accented voice. "My congratulations. You survived the venom of the Snake. Don't you think you should quit while you're ahead?"

"I'll quit," Chin said. "As soon as you hand over the pieces of the ring."

Feng Xu laughed. "Ah, Chin. When you're gone, it's your sense of humor I shall miss most of all. Even if you could take the shards from us, there are elements of the Chinese military on their way here right now to transport the ring back to its rightful home. How do you think your kung fu would fare against their machine guns?"

The tingly, uneasy feeling of the *knowing* was creeping up the back of Nass's neck and whispering in the back of his mind, but it took him a long moment to understand what was bothering him. When he realized it, it was like a shout inside his head. All their enemies were there except one. *Where was Li?*

The answer came in the form of a thud, and Nass looked over to find that Aimee had been jumped from behind. She lay on the ground now, dazed, and before anyone could react, Li had dug into her pocket and pulled out the glinting shards of glass. Aimee grabbed for her as she passed, but Li dodged with the grace of a gazelle and ran to Feng Xu's side. She deposited the shards in the leather bag he held, the drawstrings of which were attached to his belt like a medieval purse. Then she turned and smiled at her brother.

Aimee groaned and wiped some blood off her forehead as Zhai helped her to her feet.

Feng Xu laughed again. "Well, well. We were already able to snatch our prize from those fumbling government agents, and now you have brought us the final three shards! How our snake god is blessing us today," his mirth faded into a fearsome scowl. "Come now. Let's finish this!" He gestured to his men, and they sprinted forward.

Zhai gave the signal, and he and his Toppers charged.

"Go!" Nass yelled, and he and the Flatliners surged ahead, too, running into the fray.

CHAPTER 28

"DO NOT KILL THEM IF YOU CAN HELP IT!" Feng Xu called to his men as they joined in battle with the combined Flatliner-Topper forces. "We shall feed them to our lord, the Black Snake, with their hearts still beating!"

At his command, the Obies put away their long daggers and attacked with their bare hands.

The thought of being eaten alive by a giant snake was all the motivation Nass needed, and he sprang forward in a twirling, circling capoeira assault, dropping one Obie with a leg sweep and cracking another with a backfist as he went.

Although Chin's army had the Obies outnumbered, Feng Xu's warriors were much better fighters. In the matter of two minutes, Dax, Michael, Beet, and D'von were all on the ground, either rolling in agony or trying to crawl away from the melee. Benji had managed to find a pile of bricks and was chucking them at the Obies as hard as he could. Every once in a while, one of them would connect, giving their allies a moment of breathing room.

Aimee seemed to be everywhere at once. First Nass saw her off to his left, laying a wicked head kick on a short Obie with a scar on his face. Half a second later she was thirty yards away, trading blows with Li Shao. At first he thought she was moving really fast, then he realized that it was more than that—she seemed to be disappearing and reappearing. The surprising thing was: he was barely surprised. *Good old Middleburg, always bustin' out the weirdness,* he thought and kept on fighting.

Feng Xu had immediately gone after Master Chin—Nass guessed

he was hoping to finish him off—but Zhai had stepped in front of his teacher and was now locked in deadly combat with the Obie leader.

Nass felt a blast to the back of his head, stumbled forward, and landed facefirst on the concrete. He rolled over, expecting the Obie who'd blindsided him to be coming in for the kill—and he was, but at the last moment, Cle'von Cunningham flew in out of nowhere, tackling him to the ground.

A sizzle of pinkish fire scorched across Nass's face then, and he saw a shimmer to his left, as the half-invisible Black Snake God, which had been about to eat him, was blasted back by a shot of Shen delivered by Maggie Anderson. The beast recoiled, then struck at her with its long venomous fangs, passing over Nass's head as it did.

He reacted instinctively, rolling backward and striking up in a bicycle kick, just as he'd done when playing soccer in the park near his house back in Los Angeles. The kick connected and altered the Snake's course enough so that Maggie was able to escape its deadly strike.

Nass struggled to his feet. His head was ringing and his vision was blurred—between the beating he'd taken in his fight with Rick and the blow he'd just received, he was pretty sure he had a concussion, but there was no way he was going to stay down.

"Where'd you come from?" Nass called to Maggie when he was on his feet again. Behind her, he saw Kate and Dalton throwing rocks at the enemy.

"We were walking to my house when we saw the Beetmobile heading this way," she called back. "We figured something was up—and we didn't want to miss it!"

Behind them, Nass heard a taunt in a language he thought was Chinese, and he turned to find that Feng Xu had Zhai pinned to the ground. He had two sharp fingernails on each hand, and Zhai was trying to fend them off. Despite his best efforts, the bladelike nails were inching closer and closer to Zhai's eyes.

Nass charged toward him to help, but the lashing tail of the snake swept his feet out from under him and sent him sprawling. He looked up to see Chin approaching Feng Xu from behind. The kung fu teacher looked older and paler than Nass had ever seen him, but the look of determination on his face was enough to send a shiver down Nass's spine. He'd hate to be the one to take on Master Chin when he was looking like that.

"Enough, Feng Xu!" Chin growled. "This has always been our fight, ever since you corrupted the brotherhood my great-grandfather created. We finish it now."

Feng Xu managed to bury a paralyzing knee in Zhai's gut as he rose to his feet. "Yes," he said. "We'll finish it indeed." And in a vicious blur of motion, he attacked Chin.

⁊

Every nerve in Zhai's body seemed to be going haywire. The knee that Feng Xu had hit him with had struck just below his solar plexus, into a bundle of nerves that controlled all sorts of necessary functions, and the trauma left him feeling limp and achy. Try as he might, it was a long moment before he was able to roll over, much less rise to his feet. And at the rate their duel was unfolding, either Feng Xu or Chin would be dead by then. The two men's arms blasted against one another, fitting together with puzzle-piece precision in a series of strikes, blocks, and counterstrikes that transitioned so fast that Zhai could hardly comprehend their progression. As they fought, sizzling glints of Shen power arced between them, like sparks showering from a blacksmith's forge. The two combatants were equally matched in skill, speed, technique, and ferocity—but Feng Xu had the advantage in power, and as the duel wore on he drove Chin back step by step. Finally, he managed to power him off balance and catch him with a crescent kick to the face. Master Chin stumbled back, clearly dazed.

With a wicked, twisted grin, Feng Xu sprang forward, his venomous nails reaching for the kill.

Zhai's breath caught in his throat as he tried to shout a warning to Chin, and he watched as the deadly points of the nails traveled in what seemed like slow motion toward his teacher's eyes. In that moment, Zhai realized what was about to happen and a scream rose up from every cell of his body.

Master Chin was going to die.

Chin tottered on his feet as the poison fangs approached their mark and then, with the quickness of a snapping whip, his form went rigid again, as if he'd never been off balance at all, and Zhai realized it had been a trick. Xu was already leaning forward, committed to the attack, and Chin, with his usual sharpness and precision, quickly and casually deflected his stabbing fingers, trapped his forearm, and performed an upward arm break. There was a sickening crack as Feng Xu's elbow snapped. Then Chin twisted his enemy's own arm back toward him and jammed his venom-laden nails into his own neck. Feng Xu fell to his knees, quivering.

Chin was now glowing, encased by a brilliant film of Shen illumination the likes of which Zhai had never seen before. He glared down at his nemesis and cocked back his fist.

"You could have been a great disciple in the service of the All," he said, a great sadness in his voice. "Now, you will be just another cautionary tale, soon forgotten."

Feng Xu's only answer was a wheeze—Zhai assumed he couldn't speak because his fingers were jammed through his throat. Then, he realized that the wheeze was a laugh, and he saw what the laugh was for.

"Chin, look out!" he shouted. But it was too late. The half-visible snake faded into materiality behind Chin, and before anyone could react, it struck, consuming Chin in one horrific bite.

∽

"You're a slippery girl, Aimee Banfield," Li Shao taunted.

Aimee was glad she was slippery. If she wasn't, she thought, Li would probably have killed her by now. But Aimee had figured out how to integrate teleporting into her fighting and the result was pretty awesome. Instead of blocking a strike she could simply slip away and appear behind Li, or to one side of her, or ten feet away. Instead of having to use an attack approach, she could simply appear right next to Li, throw an elbow, and then slip away again. But even with these advantages, it was barely an even match. Li's speed, agility, and technique were mind-boggling, and Aimee now had a bleeding cut above her brow and her lower lip was swollen and bruised. Still she fought on, knowing that the only way to save her town—and maybe the world—was to defeat Li and the Obies and get back the shards of the ring. If she could keep Li busy, it would give Zhai and Chin a chance to get them.

Li lashed out at Aimee with a backfist, and Aimee blinked out of existence as it swung past and reappeared just behind it, in time to crack Li in the side of the head with her fist. Li, however, simply used the momentum to lean down into a side kick, and bury a foot in Aimee's stomach—so hard that Aimee almost threw up.

Groaning, cursing, and clutching her abdomen, she slipped about twenty yards away to regroup. Then she slipped back, appearing in the air directly above Li's head before falling on her knees-first, like she was doing a cannon ball into a swimming pool.

Li fell to the ground under the heavy blow, but instantly she was squirming as fiercely as a wet cat. She managed to grab Aimee with her legs in a scissor hold and flip her to the concrete. She raised a fist to strike and Aimee prepared to slip—but Li suddenly stopped. Aimee followed her gaze just in time to see Master Chin being swallowed by the Black Snake God.

Everyone on the battlefield froze, and Feng Xu rose slowly to his feet, blood pouring down his neck. Wheezing a cackling laugh, he triumphantly held the black bag filled with the ring shards aloft. Above them, they heard a rumbling sound that shook the earth, and everyone looked up to see three black stealth helicopters fly in over the treetops, heading for the roof of the factory.

Feng Xu laughed again, spat a wad of blood on the pavement, and then pointed up to the helicopters. "Well, there's our ride now," he called hoarsely to his men as the choppers started landing. "Let's go!"

He turned to head back to the factory, but a strange hissing sound made him turn around. The gigantic snake was writhing now, slithering violently back and forth. A wisp of smoke emanated from its fanged mouth, and then the bulge in its neck began to glow. A single ray of golden light burst through the snake's scales, then another, and another—and the thing hissed and screeched in agony.

"No," Feng Xu whispered, taking a step forward, and then he was yelling, "No!"

More and more light poured through the blackness where the snake was, like sunlight pouring in through a set of window blinds. In just a few moments the light had completely consumed the shadowy body of the snake, leaving nothing but light. The glow was so bright that Aimee had to avert her eyes, and when she was able to look back she saw that Master Chin now stood where the snake had been—and he was glowing with radiant Shen illumination that made him look like he was cast of liquid gold.

The minute the snake disappeared, the Obies and Feng Xu all fell to their knees, as if the life had suddenly been yanked out of them. Now made entirely of light, Chin walked slowly up to Feng Xu, then reached out, and snatched the bag of ring shards from his hand. The Obie leader made no move to resist.

Then Chin, still filled with light, lashed out, burying one hand in Feng Xu's chest. When he yanked it free, it was holding a still-beating black heart. Chin held the heart in front of Feng Xu's chest so that he could see it. "I could crush this, Feng Xu, and your life would be at an end," he said solemnly.

Xu stared at his own beating heart, transfixed.

"But I will not. Let my mercy be your first lesson in true wisdom, Feng Xu. The Snake is dead. Find another god."

With that, Chin jammed the man's heart back into his chest and stepped back. When he withdrew his hand, there was no hole in Feng Xu's chest. The wounds in his neck were healed, too.

"Go now," Chin said. "But know this: if you dare to show your face here again, you will not find me so lenient."

Feng Xu got unsteadily to his feet and backed up a few paces, never taking his eyes off of Chin. He hazarded one wary glance up to the rooftop and then addressed his men. "To the helicopters," he shouted. "Go!"

And his men retreated into the factory with him.

As she backed away, Li's eyes lingered on Aimee. "We'll finish this," she said. Then she glanced at her brother, turned, and ran away with the other Obies. After a moment, the helicopters rose up from the rooftop and their roar diminished.

Chin fell to his knees. The golden glow disappeared from his skin, and he looked exhausted. He was trembling.

"Master Chin—you okay?" Zhai asked, hurrying to his teacher. The rest of the allies—the Flatliners and the Toppers—limped and shambled closer, gathering around Master Chin.

"Yes, I am . . ."

Although he smiled when he said it, to Aimee he still seemed a bit unsteady.

"Now, let us take what was broken and reunite it," Chin said and held the bag of ring shards aloft.

∞

Zhai could see how tired Chin was from the battle with the Snakes, but his sifu still moved quickly and with purpose as he led the horde of high-schoolers up the mountain. "Let's go," he said. "According to the tapestry, the ring must be reassembled on the top of the tunnel mound."

When they reached the clearing on the summit, Chin held Feng Xu's black bag out to everyone present and asked them to take a piece of the broken treasure.

After they had all taken one, he said, "Come. Gather around and let's piece it together." They all formed a circle—Toppers on one side, Flatliners on the other—and started trying to match the jagged edges. It was like a circular puzzle.

"I think mine goes with yours," Cle'von said to Beet, and the two guys moved next to one another and fit their shards together.

"Here—these match," Maggie said to Aimee.

Zhai realized how amazing it was that all these former rivals were working as a team to reunite the ring. Soon they had the right order and, each of them holding a shard, they put them together. But there was a problem, Zhai realized with a groan. They were missing a piece.

∽

Raphael stepped into the cold breeze outside the Middleburg Materials factory, wiping a tear from his cheek. He felt completely empty and exhausted, but angry too, his chest burning with a fire that felt like it would take a thousand years to extinguish. Now, more than any moment during his exile from Middleburg, he deeply, desperately wanted to go home. But how? The train and the Magician were nowhere to be seen.

Like a sleepwalker, he wandered away from the factory and into the woods, barely aware of his surroundings. He'd only gone a few paces when he felt something hot scorching his thigh.

He looked down, and then reached into this pocket. His hand came out with the broken piece of the ring—and it was glowing, brighter than ever!

As he stared at it, it shone so bright that everything else around him seemed to fade into shadow, so that all he could see was the shard's infinite light. Then, as he watched, something strange happened. Suddenly, the light was no longer a point, but a ring.

Its illumination was so bright that he had to look away from it, and when he did he saw that he was no longer in the woods outside Middleburg Materials; he was on a mountaintop—and all his friends were around him! There was Master Chin, Nass, Aimee, Maggie, the Flatliners, and even the Toppers. They were all staring at him, laughing, and cheering in amazement. And all of them were holding on to the ring—Middleburg's restored treasure.

"Raph!"

"Thank God!"

"We missed you!"

His friends shouted over one another, their voices mingling as they all tried to greet him at once. The only one who didn't seem excited to see him was Aimee. She gave him the same flat, unrecognizing look she had in 1877, and her reaction soured the joy he'd felt just a moment before. Still, there was a lot to be happy about, he told himself: he was home.

For half a second, he was sure that he was only having a dream, that he'd wake up and find himself once more on that terrible shadow train, barreling through the oblivion of the Dark Territory. But in the next instant, he was enveloped in a massive group hug. He felt hands clap onto his shoulder, lips kiss his cheek, arms embrace him, and he knew at that moment that it was true. He was really back in Middleburg. He'd made it.

The ring was now complete and resplendent, and Raphael held it above his head triumphantly.

In that moment, however, a loud noise cut their celebration short. They all went silent, listening as the chugging rush of a helicopter echoed through the valley below, followed by the sound of an explosion.

Nass looked worried. "Great. You think the Snakes are back?"

"Or the government guys," Dalton said, and they exchanged a lingering glance.

Raphael was about to ask what was going on when a shadow suddenly blotted out the sun. He looked up to find a huge black-winged shape swooping down on him. The next thing he knew, he was lying on his back on the slab of rose quartz he had been standing on, his hand throbbing.

The ring had been ripped from his grasp.

In the next instant, the sound of a roar drew his attention to the edge of the woods, and he turned to see a demon on all fours, watching them. It looked like Rick, Raphael thought. Like Rick would look if he morphed into a demon. It was foaming at the mouth and laughing—and it stood up, raised its arms, and snarled triumphantly. In the next instant, it turned and bounded down the steep incline of the tunnel mound, moving with the grace and power of a mountain lion.

It seemed to be following the black, swooping thing, which was now bearing the Shen ring away across the sky. Raphael recognized the wide, dark, feathery wings, the long body, the jerky yet graceful movement, but Chin spoke before he could.

"Oberon is free," he said darkly.

"Yeah," Raphael finished. "And now he's got the ring."

CHAPTER 29

RICK YELLED WITH EXHILARATION AS OBERON swooped under him, picked him up, and flew around above the abandoned factory. Rick tried to touch the ring, but Oberon held it away from him.

"Oh, no, my boy—this is not for such as you," Oberon scolded, gentle but firm. "This is as close to it as you'll ever get."

Then he descended, set Rick down on the ground, and flew on through the forest, his black wings propelling him forward only a few feet above the foliage as he maneuvered around tree trunks. Even with all the power Rick's demonic body contained, alternating between sprinting like a man and scrambling on all fours like a beast, it was all he could do to keep up.

"Awesome!" Rick shouted over the wind. Killing Clarisse's drug-dealer friends was the culmination of the growing blood lust he'd felt for the last year, and he was now reveling in the afterglow. Stealing that ring from Raphael Kain fired him up even more.

"Enjoying yourself, aren't you?" Oberon shouted back at him. "I knew you would. I knew you would make a fine servant, and you have not disappointed."

It irked Rick to hear anyone call him a servant, but he was having so much fun he wasn't going to complain about it. Besides, he was already trying to figure out how he might eventually steal the ring that Oberon now clutched in his hands. It was a beautiful thing, whatever it was—a treasure—and Rick was already imagining all the fun he could have with its power when *he* was the king of Middleburg—and the Dark Territory, too.

"What do we do now?" Rick panted, still struggling to keep up with Oberon.

"First, my boy," Oberon said, "we open the doors to hell—and then we open the entrance to the higher realm so we can take Azaziel's army there and defeat the exalted ones."

∽

From the cockpit of a Black Hawk helicopter, Hackett gazed down at the rooftops of the rundown neighborhood called the Flats. In the last six hours, he'd blockaded the city and called in major reinforcements. When the police station started getting calls about military choppers flying over rooftops east of town, he'd immediately known that it must be the Chinese agents. The cops at the precinct gave the order to sound the town air-raid siren as a precaution, and Hackett had scrambled his own helicopters and taken to the air to track the enemy down. So far, however, there had been no sign of Feng Xu's forces.

"Sir, we got something!" one of his men shouted. He was staring down at the screen of a tablet computer.

"What?" Hackett shouted over the roar of the rotors.

"Major energy spike, sir."

"The ring pieces?"

"Either that or somebody built a nuclear plant in the last two minutes and forgot to tell us about it."

"Where?" Hackett asked.

The agent pointed toward the east. "Looks like its moving. Heading away from the Middleburg Materials Factory. It's moving toward town, sir."

"Take us that way, Sanders!" Hackett ordered the pilot. "And go in low and fast!" Moments later, they were skimming the treetops of the forest that bordered the train tracks south of town. "Pull the energy-tracker window up on the nav screen," Hackett shouted above the noise of the rotors, and a moment later the screen from the agent's computer display was linked with the flight computer and displayed holographically in front of the chopper's windshield.

"Looks like its right below us, moving in the same direction as we are—moving fast, sir," the pilot said.

"Jones, look out—see if you can get a visual," Hackett commanded the other agent, craning his neck to look down through the sparse canopy of newly budded spring leaves.

"There—twelve o'clock!" the pilot said, and Hackett looked through the front glass again. Ahead and below them, something was moving through the trees.

"That's it—that's the energy source!" Jones shouted.

The figure below looked like a massive bird with what had to be a fifteen-foot wingspan. Its body was the shape of a human's, but the color of a stealth bomber's paint job. Another creature, on the ground, bounded along behind it. It looked like a cross between a person, a bear, and a hairless stampeding bull partially dressed in human clothing. One of its arms (or forelegs) seemed to be made of metal, and it glinted rhythmically in the sunlight.

"What the hell is that?" Hackett said.

"I don't know, sir," Jones answered, sounding a bit shaken.

"Whatever you do, stay with them," Hackett told the pilot.

"What's the plan, sir?" Jones asked nervously.

Hackett thought for a moment before replying. "The plan is to pray that the reinforcements get here soon," he said. "Because whatever's going on in this town, it's a hell of a lot bigger than us."

At that moment, another black helicopter swooped into view, its guns blazing, and Hackett felt the chopper he was in shiver as the bullets rattled against its armored hull. Feng Xu's men must have detected the energy spike, too. They had come out to play after all, Hackett thought with a mix of terror and triumph. The battle was on.

Zhai stood with Kate atop a vast hill. A beautiful, sweeping view lay behind them, but Zhai wasn't taking in the scenery. He was staring at the smoldering remnant of the Shao mansion.

When the severity of what was happening in Middleburg became clear, Chin had ordered everyone to find their families and bring them to the Middleburg United Church. With its thick ancient stone walls, it was the city's designated fallout shelter, and by far the safest place in town. Zhai knew it was important to go after the ring, but by the time they'd reached the bottom of the tunnel mound, Oberon was nowhere to be seen, and he realized that he couldn't wait any longer. Even if it meant he would risk losing the ring, he had to find out if his dad or Lotus were still alive. Of course, Kate had insisted on coming with him—and Nass had come along too, to check on his family in the guesthouse.

The fire had destroyed the Shao mansion so completely that now only a few charred pieces of lumber jutted up from the ash and debris. Firemen in dingy yellow suits and helmets hustled around rolling up hoses.

"We're still trying to determine the cause," the fire chief was saying. He'd been speaking for some time now, but Zhai hadn't heard most of it. He was just staring, stunned, at the smoldering rubble. "As I said, there were two bodies. We believe one was male and the other female, but we'll have to use dental records to make the identification."

"It was my father and stepmother," Zhai said tonelessly. "They were the only ones home. They were having a fight when I saw them last."

The chief nodded sympathetically. "Well, I'm sorry for your loss," he said. "I'm sure they were good people."

Zhai was silent. For as long as he remembered, he hadn't felt as normal people did. Now that he was with Kate, he'd begun to experience a true emotion—love—but at this moment, he felt nothing else. Not sadness at his father's loss, not anger at his death—nothing. He felt just like the ruins of the house: charred, broken, empty. Kate squeezed his hand, and he finally looked away from ruins of what had once been his home.

The fire chief cleared his throat, took out a business card, and offered it to Zhai. "Anyway, here's the number you call to collect the remains and get the autopsy information," he said and walked away.

"Zhai, are you okay?" Kate asked softly.

Zhai shook his head. "I don't know."

"How do you feel? Your father betrayed you—are you angry? Or just sad?"

"I don't know," Zhai said again. "I really don't."

From the valley below came the long wail of the air-raid siren. It was a frightening mournful drone, and to Zhai it was the perfect sound for the moment. From somewhere in the distance came the chittering rumble of a helicopter again, too.

"What's that?" Kate asked, alarmed.

"Air-raid siren," Zhai said. "They usually only use it if there's a tornado sighting."

Residents began to come out of their houses to stand on their front stoops, looking around curiously, as if trying to determine what was going on.

Zhai heard loud voices and turned to see Nass leading his mother and father up the walkway from the backyard.

"Chin said for us all to go to the church, where it's safe," he was saying.

"You think—maybe it's just a drill?" Amelia Torrez asked hopefully.

"Definitely not," said Zhai. "Where's Clarisse? Is she with you?"

"She's gone," Mrs. Torrez said. "Back to L.A. I got a text from her last night."

"Yeah," added Nass. "She didn't tell us she was leaving. She just split. Come on—we have to hurry!"

Zhai took one last long look at what was left of his house, then he, Kate, and the Torrez family piled into the Shao's Maybach and raced down the hill.

Raphael emerged from the woods that bordered Golden Avenue and stopped to stare at the scene before him. He was exhausted, emotionally drained, and his nerves were frayed; he had no words to process what he was seeing now.

Several helicopters bolted through the gray-streaked sky above, shredding the quiet day with the deafening chuckle of machine guns and the concussion of exploding missiles. A mile or so north, a large green plane flew higher in the sky, and he could see paratroopers drifting down from it, their chutes open to catch the wind. As he was taking all this in he heard the earth-rattling explosion of a bomb detonating somewhere in the downtown area, followed by a chorus of screams. People were running—men, women, children—all flooding north from the Flats, up toward Golden Avenue.

Raphael watched as they all hurried off the roadway and onto the sidewalk. A Humvee barreled toward them, the machine gun affixed to its roof rattling off a series of deafening rounds skyward, at one of the passing helicopters. When it was gone, the fleeing refugees took to the street again, struggling north as fast as they could. It was surreal. Middleburg was a war zone.

"How long have I been gone?" Raphael muttered to himself. Whatever was happening, he had no doubt that it all had to do with the Obies, the ring, and Oberon.

While everyone else had gone down the north side of the mountain to their parked cars, following Chin's orders to collect their families and take them to the church, Raphael had sprinted straight down the steep hillside in pursuit of Oberon. It was a reckless move, maybe, but he was desperate to track down his nemesis and take back the ring. But he'd lost sight of Oberon moments after he'd disappeared into the woods. Raphael had gotten bogged down in the thick underbrush while Oberon soared above it; he had no idea where he might find him now.

He wondered what terrible calamity would strike Middleburg if he didn't.

At that thought, his mind flashed to the horrible apocalyptic visions that the Magician had shown him and Zhai after their first quest, and to the terrible, desolate version of Middleburg he'd traveled to in the future with Aimee. Could this be the beginning of a war that would bring about that miserable future? All he could hope was that whatever was going on, he and his friends could somehow find a way to stop it before the whole town—and maybe the world—got destroyed. But how?

And then he heard a series of screams off to his right, further up Golden Avenue, and he caught sight of a flurry of black wings, flying low in the sky. It was Oberon, and he was heading straight toward Middleburg United Church. Rick was on the ground below him, running at full speed and occasionally glancing up, keeping the fallen angel in sight. Oberon did a gliding turn, and Raphael saw that he still had the ring. Without hesitation, Raphael gave chase.

&

Savana Kain's screams echoed through the stone-walled room, but that wasn't what was bothering Aimee. It was the increasing sounds of explosions and machine-gun fire coming from outside.

As soon as Chin had instructed everyone to go and look after their families, Aimee had thought of Savana, who was at Lily Rose's house, going into labor. Immediately, she'd slipped there. The wise old woman had assessed that Savana's baby was coming soon, and she'd told Aimee to teleport them to the church.

"Not the hospital in Benton?" Aimee asked, confused.

"No," Lily Rose had replied firmly. "This baby's got to be born on sacred ground. Just get us there—as fast as you can!"

As soon as they arrived, Lily Rose had set up a makeshift delivery room in the kitchen, and they'd been there for about ten minutes when the explosions outside had started and people began streaming into the church. Aimee hadn't stopped moving since then. Dalton arrived as the first of the Flatliners and Toppers began to straggle in with their families, and Emily Banfield was already there, acting as assistant midwife. Emily put Aimee and Dalton to work, telling them to bring Lily Rose towels and hot water and try to keep Savana comfortable. Not knowing what else to do, they adjusted Savana's pillow and wiped the sweat from her forehead. In every spare moment Aimee was stealing glances out the window, where the signs of battle seemed to be increasing, and running out to peek into the nave of the church, where the crowd of frightened citizens was growing ever larger.

She was staring out the window with a rising sense of dread when she saw a nightmare vision that she'd hoped never to see again. It was Oberon, in his natural form. As she watched, he winged his way upward, toward the top of the church, and disappeared from view. Aimee thought for a second that he'd simply flown over the church. Then, a deep boom vibrated the whole building.

"Um, Lily Rose . . ." Aimee said.

The old woman looked up from her patient. "I know," she said wearily. "That shadow train's a steamin' into town again, bringing a whole freight load of destiny with it. You go out and fight, if you need to. Hold 'em off for as long as you can. I'll be here, bringing this baby into the world. Go on—I'll bolt the door behind you."

"What do you mean, fight?" Emily protested. "Okay—you were pretty impressive in old-time Middleburg, but I'm not going to let you—"

Aimee grasped her hand, interrupting her. "I'm different than when you left, Mom. I'm stronger. I'll be fine," she said.

That left her mother momentarily speechless. Then Emily nodded. "Okay, honey. Okay. Just be careful," she said.

Aimee hurried away. In her excitement, though, she was too impatient to wait for her feet to carry her into the sanctuary. She slipped there instead and appeared in the middle of the crowd, startling everyone. Most of the people she knew in town were already assembled there, including the Toppers and Flatliners and their families. Maggie's cheerleader pals were also there, gathered in one corner and talking in voices that were shrill and hysterical.

Her dad was there, too, pacing up by the pulpit in his customary gray suit and yelling into his cell phone. "I don't give a damn what your protocol is! You put me on the phone with the governor! You tell him if he doesn't have the entire Kansas National Guard up here within the hour, he can kiss his reelection goodbye!"

Aimee shook her head. At least some things never changed.

She was crossing the room, heading for the place where Zhai, Nass, and the rest of the Flatliners and the Toppers were gathered, talking to Master Chin, when she felt a sudden vibration shoot through her body. Instinctively, she stared up at the ceiling. Several people around her did, too. There was a strange sound coming from above, a massive vibratory hum that seemed to rattle every cell inside her, every molecule of the air, and every stone of the church.

Great, she thought, what *now*?

∞

Raphael had cut through the woods and was charging ahead, dodging the ancient headstones that filled the churchyard, when he caught sight of Oberon again. He had flown up to the bell tower of the church and disappeared into its arched opening, even as dozens of terrified people crowded into the broad entrance of the church below. Raphael gritted his teeth and ran faster. *What could Oberon be planning?* he wondered. Was he going to use the ring to bring the whole structure crashing down on everyone in the town? Or something even worse?

Raph had taken only a few more steps when he saw an explosion of blue-green light rip from the bell tower, in three concentric circles. The shockwave of energy seemed to blow a fuse in Raphael's brain for a second, and the blast knocked him off his feet. When he sat up again, he saw that a great beam of white light was shining out of the arch in the bell tower, blasting like an impossibly bright spotlight toward the south.

There was another fainter, vaguely spiral-shaped shaft of light that shone straight upward, as far as he could see, until it vanished in the clouds. As Raphael watched, two figures—Oberon and Rick—stepped out into the beam of light, and it carried them south at incredible speed before disappearing above the treetops.

Raphael groaned, exhausted by the prospect of chasing Oberon back the way they'd come. After a second, however, another round of machine-gun fire roused him, and he stood.

He had to track Oberon down, he decided. But first he knew he should go and investigate the two lights now shining out of the bell tower. They must have something to do with whatever Oberon was up to, he thought. If he could shut them off somehow, maybe he could avert the disaster the Magician had foretold. With a sense of renewed determination, he charged once again toward the church.

෨

Inside one of the black helicopters, Feng Xu sat, grinning.

"Excellent," he said into the cell phone pressed to his ear and ended the call.

Chin might have managed to kill the Black Snake God, but the Chinese government would not be so easily vanquished. Earlier, Feng Xu had called for reinforcements. Now, the members of dozens of secret spy cells were converging on the town with enough firepower to level Middleburg. Of course his opponent—the foolish, overcautious Agent Hackett—would have called for reinforcements, too. Most of them had already arrived. But they, like Hackett, would be cautious, fearful of needless destruction or the taking of innocent lives, and that is why Feng Xu would be victorious. That is why, within hours, the ring would be his. They had already located it: it was in the tower of the church, and it was emanating an unmistakable beacon of light, like the beam of a lighthouse. Now, all that remained was to gather his forces, go into the church, and take it.

"Damn it! You're sure?" Hackett snarled over the deafening rotors of the helicopter.

Agent Jones nodded.

So the ring was definitely inside the church—which was also where hundreds of civilians were now gathering. *That's just great,* Hackett thought. It was a nightmare scenario. Either they go in and snag the ring, which would likely result in a firefight with perhaps dozens of civilian casualties, or they sit back and let the Order grab it and try to catch them with it afterward—and risk letting them escape. He knew that the latter choice was not an option. If Feng Xu's people got their hands on the ring and weaponized it, that could result in *millions* of casualties. He had to go with the lesser of two evils. They had to get the ring now.

"Lieutenant Sanders—what do you think about dropping some snipers on the roof of the church?" Hackett shouted up to the pilot. Sanders looked down at Middleburg United, then shook his head.

"It's a no-go, sir," Sanders said. "The pitch is too steep. The roof is slate—it's slippery—and it's too windy."

With a mumbled curse Hackett sat back in his seat, frustrated. How had this operation gone sideways on him so fast? Only yesterday he'd been confident that this mission was going to be the key to a big promotion, a fat salary, and a cushy desk job in D.C. Now, there was collateral damage and probably civilian casualties as well, and if he didn't secure the ring now, he'd be lucky to avoid a demotion—or worse, World War III.

"All right, bring us down," he said finally. "We'll have to do this the old-fashioned way. Have all units rendezvous in the field north of Spinnacle Restaurant. We'll proceed south on Golden Avenue by Humvee and on foot. We'll surround the church and secure the ring while you provide air support."

Jones looked at him, wide-eyed. "There are hundreds of civilians down there, sir. If we get into a fire fight in front of that church—"

"No one asked for your opinion, Jones," Hackett snapped. "I don't care if Black Ops has to come in and bulldoze this whole miserable town. I'm getting that ring, and I'm getting it now."

ↄ

The sounds of gunfire and explosions outside had risen to a terrifying cacophony. Aimee's hands were trembling, and it was all she could do to keep from slipping out of Middleburg altogether and going someplace calm—like the Bahamas. She pushed the thought out of her mind and tried to focus on the conversation that was happening as she, Zhai, Nass, Maggie, and Chin discussed what to do next, but her eyes kept drifting to the faces in the crowd around her: the frightened children, the concerned mothers, the blustering fathers. Anne Pembrook and Mr. Brighton were walking among them, trying to keep everyone calm.

At that moment, the huge wooden door to the church swung open and a young man came in.

The Flatliners and Toppers stood in a restless group at the back of the church talking among themselves. When the intruder came in, they all hurried to his side. He was the boy who had appeared from thin air when they'd assembled the ring on the mountaintop, Aimee realized. When he'd appeared, she thought he seemed familiar. Now, suddenly, she recognized him. He was the mysterious gunslinger who'd saved her life in 1877 Middleburg. She also knew his name—Raphael—and she remembered Dalton and Maggie talking about him. Still, she couldn't quite figure out how she knew him.

And then, over their heads, he was looking right at her. He passed through the crowded church and walked right up to her.

"Aimee," he said, and the sound of her name on his lips sent a shockwave through her soul.

"What?" she began. "You—you're that guy—how did you get here?"

"Aimee, it's me—Raphael."

A sudden emotion she couldn't understand came over her.

"You know me," he went on gently. He took her hand. She was surprised at how natural—how right—it felt.

"Okay," she said. "Dalton, my friends, they all told me that I went to the homecoming dance with you, but honestly, I don't remember that."

He moved closer and put his arms around her, and she looked up at him, into his awesome blue-green eyes. "Do you remember this?" he whispered, and he kissed her softly, slowly.

And it all came flooding back to her like a tidal wave, every memory of every moment they had spent together. With the memory, her love came flooding back, too—filling her with the splendor she'd known with their very first kiss.

"Raphael," she said, tears welling in her eyes. Eagerly she kissed him back and then hugged him close as he held her tightly, his sweet breath caressing her neck and ruffling her hair. She felt like she was waking up from a very long sleep. "How could I forget you?" she said.

"It wasn't you." Maggie came forward then. "It was Orias." She looked at Raphael. "He put some kind of spell on her. I'm not sure how he did it, but she kind of lost touch with all of us for a while."

"Oh, God—Orias," she said. "Raphael, how will I ever make that up to you?" She wanted to say more, to try to find answers, to explain—to herself, most of all—but at that moment Chin approached.

"Master Chin, Oberon is here," Raphael said. "He took the ring up to the bell tower—and now there's this crazy light coming out of it."

A shadow of worry crossed Chin's face. "Let's go," he said.

∽

Maggie fought to hold back her tears as she watched Aimee and Raphael. She had imagined many times what Aimee and Raphael's reunion would be like, and she'd always imagined herself crying tears of bitterness and rage, but that's not what she felt now. She actually felt happy for them. All the jealousy she'd felt for Aimee over the last few months had somehow melted away, like snow on the first warm day of spring. She couldn't believe how mean and selfish she'd been. Aimee loved Raphael, and he loved her. They were both her friends, and if their happiness meant she would have to forget about her feelings for Raphael, then that's what she would do. Anyway, there were more pressing things to worry about than her miserable love life.

After some discussion, the group settled on a plan: Nass, Benji, Josh, and Beet would remain downstairs with Michael, Dax, D'von, and Cle'von so they could bar the door and make sure everyone stayed safe, while Chin took Raph, Zhai, Aimee, and Maggie up the stone steps leading to the bell tower. As they passed through the narrow weathered door that led to the area where the bells hung, Maggie braced herself for the sight of Oberon's face, which Aimee had described as scarred and black but also eerily beautiful—but instead she found only a wooden platform with three huge bells hanging above it, all silhouetted by a blinding light. Chin led them to the other side of the bells, and there they found the source of the glow.

It was the ring.

Middleburg's treasure was set into an ancient ornately carved stone altar that looked as if it had been made specifically for the ring to sit in. The illumination that filled the space shone out of the south-facing arch of the bell tower in a powerful beam.

After taking in the sight of the ring, Maggie looked in the direction the beam was pointing. She felt a sense of vertigo, as if she were staring into a telescopic lens that was zooming in at hyper speed—and suddenly she could see all the way across town, to the mouth of the north train tunnel, perhaps two miles away. Its black entrance was now ringed in a bright, sizzling purplish light, and from it poured thousands of creatures: hideously deformed men, snarling demons, beautiful shadow angels with skin the color of ash and wings as black as midnight. They bore heavy shields, glinting swords, wicked machine guns, chain saws, spears, pitchforks, scythes, and hand grenades. She watched, appalled, as they formed columns and began marching toward her—toward the church. That's when she heard Aimee calling her name. The vision disappeared, and she fell to her knees.

"Maggie—are you all right?" Aimee was asking, concerned.

Maggie blinked as everything around her came into focus again. "The gate to the Dark Territory is open," she said hoarsely. "A horrible army is coming this way."

Chin nodded gravely. "Aimee," he said. "Can you take me to my house, fast? I have weapons there that will help us."

"Yes," Aimee said. She looked at Raphael and kissed him again. "This is going to seem very strange," she said. "I'll tell you all about it when we have more time." And then she took Chin's hand and slipped.

For a moment Raphael stared at the spot Aimee had vacated, and then he shook his head. Nothing that happened in Middleburg should surprise him anymore, Maggie thought.

Raphael helped Zhai get Maggie to her feet.

"You okay?" Raph asked, and Maggie waited for the rush of feeling and the rapid heartbeat she always felt whenever he touched her—but it didn't come. It was kind of sad, she thought. But it was also a big relief.

"Yeah, I'm good," she said. "What now?" She looked from Raphael to Zhai.

"I'm not sure," Zhai said.

"I don't suppose we can just grab the ring and shut the portal?" Raphael suggested. They all looked at the ring. The altar was made of rose quartz and carved with all sorts of strange symbols. The ring sat perfectly in a circular groove that had been carved into its center.

Zhai reached for it, and then stopped. "I don't know," he said. "It looks like this is where it belongs—where it's supposed to be. Where it should have been all along."

Raphael nodded. "Shen is telling me the same thing. Anyway, Maggie said the army was already through the gate, right?"

Maggie nodded.

"No point in taking it out of its rightful place, then," Raphael said. "It's probably safer here, anyway."

He looked up, and Maggie noticed that there was a spiral staircase leading upward from the altar where the ring sat. And it was made of pure light.

"What do you think is up there?" she asked.

"Beats me," Raphael said. "But I don't think now is the time to explore it and find out." He gazed out of the bell tower. Off to the northwest, they could see the U.S. troops forming up in the field behind Spinnacle, as if preparing to march. Downtown, several large Obie helicopters had landed on building rooftops. Black-clad snipers were positioning themselves on the corners of buildings while the rest of the Chinese troops streamed down fire escapes to the street below, where they moved toward Middleburg United like columns of swarming ants.

"I guess we go back down and get ready for the war the Magician warned us about," Raphael said.

"A war to end all wars," Zhai agreed darkly. He headed toward the steps, but Raphael stopped him.

"Hey, Zhai," he said, and his rival turned around. Raphael stared at his shoes for a second before raising his eyes to meet Zhai's. "Before we do this . . . in case something happens to one of us . . . I owe you an apology. While I was gone I traveled through time. I was in Middleburg, the day that my dad died in your father's factory. I saw what happened. It wasn't an accident. Oberon and Jack killed him."

"Oberon and Jack?" Zhai repeated.

Raph nodded. "I made a mistake when I accused your family of being responsible for his death. I was just so angry . . . I guess I had to blame someone. But I was wrong, and I'm sorry."

Zhai took Raphael's outstretched hand and shook it.

"Apology accepted," Zhai said.

"Good, then let's go," Maggie said impatiently. "Those armies are coming fast."

When they'd reached the bottom of the bell tower's staircase, Dalton appeared from the crowd and grabbed Raphael's arm.

"It's about time you got here!" she exclaimed joyfully. "Your little brother or sister is about to be born—right now. Come on!" And she pulled him toward Lily Rose's temporary delivery room.

❧

Minutes later, Raphael was holding his mom's hand, and between contractions she was kissing it and telling him how glad she was to see him. It wasn't long before Nass came rushing in.

"Hey, Raph—whoa," he said, averting his eyes when he saw Raphael's mom lying on the delivery table, her knees up and one of the church's white linen tablecloths draped over her lower half.

"Come on in, Nass," Savana joked. "Pull up a chair."

"Yeah," said Emily Banfield. "The more the merrier."

"No," said Lily Rose, serious. "Say what you came to say and then get on out of here. I need room to work."

"We've gotta go," Nass said, still embarrassed. "Come on, Raph. They're back."

Raphael followed him out to the church's courtyard where Chin and Aimee were waiting. The four black horses Zhai had given Chin for his last birthday were there, fidgeting nervously as two fighter jets streaked past overhead. Three large black steamer trunks sat on the ground, and Master Chin was throwing them open.

"Time is short!" he said. "Assemble everyone now. We must protect the church and the Staircase of Light. Get the others."

"You got it," Nass said and headed off. "Hey, guys!" he shouted as he went. "Come out here!"

Zhai had found his way out to the courtyard, too, and Raphael walked over to the open trunks with him. One was filled with weapons—swords mostly, with some clubs, maces, knives, and other assorted weapons, and even a few guns mixed in. There were also sais—pointed metal batons with curved prongs attached to the handle. The second trunk was full of what looked like a bunch of white T-shirts, except they were made of shiny cloth that Raphael guessed was satin or silk.

"Put one on and grab a weapon. We got your swords, too," Chin said, handing Raphael the samurai sword he'd taken from the creepy dead samurai warrior he'd vanquished in Maggie Anderson's house a couple of months before. Chin handed Zhai a medieval hand-and-a-half sword that Raphael knew he'd pilfered from the four knights he'd conquered in the locomotive graveyard during that same strange battle.

Zhai was pulling on one of the weird T-shirts, and Raphael noticed that Chin and Aimee had already put them on. "What are these?" he asked, pulling one on over the shirt he was already wearing.

"Lily Rose made them. They'll protect you," Chin said, adjusting one of the horse's saddles. Raphael remembered how Dalton had survived the collapse of Middleburg High's gymnasium while wearing a dress Lily Rose had made for her. He wasn't sure if her shirts would stop a bullet or a supernatural sword, but it sure wouldn't hurt to be wearing one.

By then, the rest of the Toppers and Flatliners had assembled in the courtyard, and they had all picked out weapons. Benji had a pirate cutlass and Beet was holding a spiked mace. Josh grabbed a bow, a tomahawk, and a pair of brass knuckles. The Cunningham brothers each took a massive bastard-sword, while Michael and Dax picked out a couple of guns and hunting knives. Nass grabbed a pair of sais that he thought would work well with his capoeira fighting style. Kate took a shotgun.

"I don't know if I can use this thing," she quipped. "But I wouldn't want to take a sword to a gun fight, to be sure." She also found a satchel of hand grenades and slung it over her shoulder. Maggie was hanging back, and Raphael smiled as he watched Aimee approach her.

"Here, Maggie. I swung by the school and got this for you," Aimee said as she took something from a backpack. It was the Middleburg High homecoming crown that Maggie had worn twice before—once at the dance and once when she was fighting off the terrifying Black Snake God of the Obies. "I thought you might like it better than a bazooka or something."

"Thanks, Aimes," Maggie said, placing the crown on her head. Instantly, she was bathed in a glow that was beautiful—and a little scary.

"We'd better get ready," Nass said nervously. "I can feel all three armies getting close."

Chin nodded to Raphael. "Raphael, you, Zhai, Maggie, and Aimee will ride the horses and lead the charge. The rest of us will follow you."

"Me?" Aimee asked, incredulous.

"Have a little confidence in yourself," Zhai said. "I've seen you fight. You're good."

"And you rode horses at that boarding school of yours, didn't you?" Dalton asked.

Aimee shrugged. "Almost every day but . . ."

Raphael stepped close to her and squeezed her hand. "You can do it," he said. She smiled up at him, and it was all he could do not to grab her and kiss her again. She took the reins of her horse and climbed on.

They were all ready to ride out when Chin turned to Dalton. "One last thing," he said. "We can't have the people inside the church panicking when this all goes down. Dalton, maybe you can sing them a little lullaby to keep them calm and safe?"

Dalton smiled. "Don't worry," she said. "I'll sing until I sing 'em through to the other side." And she headed back into the sanctuary.

Raphael mounted his horse and glanced from Aimee to Maggie and finally to Zhai as they rode to the front of the small column of soldiers.

"The Army of Light," Chin declared proudly when they were all in place.

Raphael tried to give him a confident smile, but his heart was thundering in his chest. Weapons or not, they were just a bunch of teenagers. But if they didn't fight, who else would? "You guys ready to do this?" he shouted.

"I was born ready," Maggie said.

"I guess," said Aimee.

"Let's do this, my brother," Zhai said. And the Army of Light rode forth.

CHAPTER 30

ZHAI TOOK IN THE BATTLEFIELD at a glance, and he felt like his heart would turn to lead inside his chest. To their right, northward, a caravan of Humvees and U.S. troops on foot swept south down Golden Avenue, heading toward them. Straight ahead, a battalion of Obies and Chinese soldiers was leaving the downtown area and moving down Church Street—which dead-ended in the churchyard where he now sat astride Chin's black horse. From his left, or southern flank, Zhai could hear the sounds of the approaching Dark Territory army, their gut-thudding drums rattling, their earsplitting trumpets braying into the impending dusk. As he looked, he began to see glimpses of red snapping banners and glinting swords as the force made its way through the woods, and then up a small embankment from the railroad tracks that ran behind the church.

Zhai looked at Raph, Maggie, and Aimee, their heads high as they rode forward, and then he glanced back at the rest of his small battalion: Michael, Dax, D'von, Cle'von and Benji, Beet, Josh, Nass, and Kate.

Finally, there was Master Chin, wearing the samurai helmet Raphael had given him as a birthday present. Their sifu was standing firmly at the front of their little phalanx. Fourteen of them, against who knew how many trained soldiers and demonic fiends.

It was to be a clash of four armies, and theirs was by far the smallest. Still, Zhai would not allow himself to be afraid. If there was ever a moment that his years of training had been meant to prepare him for, this was it, and he forced his hands to stop shaking.

Raphael's horse stamped impatiently, and he pulled back the reins, keeping the beast steady. "Should we split up and each of us take a flank?" Raphael asked Master Chin.

The old teacher shook his head, drawing the ancient-looking Chinese sword that hung at his side. "No. We'll all stand and fight together," he said. "Wait until they've crossed through the gates of the churchyard, then charge. No matter what, we must not let them get the ring—or ascend the Staircase of Light."

Everyone nodded solemnly; there was no more time for talking. The Chinese and U.S. forces were already exchanging fire and sweeping toward them. Zhai's eyes found Kate's and he gave her a reassuring smile, then gripped his sword tighter and stared out across the grave-filled churchyard, waiting for the battle to come.

ℴ

Raphael watched with admiration as his *sihing*, Zhai, with his usual nerves of steel, was the first to charge into the fray. He galloped into an advancing phalanx of Obies and Chinese soldiers, his sword flashing. Kate was a few steps behind chucking grenades, and the rest of the Toppers plunged into the battle, too, fearlessly following their leader into the storm of bullets. Raphael had been bracing himself for a bloodbath, but as he'd hoped, the shirts Lily Rose had made them seemed to have some sort of protective properties. The raking streams of bullets seemed to have no effect; they passed right through the charging Toppers as if they were ghosts.

"Raph . . ." Nass said nervously, and Raphael looked in the direction he was pointing. The Dark Territory army had made it up the hill faster than expected and was already swarming through the wrought-iron gates of the churchyard, led by a flock of scary-looking half-women half-birds bearing swords, which Raphael guessed from a couple of books he'd read could only be harpies.

"Charge!" he shouted and kicked his horse into a gallop, hacking the wings off the first two bird-women as he went. Immediately, a sea of sickeningly deformed demon-men in rusty body armor surrounded him. They lashed at him with everything from pole axes to bullwhips, broken bottles to stumps of table legs. He hacked at them furiously and managed to get free of their swarm, but not before his horse had suffered a few serious wounds. As he circled for another charge, he saw that his comrades were all battling with everything they had.

Beet, who was a head taller than any of the deformed soldiers, was swinging his mace in wide arcs, mowing them down like bowling pins. Josh was picking the harpies out of the air with his bow, until one swooped in from behind him and tackled him with her talons. Benji got to him quickly, though, slashing the harpy with his cutlass and helping Josh to his feet.

Aimee seemed to be everywhere, stabbing an Obie with the slender blade of her rapier one moment and then the next, slipping to a spot thirty yards away and slashing a harpy out of midair.

So far things were going okay, but when Raphael looked out in the direction of the tracks, he saw trouble coming. Hundreds, maybe thousands, of onyx-skinned or ash-colored beings with black wings were flying toward them, wielding flaming swords. They advanced on the churchyard in numbers large enough to nearly blot out the southern sky.

Raphael had seen creatures like this before. *They look just like Oberon,* he thought. *They're fallen angels.*

"Oh, crap," he whispered as their army winged toward them. "Chin! Zhai!" he shouted, his voice cracking with fear.

He turned to see a series of explosions (probably from the grenades Kate was lobbing at the Obies). A moment later, Chin appeared from around the southwest corner of the church, with Zhai and Maggie in tow. They all hesitated when they saw the cloud of Irin approaching, then Maggie's eyes narrowed. The homecoming crown on her brow pulsed, and she leaned back like a baseball pitcher winding up. When she threw both hands forward, a typhoon of pinkish fire exploded from them. It decimated everything it touched, snapping treetops and setting them aflame, leveling tombstones, and sending scores of fallen angels tumbling from the sky.

The whole Army of Light cheered, but Maggie fell to her knees, spent from the effort of her mighty Shen attack. And the Irin were still coming.

◊

Aimee understood the situation instantly, and she knew that if they didn't do something fast, the fallen angels were going to overpower them. Instinctively, she slipped to a spot just above a wicked-looking Irin, teleporting into just in the right spot to fall on top of it and impale it with her slender sword. The dark angel gave a piercing scream and fell from the sky, and Aimee rode it down to the ground, ramming her sword in deeper as they fell. The moment they struck the earth, the Irin burst into flames, and Aimee had to step back fast to avoid being torched. In seconds, the fire completely consumed the winged body, leaving nothing but an outline of fine gray ash. Aimee stared at it for a second, trying to understand what had happened.

Then she remembered something Orias had told her: the Fallen were not permitted to touch consecrated ground. It wasn't Aimee's sword that had burned the evil Irin; it was the churchyard!

She looked up and saw Raphael battling two of them. Both hovered two feet above the ground as they flapped their massive wings. "Raphael!" she shouted. "Pull them down! They can't touch consecrated soil!"

"Right!" he yelled back, ducking one flaming sword and parrying another as a third Irin came up behind him. Aimee watched it happen as if in slow motion: the flaming blade ramming through Raphael's chest and coming out the other side. A scream died in her throat, and she slipped over, stabbed the Irin behind him in the throat with her sword, and pulled the flaming blade free of Raphael's chest. When he spun to face her, however, his eyes were not glassy with the shock of a mortal wound—he looked fine. There was no wound there. He smiled.

"I'm fine," he said. "It's Lily Rose's shirt. Stuff just passes right through it!"

But there wasn't time for another word. An Irin swooped down on him from above and he managed to parry the strike, grab the angel's forearm, and yank it toward the ground. The moment the Irin hit, it was engulfed in flames and in seconds there was nothing left but ash.

"Army of Light! Pull them to the ground!" Raphael shouted. "They can't touch the ground!"

Instantly, two other flames sparked as first Beet and then Zhai each managed to drag one of the hellish creatures down low enough to touch the sanctified soil of the churchyard.

But, Aimee soon realized, reaching the door of the church wasn't really the Irin's strategy anyway. Most of them were flying over it, entering the bell tower and swarming up the Staircase of Light that rose from it, all the way into what had to be outer space.

"Raphael! Master Chin!" she shouted. "Look up—they're getting up the stairs!" She expected Raphael to take some drastic action, but he stood frozen in place, staring away from the church, out across the churchyard. She followed his gaze and understood. Leading the Irin army were Oberon and Azaziel, and they were wearing wicked-looking black armor and holding swords of simmering red flame. And they were moving toward Raphael and Aimee.

She braced herself, preparing to watch the duel that was about to take place. Chin tapped her on the shoulder, and she looked around to see that his face was smeared with blood from a deep gash on his forehead— but he looked as determined as ever.

"They must not be allowed to ascend the staircase," he said quickly. "Teleport us up to the bell tower, Aimee. We have to get the ring."

∾

Raphael glanced to his right, where Zhai was locked in what seemed to be a death battle with his sister, Li. To his left, Beet was fighting side by side with Michael Ponder. Benji and Josh were saving Dax Avery from an Irin and a swarm of harpies. The Cunningham brothers were standing back to back, swinging their swords wildly at the tangle of Irin and deformed knights surrounding them. Maggie was using what was left of her Shen energy to blast a series of pinkish fireballs at Rick, who bounded toward her, his mouth full of jagged, gaping teeth, like some kind of demonic shark. Raphael took all this in just seconds and then turned his attention back to the two supernatural beings coming toward him.

Oberon grinned in recognition as he approached Raphael, and Raphael saw that there were strange, translucent, glowing eyes hovering in his scarred eye sockets—which was somehow even creepier than the empty spaces would have been. The fallen angel who was with him— an even taller, more beautiful being who wore a strange black crown— seemed to be fixated on Raphael as well, but he stood back at the edge of the woods outside the churchyard, apparently happy to let Oberon do his dirty work.

"An eye for an eye, they say!" Oberon shouted at Raphael. "But I think I'll take much more than that from you. And as for that pretty shirt of yours, it won't protect you from my ancient Irin weapon."

With an evil laugh, Oberon charged.

Raphael didn't hesitate. As soon as Oberon drew close, he snarled and attacked, clashing swords with him, dodging a slice from his flaming blade, then striking back, settling into the flow of combat.

He wasn't thinking of the fight blow by blow. The whole thing was one great, fluid motion. Each strike, each block, like the crashing and receding of the ocean, was part of the same unending flow. Oberon's flaming weapon crackled and hissed like a lightsaber as it whooshed toward Raphael in a seemingly endless series of strikes and feigns—and he was good with a sword. In the first two minutes of the duel, Raphael's leg was scorched and his left arm slashed and burned. Still he fought on, even more furiously than before, ducking a wild strike and countering with a slash to Oberon's face.

Now that the fallen angel was wounded, Raphael redoubled his effort, driving him all the way back to the iron fence. He threw a feint and got his enemy to overcommit, then managed to nick his hand with the tip of his samurai sword. Oberon's flaming blade fell to the ground, and Raphael cocked back to give him the deathblow.

But at that moment there was a massive change in the air, and Raphael looked over his shoulder to find that the staircase leading up from the church spire had now disappeared, as had the beam that shot into the tunnel. Someone must have moved the ring.

The distraction lasted only an instant, but when Raphael turned back to Oberon, he saw a black bar speeding toward his head and recognized it as part of the churchyard fence that Oberon had pulled free. He heard more than felt the metallic thump as it connected with his head, and the next thing he knew he was on his knees, his vision blurred, and his head spinning. Raph's weapon fell from his numb fingers. He felt hot blood flowing down his face and looked up to see a flaming sword raised above him.

And then it came down.

Raphael tried to throw himself backward, out of the way of the strike. He managed to avoid the head blow that Oberon was attempting, but when he tried to shield himself from it he felt a sharp, paralyzing pain in his forearm as a flaming blade slashed him to the bone.

He lay on his back now, scrambling backward as the fallen angel advanced toward him, the fiery sword in his hand poised to deliver a final strike.

There was the sound of an impact on Raphael's left, then another on his right, and both were followed by bursts of flame. He realized with a shock that the Irin were falling from the sky. Somehow when the staircase disappeared, it must have stunned them or something, because they weren't using their wings, they were just plummeting to the ground like huge black raindrops.

Raphael looked up and saw one falling right toward him, along with the flaming sword it must have dropped when the staircase disappeared. Oberon saw it too, and backed away.

At the last second, Raphael executed a quick shoulder roll and managed to avoid getting blasted. As he did, he grabbed the Irin's blazing sword out of the air.

A movement caught his eye, and Raphael glanced over to see Master Chin and Aimee materializing at the foot of the church wall. They had retrieved the ring, and Raph realized that's what had caused the Staircase of Light to disappear. As soon as they showed up, Feng Xu was there, renewing his battle with Master Chin.

Oberon had seen Aimee, too. Before Raphael could take a step to follow, he was already flying, speeding across the battlefield toward her.

⁊

At that moment, a deep voice thundered across the battlefield, and Aimee froze, holding the glowing crystal ring tightly. Oberon was still in the air, hovering perhaps thirty yards away, his wings slowly churning to keep him aloft. He held a flaming sword in his hand, but as Aimee watched, it twisted and curled, changing shape until it was no longer a sword but a flaming machine gun—and he had it pointed directly at her head.

"Hand over the ring," Oberon ordered. "Or die."

The entire battle had ceased, and all eyes were now on Aimee and Oberon. She clutched the ring to her chest and shook her head.

"No," she said calmly. "I won't give it to you!"

⁊

Raphael stopped running and stood as still as the tombstones around him, watching along with everyone else as Oberon held Aimee at gunpoint. He was terrified that if he made a move, Oberon would simply pull the trigger and kill her. Cold dread ran through the crowd, and Raphael held his breath. Across the churchyard, Oberon raised the gun to his shoulder and took aim.

But there was a blur of motion, and suddenly Li Shao was standing in front of Aimee.

"No!" Li said adamantly. "You'd better give that ring to me, Aimee."

"Give me one good reason," Aimee retorted.

"She's one of them!" Zhai shouted. "She's one of the Obies! Don't let her have it." He ran to Li, but Raph couldn't tell if it was to protect her from Oberon's weird gun or to protect the ring from her.

Again Oberon seemed ready to fire, but Kate rushed in, stepping in front of Zhai. Then Maggie hurried in to shield Kate. Raphael was on the other side of the churchyard, but he was moving forward now, certain that Oberon would shoot Maggie if he didn't intercede.

"Out of the way, or I'll kill every one of you!" Oberon growled.

But before he could, Aimee slipped again and appeared in front of Maggie.

"She's my friend," Aimee said. "You want her, you've gotta shoot me first."

Raphael was running now, desperate to avert Aimee's death, but Nass was closer, and he stepped in front of her. The rest of the Flatliners crowded in, too, shoulder to shoulder, forming a protective wall, and the Toppers lined up in front of them, making a second wall.

"Move!" Oberon screamed in a fury. "Give me the ring or I will kill you all!"

At last, Raphael reached his friends and stood at the head of the Toppers, directly in line with Oberon's gun barrel. Raphael met Oberon's stare and refused to look away.

"Do it, Oberon!" the dark angel in the crown commanded from the edge of the churchyard. "Destroy them!"

"You can kill them," Raphael said. "But you'll have to go through me to do it." He began striding slowly, deliberately, toward Oberon, who raised the wicked hell-gun to his shoulder once more.

"With pleasure," Oberon snarled and pulled the trigger.

CHAPTER 31

Raphael felt the blast from Oberon's gun splinter every bone in his chest and liquefy his organs with the heat of a supernova star. What he felt was too catastrophic, too complete, to merely be called pain. It was like every neuron in his brain lit up at once, and it felt in that moment like his whole body had been dosed with a nuclear explosion of Shen energy powerful enough to decimate the entire planet. For a second, all he could do was experience the physical sensation of his own destruction—and then he looked down incredulously and saw the smoking hole in his chest. He managed to look over his shoulder and saw that Nass, behind him, had already fallen to the ground, as had all his friends. The bullet had gone right through him and hit them. He swayed on his feet, then, and his legs gave out and he fell to his knees.

A deafening cheer went up from the remaining Irin warriors, and Oberon's low, virulent laughter punctuated the sound—but Raphael could hardly hear it now. The world was fading fast, like a sidewalk chalk drawing washed away by rain.

It was strange, he thought. All his life he'd fought, clinging to his own hope of finding fairness, justice, and happiness in an utterly unfair world, but all he'd ever found were the little scraps of goodness that he and his friends had somehow created themselves. Still, in his final moments, he'd believed with all his heart that by doing the right thing, by protecting his friends, somehow, some way, everything would work out okay.

It was not bitterness he felt as he slumped to his hands and knees on the muddy earth: it was bewilderment. Even now he expected his happy ending, and yet it did not come. He was dying.

The wind rose in a big, howling gust as Oberon raised both hands over his head in triumph. Glancing up from his place in the dirt, Raphael saw that the other fallen angel watched as Oberon passed by him on his way to collect the ring from Aimee's lifeless hand.

But the wind continued to rise, until it was so powerful that it was pushing Oberon backward, away from the ring. He struggled to proceed, but the wind became a roar, and Raphael saw a blinding white light streak down from above to blast the earth directly in front of Oberon, like a falling meteorite.

When the dust settled, there was a figure standing in the crater. It was a tall man with long, black, hair and a pale green robe that blew and flapped in the wind.

Raphael lay in the mud now, and he felt the last of the life draining out of him. His eyes were about to close for the last time when the man in the crater turned to him and gave him a mischievous wink. The narrow eyes, the harsh, gaunt face, the pointy beard were all familiar. It was the Magician.

At his appearance, all the other warriors—the Obies, the U.S. troops, and the Dark Territory monstrosities—had stopped fighting and most were standing frozen in place, as if they were statues in a sculpture garden. They looked at him in awe, and a few of the soldiers dropped to their knees and made the sign of the cross.

He gestured to Raphael, and in his mind, Raphael heard the word *rise*. He was stunned to find that despite his wounds he was able to stand, and behind him his friends—the Army of Light—rose, too. Chin came to the edge of the crater and humbly bowed before the Magician, the Man of Four, the Dark Teacher.

Oberon, however, did not seem impressed. His gun turned back into a flaming sword and, still airborne, he moved slowly forward, preparing to cross the crater. With a look of amusement on his craggy face, the Magician looked up at him.

"I don't know who the hell you are, and I don't care," Oberon growled. "Out of my way."

"Indeed?" said the Magician. "Tell me, Oberon, what *do* you care about?" The familiar, mocking tone Raphael knew so well almost made him laugh.

"Last chance," Oberon said, raising the sword.

"My last chance—or yours?" the Magician mocked.

Oberon raised his sword and slashed the Magician across the chest with it. Raphael winced, waiting to see the Magician fall, but instead, a gaping, smoldering wound opened across *Oberon's* chest. He howled in pain, staring at the Magician with incredulous fury. Then, he reared back and stabbed the Magician in the heart with his flaming blade. Still the weapon did not harm the Magician. Instead, when Oberon pulled his blade free, it was his own chest that bore a livid oozing wound that looked as if it went directly through his black heart. He slumped, dark blood bubbling from his mouth. The sword fell from his hands, and his eyes rose questioningly to the Magician's. His wings slowly ceased their flapping, and his body began to transform, his skin changing from the slick, scaly black of a snake's flesh to the flat gray of granite. As Raphael watched, he thudded to the ground, a lifeless gargoyle. Oberon had turned to stone. He was dead.

The Magician turned his gaze on Oberon's Irin companion. "Be gone, Azaziel. You're finished here," he said. The tall dark angel in the black crown took wing. With one last defiant, rageful shriek, he wheeled and flew away, heading for the Middleburg tunnels.

The Dark Teacher was changing, too. His head rose as he grew even taller and the green color faded from the robe, leaving it a sparkling white. When he turned to look at Raphael and the rest of the Army of Light, his face was as clear and bright the sunshine on a new spring morning, and his hair was long and silvery white—although he looked as if he were no more than twenty years old. A pair of great, golden, feathery wings spread from his back. He was splendid, dazzling, and so bright Raphael could hardly look at him.

"You're—an angel," Raphael stammered, then felt like an idiot for stating the obvious. The angel smiled.

"Rise, Army of Light," he said. "You have stood your test and carried your weight. Rise and be joyous."

Raphael obeyed. He felt a tingling in his chest as he did, and he pulled away his shredded shirt, amazed to see his deadly wound healing before his eyes. In two seconds, it was gone—there wasn't even a scar—and he felt rested and renewed, better than he had in days.

"Raphael . . . Zhai," the angel said. "Brothers in spirit. Come to me."

Raphael glanced at Zhai, and together they went to stand before the celestial being.

"I'll be leaving you soon," the angel said. "But before I go, I'll answer your questions."

Raphael opened his mouth, but the angel raised a hand, silencing him. "No need to speak," he said. "I know your questions before you ask them. I am Halaliel, Archangel, enforcer of the Law of Cause, also known as the Law of Sin, also known as the Wheel of Karma."

Raphael stared at him in awe.

"I want to thank you for allowing me to be your teacher," Halaliel said and bowed to them. "It has been a privilege to serve you."

Raphael laughed. "*You're* thanking *us?*" he said.

Halaliel's smile was genuine. "Absolutely. I try to teach everyone I encounter, but so few are willing to learn my hard lessons. But you—all of you—have done well."

Raphael glanced over his shoulder. The Toppers and Flatliners, still standing together, stared in amazement at what they were seeing. They *had* done well, he realized. He just wished Emory could have been there to see it. They had made some mistakes, but they had learned, and that was the important thing. He was certain that, if nothing else, the gang battle in Middleburg was over forever.

"There have been many Armies of Light since the Four Wheels and the Four Staircases were first created, and you are among the worthiest. I believe you will do well."

"Excuse me, Halaliel sir, but do well at *what*?" Zhai asked politely.

The angel's smile grew even more radiant. "At protecting the ring, the Wheel, and the staircase. Aimee . . . the ring, please."

Aimee went to him and placed the glowing Shen ring into his outstretched hand. He gently lifted it up and let it go, as if releasing a bird into flight. It rose upward, before finally disappearing into the arch of the church's bell tower and instantly, the spiral staircase leading up into the heavens was illuminated once more, along with the beam that shone into the railroad tunnel in the side of the mountain.

"Now, the fourth and only remaining staircase to the celestial realm is restored, and souls that have earned their way will once again be able to ascend to the heaven. It will be up to you, Raphael, Zhai, and the Army of Light, to make sure that the ring remains safe and intact."

Raphael exchanged a glance with Zhai.

"We're honored, sir," Zhai replied.

"We'll do our best," Raphael said.

"The All requires no more of you than that. Do your best and the world will rejoice. But my time here grows short, my friends. There are other worlds, other times, other realms that require my attention—"

"Wait!" a voice rang out, interrupting him, and a tall military-looking man came striding toward them. He stopped in front of Halaliel, facing him squarely. "What am I supposed to tell them in D.C.? I came here to investigate an energy spike. Angels, monsters, demons? Come on—how am I going to make a report that doesn't sound completely insane?"

"Are you still worried about your promotion, Agent Hackett?" Halaliel asked. "What if you were to tell them that energy spike was created by some teenage prankster who hacked into a government computer mainframe, and you resolved the problem? What if you were to tell them that in doing so, you found that Middleburg is the perfect place to develop wind and solar power? A government energy project would create a lot of jobs for the good people of Middleburg, would it not?" Halaliel asked.

"You're telling me to lie to my superiors?"

"Am I?" Halaliel sounded, Raph thought, like the Magician again. The angel gave a slight shrug. "Or perhaps you could make your report all about angels. Would you like me to spell my name for you?"

"That won't be necessary. I guess I could tell them—you know—what you said."

This Hackett guy must be pretty shrewd, Raphael thought. It looked like he was buying into it.

"Perhaps you will get your promotion after all," Halaliel told him, and Hackett walked off, seemingly in a daze.

"Now," Halaliel said. "Does anyone have any more questions for me before I go?" He glanced at Aimee as he spoke, and Raphael was surprised when she stepped forward.

"I do," she said. "Sir." She sounded a little nervous but she went on. "It's about Orias. He's imprisoned in the Dark Territory. According to some really stupid rules, as a Nephilim he's doomed. He says he has no soul and he's supposed to live a completely miserable, long, long life. Azaziel says he's as repulsive to those above as he is to those below and he's damned forever. But that doesn't make any sense."

Halaliel arched his eyebrows in surprise. "Indeed? And you are aware of what a Nephilim is?" he asked.

Aimee nodded. "Yeah—half human and half fallen angel."

"And you're aware that as a Nephilim he has no claim to heaven or to eternal salvation?"

"But that's not fair!" she protested. "His human half has a soul. What about that?"

"I'm sorry," Halaliel said. "Those are the rules. I didn't make them."

"So you're telling me that no matter what he does—no matter how good he is . . . or becomes . . . he can't ever get into heaven?"

"That's exactly what I'm telling you," he said.

She didn't say anything for a long moment, as if she was considering this. "Well, then," she said at last. "I won't go either."

"Aimee!" Maggie put in. "Do you know what you're saying? You can't mean that!"

"But I do," Aimee insisted. "What kind of heaven can it be if it's so unfair? He has a human half and that human half *must* have a soul—and yet he is not allowed to repent and try to make up for his mistakes. It's just not fair."

"But, Aimee," Kate began.

"No," said Aimee. "If there's no way—ever—that Orias can get to heaven one day, then I won't go either."

Halaliel gazed enigmatically at her. "You would give up your chance for the sake of another?"

"Yes," she said. "I would."

There was a heavy silence as both crews—the Flatliners and the Toppers—stared at her. Raphael thought she was the bravest person he'd ever met.

Halaliel smiled and winked at Raphael again. "I hope you appreciate what you have in this truly remarkable girl," he said, taking a scroll from the pocket of his white robe. He held it out to Aimee.

"What's that?" she asked.

"A celestial pardon," he told her. "Present it to Azaziel, and he will release Orias."

"Really?" she said as she took the scroll.

"Really," he assured her. "Azaziel won't like it, but there's nothing he can do about it. He'll have no choice but to let Orias go."

"But . . . how?" Aimee asked. "I don't get it."

Halaliel laughed and the sound was like wind chimes. "You have found the loophole, my child. I couldn't tell you about it—you had to get there on your own. As it is written in *The Good Book,* 'Greater love has no man—or, in this case, girl—than to give up his life for another.' You can multiply that by at least ten when it comes to the soul."

"Wait," said Raphael. "She has to go into Dark Territory to deliver it?"

"Have no fear. No harm will come to her," Halaliel promised. "Her spirit is filled with the light of pure love."

Raphael felt a pang of jealousy, but he managed to contain it.

She gave Raphael an apologetic glance. "I'll do it," she said. "I care about him, Raphael. I don't love him like I love you, but he was really good to me. I can't let Azaziel have him."

"I get it," Raphael said, even though he didn't like it much. But he knew that whatever had been going on between her and Orias, it was over now. Besides—what Aimee felt for Orias was not romantic love, he reminded himself. That made her wanting to help him a selfless act of humanity. It made Raphael feel humble.

"You must remember, though, that there are conditions," Halaliel said to Aimee. "Once his half-soul is made whole, he will no longer be Nephilim, but human. Mortal. He will live out his life—a normal life span—and then he will die. And he must repent his bad choices, but repentance is not enough. He must find a way to make restitution. You must make sure he reads the scroll carefully and signs it . . . and then it's done."

"Thanks," she said. "I will."

"Can I go with her?" Raphael asked. "To deliver the scroll?"

"You certainly can," said Halaliel, and he turned his attention to the entire group. "Farewell now, Army of Light," he said. As he spoke, a golden halo appeared behind his head. In seconds it was so bright that Raphael had to look down. Even the black dirt at his feet soon became illuminated, like an overexposed picture, and he shut his eyes.

A moment later, when the glow behind his eyelids dimmed and Raph looked around again, the Magician, the Dark Teacher, the Man of Four—the angel Halaliel—was gone.

Raphael was amazed. Even though the sun had been setting a moment ago, it hung high in the sky now, as if time had reversed to the moment before the battle had begun.

The Dark Territory hordes had completely disappeared. Every wound anyone had suffered was healed. The Obies and the U.S. soldiers looked at one another warily, but all the weapons, even the flaming sword Raphael had carried, had disappeared. Without their guns or other weapons, the two factions realized that the fight was over and began walking away. When Li started to follow the Black Snakes, Zhai caught up to her and took her hand.

"Wait—Li, where are you going?"

The look she gave him was full of contempt. "Leave me alone, weakling. They are my people now. I'm taking our father's fortune, which my mother made sure would all come to me one day—and I'm leaving this stupid town. There are better things out there than Middleburg, and I'm going to find them—and enjoy them all."

"Come on, Li—you're my sister. We can figure this out together."

"Are you deaf as well as stupid?" she demanded. "I have no more use for you, Zhai. I'm out of here."

And she followed her comrades off the battlefield, running into the woods with them as the U.S. troops gathered into a small knot on the church steps, arguing about what to do next.

"Check it out!" Benji said, pointing. A house just outside the church-yard that had been blown up had been miraculously restored. Even the treetops that had been snapped by Maggie's Shen blast were back to nor-mal, waving serenely in the breeze, and down the street they could see the marquee of the Starlite Cinema advertising the latest action flick, just like always. Middleburg seemed none the worse in spite of the brief war—

with one exception. The only place that wasn't restored was a big Victorian house a half a block away from the church. It was Oberon's house, Raphael realized, and now it was completely demolished.

The rest of the town was fine.

"We did it," Raphael whispered, although he still barely comprehended exactly what they had done or how they had done it.

"We did it!" Zhai repeated, and everyone took up shouts of exultation, pressing together in a wild frenzy of hugs, high-fives, and howls of joy.

❧

Maggie was grinning as she surrendered to her classmates' massive group hug, but the smile left her face for a moment when she saw Aimee and Raphael kissing. She averted her eyes, sighed, and walked a few steps away from the crowd. She was happy for them—she really was—but it might take a little while to get used to seeing them together again.

Her head was still throbbing from the fight and she had a feeling she was going to end up with a wicked shiner. Black, puffy eyes were so not in this season. Feeling a little dizzy, she wandered over to lean against one of the tombstones when something above and to her left caught her attention and she squinted up into the sunlight. It was hard to make out in the glare, but she could see—very faintly—the staircase made of light, ascending heavenward from the top of the church steeple. And moving up the long, long staircase was an endless series of disembodied auras: pink ones, blue ones, orange ones, reddish ones, deep greens, pale greens, and almost-whites, all spiraling upward. She remembered the dark, shadowy shapes she'd seen lingering around from time to time since she'd gotten her ability to "see things right," as *The Good Book* said. Now, she understood that they were spirits, trapped on the earth because the Four Staircases had been closed. Because of what they'd done here today, this one had reopened, and they were able to move on to a better place. And she could move on, too.

"Hey," a voice said, and she turned around. It was Rick—but he wasn't talking to her. Somehow he'd returned to his human form—by Halaliel's magic, maybe—and he looked distinctly concerned as Johnny the Cop and Detective Zalewski approached him.

"It's a good thing you two are here!" Rick continued. "These Flatliner punks have been starting trouble again! I have a dozen witnesses that will tell you—"

Johnny rested a hand on his gun. "Okay, Rick—hands where I can see them!"

"What?" Rick said, incredulous. "What the hell do you think you're doing?"

"Rick Banfield, you are under arrest for the murder of Emory Van Buren. Hands behind your back, kid," Zalewski said.

Rick seemed stunned as the cuffs clicked tight on his wrists. "This is ridiculous," he said. "Are you guys insane? Do you have any idea who my father is?"

"Yeah, yeah, yeah, everyone knows who your father is," Zalewski said. "And nobody cares." He and Johnny escorted Rick toward the waiting cop car, while the Army of Light stood and watched. Rick was cursing and shouting all the way.

∽

Even though Aimee could have teleported them straight to Azaziel's throne room, she suggested they go by way of the tunnel and the Wheel of Illusion. She wanted time to apologize to Raphael again and to try to explain about Orias. Maggie had already told him that Orias had put some kind of spell on her and he'd told her no other explanation was necessary, but she felt she had to say more. She was sure he had so many unanswered questions.

When Nass heard that Raphael was going with her, he'd insisted on going too, and Dalton told them there was no way she was staying behind. So the four of them had set out with flashlights and backpacks full of water bottles and snacks, walking deep into the tunnel. When they stopped for a moment to take a break and Nass and Dalton were busy looking at the strange carvings on the tunnel walls, Aimee took Raphael's hand and led him a little away from them. She could see in the dim glow of their flashlights that he was frowning.

"Raphael," she ventured softly. She'd thought a lot about what she wanted to say. He looked down at her. "I'll never be able to make it up to you—what happened with Orias," she said. "But if you'll let me, I'll spend the rest of my life trying."

He didn't speak for a moment, and she was afraid he was going to turn her down. And then he said, his voice catching slightly, "There's just one thing I need to know."

"What?"

"Did you and Orias—I mean—how far did it go, exactly?"

She thought he was holding his breath, as if he dreaded to hear her answer and she hastened to reassure him. "No—oh, no," she said. "It never went beyond kissing. He was very respectful about that. He didn't try—you know—anything like that."

"Good. I don't know if I—" but he didn't finish the thought. He grabbed her and pulled her to him in a fierce hug. "I just want to forget all about that, once we get this over with," he said. "The important thing is we're together again. I love you." He grinned. "And yes—I'll definitely let you spend the rest of your life making it up to me."

She laughed, relieved. "Okay, then," she said. "Let's get this done." She waved Nass and Dalton over and they continued their trek.

It was amazing, Aimee thought, how different the tunnels felt now that the ring was in the church tower and the staircase to Heaven had been reopened. There didn't seem to be any murderous monsters waiting in the shadows, and the frightening, oppressive feeling that the tunnels always held seemed to have been swept away.

When they reached the center of the Wheel, Aimee instructed them to all hold hands. "Here we go," she told them, and they slipped.

ℂ

Orias was still in the cage. His shirt hung in tatters around his torso, and lash marks from the whippings he'd received oozed blood down his back. He could still see the hundreds of Irin assembled there, their dark, expressionless faces gazing out from the shadowy ring of columns surrounding him. The war was over, and somehow the fallen angels had lost. Azaziel had returned with what was left of his Irin soldiers and wasted no time in taking his fury out on Orias. Somewhere close but unseen, drummers pounded out a solemn beat on a pair of massive kettledrums. The black, flittering shapes of disembodied demons flittered around his head, looking at some moments like bats, at other moments like circling vultures. They cackled and whispered taunts in Orias's ears, and occasionally paused to take small, painful bites from his flesh.

He was thankful that Aimee would never see him like this, but his gratitude didn't last long. She materialized in the throne room to stand right before the astonished Azaziel. Dalton, Nass—and Raphael—were with her.

"Let him go!" Aimee ordered, looking defiantly up at Azaziel. Slowly he descended his throne.

"Why should I?" he snarled.

She held Halaliel's scroll out to him. "He has received a celestial pardon," she said. "You lose! Read it and weep."

Azaziel took it from her, broke the seal, and perused the document. And then he laughed. "He'll never go for it," he said.

"Betcha anything he will," she retorted. She took the scroll back and went to the cage.

"Aimee, what's going on?" asked Orias. She held the scroll out to him.

"It's true," she said. "I talked to Halaliel and—"

"And she offered to sacrifice her soul for yours," Raphael broke in. "Which is a lot more than you deserve."

He looked at Raphael. "You're right about that," he agreed, and then he took the scroll and studied it. "Why would you do this, Aimee?" he asked. "After the way I used you—manipulated you."

"Yeah," Raphael said bitterly. "It was all about getting the ring."

"At first," Orias agreed. "But then I fell in love with her—and I thought, in time, I could make her love me."

"Well, it didn't work," said Raph. "Just so you know—it's me she loves, and after this, I'm going to do everything in my power to see that she never gets near you again."

Aimee took Raphael's hand, quieting him. "You don't have to worry," she told him. "I do love you—only you—and that's not going to change." She turned to Orias. "But even though you thought you were just using me, Orias, you were good to me. You gave me a safe haven when I needed to get away from my father. You taught me I could slip. You helped me to be strong. For that I'll always be grateful."

Orias held up the scroll again, his eyes filled with deep sorrow. "And . . . this is for real?"

"It's for real," she said. "But there are conditions. You have to agree that this is what you want and you have to be truly sorry for all the bad things you've done. And somehow, whenever you can, you have to find a way to try to make it right—restitution. That's what the scroll says. You have to sign the pardon—and then you'll be mortal. You'll live a normal human life span, you'll get old and you'll die, just like the rest of us. And you won't have any more super powers. You'll be a regular guy. But your half soul will be whole, and you'll have a right to heaven, just like all humans."

He read the scroll again. "I'll sign it in blood, if that's what it takes," he said.

"We can make that happen!" said Azaziel, reaching out his taloned hand and slashing Orias's forearm with a claw. "If you're sure that's what you want. Don't you realize you'll be giving up a nearly immortal lifetime? Thousands of years of partying and pleasure. Don't be stupid. Don't sign it, and I'll let you go. You can return to your almost unending life of debauchery. Or perhaps we could work together. With your father gone, I could use someone with your skills. Think of the glory. Come on, what do you say?"

Orias looked at him with contempt. "I say go to hell." And he dipped one finger in the blood oozing from his wound and with it signed the document and gave it to Azaziel. As soon as the Irin touched it, it vanished in a plume of sparkling purple smoke. Instantly, the cage door sprang open.

Aimee grabbed his hand and Raphael, still holding her other hand, grabbed Dalton, who grabbed Nass. "Let's go," she said, and they slipped back to the tunnel mound in Middleburg. The last thing they heard was Azaziel's thunderous roar of rage.

಄

When they'd finished materializing back in their own normal world, Nass laughed. "Wow!" he said. "We've literally been to hell and back. That was wild."

"Yeah," Dalton said. "You did it, Aimee. Let's go home."

They all started walking away, except Orias. When Aimee looked back, she was surprised to see that all his wounds were healed—but his eyes still looked tortured.

"Aimee, wait," said Orias and he sounded sincere, Aimee thought. Not arrogant, like he usually did. "I promised restitution, and I want to start with you. How can I make you know how truly sorry I am for what I did to you? I did love you—I still do—and I've lost you. I think that's the worst punishment I'll ever have. I will never feel anything more painful than losing you, but letting you go—I guess that's my first step at making things right. I can never thank you enough for standing by me."

She smiled. "Just go home—and have a good life," she said.

"Uh . . . there's just one small problem with that," said Nass, and they all looked at him. "His house blew up. It was the only one that wasn't restored after the battle. He's got nowhere to go."

After a moment of silence, Dalton spoke up. "Oh . . . all *right*," she said. "My grandma would skin me alive if I didn't offer him shelter. We've always got room for one more. Come on, Orias—but be prepared. She's a real stickler for that restitution thing. She'll be on your case twenty-four seven."

They all laughed and walked down the tracks together.

CHAPTER 32

FOUR DAYS LATER, MAGGIE WAS WALKING UP to Hilltop Haven with Aimee. Aimee and her mom had been staying at Maggie's house, and it was such a beautiful day, they'd decided to walk home from Emory's funeral instead of catching a ride with the guys in the Beetmobile. The Flatliners and their families had all attended and even the Toppers were there to honor his memory. Myka and Raphael had given the eulogy, and Dalton had sung "Swing Low, Sweet Chariot" as a special tribute.

"Hey, Aimes, you want to hang out?" Maggie asked. "You can come with me to Bran's if you like. I want to see how he's doing, and he wanted to hear about the funeral."

"Can't," Aimee answered. "Family meeting. My mom's had the divorce papers drawn up. I don't want to miss that."

They both laughed, and when Maggie turned up the walkway that led to Bran's door, they parted ways. Maggie's old crew had just come out of Bran's house, and they were chattering about how cute he was when they caught sight of her. They all averted their eyes, and Lisa Marie bumped Maggie with her shoulder as she walked by. As they passed, Maggie could hear them mocking her.

"Nice black eye."

"I know, right? Ugly much?"

"And now she's hanging out with Aimee?"

"Freaks. They're two peas in the same loser pod."

Maggie watched them walk away, feeling a kaleidoscope of emotions exploding through her like starbursts, from hurt, to outrage, to sadness—

since she knew that only a few months ago, she had put Aimee through the same torture. But to her surprise, those feelings evaporated and she giggled, then chuckled—and then laughed out loud. Because she now understood: some day, all those girls would be outcasts, and someone else would make them feel like crap. *The Wheel of Karma,* she thought. And it would serve them right. Maybe it was the only way they could learn.

Bran's mother greeted Maggie at the door with a smile and directed her up the stairs to Bran's room. He was lying in bed watching ESPN, tossing a football up in the air and catching it, clearly restless in his current, injured state. The room was filled with a half dozen Mylar balloons with messages like *HANG IN THERE* and *GET WELL SOON* written on them in bright, shiny letters.

"Hey," Maggie said awkwardly, and she realized suddenly that she'd never had a one-on-one conversation with Bran. To her, he'd always been nothing but Rick's best friend, and he was her friend only by extension. Most of the time, they'd barely looked at one another. But they looked at each other now, as Bran pointed to a chair near the bed, gesturing for her to sit. They *really* looked.

"How'd it go?" he asked.

"Sad," she said. "You know. But everyone was there and Dalton sang. It was nice. Emory would have liked it."

"Yeah."

As Maggie sat down, she took a big Toblerone chocolate bar out of her purse. "Here," she said. "I didn't know what to get someone who's been . . . you know . . ."

"Shot in a gang fight?" Bran finished in his charming Southern drawl. "I believe a do-rag and a bullet-proof vest are the traditional gifts, but chocolate always works for me. Wanna split it?"

She nodded. Bran unwrapped the bar and held one end of it out to her. Their hands touched briefly as they broke it apart. As they each took a bite, his eyes caught hers. She was amazed at how blue they were, and when she looked into them, she was convinced that Bran was exactly what he seemed to be: a kind, good, caring, honest, funny guy. His aura was blue, too—a rich, unwavering cobalt that was as constant and lovely as a clear summer sky. She realized he was staring as much as she was, and self-consciously she touched her swollen eye.

"Sorry," she said. "I look like a monster right now."

"No, you don't," he told her, shaking his head. "You look amazing."

His words were so rich with meaning, and the connection between them was sudden and so deep that for an instant, Maggie felt breathless.

"Oh, I'm so sure," she said, and the tension that mounted within her became a quivering in her chest, and the quivering became laugher. Soon, Maggie and Bran were cracking up together, like a couple of best friends.

ဆ

Aimee walked into her father's study with her mom, who was dressed in a lovely beige suit, her hair beautifully coiffed and her nails freshly manicured. Unlike Emily Banfield, who seemed perfectly calm, Aimee felt tension building within her. Her father was always like a volcano on the verge of erupting, and since Rick had been arrested, it was worse. The scandal of Jack's bigamy had spread all over town, and it was tainting his so-called clout. Savana Kain had filed papers to have their marriage annulled on the same day that Aimee's mom had filed for divorce. Emily had hired the best attorney in the state, and Aimee had overheard her telling Violet Anderson that she wasn't going to settle for less than half of everything Jack had.

"And believe me," she'd confided to Maggie's mom. "I have my own ideas about what to do with his property and companies, once I've taken over my half of them—especially when it comes to the Flats. He won't be bulldozing people's homes on my watch."

Things weren't going any better for Jack in his bid to win custody of Raphael's little brother. Savana was now denying that he was the father, and despite his repeated requests, she refused to submit to a paternity test.

But even in the midst of this major life implosion, the thing that seemed to gall Jack Banfield the most was that Aimee and Raphael were seeing each other again, and no matter what he said or how he threatened her, she refused to stop.

"Thanks for coming," he said to Emily when he opened the door. "I know that if we both behave like civilized people we can work all this out." His voice was sickly sweet, even smarmy, and Aimee hoped her mother knew better than to trust him.

"There's nothing to work out, Jack—except the divorce settlement," Emily told him as she handed him the papers. "I know you've already been served by a disinterested party, but I couldn't deny myself the pleasure of giving the papers to you myself. My attorney says it'll go better for everyone if we can come to some kind of agreement before we go to court."

His attitude changed. "Yeah, well—we'll see about that. There's nothing I can do for Rick, it seems, but I want my daughter to come back home."

"That's not happening," said Aimee.

"No way," said Emily.

He ignored his wife and turned to Aimee. "Come on, sweetheart. Don't you miss your room? I'll double your allowance and we'll start shopping for a car for you—"

"No, thanks," she said.

So he got tough with her. "Look—you either come back home right now, or I will personally take you back to Mountain High Academy and instruct them to lock you in and throw away the key."

Aimee shook her head sadly. "What is your problem, Dad? Why do you think you have to control everything?"

"You are my daughter, Aimee—and you will not throw your life away by spending it with losers," he told her. "You will live up to your potential, and you will appreciate the sacrifices I've made for you and for this family."

"What family?" Aimee said calmly. "Your family is gone—because of you."

Her father leaned close to her, his face white with anger. "You be very careful, young lady."

"Sorry, Dad," she said gently. "That just doesn't work anymore."

Jack snorted. "Well, we'll see about that," he scoffed.

"That's enough, Jack," Emily said. "Aimee will continue to stay with me at Violet's until our apartment is ready. She isn't going to stay with you, and if she doesn't want to see you, you won't even have visitation."

"You shut your mouth—you're done here," he said and was as stunned as Aimee when Emily laughed at him.

"You're right about that," she agreed. "And when I get through with you, you'll be done in Middleburg. Now that Orias has signed over his shares of your business ventures together over to me—plus what I'll get in the divorce—I will wipe you out and take great pleasure in doing it. Come on, Aimee. Let's go home."

ॐ

Jack followed Emily and his daughter to the door when they left and slammed it behind them, letting out a string of the vilest profanity he could come up with. After that, he went into a rage that destroyed his living room, breaking into bits the lamps and bric-a-brac that Lily Rose carefully dusted every other day.

He smashed the coffee table into kindling, kicking it and banging it violently into the wall, and he used one of its splintered legs to slash a painting—an expensive Thomas Kincaid—like he wanted to slash Orias's face.

How could that pompous, self-important son of a bitch just give his shares of Jack's businesses to Emily like they were bubble-gum trading cards? How could his once mousy, mealy-mouth about-to-be ex-wife think she would get away with taking what he'd worked for years to accumulate? How could his ungrateful wretch of a daughter treat him so disrespectfully? Rick was the only one who'd shown any promise, and he'd been stupid enough to get himself arrested for giving some Flats rat a beating that he surely deserved.

Well, Jack thought, *damn them all to hell.* He didn't need any of them, and they wouldn't take him down. He'd build his holdings up again, bigger and better than ever. He'd show them all—but first, he needed a drink. In fact, he needed to go to the nearest bar and get rip-roaring drunk like he hadn't been in years.

He felt in his jacket pocket for his car keys and came up with a small vial—the vial Orias had given him, filled with some kind of herbal remedy he'd said was good for Aimee's nerves. And if there was anything Jack needed at that moment, it was something to steady his nerves.

He screwed the little silver top off the tiny bottle and slugged back the contents, which actually tasted delicious. As soon as he swallowed, he felt an infinite calm stealing over him, and then he felt nothing. Nothing at all. Every care he'd ever had drifted away . . . never to be remembered again.

�৪ও

When Maggie got home, after she had spent a pleasant afternoon with Bran, she found a strange car in the driveway. She entered the house calling her mother's name and went directly to the hallway to find her with Vivian Gonzalez, Middleburg's only art framer and a part-time travel agent. The two stood together gazing up at Violet Anderson's completed final tapestry.

There it was, the battle of Middleburg, framed and laid out in exquisite detail, everything from the government choppers to the Obie daggers, from Orias's resurrection to the Staircase of Light. And in the center of it, resplendent in white, stood the angel Halaliel, holding up the glowing Shen Ring, surrounded by the Army of Light.

"It's stunning, Mom. A masterpiece," Maggie said, shaking her head in awe.

"Yes," her mother said wearily. "I don't think I'll ever do another. After everything that's happened, I'm quite ready for a break."

"And you've earned it," Ms. Gonzalez said, handing Violet an envelope. "Bye, ladies," she said and headed out the door.

"What's that?" Maggie asked, gesturing to the envelope. Violet smiled.

"It's for you. For us. Open it," she said, and Maggie took the envelope and ripped it open. Inside, she found a set of three tickets with the words *CARNIVAL CRUISE LINES* on them.

"I've always wanted to go on cruise," Violet said wistfully. "Now I will. *We* will. As soon as school's out for the summer."

"There are three tickets," Maggie pointed out.

"I thought you might want to bring someone," Violet said.

Maggie blushed as she thought of Bran and wondered if he'd accept her invitation to go on a cruise. Just asking him would be a major step, and they weren't even officially together yet. But it sounded divine—Bran with her onboard a ship in the middle of a sparkling aquamarine sea. But it didn't matter. They couldn't go anyway.

"What about the doorway?" she reminded her mother. "We have to guard it."

Violet smiled. "Not anymore," she said. "Take a look."

Maggie gave her a quizzical glance and brushed past her, unbolting and opening the basement door. She braced herself to see a tunnel of endlessly descending blackness, maybe even a monster or two waiting there to ambush her, but instead she found something much more surprising: nothing.

It was just a normal basement staircase.

She could see beige tiles covering the floor below, and she looked at her mom, confused.

"Now that the Wheel of Illusion has been restored, this back door to hell is closed," Violet explained. "We don't have to worry anymore about residents of the Dark Territory using it to make their way to earth. An angel—a very tall angel—came and sealed it up."

Maggie was speechless.

"Go and check it out," Violet urged, and Maggie raced down the steps. The basement was gloriously normal, filled with a Ping-Pong table, a pool table, a wet bar with a mini-fridge, a couch, and a big-screen TV.

She walked through it, taking it all in, and then she flopped down on the couch and sobbed, great tears of joy and relief pouring down her cheeks and onto the new leather sofa. She had expected to spend her life as her mother had spent hers, locked up in this house and guarding the basement door until she slowly lost her mind with loneliness. Now, she was free.

"You like it?" her mother shouted from above.

"I love it!" Maggie shouted back, her voice choked with emotion. "And we're totally going on that cruise this summer!" she said, and the invisible ghost crown on her brow throbbed in time with the beating of her happy heart.

∾

Zhai and Kate embraced in her little train-car home for what he feared would be the last time. She'd told him again that she had to get back to her real home, in her own time, and he couldn't bear to think of what his life would be like without her.

The last few days had been a whirlwind of activity as he made arrangements for his parents' funeral, found a temporary place to live, and met with his family's lawyers to check on his father's will. What Li had told him was true. Somehow, Lotus had either convinced Cheung Shao to leave Zhai with nothing, or she'd forged his signature on a new will. He'd insisted that Nass and his folks keep the guesthouse until they found something else, or until Li's guardian, who Zhai knew had to be the new leader of the Black Snakes, evicted them.

To his surprise, Raphael and Savana had insisted he bunk with them for a while, until things got sorted out. He'd also had to find a job, which hadn't been as difficult as he'd expected. When Orias had returned from Dark Territory, he'd started his restitution thing right away. The first thing he'd done was sign all his interests in Jack Banfield's enterprises over to Aimee's mom, and then he gave his coffee shop, Elixir, to Savana so she and Raph would have a steady source of income. Savana had happily hired Zhai to work there, too.

Zhai also had to keep up with his schoolwork and, at Kate's insistence, he'd also made time to grieve for his dad and play his violin. Today, she had asked him to meet her in the train car for a special talk. He'd shown up with flowers and as usual, she scolded him for spoiling her and then led him inside. They sipped tea, kissed, and gazed into each other's eyes before she grew serious and got down to business. She took out a book—*A Local History of Central Ireland*—and opened it.

"I borrowed this from Miss Pembrook," she said as she placed it before Zhai and pointed to a picture.

"That's me," she said faintly, then sat back, waiting for Zhai's response.

The picture was labeled St. John's School for Girls, August 1915.

Zhai looked from the picture to Kate. "You were adorable even back then," he said and kissed her freckled nose.

She smiled sweetly at him. "Well, you know I'm a time traveler, but I haven't told you how it happened. I was out digging potatoes from our garden one day when my mother called me in, crying hysterically, saying my brother was on his way to Dublin to enlist in the army so he could go and fight the Germans. She shook our last bit of money out of the can where we kept it and told me I had to go and find him and talk him out of it. He was too young to sign up, but she knew that once the soldiers had him they wouldn't let him go."

"And you took the train?" Zhai guessed.

"Aye," she said. "But I was soon to learn it was no ordinary train. I was the only one on the car I boarded, but for our small village I didn't think that was anything unusual. I figured more people would be getting on soon. But we left the station and somewhere along the way, the train started glowing and picking up speed, going faster and faster until I got so dizzy I must have fainted. When I came to, it had stopped. You can imagine my surprise when I found out I was no longer in Ireland, and it was no longer 1915."

"I can't imagine how hard that must have been for you—never to have seen all the modern technology we have—TVs, cell phones, airplanes. And no money to live on. I think you're a genius—I don't know anyone who could have made a home here in the locomotive graveyard and survive on fish and berries, with no electricity and no running water."

"And don't forget—I'd found a couple of gold coins around these old wrecked trains. That helped a lot." She frowned. "But I have to go back, Zhai, if there's a way. I've got to complete the task my mother sent me on. If I don't, my brother could die in the war. I've got to try and get back there." She had tears in her eyes.

"I know," he said. "And I've been thinking . . . maybe I'll go with you, if that's okay."

"But what if something happens, and you aren't able to get back here? Are you absolutely certain that's what you want?"

Zhai nodded. "I'm sure. I'm hoping that with Aimee and the Wheel, we'll be able to come back once in a while—but even if we can't, I don't want to lose you."

She kissed him, then, in a way she'd never kissed him before, and the kiss told him all he needed to know. "I don't want to lose you, either," she said when she finally pulled away. "The only thing I can't figure out is why the train—or Halaliel, or the All—brought me here in the first place. I mean, sure I was a grenadier in the Army of Light, but you certainly could have won without me. . . ."

Zhai shook his head. "I couldn't have won without you. I couldn't even live without you. Kate, you taught me to *feel,* to need something, to open myself up to other people," he said vehemently. "I never could have gotten through any of this without you. You taught me to love." He reached into his pocket and took out the lock of hair she'd given him so many months ago. It felt like a lifetime.

"I've kept it with me ever since," he said softly. "And I'll always keep it with me."

Her smile was radiant as she went into his arms again. Not long after, they got together with Aimee, Maggie, and the Flatliners at Lily Rose's house for a special victory dinner. Even Orias was included in the celebration.

When they told everyone that Kate was going home and that Zhai was going with her, Lily Rose gave her a copy of *The Good Book.*

"This will help you both in your spiritual journey," she told them. "But it'll do more than that. We want you to keep in touch, to let us know how things work out for you. "

Kate looked at the book in awe. "How does it do that?" she asked.

"Just write me a letter and tuck it inside the book," said Lily Rose. "And let your heart fill with love when you think of us. The book will do the rest."

"Zhai," Raphael said. "It's a major decision, man. You sure you want to do this?"

"I'm sure," Zhai said. "You know I've always felt a little out of step with these times—and all the plans my dad had made for me to take over his business. I've always felt a little like I didn't belong here. There's nothing left for me here—and I can't live without Kate."

Orias cleared his throat. "I'd like to go, too," he said. Everyone looked at him, surprised. "I have a lot to make up for," he continued. "It wouldn't hurt to go back about a hundred years and get a head start."

෨

It was the earliest and most resplendent spring anyone in Middleburg could remember. As the days passed, neither the Flatliners nor the

Toppers spoke of that terrible day filled with fighting and destruction. Most Middleburg residents, once they woke up from Dalton's song-induced sleep at Middleburg United, seemed not to remember the events at all. After the battle, they'd simply walked, squinting, into the unusually bright afternoon sunshine, heading back to their homes after what they'd thought had been a tornado warning. They hadn't even seemed to notice when Agent Hackett and his men climbed into their helicopters and Humvees and rolled out of Middleburg. The Obies who'd survived the fight had quietly left town. In place of the destruction that now seemed like an odd half-remembered dream, the ruined houses and buildings were now miraculously intact—except the one that had belonged to Oberon and Orias. The lot it had stood on—the whole town, in fact—was overrun with so many varieties of beautiful wildflowers that it looked like Lily Rose's garden had exploded. Orias had donated the property to Middleburg, along with some money, with the understanding that a park and teen community center be built there.

Nass had made good use of the early bloom. Every day after school, he'd spent hours gathering flowers, making them into bouquets and surprising Dalton with them at every possible occasion. Soon, she'd said she'd date him, run away with him, marry him—anything to get him to stop giving her the darned flowers. Her house was full of them, and she was getting tired of vacuuming up the petals. He said he'd be content if she would just forgive him—and she did. Nass and Dalton were officially Middleburg's most entertaining couple once more.

Raphael had enjoyed the beauty of the early spring only in passing; he'd been busy with school and rebooting his relationship with Aimee. He also had to help his mom run Elixir, and he'd managed to find housing for Emory's family. The rest of the Flats families had gotten a reprieve from eviction, since Jack Banfield had been found wandering around on Golden Avenue with no idea who he was. Aimee's mom had committed him to the state asylum, and she took over running his companies—after she and Aimee moved back into the Banfield mansion. Every Sunday Emily faithfully went to the county jail, where Rick was being held until his trial, but he continued to refuse to see her or respond to her letters.

Raphael tried to get to know his new baby brother, who his mom had named Gabriel, but Lily Rose was helping take care of him and she would let Raphael hold him for no more than a minute or two before she spirited him away to rest. Raphael wasn't worried about it, though. He'd have the rest of his life to get to know the little guy, and he trusted Lily Rose's judgment in all things, especially when it came to babies.

There hadn't been time, after what he'd come to think of as the Great War, to have a big celebration, and the Flatliners and the Toppers had mutually agreed to put it off until spring break. They had learned to peacefully coexist and there were no more gang fights and hardly ever any disagreements. They were all getting along so well that the Cunningham brothers joked about combining them into one group and renaming it the Flat-Toppers, and Nass had quipped that nobody'd better expect him to get some kind of loser retro haircut to go along with it.

The economic situation was improving, too. Agent Hackett had made good on Halaliel's suggestion about developing wind and solar power in Middleburg and not long after that, when Beet, Benji, and Josh were poking around in the old train graveyard they found an old safe that was full of gold coins. The best they could figure, it had been exposed when all the explosions shifted some of the old boxcars around. Letters in the safe dated it back to 1877, and laughing as if it was the biggest joke in the world, Aimee and Maggie had explained to them that it was the lost payroll the outlaws had been after when they'd gone back in time. It was Benji's idea to turn the locomotive graveyard into a train museum and charge admission. Every chance they got, they worked on cleaning up the place, and Josh built a website to promote it. Already, it promised to become some kind of cool tourist attraction. There was a lot to celebrate.

The party was going to be at Master Chin's farm and everyone in town was invited. The flyers Raph and his friends had posted downtown had billed it as a spring festival, but those who were in the know understood that it was a celebration of the Army of Light's victory over the Dark Territory hordes, and the restoration of the celestial staircase. Already the creepy feeling that had permeated Middleburg for so long seemed to be dissipating. Raphael wasn't sure why, but he guessed that maybe a backlog of ghosts and darker entities that had been loitering there were now moving on to a better place.

On the night of the party, Raph and his friends crammed into the Beetmobile and rolled up to Master Chin's farm. They found it transformed into a carnival, complete with rides, a live band, and dozens of food vendors.

Beet, Benji, and Josh insisted on using part of the money from the safe to pay for the party.

"It's like Disney World, right?" Benji asked.

"Like you've ever been to Disney World," Beet scoffed.

D'von Cunningham was riding shotgun next to Beet. Ever since Beet found out D'von was into cars, they had been hanging out quite a bit. He glanced back now. "You've never been to Disney World?" he asked Benji in amazement.

"Of course not. You have any idea how much it costs?" Benji said.

D'von shook his head sadly. "I'm taking you there some time," he said decisively. "Y'all are deprived."

"Not as deprived as you losers," Benji joked. "Our train museum is going to make a load of money. How about I take *you?*" And everyone laughed.

As soon as the car stopped, Raphael was out, and he and Aimee hurried, hand in hand, through the labyrinth of smiling faces and twinkling lights.

Master Chin's barn/kung fu school was at the center of the festivities. Its doors were shut, Raphael knew, because this was the V.I.P. area, the party within the party—the area reserved for members of the Army of Light and their families. Inside, Master Chin's *kwoon* was decked out, its rafters festooned with glowing paper lanterns and filled with potted flowering plants. Against one wall, there was a table full of all kinds of fancy gourmet food catered by Spinnacle, with servants in white linen uniforms dishing out delicious-looking portions of steak, au gratin potatoes, grilled salmon, salads, rolls, desserts—the works. Against another wall, there were burgers, barbecued ribs, hot dogs, and French fries supplied by Rack 'Em and served buffet style.

Master Chin stood amid a knot of partygoers, relating a story that had happened long before any of them were ever born, when he'd had a run-in with Oberon and had taken out one of his eyes using snake-style kung fu. When Raphael and Aimee approached, however, he ceased his tale and embraced them both.

"Ah, so lovely to see you two!" he exclaimed. "Now everyone is here!"

"Sorry we're late. *Someone* takes forever to get ready," Raphael said, elbowing Aimee playfully. She stuck her tongue out at him.

"Tell me about it," exclaimed Nass, looking at Dalton who gave him a playful shove.

Everyone was there: the Cunninghams, Dax, Michael, Beet, Benji, Josh, Myka, and Bran Goheen. Bran was quite a bit more subdued than when he'd been hanging out with Rick Banfield, but he looked happy. He and Maggie Anderson were holding hands. Everyone was surprised when they started going together, but they seemed perfect for each other.

"I wish Zhai and Kate were here to see all this," said Maggie, taking in the room. She looked at Lily Rose. "Have you had any word from them?"

"As a matter of fact, I have," said Lily Rose, her eyes twinkling as she took *The Good Book* out of her oversized purse. "I looked this morning and found something waiting for me. It's a letter from Kate."

She opened *The Good Book* and read it to them.

"Dear lovely friends," Kate had written. *"We got back safely. Aimee was*

able to teleport us right to the enlistment office in Dublin—but it was too late for me to get my brother out of the army. Have no worry—he survived the war, and I'll explain how in a minute. To our surprise when we materialized on the other side, Orias was wearing a priest's collar, of all things. He laughed and said he thought that was fitting. He was willing to live a life of service to others and thought maybe there was some good he could do. He enlisted in the army as a chaplain and went off to minister to the soldiers.

"Not long after we returned to my little village, Zhai and I were married. None of my neighbors had ever seen an Asian gentleman before and for a while they were sure I'd brought back some kind of exotic leprechaun (ha ha), but they soon got used to him and realized they weren't going to find a pot of gold by following him around. We haven't found one either, although Zhai has made a good living as a music teacher and he never lacks for students.

"Now about my little brother. He came home from the war unscathed, thanks to Orias. He wasn't even wounded, for Orias jumped in front of the bullet that was meant for him. I'm sorry to inform you that Orias didn't make it. But, according to my brother, his last words were, 'I can see the light. I can see it! I'm going home now . . .' and he died with a smile on his face.

"We miss you all terribly and hope to see you again someday soon. Meanwhile, we are happy in our little country cottage and will soon add to our family with our first child. I hope it will be the first of many.

With all our love, Kate and Zhai."

Everyone was silent for a moment when Lily Rose closed the book. Raphael looked at Aimee, concerned, and when she gazed into his eyes hers were misted with tears.

"It's okay," she said. "He's okay, now. He did it. He made his restitution."

"Yep," said Lily Rose. "I knew that boy had it in him. Orias found his road to glory."

Above them, from one of the barn's rafters, hung a flag that Violet Anderson had made for the Army of Light. Against a white background, it featured a spiral staircase rising from a ring stitched in blue. At the corners of the flag were the four items the Magician had sent Raphael and Zhai to find in their first quest: a pocket watch, a wedding ring, a rosary, and a lock of hair.

"Cool flag," Raphael said, gazing up at it. It reminded him of a conversation he'd had with Zhai before he and Kate left.

"The one thing I'm still trying to figure out is that first quest, where the Magician had us get those items," Zhai had said. "And then we had to get the key. I mean, I understand the key—you couldn't have rescued Aimee without unlocking the Wheel of Illusion—but the rest of the stuff?"

Raphael had nodded and replied, "I thought about that a lot on my train ride through the Dark Territory borderlands. I think each item had a lesson; the Magician is called the Dark Teacher, after all. I know for me, the pocket watch symbolizes time." He'd tried to channel the Magician's creepy voice, which had made Zhai laugh. "Time is an illusion," Raph had said. "And we can travel through it. But it's also precious and limited. Like my time with my dad. And I think Mrs. Anderson's wedding ring symbolizes commitment," he said, thinking of Aimee. "Plus, I never would have become friends with Maggie if I hadn't gone to find it."

Zhai had considered Raphael's words carefully, and then he'd said, "After our quest, Lily Rose told me to heal Li with faith. That could be the rosary...."

"And what about the lock of Kate's hair?"

At that Zhai had grinned. "That's easy," he'd said. "It's love."

When they'd told Chin what they thought, he'd nodded proudly. "Time, commitment, faith, and love," he'd said. "All necessary ingredients to becoming a Soldier of Light."

"Yeah, well he sure didn't teach us the easy way," Raphael had said.

Chin clapped him on the shoulder. "He never does," he'd said.

Remembering his conversation with Zhai made Raphael miss his old friend, but he knew that somehow, somewhere, he would see him again.

Aimee's voice brought Raphael back to the present. She was addressing Master Chin. "I never got a chance to thank you for those telepathic kung fu lessons you gave me while you were in your coma," she said. "I'll always be grateful. They saved my life more than once."

"Of course," Chin smiled. "You were an excellent student."

"You know . . . if you'd ever let me take lessons sometime when we're both awake, that would be amazing," she suggested.

Chin eyed her playfully. "Do you remember what I said when you asked the first time?" he asked, and then he reached into a cabinet and took out a thick wooden board.

"You said when I could break that board you'd train me."

"Right," Chin said. "You think you can do it?"

He held up the board and braced himself, ready for Aimee to strike it as she had the first time she tried. The rest of the Army of Light surrounded her, watching eagerly.

Aimee looked at the board for a minute, crestfallen, and then shook her head. "I can't do it," she said. "It's too thick. There's no way."

Chin laughed and set down the board. "Then I'll train you," he said.

Aimee's face lit up. "What? Really?"

"I cannot train someone unless they understand their own limitations. Now you understand yours," he explained.

Aimee smiled and gave her new kung fu master a bow.

"And I have a surprise for you, Sifu," Raphael said, and everyone gave him their attention. "I've finally figured out the Strike of the Immortals."

Aimee looked at Raphael, confused, and he explained. "The most advanced technique in all of kung fu, the move that can never be defeated, that can't be taught, only figured out."

Chin nodded. "Very well," he said, gesturing toward his Mook Jong, the kung fu wooden dummy that stood in the corner. "Show me."

Raphael nodded. With everyone watching, he walked over to the Mook Jong, but instead of attacking it he just stood there.

"Go ahead! You can do it!" Josh said.

But Raphael simply looked at the dummy for a moment longer before turning back to Chin.

"Do it, Raph!" Nass said eagerly, but Raphael only smiled.

"He did do it," Chin said, beaming with pride.

They all looked confused.

"Come on," said Beet. "Show us the move."

"That's it," Raphael explained. "That's what the move is—nothing."

"The Strike of the Immortals is the strike not thrown," Chin said softly, his eyes a little misty. And then he grinned. "It is peace. And nothing—*nothing*—can defeat it." He gave Raphael a tearful embrace. "You're a master now," he whispered. A moment later he pulled away, wiping tears of joy from his eyes. "And now, we dance!" he said exuberantly, taking a remote control from his pocket and aiming it at the impressive sound system he'd set up on one side of the barn.

"Just a second," Raphael said. He had spied his mom at the far end of the room, holding his little brother. "Hey, Mom," he said, meeting her in the middle of the barn.

"Hey, kiddo," she said, bobbing the baby up and down in her arms. "You want to hold your little bro?"

Gingerly, Raphael took the baby from his mother. "Hey, Gabe," he said. He was getting more and more comfortable holding him. "What's up, little guy?"

Maggie, Aimee, and Dalton gathered around, oohing and cooing at the adorable child.

"I've got to ask," said Dalton. "How did you decide what to call him? Is Gabriel an old family name or something?"

Savana smiled. "It was an easy choice. Raphael is named after an angel. I thought it would be appropriate for this one, too. My two angel boys."

"Mom—come on," said Raphael. "Stop before you embarrass me."

Savana laughed, and Gabriel squirmed in Raph's arms. He looked up at his big brother and a huge smile spread across his tiny face. Suddenly, a halo of golden light surrounded his perfect little head, causing everyone watching to gasp. Then, the baby was glowing all over, bright and beautiful, just like he'd glowed in the womb. Everyone stared at him in stunned silence.

Chin approached, glanced at the baby, then at Raphael and he clapped Raph on the back. "Well, it looks like the new generation of warriors for the Army of Light is already among us," he said pleasantly. His smile was infectious, and soon the others were smiling and laughing, too, even Raphael.

"He's going to be great—especially with a big brother like you," Aimee said, kissing Raphael on the cheek.

"So . . . can we dance already?" Chin asked with boyish impatience, and they all laughed.

"Yeah!" Aimee and Maggie said at once.

"All right, *Sifu,*" Raphael said. "Let's dance."

The End

ACKNOWLEDGMENTS

This book is dedicated to you, reader. You, who have come on this nearly 1,500-page journey with us. You, who have persevered to the end. You, who have learned the Strike of the Immortals. Thank you.

Thanks also to: Carol, Kim, Peter, and everyone at HCI Books, Robert Vahovich and the Battle Creek Traditional Wing Chun Club, my extraordinary family, Charlene Keel, and the gorgeous, peerless, fearless Melissa Kay Hart.

—J. Gabriel Gates

For all the inspiration that happy childhood memories provided, I want to thank the playmates of my youth: my siblings, Bennie, Mike and Becky; cousin Margaret Ann and Willie Howell's brood—Sandra, Elaine, Gloria, Charles, David, Edward, Charlotte, and Allen; Pat, Wayne, Jimmy, Billy, and Jaylene Mitchem; all the Keel cousins, especially Larry and Sandra, Diane and Douglas, Frank and Bobbi Jean, George and Nancy, and their Susie and Lloyd; Jot and Phyllis Coker; and my first best friend, Sally Sellers. And most especially Lugene Lewis, my very own Lily Rose. I treasure all the hours of make believe, laughter, love, and encouragement they gave me.

—Charlene Keel

ABOUT THE AUTHORS

J. Gabriel Gates is a Michigan native and a graduate of Florida State University. He has worked as a professional actor, written several Hollywood screenplays, and coauthored the teen fantasy series The Tracks. His novels include: *Dark Territory*, *Ghost Crown*, *The Sleepwalkers*, and *Blood Zero Sky*. For more information, visit his website: www.jgabrielgates.com and follow him on Facebook and Twitter.

Charlene Keel is an author and screenwriter whose TV credits include *Fantasy Island* and *Days of Our Lives*. Her other novels include *The Lodestone*, *Seventh Dawn of Destiny*, *Dark Territory:* (The Tracks, Book 1), and *Ghost Crown* (The Tracks, Book 2). For more information, go to www.charlenekeel.com and follow her on Facebook and Twitter.